25 CENTS. This BILL will be received in payment of any debt, or redeemed in current Bank Notes, on demand, at my House in WORTHINGTON, for TWENTY-FIVE CENTS

No. 160

WORTHINGTON.

TWENTY-FIVE CTS.

Sept. 23d 1816

Ezra Griswold

S. &

1 1

President

Directors & Co.

The BANK of DELAWARE Promise to pay

or bearer One Dollar on demand

Delaware Novr 2 1814

Cash.

Moses Bybbe Pres.t

ONE

Recd.

OHIO

1

ONE

No. 227

A

ON demand I promise to pay

in current Bank Notes at my Office, in Wo

ONE DOLLAR.

Worthington,

Attest,

Ezra Gris

JONATHAN BLAIR:
Bounty Lands Lawyer

JONATHAN BLAIR: Bounty Lands Lawyer

by *William Donohue Ellis*

Cleveland and New York

THE WORLD PUBLISHING COMPANY

C. 3

Library of Congress Catalog Card Number: 54-10451

SECOND PRINTING

2 HC 1054

TO

Helen Naiden

CONTENTS

BOOK I

BOOK II

BOOK III

"This certifies that there is on deposit in the treasury of

THE UNITED STATES OF AMERICA

ONE DOLLAR

in silver payable to the bearer on demand"

THE READER will find in his own wallet this contract between himself and his government. It has been perhaps the most eventful contract ever written, the burden of it sometimes falling on the party of the first part, sometimes on the party of the second, but ultimately on both. Like any agreement which requires to be written down, it began in disagreement. Before finding its way into the reader's wallet, this writ began to be conceived in many places, one of them being a frontier place called Mesopotamia where Jonathan Blair was observing certain nervous events which follow.

WM. D. E.

BOOK I

Chapter 1: HARD MONEY

IF IT actually happened, Blair would probably be for the defense . . . afterwards, for that was pretty much the nature of Jonathan Blair.

But more important to the town . . . where would he stand *while* it happened? For that was always the attitude of Mesopotamia.

In the next sixty seconds, it looked as though the town would finally find out how much silver was in the barrel at the bank or else they'd find out how much iron was in Sam Hosmer's spine.

It was typical of Jonathan Blair, that even as he watched young Hussong's thumb grip the hammer of his rifle, his thoughts wandered from the particular fact that old Sam Hosmer could be shot in the next few seconds . . . to the generalization that if all the Joe Hussongs in the Northwest Territory took this method of redeeming their wild-cat paper dollars in hard money, the West would go back to war, internal.

Even though there were nine persons in the store of Samuel Hosmer in the place known as Hosmer's Village, and officially named Mesopotamia, in the Ohio part of the Northwest Territory, they stood so still that everyone could plainly count the six clicks of the lock on the rifle of Joe Hussong as his thumb pulled back the hammer. Since the seven men and two women all used Stikes' rifles, they knew Joe Hussong was now at half-cock. Worse, they knew he was half-crazed. But worse still, he had a right to be; and he said to Hosmer what the others would say, if they dared.

"Sam, I don't want to scratch a hair of you. But stand back so the ricochet don't get you. I'm gonna blast the lock off that iron frame. I'm gonna open the gate and walk back in there and I'm gonna give you one hundred paper dollars. Then I'm gonna take one hundred silver dollars out of that barrel of yours. And I'm gonna take 'em down and pay the Chillicothe land office my fifth land payment. Everybody here knows that's fair."

Hussong looked around for corroboration, but if any man had had in mind to speak, which is doubtful, he was stopped dead still by the

kind of answer which came back now from the storekeeper-banker—
six clicks from Sam Hosmer's rifle.

Hosmer's seventy-year-old arm was not as steady as young Hussong's
but he firmed it up by resting it on one of the iron bars behind which
he sat. And he rested his case, reasonable or unreasonable, on the
barrel of silver on which he sat. Old Sam Hosmer was the banker.
But since the bank had been robbed of some of its silver—how much
Hosmer never said—old Sam had refused to let any silver go out, even
though it said on the face of every Mesopotamia Hog & Trust bank
note that it was redeemable in silver at the bank. This, over Sam's
signature in the lower right-hand corner.

Because of Hosmer's stubbornness and because everyone knew that
Hosmer was holding onto the silver in the bank, Mesopotamia Hog &
Trust dollars still circulated at very close to par as far as a hundred
miles from Mesopotamia. This was an achievement, because most of
the thirty-five other kinds of money circulating in the West wouldn't
transfer for half-value fifty miles from the issuing bank. John Piatt
bank notes in Cincinnati were perhaps best, but a John Piatt dollar
was worth only eighty cents in its own home town of Cincinnati. At
Fort Pitt, lately called Pittsburgh, a John Piatt bank-note dollar was
accepted at a rate of sixty-five cents. Farther east at Harrisburg it
brought sixty cents. At City of New York a John Piatt dollar would
bring fifty cents. At Boston it wouldn't buy a draught of ale.

Bank of Vincennes notes were fair. But fifty miles from Vincennes
they were only souvenirs. Same with Detroit in the Michigan Territory,
Kankakee in the Illinois Country, and notes on the Dayton Bank.

Besides that, you had to watch from day to day. Mike Stikes had
taken a fistful of Owl Creek Bank notes in payment from Amos Exeter
on Sunday. Sunday night talk got out that Owl Creek Bank dollars
were only backed up ten to one with silver. Monday morning it was
twelve paper to one silver, and before Stikes could ride down to County
to pay his taxes, the Owl Creek notes had become rifle wadding. Stikes
threw them in the face of the county tax collector. They fell to the
floor. Nobody picked them up.

But through it all people were still accepting Mesopotamia Hog &
Trust notes without much question, down at Boxford's Cabin, down
at County and even south of that at the Borough of Columbus. That
was because old Sam Hosmer's name was signed to them, and everybody knew how he was holding onto what silver was left in the bank

after the robbery. Only place that wouldn't accept them close to par was the United States Land Office.

Sam Hosmer wasn't about to let that change. He had let Caleb Wright's farm go under Emanuel Ault's auction hammer when Wright tried to redeem his Mesopotamia notes in silver to pay the Land Office. He had stood by while Wright loaded his family in the wagon to go back east.

That took either guts or cussedness. Hosmer had both, and when his hammer was at half-cock he said, "Hussong, ye'll be needin' *two* guns. Because after ye fire off that padlock, ye'll have to shoot me. I'm servin' notice if ye open that gate, I'll fire."

"Then you better aim sharp," Hussong said. "Because I'm comin'."

Hussong shoved Camelia Flannerty away from him and he lowered his piece to rest his elbow on the counter. Everybody could see he was lining up his front sights on the Stikes-built padlock that held the iron grill.

Jonathan Blair, the lawyer, watched. And he wished, as he had never wished before, that he had built himself some stature in the fifteen years he'd spent up here in the big woods, enough so that he could step in there now and say something to stop it. Not that he knew what to say. For Jonathan Blair's trouble now, and for the last fifteen years, was that he could see both sides of the question. And to build a standing in Hosmer Village or anywhere in the Northwest you took a stand on one side or the other and then you laid everything you had on the barrelhead. Hosmer right now put his life on a barrel of silver. When it was over he might be dead, but by God he'd be somebody.

That's how Hosmer had got to be Hosmer. If his name was on it, his life was on it.

Strangely enough, Blair's sudden desire for some standing in this place was not to save the life of Hosmer or Hussong. It was because across the store Hope Emerson was right now looking at him to stop the fight. She had brought Blair to the store for that purpose. And the lawyer was only due for about one more chance from Hope.

She stood nearest the padlock. Hussong said, "Blair, you better get your future wife back from that padlock or she'll be getting brass splinters."

But Hope only said, "Joe, that gun won't bust this lock, anyhow."

"Yes, it will, Hope. Stikes made the gun."

"Stikes made the lock, too," Hope said.

There was something about the presence of Hope Emerson which firmed a man in his purpose. A man tried somehow to match her. And if Joe Hussong had any quaverings about firing, he wouldn't be apt to back off now, after Hope heard him say he'd fire.

Hussong said, "Step to one side a little, Hope." There were four more clicks as Hussong pulled his hammer back to full cock.

They were answered by four more as Hosmer pulled back.

Hope said, "Joe, wait!"

Hussong raised his head from the sights, but not much.

"When I went out and brought back Blair," Hope said, "it was because he knows about these money things. We haven't had use for a lawyer much 'round here. But now we have, and we got one. Tell them, Jonathan."

Blair said, "Joe, if you take your full hundred dollars silver out, then everybody's entitled to full silver for their bank notes. Sam said there isn't that much in the barrel since the robbery. Why should *you* get full value?"

Hussong flared at Blair. "Because I'm the one whose payment is due right now. Because I'm gonna lose that two hundred acres that I broke my back clearin'. Or would you understand that?"

"The others have payments coming due just as ——"

But the lawyer never finished. Hussong yelled. The explosion and the smoke filled the store. But as the smoke rolled up to the rafters and spread under the ceiling, it was sucked out through the bullet hole in the roof. The crowd saw Hussong's rifle pointed to the roof, held straight up by the corded arm of Mike Stikes whose veins stood out as he strained against Hussong. Gavagan grabbed Hussong from the rear. Stikes ripped the gun from Hussong's arms and they dragged him outside. Hope followed them out, turning her head briefly toward Blair in a fleeting appraisal, not freighted with admiration.

Hosmer slowly eased forward the hammer of his rifle. He unlocked the iron grill and came out into the store. The others exhaled now and moved around.

There were no congratulations for Hosmer, nor expressions of relief. For each man in the room would soon face the same dilemma as Hussong. And they had just had a sample of what they'd have to face to get silver out of the Mesopotamia Hog & Trust in exchange for bank notes. You didn't coddle up to a man like Hosmer, because you might have to fight him tomorrow.

There was an aristocracy in Hosmer Village as blunt as the hand of Sam Hosmer and as inevitable as survival.

Jonathan Blair knew this as clearly as he knew why he was at the bottom of it. And as he studied the brown face of old Sam Hosmer which was myriad-wrinkled as the neck of a turtle, he knew why Sam Hosmer was at the top of it. Hosmer had built a hierarchy of survival. And when a man could contribute to the survival of Hosmer Village —or Mesopotamia, as Homer tried to have it called—he moved instantly to a place in the village commensurate with his usefulness.

And law, well, they weren't using much of that in these woods.

Old Sam Hosmer had come out here two years after the Ordinance of 1787. He had found this place, measured it off, built a cabin and then gone back for his wife and two of the others.

Mike Stikes, the lank, white-haired blacksmith stood next to Sam Hosmer because for the first seventeen years of it, Michael Stikes had kept the rifles of Mesopotamia functioning well enough so that three cabins had grown to thirty-three despite Captain Michael's howling Wyandots.

Stanley-the-Slasher stood next to Stikes, for he was the slasher. He had a particular genius with an axe which had become legend and which put him in demand all along the whole south length of the Greenville Treaty Line. For Stanley-the-Slasher, by judiciously slashing cuts into a stand of timber, and then by selecting the key tree to topple, could bring down an acre of timber in a single day, using gravity as in knocking down a row of dominoes. And the genius of Stanley-the-Slasher could in one day save the backs of ten men from two weeks work.

Beside Slasher stood Asa Buttrick, and he stood there because in the two winters of famine which drove half of Mesopotamia back down to Cincinnati and back east to Fort Pitt, Asa Buttrick, the trader, had managed to steal and deal for enough corn to get the other half through the winter.

And next to Asa Buttrick stood young Joe Hussong. It should have been Thomas Woodbridge, but Woodbridge had left for the Illinois Territory shortly after the bank had been robbed. Young Joe Hussong, though, had learned enough of hog husbandry from Woodbridge to supply the town with pork and breeders.

The others occupied positions in proportion to their ability to sustain Mesopotamia. That put a lawyer pretty far down the list.

They had wondered why Blair had come in the first place with his fluff-fronted shirt and his talk of improvements. They had wondered then why he had stayed, frittering with an occasional case of law and his newspaper, *The Tabulator,* and his trips to visit the legislature. And then they had ceased finally to wonder about him at all. Except Hope Emerson did sometimes.

But today Sam Hosmer wrapped a piece of greased doeskin around his rifle, swung it back on the dowels behind the counter and turned on Jonathan Blair.

"Damn it, Blair, if the whole of us can't make our land payments to the Government Land Office, what can they do to us?"

"Foreclose."

"You sure?"

"Positive."

"We held off the Wyandots in 'ninety-five, ye know, and again in 'o nine and in eighteen 'leven."

"But you can't hold off the Land Office."

"We held off the government troops out of Fort Washington when they said we was squatters."

"Government Land Office will be different."

"How do you know, damn ye!"

"They're already foreclosing down around Columbus. They're better about fifth payments. But on third and fourth payments they're not playing any more."

"But if the whole of us stick together and plain refuse to git off the land, what they gonna do about that?"

"They tried that down at Zanesville. Government just moved troops right in for the auction. Transferred title right there."

"Well, just don't stand there, Blair!" Sam Hosmer took it out on Blair because he couldn't get a grip on anything else. Blair knew this.

When the Wyandots started raiding down across the Greenville Line, old man Hosmer had grabbed an axe and built the blockhouse. When the Miamis sneaked up and walked off with twenty head of Hope Emerson's sheep, Hosmer had grabbed a rifle and fourteen men and brought back the sheep. But when the forty different kinds of Western currency began to go to rot, Samuel Hosmer could get no grip on that kind of trouble with his hard, dry hands.

"Damn it, Blair, ye're no hand with an axe, but ye're *s'posed* to know

what to do about money and law and politics and like that. After all,
ye *did* set up the legal papers for our bank, and ye *did* make the legislature, even if we are mostly the only people in your district. What do
we *do?*"

"I told you. You've got to get to Gideon Schaacht in Chillicothe and
get a United States Bank loan for our bank."

"We tried. Buttrick went down."

"What did Schaacht say?"

"Wouldn't even talk to Buttrick."

Buttrick blustered to defend his own prestige. "Well, that is, he
wouldn't talk to me about a *loan.*"

"Naturally," Blair explained. "Schaacht was sent out here to establish a branch of the United States Bank to stabilize the currency of the
West, not to make small loans to settlements this size. We've got to get
somebody important to talk to Schaacht. I told you to ask General Harrison."

"He never answered my letter," Hosmer said.

"Try Governor Worthington."

"Nobody here knows him."

"Nicholas Longworth or Jacob Burnet down at Cincinnati could
talk to Schaacht."

"Yeah," said Matt Gavagan. "But who in hell can talk to Longworth
or Burnet?"

Stikes returned to the store. Hope Emerson was with him. She
handed a letter to Sam Hosmer.

"Elizabeth sent this over. Said it was from General Harrison. Maybe
it's good."

The crowd wished Hosmer through the motions of breaking the seal.
He held it at arm's length and read it through silently. Then he said,
"The General writes, 'Dear Mr. Hosmer, I have laid the case of a
United States Bank Loan for Mesopotamia before Gideon Schaacht.
I have explained the services you performed for our army during the
war, and Gideon Schaacht has assured me that he will receive a repre-
sentative from your town to discuss this possibility. Your servant, Wil-
liam Henry Harrison.' "

It further advanced Hosmer's standing that he showed no surprise
or elation at receiving a letter from General Harrison. But in that same
proportion it added to his responsibility. Asa Buttrick said, "That

settles it, Sam, if you can get an answer from General Harrison, *you're* the one to go see Schaacht. You can get the general to take you in to Schaacht."

"No. I stay here to keep charge of the bank."

Gavagan bawled, "What's there to keep charge of? Ever since the robbery you never said how much silver is left in that barrel ya guard so close."

"You want to run the bank?" snapped Hosmer.

"No. But you could tell us how much silver we got left."

"Enough so's Mesopotamia dollars are at least better than most of 'em! It's gonna stay that way!"

Buttrick said, "Then let's send Stikes to see Burnet. He met him once. Get Burnet to see Nicholas Longworth. And get Longworth to see Schaacht."

Hope Emerson didn't move, but Blair noticed that when she spoke she became the center of the room. "Seems to me we're goin' the long way round," she said. "We have in this room here the right person that should go direct to this Gideon Schaacht. We have a lawyer that knows about those papers and such. And he's a state legislator. That ought to be good enough to talk to this Gideon Schaacht or anybody else."

The eyes of Mesopotamia converged on Blair as if they saw him for the first time. But Blair said, "Hope, you don't understand about this Gideon Schaacht and ——"

"I understand he's only a man. Can he be so darnation fearful?"

Buttrick spread his coat and hooked his thumbs in the pockets of the vast waistcoat which was unveiled. "Hope," he said, "the way it works with sending a man like Blair to talk to a man like Schaacht is ——"

"Is like anything else, to my notion," said Hope. "When we needed a good shot we got Slover Navarre. When we needed a trader we got you. Now we need a man that understands money and papers. We got Blair."

She snatched the letter from General Harrison. Hosmer reached to retrieve it. But she passed it to Blair.

"You'd best have this letter with you, Jonathan. And you'd best hurry. The Land Office won't wait much longer for our payments. You *see* Schaacht . . . some*how*."

Buttrick laughed. "Fat chance. Set her straight, Blair!"

But Jonathan Blair folded the letter into his pocket and for some preposterous reason he said, "She's already straight, Buttrick. I'll get the loan."

Matt Gavagan curried Blair's bay as if Gideon Schaacht personally might inspect it. Mike Stikes bent new iron and replaced all four shoes. Stanley Slasher carved black-walnut buttons for Blair's faded-blue wool army shortcoat. Hope Emerson bleached his buckskin trousers so at a distance they looked like Cincinnati cloth pants. Blair stuck Hosmer's letter from General Harrison in his coat pocket and headed the bay south.

At the ford Sam Hosmer stopped him and grabbed the bridle. Blair looked down into the watery old eyes.

"Yes, Sam?"

"Blair, bring back the loan. I can't hold out much longer."

"You can't what?"

"Just bring back the loan, understand? Bring back the damned loan."

Blair splashed across the ford and into the woods . . . south.

During fifteen years in the upper woods, Jonathan Blair had forgotten that it could be infinitely more difficult to traverse twenty feet of political corridor than two hundred miles of wilderness. Thus, after riding all the way south from the Greenville Treaty Line over the old Harrison War Road through the little clearing of Columbus and then on down over the old Scioto Trace to Chillicothe, he finally stood within twenty feet of the great man. Yet he might as well not have come to the United States Bank in Chillicothe. For he was separated from the great Gideon Schaacht by twenty feet of hallway and the thickness of a young clerk's ego. The clerk said, "I'm sorry, sir, but Mr. Schaacht has no record of an appointment with you. And he remembers no letter from General Harrison mentioning your bank."

The clerk sat down and resumed writing, leaving Blair standing there with cold-reddened hands hanging out of his sleeves.

"Look, I'm all the way down from Hosmer Village. Blair's the name. Jonathan Blair."

The handsome young clerk stopped his writing and looked up, studying Blair's leather breeches with complacent interest.

"Some new settlement in the Michigan Territory?"

"No. Mesopotamia is the real name. And it's right here in the State of Ohio. I represent eighty-three people and I've got to see Gideon Schaacht."

The young man pulled out a map of the Northwest Territory. On it Blair could see Cincinnati, Detroit, Vincennes, Louisville, Dayton. Columbus wasn't even on it yet. How could you explain to a fluff-shirted young clerk who'd obviously never been north of the tame Indian belt that there were eighty-three persons in a place called Mesopotamia and a few thousand more scattered in settlements up through the big woods who had more right to call on the help of Gideon Schaacht and the United States Bank than all the Ohio River merchants who still thought the frontier was just north of Chillicothe and just west of Cincinnati.

Blair pointed four and a half inches north of Chillicothe. "Up here it is."

"Up there? That's Indian country still."

"Not legally, it isn't. The Greenville Treaty Line is a few miles north of us. We've been there over fifteen years. If we hadn't been, you wouldn't be here now."

The clerk smirked and rolled up the map asking, "And you're the state legislator from there?" His eyes raked Blair's spattered boots. The outfit which had looked ridiculously fancy up in Mesopotamia was ridiculously crude in Chillicothe.

"That's right. I haven't sat yet," Blair said. "But I will, next legislature."

"And you're here to get a United States Bank loan, and since you represent a town of eighty-three people, you should go *right* in to see Mr. Schaacht . . ."

Blair took a step down the hall toward where he could see the great man's boots crossed under a writing desk. But a white bar swung across the aisle blocking him and the clerk finished his sentence.

"You should go right in, while over there, waiting, sits a man from Dayton which already has one hundred thirty houses. Over there sits one from Steubenville which has eleven factories. There sits one from Vincennes which has 1,200 people and eighteen stores. And all those others. All waiting to see Gideon Schaacht. You should go in? I'm afraid not, Mister."

Blair sat down under the stares of the others.

Three days he sat in that waiting room in the bank while the distressed merchants from the major cities along both shores of the Ohio

River came by appointment only to ask loans of the fabulous Gideon Schaacht who held the economic destiny of the West in his long-fingered palm, and in the thick vaults of his United States Bank.

Blair saw the great men of the West stride down that corridor confidently to the office of Gideon Schaacht. Then he saw many of them slink back out, slowly, followed out the door by the all-wise eyes of the clerk whom he now knew to be named Justin Bolding.

Bezaleel Wells, who had built up Steubenville, barged in aggressively, minced out quietly. John Piatt, who had supplied General Harrison's armies, came begging for his struggling bank. Colonel Cook, hero of the battle at Thames, came in with a loud patronizing greeting to Bolding, and he slunk out ignoring Bolding's patronizing goodbye.

Yes, they had bought too much land. Yes, they had loaned too much money to others who bought too much land with it. Yes, it was their fault. But they had banked on the big immigration. That was why these men had knocked Proctor out of the West and driven him back into Canada. That was why they had torn the West away from Tecumseh and driven Rontondee and Captain Michael and Silver Pigeon up north of the Greenville Line.

Now the wilderness was ready for the immigrants, and these frontiersmen had bought up huge hunks of it to sell to the horde that was sure to come with silver in its pockets. But the horde had not come with silver. The horde that came had been ragged, broke; and it had not been such a horde at that.

The West was mortgaged to the United States government, now creditor to its heroes who had created a Western paper money which was rapidly becoming worthless. But the Congress and Mr. Monroe had created the United States Bank to remedy this. And he had sent out a branch of it, in the person of the brilliant Gideon Schaacht, to save the West . . . at 6 per cent.

The name of the savior rang through the big woods from Pittsburgh to Vincennes to Louisville with various effect. Blair had heard it rolled off the tongues of judges on the court circuit, "Gideon Schaacht," with a powerful tone that built some supra-judiciary deity. He had heard it pronounced brusquely by lawyers on the circuit court, "Gideon Schaacht," as a kind of threat. In political discussions at Exeter's Tavern, Blair had heard it hushed about, "Colonel Schaacht says," picturing some powerful chess player whose influence crossed all appointments, military, postal, civil, judicial . . . federal, state and county.

But at this moment the man who paused at the clerk's desk on his way out spat out that name so it shattered the afternoon.

"Schaacht! Hah!"

The speaker broke his cane over the rail in front of the desk of Bolding, who did not give him the satisfaction of removing the broken stick from his desk. The clerk now beckoned to Blair, who went up to him, hat in hand.

"We still find no record of an appointment for you with Gideon Schaacht. But go down the hall and into the room at the end." As he walked the twenty feet into the large office, Jonathan Blair rehearsed his speech for Gideon Schaacht. The heavy-set man at the writing table did not look up from his writing.

He said, "Yes?" He had a stack of letters at either elbow. Two other quills lay on the table. The desk was as cluttered and as busy as the man. He repeated, "Yes?"

"It's about the Bank at Hosmer's Village, sir, that is, Mesopotamia, up under the Greenville Treaty Line."

The big man looked up and appraised Blair as if he were collateral.

"Do you tell me, sir, that while we are trying to pump good currency into the West to lift the entire Mississippi Valley out of economic crisis, you come to talk to me about a bank in a place called Hosmer's Village or Mesopotamia?"

"I believe you had word about us in a letter from General Harrison, one of your directors. Blair's my name."

"I had no such word."

"But there *was* a letter."

"When?"

Blair suddenly remembered that Hope had given him Hosmer's letter from Harrison. He dropped the folded letter on the table. The big man snapped it open, read it, spiralled it back in front of Blair.

"I see you didn't think I would really read it. Good trick, Blair. But it didn't work."

Blair was mystified. He read the letter for the first time.

"DEAR MR. HOSMER:
I am sorry it is necessary to advise you I have not found it possible to write to Colonel Schaacht recommending a loan for the Mesopotamia Bank. As you know, the United States Bank's mission is to give the West a stable and honest currency. To accom-

*plish this vast object, Colonel Schaacht must place his loans very
well and carefully and on large scales. He will need to concentrate
on the large centres of populace and on the large manufactories.*

Your servant

WILLIAM HENRY HARRISON."

Blair looked up, surprised. The man behind the desk said, "They
have tried everything on me."

But the fierce mask before him now about-faced to such a pleasant
expression of alertness that Blair felt the great man must sympathize
with his predicament. But the change was not for Blair.

Some presence had entered the room. From behind Blair a deep, extremely relaxed and granulated voice said, "Riddle, how badly was
Pittsburgh discounting the notes of the John Piatt Bank last week, also
the Western Reserve Bank, Marietta Bank, Vincennes Bank and the
Bank of Lake Erie? And how were those notes holding up as far east as
Harrisburg?" The new speaker was an enormously tall man and as he
talked he strode to the empty table with his hands in his pockets.

The questioner obviously was not about to repeat the involved question, nor was it necessary, for the man opposite Blair had listened
with nervous attention, moving his lips to make sure he had gotten it
all. He said, "Got it right here, Gideon," and he attacked the pile of
papers on his desk.

Blair had mistaken someone else for Schaacht. Riddle had looked
and acted like the legend of Schaacht. It was amazing to Blair that
there could be a man on earth who could so instantly dwarf the giant
he had believed to be Schaacht. But Schaacht's presence in the room
changed Riddle to a boy. Riddle hurried over to Schaacht and extended a paper. Schaacht did not take his hands from his pockets, only
turned his head to study the paper which James Riddle held steady
for him.

Schaacht's was a face which presumed that everything in the room
would accommodate to him . . . as in fact it did, for as Schaacht studied
the paper, his left hand groped on the desk for a pen where there was
no pen. One appeared suddenly, though, for Bolding, the alert clerk
passing by on another errand, placed a pen in front of Schaacht's grop-
ing hand.

Everybody else in this building moved fast . . . scurried, in fact. But
Schaacht moved slowly. He touched nothing. People came to him with

questions, followed along beside him while they received answers, and then left him without ever changing the big man's course, nor even causing his hands to leave his pockets.

It was distasteful to Blair that he found himself watching Schaacht with such concentration, but he did watch. Schaacht's head seemed mostly cranium. The forehead was vast and bony, the eyes were deep-sheltered under it in sockets of shadow. The face was wide where the jawbones made sharp corners under the ears, but the cavernous cheeks then slanted in toward the nose so abruptly that the face came to a knife edge at the nose which seemed to slash through the room and through the West.

It was a large head, but it seemed small because of the breadth of shoulder. The man was vital, and as he moved, the rippling folds in the new cloth of his clothes outlined muscle. There was a vigor out of keeping with finance, and Blair could imagine this man had surprised many professionals on his way up. "On his way up," Blair thought, because this man had obviously come from somewhere, and was going somewhere.

Schaacht looked over at Blair, who rose from his chair. "Mr. Schaacht, I came down from Mesopotamia to see about a loan for ——"

But Schaacht looked to Riddle who explained, "Mr. Blair was just leaving."

"But I came all the way to see Mr. Schaacht. I represent eighty-three people who ——"

But Gideon Schaacht walked out of the room into the adjoining office followed by Bolding who held out a paper.

The bay shook his neck and head in puzzled impatience at Blair's restraining hand on the bridle as they traveled north over the Scioto Trace toward Mesopotamia. Blair was in no hurry to return. Up until one hour ago, Jonathan Blair, the lawyer, had had a chance to take a place in Mesopotamia beside the slasher, the gunsmith, the hog farmer, the hunter and the marksman, the men who had built Mesopotamia without the help of the lawyer. When the opportunity had finally come to show Mesopotamia and himself that the Blairs of this world were also contributing, the lawyer had botched it.

He slowed the bay to a walk and he wondered how you tell Sam Hosmer and Asa Buttrick and Amos Exeter and Mike Stikes that you didn't get a loan for the Mesopotamia Hog & Trust Bank. How do you explain that you didn't even get to talk to Gideon Schaacht?

Blair remembered about the letter. He boiled at Hosmer's trickery, and he took it out on the bay's tender mouth. Hosmer had pretended to read the letter, but obviously he had made up the words to encourage someone to attempt the loan. Blair wanted Hope to know this.

At Circleville, Blair dismounted at the blacksmith shop. He said, "Mike Stikes in my town told me to stop here. He said to get a three-pound bar of brass from you suitable for making trigger guards and rifle sears."

The smith handed him the bar. Blair pulled out his paper money. "How much?"

"Depends."

"You can see what kind I've got," Blair said. "Here's some Zanesville Bank notes. You know that bank."

"Three dollars."

Blair peeled off three Zanesville Bank notes.

"But I see you got Mesopotamia Bank notes, too. I'd rather have one of those than three of the others."

Blair looked at the smith, surprised.

"Got that old man Hosmer's signature on it, hasn't it?"

"You know Hosmer?"

"There's a story goin' round that he's got every one of the Mesopotamia Hog & Trust notes backed up with damn near a dollar's worth of solid silver. He'll do anything to keep it that way."

"People know that this far down?"

"And they say, too, he's got a lawyer down at Chillicothe gettin' a loan of good United States Bank notes from Gideon Schaacht. That'll make Mesopotamia dollars solid as gold."

Blair continued north, but slowly. "He'll do anything to keep it that way." Jonathan Blair got a new picture of Samuel Hosmer.

The bay shook his head, neck and bridle and slathered sideways fifty feet, refusing to believe Blair really meant to haw back south. Once turned back south, Blair raked the bay's belly with his heels and closed the distance to Chillicothe and Gideon Schaacht.

Outside the United States Bank in Chillicothe Jonathan Blair stood watching the men come out. The ones who walked fast, he let go by.

But the ones who walked *very* fast, and the ones who walked *very* slow, he studied for a particular facial expression—a particular combination of anger and despair. He stepped in front of a short thin one.

"Blair's my name. Jonathan Blair." The thin one looked up at Blair and stepped around his outstretched hand. He walked to the hitching rail and untied his lines. Blair said, "No luck, huh?"

"How do you know?"

"They told you the United States Bank loans were only to be given to big banks and big merchants where they could influence the whole currency."

"Look, Mister. I was sent back here from Lebanon." He swung into his saddle. "I got a long way to go."

The thin one pulled his mount around. But before he had gone three rods, Blair raised his voice, "What are you going to tell them back there?"

The thin one hawed around again, looked at Blair for a moment, then rode off, but slower.

Blair walked along the line of patient horses that were tied to the rail. They were well groomed and harnessed for the most part. But one large hunter had an untanned rawhide bridle, a very dusty saddle bag with sweat stains around it, and he was splattered to the shoulders with dried mud. Blair waited in front of that horse.

He guessed the owner as soon as he came out of the bank building. He was perhaps the one man in Chillicothe who wore more buckskin than Blair, and he looked even more out of place. Blair noticed that his boots matched the mud on the hunter and the friendly arrogance of his face matched the enormity of the horse. The leatherclad individual accepted Blair's hand with unguarded interest.

"Blair's my name, sir."

"Jackson Garth."

"From far?"

"Piqua, near the Indiana Country." Garth rubbed the sides of his horse, crumbling cake mud to dust. "I should have known better'n come here," he continued. "But we need currency. Most of us are coming due for second and third land payments out there. No money. Land Office is gettin' mean."

"Did you get a loan?" Blair asked.

"From Schaacht?" Garth spat. "Hah!"

Garth disappeared around the other side of the horse and bent to dust off the shoulders and belly. His voice floated under the horse. "They said loans to the territories and the northern parts won't help stabilize the money. No influence on the trade."

"Maybe we'd look more like an influence if he'd see us in a bunch," said Blair.

Garth's head appeared above the saddle. "How do you mean?"

Jonathan Blair started to propose an idea to Jackson Garth. In the middle of it the thin one who had ridden away, came back. He dismounted and listened, saying nothing. As the two of them listened to Blair, a third man came out of the bank building dressed somewhat like Garth. Garth yelled to him. "Adonijah! Get over to the tavern and bring back any of that Wabash crowd that was with us. Go ahead, Mr. Blair. This is kind of int'ristin'."

The thin one was some help. Not much. Jackson Garth was a big help. He stayed with Blair outside the door for two days, talking to the men who came out.

Garth was neither so careful nor so discerning as Blair, but more direct and less respectful of brocaded waistcoats. Blair let one brocade waistcoat go by. But Garth stopped him with his usual approach, "Did that high-belted bandit give you the same runaround, *sir?*"

The way Garth pronounced "sir" it was no "sir" at all by eastern manners. It was the territorial kind of "sir" which gave the stranger temporary benefit of any doubt, demanding the same in return. The brocade vest returned him the Chillicothe-Cincinnati variety, "Sir!"

"I mean, did the old ——" Garth looked at the lady on the arm of the brocaded vest and he amended. "Did Schaacht give you a loan? We're gettin' up a little meetin' over in the old statehouse there. Aim to invite highpockets over to explain us a few things about how this Younited States Bank works."

The girl disengaged from the arm of the brocaded vest and walked briskly back toward the bank.

"Now what did I say that she left so quick?" Garth asked.

"That happens to be Virginia Schaacht, the daughter."

Blair overheard the explanation and he saw the decision in the girl's march. He immediately walked to the door ahead of Miss Schaacht. As he opened the door, she started to go through, but Blair preceded her, leaving her to face closed panels and the necessity to remove her hands from her muff to open them.

Blair stopped at the clerk's desk. But Bolding was not there. He heard Virginia Schaacht open the door behind him and he hurried down the hall to the big office ahead of her. He stepped into the office and said, "Mr. Schaacht!"

But he faced the broad, tailored back of Schaacht. Schaacht was not in the habit of turning to answer everyone who called his name, and he continued listening to the clerk who now hurried his story. Like many a bright young assistant, Bolding had let Blair's threat grow into a good one before he reported it; and then he arrived complete with a suggested solution. Blair heard him conclude.

"So they plan to invite you to address all the disappointed loan applicants, Mr. Schaacht, and by weight of numbers to bring pressure. So I suggest, sir, you send me or Mr. Riddle to handle the meeting while you leave for the business in Cincinnati."

Bolding was disappointed in Schaacht's reaction, mainly because there was none. The tall man continued studying a paper.

Virginia Schaacht came bursting past Blair and confronted Schaacht. But apparently even the daughter was trained, for though eager to speak, she only placed her hand on Schaacht's arm while he finished reading.

Bolding said, "I told him, Virginia."

Schaacht handed the paper to Bolding for disposal and when he finally spoke, Blair experienced an admiration for him. He said, "Very shortsighted, Bolding. Do you think that the United States Bank is some private secret to be kept from the best men in this territory? You are no longer in Philadelphia. Men who are sent here to get loans of us are leaders of their territories. Thank Mr. Blair for arranging this opportunity to explain my ideas. Tell him to send for me when his people are assembled and seated."

"Yes, sir."

As Bolding approached to tell him what he had already overheard, Blair watched the face of Virginia Schaacht which smiled at him in victory. Blair touched the broad brim of his flat felt hat, and he left before Bolding repeated the message.

Blair noticed the great power of the man by the stillness of the audience and by the skillfulness of Schaacht's opening remark.

"This meeting was an excellent idea. I should have thought of it myself. It is very important to me to have this particular group understand the mission of the United States Bank. You are necessarily the men who must explain these matters to your people."

There was no flattery. It was true. The men leaned forward, and Gideon Schaacht's deep voice drained their anger and asked them for assistance in his tremendous assignment. He explained that the United States Bank branch in Chillicothe and the other one in Cincinnati had been created to abolish the forty different kinds of defective wildcat currency that was bankrupting the entire West. His mission was to give the West a dollar bill that was worth a dollar *anywhere*, not just in the town where it was issued.

The men felt the pressure which was on this man and they felt ashamed. And Gideon Schaacht spoke the truth and nothing but the truth. If it was not the *whole* truth, it sounded like it.

When he had finished explaining that he must lend United States Bank notes where they would best stabilize Western currency, heads were even seen to nod understandingly. Schaacht then added hope that the United States Bank loans would gradually extend farther and farther north and west to spread sound money up through the big woods.

Blair stood up. "Excuse me, sir. But will not the good United States Bank notes flow back east to pay our debts back there, leaving your bank without notes to loan?"

"Yes. But we will get more notes from the mother bank at Philadelphia."

"Then, will they not become watered down as our own wildcat money?" Blair asked.

"No," said Schaacht. "As we make more loans, which money may flow back east, we will replace missing specie, of course, by mortgages against your property. So the value still remains here. It matters not whether a dollar bill is backed up with a chunk of silver or a mortgage on a farm."

"Yes, but mortgages don't circulate, do they?"

Schaacht colored some. But the men in the room were not interested and Gideon Schaacht knew it.

"Mr. Blair, this gets a little abstruse. I'll be glad to talk in my office."

A few heads turned to Blair wishing him to sit down. But he asked, "One other question, Mr. Schaacht. You refer always to the United States Bank as though it were an official institution of the government.

But actually, isn't it just a private house of business in which the government happens to hold some stock? And are you not a principal stockholder in it?"

"Mr. Blair, I suggest we release these men and continue this discussion in the office." Gideon Schaacht walked out of the old statehouse a hero to the men whom he had refused, and that is power. Blair knew it.

When Blair re-entered Schaacht's office the third time it was upon an entirely different footing. Riddle, the cashier, shoved a chair toward him. Justin Bolding paid him the honor of glaring at him instead of grinning. Gideon Schaacht now even listened attentively.

Now an attitude of attention from Gideon Schaacht was in itself formidable. It was not mere courtesy. It was scrutiny. Though his long face was relaxed and his body was slouched in the chair with arms folded, boots extended and crossed under the table, his eyes were alert and direct. The cranium inclined toward Blair so that huge black brows had to lift a little to let the eyes look out at the visitor, much as Blair had seen Slover Navarre hold his eye to the sights of his rifle for minutes on end patiently waiting for a Wyandot to crawl to a place where he could be shot handier.

"Mesopotamia, you say, Mr. Blair?"

"Yes."

"Bolding, get the map, if you please."

While Bolding went for the map Blair felt awkward sitting in the silent rays of Schaacht's scrutiny, the more so because Virginia Schaacht also sat watching, as though she were at some sporting event. In fifteen years up in the big woods among the Faith Hawkinses and the Hope Emersons and Elizabeth Buttricks and the Wyandot girls, Jonathan Blair had forgotten the sounds of silk and the smells of eastern perfume and the transparency of the skin of a woman who stayed in the house and didn't wear leather. But even as he remembered them now, he still did not remember any time when these things had combined to create such a presence in any room. Without looking directly at her, he was overwhelmingly aware of the little rustlings as she changed her position in her chair, and he was aware of an area of whiteness of face and throat so delicate that it should be covered against the dust and gaze of the world.

He further felt that she must know what he was thinking. And to break it he said, "Mr. Schaacht, the men who sent me to ask for this loan have every confidence in the land. We are north and west of the Borough of Columbus. The dirt is black eighteen to thirty inches down. The land will repay many times the money we need to hold this ground."

"You don't look like a man that would care about the blackness of the dirt, Mr. Blair. In fact, you wear the clothes of a frontiersman, but you act like an easterner. In fact, you seem out of place in either place. I can't figure you."

"I've been up there long enough to know that those people are all on their fourth and fifth land payments to the government," Blair said. "And I know now that the bad money in the West is only a symptom of something else. Your real object should be to keep that ground in the hands of the men who have held it this long already. If you can do that, the currency will correct itself."

"How should I do this?"

"Give a loan to Mesopotamia so that they can make their fourth and fifth payments to the Land Office. They'll make the land pay."

"Hah!" Schaacht sat up and shoved a long skinny finger into Blair's face. "You were making sense until you said that. But that's the trouble. They have *too* much confidence in the land. That's why they borrowed too much money to buy too much land. That's why they contracted to buy four hundred acres of land from the government, and now they're scratching to pay for forty."

Blair had no answer.

"Furthermore," said Schaacht, "I am already forced to become depository for the monies received by the United States Land Office across the road. Every day they bring in bales of the wild paper that you people are paying into the Land Office. What am I supposed to do with the stuff? Paper the walls? What would *you* do with it?"

"When you have stabilized the currency," said Blair, "why couldn't you loan it back out?"

Schaacht considered the suggestion seriously.

Bolding brought in the map, and like a good aide, he had made a mark indicating Mesopotamia. This brought more life to the face of Gideon Schaacht than anything yet. He left Bolding holding the map, but he tapped it with his finger.

"That's in the Indian country, Blair!"

"No. Just under it."

"Draw the line in."

Blair drew in the Greenville Treaty Line. Schaacht said, "No, down here a little more."

Blair said, "Oh? How come you know something about it?"

Schaacht snapped his head to Blair, but apparently found no danger. He said, "Well, now that the Wyandots have ceded most of that area under the new treaty, I'm naturally interested. Do the Indians seem to be content with the treaty?"

"No."

"No?"

"That's right," Blair said. "Is that important to you?"

"Well . . . uh . . . the sooner those Indians are moved off the land, under the terms of the treaty, the sooner those lands can go up for sale. Sooner they go up for sale, the sooner we can get some eastern money out here . . . eastern buyers."

Schaacht studied the map slowly, not noticing that Bolding's arm was quivering from holding it up so long. In a new mild tone of voice Schaacht said, "Blair, tell me, are you familiar with these chiefs up here?"

"We all are. As soon as the Indians evacuate the land under the terms of the treaty our people want to move in and stake out new farms."

"Why?"

"Because it looks like they're going to lose the farms they now have to the Land Office. Starting on a new piece of ground, though, they start with new credit from the government."

"Huh. Is there as much black walnut up there as they say?"

"There's a lot."

"I hear there's salt, too."

"That's another thing we've got our eye on."

Abruptly Schaacht turned back to the other subject.

"Blair, you may tell your people that . . . uh . . . perhaps we can work out a loan for the Mesopotamia Hog & Trust Bank."

Blair drew his chair closer and waited for more. But there was no more. Gideon Schaacht rose and offered his arm to his daughter.

"When, Mr. Schaacht?"

"Later. I'll send a man up to examine the properties on which such a loan could be secured."

"When?"

But Gideon Schaacht left the room with his daughter.

Blair could see Mesopotamia lose interest immediately after Sam Hosmer asked his pointed question.

"*When* will he come up to look us over for the loan?"

"He didn't say," Blair answered.

Stikes and Hussong were already turning away to leave the store. But Hosmer clung to the last.

"But what did he do when ye asked him when he would come?"

"He walked out of the room."

The store began to empty. Hope Emerson stepped to the center of the store. "Don't act like it wasn't better than nothing," she charged. "Did you expect Blair would be packing the money back in his saddle bag?"

But they turned and left. In Mesopotamia when a Wyandot had to be shot, he had to be shot right now or sooner. When a cabin had to be raised, it had to be done now, before snow.

They needed currency now, and Jonathan Blair had not brought it.

That's why it seemed a great day for the lawyer when a young man from Chillicothe rode into Hosmer Village and asked for Jonathan Blair.

The village had seen the splotch of white at the young man's throat when he rode in. They noticed he wore a side arm instead of a rifle, and that he wiped his feet before he entered the store. Then they saw Camelia Flannerty hurry from the store over to Blair's cabin in the center of the village. They saw Blair follow her out and head back toward the store. And almost simultaneously that morning the settlers of Hosmer Village remembered errands at the store.

It was easy for everybody to see they were two of a kind. The young lad was like Blair had been fifteen years before; dressed fine and somewhat arrogant and looking out of place like a pig in pants. But that was all right. If Blair could understand this young whippersnapper and get a loan out of him for the town, it didn't matter what the two of them looked like.

The young man, whose name was Justin Bolding, was looking around as though he wasn't used to conducting his business in front of everybody. Blair said, "It's all right, Mr. Bolding. It's just as well they're all assembled. These are the people whose property you'll want to appraise for the loan to our bank. We're all stockholders in our bank. And we're mighty glad you're here. We were beginning to think you weren't coming."

"You mean you were expecting me?"

"Schaacht said we'd get a United States Bank loan."

Justin Bolding looked around the store. "Oh, is that what you think?"

"Well, you're from the bank."

"No. I'm not here for the bank."

"Not for the bank?"

"No. And I'm afraid you'd best give up that loan idea. Mr. Schaacht perhaps spoke too quickly."

They stared at him.

Hosmer said, "If you didn't come about the loan, what then?"

Bolding addressed Blair. "I came up to ask if I could read law under you. Wondered if you'd be my preceptor."

The crowd left the store.

In his own cabin, Blair looked across at the fancy young man. "You said you knew Judge Burnet in Cincinnati, Bolding?"

"Yes."

"And you know Governor Worthington?"

"Yes."

"And you know Corwin of Lebanon and Wells of Steubenville and Sloo in Cincinnati?"

"Yes. But what has that to do with it, Blair?"

Blair rose and walked a few paces. "If you know these, the most prominent lawyers in the West, what do you want to read law under *me* for? I've got three law books and outside of this last year I haven't tried ten cases a year."

Bolding looked with unconcealed contempt at the three rain-stained volumes over Blair's door. "I brought my own books," he said.

"The devil with your books. Why did you pick me for preceptor?"

"I thought you knew. Your brilliant reputation, of course."

Blair stared at the impertinent brat. He said, "Bolding, you might be just mean enough to get along up here. I'll take you on. But you'll find your own quarters. You'll execute all documents I ask for. You'll furnish your own horse and found. And I still doubt like hell if I ever recommend you for the bar."

Bolding grinned. "I doubt if I'll need your recommendation."

Blair said, "Get your boots off my bunk if you don't mind."

Chapter 2: COURT DAY

JONATHAN BLAIR believed that it was patience that would save the West, patience and waiting; and he wondered if these men would wait. While opposing counsel fanned their anger, Jonathan Blair further wondered what he could do about it if they did not wait.

His glance circled the courtroom while the auditors stared at the Indian defendant in the dock. It was only the first time the old blockhouse in Mesopotamia had been used for a courtroom, and certainly it would be the first time the old blockhouse had administered justice instead of bullets to a Wyandot. That is, it would be justice if these men would be patient.

But Blair saw no patience on the crinkled leather face of old Sam Hosmer who sat as a matter of course in the middle of the first row of puncheon benches, leaning forward. He strained old eyes to glare at the Wyandot with a concentration he once saved only for the sights of his rifle.

Hosmer was founder, father and patron saint of Hosmer Village or Mesopotamia, as he tried to have it called. He had no patience for anyone who deterred settlement here. The Indian who sat in the dock would cost the settlement a good Merino sheep farmer, and Merino wool was beginning to look like an escape from bankruptcy. More than that the Indian was costing them their self-respect. For Mason Irving, the new settler, had now seen the depths of their poverty, the height of the mortgages on their land, and the treachery of Western money. He would report this when he went back east, and the report would slow up immigration here, further postponing the dream for which old Hosmer had paid a lifetime and two sons.

Blair saw no patience on the massive, jutting jaw of Brutus Christofferson who sat next to Hope Emerson, hoping to comfort her with the nearness of his muscled bulk. Blair saw no patience either on the dark face of young Joe Hussong who looked at the Indian as though he remembered the crimson splurting from his father's right eye through the fingers of his hand, running down his bare forearm and streaming off his elbow. Blair saw the sweat of Hussong's hand wet the iron rifle barrel . . . though the day was cold.

There was no patience on the good blunt face of Jim Dolk who remembered when Hosmer Village scalps were bringing $4.50 at the British fort at Detroit.

Captain Michael, the ancient Wyandot in the defendant's dock, inherited all that. But worst of all, Captain Michael inherited the enmity of all the friends of Hope Emerson. They remembered the singing whing of the Wyandot bullet that had widowed her. More than anyone else she sealed the Indian's doom, for it was *her* brother who had been tricked by the Indian. Her brother was the prospective settler. His arrival had been long-awaited by the village for two reasons. First, he was to bring to the village two more rams and eight more ewes of the fabulous new Merino sheep to augment Hope's flock. Second, he was Hope's brother, and Hope Emerson was much loved here. And on Hope's face, there was no sympathy for the Indian.

There was another side to the story, too, but the eloquent young opposing counsel was not bringing that into the courtroom right now. Stuttgart was his name, and he was good. He was up from Kentucky to travel the Ohio court circuits, and he gave these Mesopotamians a taste of the show and the eloquence which Kentucky attorneys had brought up to the Western bar. Blair had lost four cases to him in four different towns in the Western circuit this month.

Fortunately there was no jury for there were no peers here for Captain Michael, the old Wyandot chief.

Opposing counsel half-faced to the crowd and lowered his voice to the lush baritone, which Blair now recognized as the beginning of his close. Stuttgart was laying out for the crowd the Indian's vast treachery.

"The plaintiff . . . then breaks his way west across the Allegheny Ridges in his wagon with his family. He is looking forward to joining his sister . . . your widowed Mrs. Emerson. In his pocket he has his savings. At your borders he meets this Indian who professes to be heading east and in need of eastern currency. The Indian persuades Irving that he will need Western currency to make any purchases in the West. The Indian agrees to swap his filthy Western money for Irving's good Boston Bank notes, on seemingly attractive terms. The unsuspecting Irving then swaps his hard-saved pocketful of money for two pocketfuls of the most illegitimate collection of Western wild-cat paper that I have ever seen.

"The plaintiff, Irving, arrives at your town to find that his two pocketfuls of paper trash will not even trade at Hosmer's store for a one pound package of gun powder. The culprit—yes, the robber—sits here in your midst and your own Mr. Blair says we cannot force him to return the plaintiff's good money, nor even confine him. Your Honors, we rest on your decency."

Each man in the room leaned back as though he had spoken the words himself.

Blair rose from the small slab table, walked slowly past Captain Michael without looking at him, halted halfway between the two judges and the opposing counsel. He seemed to address the rifle port over the head of Stuttgart.

"Opposing counsel's outrage at our failing Western currency is understandable," he said quietly. The stir in the blockhouse said, "Amen to that." They leaned forward again to see how Blair would slip out of this one.

"But do we not forget that the so-called worthless dollars which this Indian handed to the plaintiff from Boston are white man's dollars. It says on the face of each 'one dollar.' The Indian did not make them worth less than one dollar."

The Kentuckian was on his feet. "Everybody knows they aren't worth the echo off a steamboat whistle! The Indian knew it!"

"Yes." Blair waited for the stir to settle. "But we have required each man to be his own watchdog about what kind of money he will accept. Whenever any of us in this room can unload our bad currency on a downstater, we congratulate ourselves. Should we expect more of an Indian?"

"But Irving didn't know! Nor did he have any idea that his own money was better than any in Ohio, or Indiana, or in the Illinois Territory!"

Blair seized Stuttgart's statement. "The real anger in the room is not that a man was cheated, but that the brother of Hope Emerson was cheated . . . or seemed to be cheated."

Brute Christofferson rose up from beside Hope Emerson, like a tidal wave cresting. "Blair, it seemed to me you just said it. A man was cheated. Now let's stop talkin' and start hangin'!"

Blair had in his pocket a slip of paper with a list of names on it which should by all logic shut off all further argument on the subject. He pulled it out and fingered it while they watched him. But studying their faces he decided that at this heated moment a victory of logic would bring a verdict of violence. He had asked the judge to entertain the case in hopes a trial would break the edge of the vengefulness. The formality of the court *had* cooled some of them. Blair put away the paper. He turned to Judge Pease.

"Sir, we cannot here open up the whole question of the deficiency of our monetary system and our poor land-sale system. Defense therefore requests dismissal of the case."

The men of Hosmer Village looked at each other, startled. Stuttgart was quick. "On what grounds!"

"Grounds," continued Blair, "are that this court is not competent to try a case between a citizen of the Republic of America and a member of a foreign nation."

The judges did not look surprised. But Stuttgart was on his feet. "Foreign nation?"

Blair held up from under his arm a rolled parchment and his voice trailed off as if it were of course the most patent and obvious of truths. "The Wyandots are officially a foreign nation, witness this treaty which I have at this moment in my custody for execution between the United States and the Wyandots and five other Northwestern tribes."

Stuttgart melted to his bench.

Judge Pease rapped for order. The court would recess while he and Judge Ethan Allen Brown considered the defense's last request, at length, Blair hoped. He needed time.

The crowd rose, muttering. But it sounded to Jonathan Blair's sensitive ear as if they would at least wait to hear the judges' decision. That should give him an hour to find a way out.

The Indian looked a question at him, but had sense enough not to speak.

Blair waited until the grumbling crowd began moving out the door for the recess. Then he also moved toward the door, slowly, careful not to rub against anybody. At the doorway his exit was blocked by the broad back of Matt Gavagan who laughed to Joe Hussong, "It's a mighty pity that Jonathan don't remember 'thirteen and 'fourteen and before, when Yankee hair was bringing fancy prices in Canada, huh? Might not be so mixed up about them red devils."

Blair walked out between them. As he crossed the common toward his cabin, he felt small groups studying him. He slowed up to let Stikes cross to his forge well ahead of him. And he moved slowly to his cabin.

Some in Hosmer Village thought Jonathan Blair was a "man of good will," others thought he was a misfit. He had been a misfit, the older settlers said, from the day he had come out here in 1801 with his ruffled shirts and his bright, eastern, legal reputation, and no knack with an axe. At a time when there was no use for lawyers in the West, Jonathan Blair had been a lawyer. But now, when it seemed there were law matters coming up, Jonathan Blair could hardly be called a lawyer any more, unless settling local arguments and arguing a few dozen cases in a dozen years, out of a rain-stained copy of Wood's Institutes, made a lawyer.

There had seldom been anything that Wood's Institutes could do for Hosmer, the storekeeper; Slasher, the woodsman; Stikes, the blacksmith; Navarre, the trapper; Woodbridge, the hog farmer, that they couldn't do better for themselves with their own big hands and bull heads. But now the strong men were getting themselves onto subtler ground.

In the last six months the currency of the West had gone to water, the pressing of Indian cessions was beginning in brutal earnest. Indiana Territory had become a state, Illinois Territory was trying for it. Neighbors were still apt to be three stream-beds apart, but even at that distance their rights and privileges and fence lines were getting tangled now, and there was now law work to do.

Blair looked behind him. The crowd had not moved far from the blockhouse.

Wood's Institutes had no instructions to offer that much helped a frontier lawyer. The law work here required new laws and new books and it required invention. And who was coming out to do it? A race of hard young whippers like that Bolding who never saw how good it was here when the West did its business without paper dollars.

Blair stepped into his cabin. He would have liked it if his student had hopped up and asked, "Did you get the Indian free, sir?" He remembered how he had treated his own preceptor. But Bolding remained seated and he grinned, "Well, have the good judges discovered yet that they have no jurisdiction over Wyandots?"

"The good judges know well enough what they're about," said

Blair. "Have you finished making a copy of the Wyandot treaty? We'll need it tomorrow. Chief Silver Pigeon should be here by then. And if we haven't hanged his father, we may have a chance to get him to comply with the treaty."

"I'm down to Article Ten."

"Leave it for now and go over to the blockhouse to watch the Indian."

"Why?"

"Just see that nobody grabs him. If that happens we'll never get the treaty executed tomorrow."

"What should I do if anybody tries?"

Blair sat down at the table which served him as a desk. He rubbed the heel of his hand up the center of his forehead.

"I don't know," he answered. "But at least you can tell me if there's trouble."

But Bolding did not leave. For into Blair's cabin strode Mike Stikes. Stikes bent his grey-spiked head to clear the cabin doorway. His leather apron was molded to his long skinny shanks. The forge hammer hanging from his right claw was a natural extension of his sinewy arm. The awkward load he carried was in his other hand. It was a piece of paper, and he carried it with the frontiersman's hopeful respect for a land document.

Blair found no insult in Stikes' opening statement nor in his extremely blue eyes. Stikes was just sticking to what he could afford. He said, "Blair, they tell me the way the land titles are bein' fouled up, I'd ought to go down to Franklinton and hire me one of those fifty-dollar lawyers. But I can only afford about a five-dollar lawyer. Would that cover you?"

"Probably so, Mike." Blair reached for the paper with a wan smile. But it was wiped off by the big grin on young Bolding's face. Bolding straightened his face and left for the blockhouse.

"What's your problem, Mike?"

"Put it this way, Blair. You're in charge of executin' that treaty with the Wyandots, aren't you? The one Cass and McArthur made?"

"Yes."

"You'll be the first to know when they're finally moved off the territory and crammed up into that one hundred fifty thousand acres at Upper Sandusky?"

"Probably."

"Then you'll be the first to know when that ceded land is open to settlement by the likes of me, won't you?"

"Should be."

"Well, that's my land grant from the Governor for servin' with Harrison. Grants me a hundred fifty acres. Soon as that ground is open for settlement—that is, soon as the Wyandots get off it—I want you to cash in that warrant and get me title to a hundred fifty acres up there. I got it picked out . . . the ground I want."

"I'll handle it, Mike. But why you going to move up there?"

"Because I'm going to lose my land down here, same as most of us will. Man can't get hold of a dollar that the government'll accept. I still owe fourth and fifth payments on my place, same as most of 'em. I've got money. But Land Office says it ain't money. It's only paper."

"The new United States Bank is supposed to fix all that, Mike."

Stikes waved his bony claw in dismissal of the United States Bank. "Blair, we're countin' on you executin' that treaty and gettin' them red devils moved outa here so's we can move in . . . on ground that's free and clear. That's what the big meetin's about isn't it, that you're havin' with the Wyandots tomorrow?"

"Yes, Mike. But what we do to Captain Michael over there today will have a lot to do with whether Silver Pigeon will cede the ground tomorrow, and how soon you can get your land."

"The treaty's signed. You got the government money to pay 'em. They got to get out."

"What's to make them get out?"

"You."

"All I've got to work with is words, Mike."

Mike looked at the hammer in his hand.

"You picked your own kind of work tools, Blair. If you don't know how to use 'em, you got a lot of us in trouble."

Stikes left.

Blair stepped to the doorway.

"Mike, what keeps you from the court today?"

Stikes turned to face Blair. "Some of them are havin' me to do a little work on their rifles all of a sudden."

"That's what I was afraid of."

Jonathan Blair glanced at the crowd which was already drifting back toward the blockhouse. He noticed the smoke of new logs coming out of the blockhouse chimney and it seemed a devil of a time for the judges to be warming themselves. It would be hot enough without a fire before long no doubt.

Blair placed Stikes' land grant in a stiff leather pouch. He opened the waterstained client book on his table and turned past many blank pages to the page marked, "December, 1817", where there were three other entries. Under these he wrote:

Mike Stikes . . . convert land grant to title, 150 acres.

Just above that entry was the notation:

Treaty 1817. Principals for U.S., Gen'ls. Cass, McArthur.
Principals for Wyandots, Captain Michael, Silver Pigeon.
Cession of northwest Ohio, parts of Indiana and Michigan Territory. Execute.

How do you execute a treaty with an Indian who is on trial by your own people? He remembered the day he had got that assignment. Major John Armstrong had walked into Blair's cabin, spread the seven-page parchment out on Blair's table and slapped his gloves on top of it to keep it from rolling up.

"It's yours to execute, Blair. I don't envy you."

"Mine?"

"That's right. McArthur and Cass got the Indian signatures . . . whatever they're worth." He laughed. "Now all you got to do is see they get off the land like they said they would. I'm to swear you in."

"Swear me in? As what?"

"Sub-Indian agent to the Wyandots."

"I don't want it."

"There's twelve hundred dollars a year in it for you, Blair."

Blair sat down and read the treaty carefully, skipping only the long list of special payments to privileged individual Indian chiefs and the long lists of meaningless Indian signatures. Then he asked Armstrong about the details of the appointment. Armstrong explained; and Blair said, "I don't want it."

Armstrong rolled up the treaty and stuck it in his breast pocket. "I warned the Old Man you wouldn't take it. Damn few would."

Blair said, "Why did they pick me?"

"Well, they picked you because Silver Pigeon and Captain Michael specifically requested you."

"Requested *me*?"

"That's right. And we're in a 'concessionary phase' now . . . the way they put it. Grant any reasonable request they make, and drive 'em out as fast as possible. The official phrase is, 'Gain concessions with all possible haste and/or methods short of bloodshed.' "

"Silver Pigeon requested me?"

"That's right. In writing. And he can write better English than I can."

Blair sat thinking. Armstrong started to leave. Blair asked, "Who'll get the job if I refuse?"

"I don't want it," Armstrong said. "But I guess I'll get it if you refuse. Johnson's already been assigned to work on the Miamis over in Indiana and Michigan Territory. Huh, and I won't even get the twelve hundred dollars, bein' on army pay already. I won't fool with 'em. I'll just pay 'em and move 'em."

Blair said, "Armstrong, I'll take the job."

"Huh? By God, you're a funny one, Blair."

That's how it had happened. When the money came to finalize the treaty, Blair chose to hold the meeting of the Wyandot, Shawanee, and Ottawa sachems and chiefs in Hosmer Village. When Hosmer Village found out about that they were mad. Hosmer had asked, "Why, *here*, Blair?"

"You want the treaty executed, don't you, Hosmer?"

"Yes, and fast. But why *here*?"

"Because when you do business with an Indian in his own surroundings, he's hard to deal with. But they're not so tall when they step out of their own Indian towns. In fact I want to hold the meeting right in the blockhouse so they'll be reminded of the . . . of what went on there."

"Makes sense," Hosmer had snorted. "But you're askin' for trouble. There's been too many bush fights lately, and they'll find the air around here awful thick."

"That's all I've got for a lever," Blair said.

And so he had sent word up to Upper Sandusky for Captain Michael to round up the sachems and signers and bring them down to Mesopotamia. He had been careful to address the message to Captain Michael, but it would be his son, Silver Pigeon who would handle it.

Old Captain Michael had arrived eight days ago, and each day thereafter there had straggled in chiefs from the Ottawas, Potawatomies, Shawanees, Miamis. That meant that Silver Pigeon was out riding through the big woods, sending them in.

Everything had been going along fine until Hope Emerson's brother had arrived in Mesopotamia and spotted Captain Michael as one of the Indians who had bilked him of his good Boston money and loaded him up with good-for-nothing Western wildcat paper. That's what sent the guns over to Stikes' forge for new frizzens and borings.

Blair closed the client book.

Through his doorway he could see that the little groups of men had not tired of waiting, as he'd hoped they would. Their interest, in fact, had heightened because Blair could see their glances converge on a lone figure which strode toward Blair's cabin. If Blair was on the wrong side of the argument before, the presence of Major John Armstrong in his cabin made it official.

Armstrong gave his boots two perfunctory passes on the footscraper and stepped in.

"I heard you might need help, Blair. Came up. Six men coming behind me."

"I sent word for you *not* to come," said Blair. "You won't have enough troops to do any good. Just enough to make everybody sore."

"Sore?"

"Look behind you."

Armstrong turned to look at the men across the common who had assembled around Armstrong's horse and were now gazing at the Blair cabin.

"Never mind that," Armstrong chuckled. "If they hang the Indian you'll never get the treaty executed."

"If they decide to hang the Indian, six men won't stop them. Go back and stop your men."

Armstrong shrugged agreement. "But just remember I tried to help you. And there's no excuses bein' accepted by the War Department for sub-agents that can't execute their treaties."

"War Department is the least of my concerns, Armstrong."

Armstrong chuckled, "Y'know Blair, I really believe you accepted this job just to see the Wyandots get fair contract."

Blair thought about this, asking himself why he had taken the job.

"And if you got any ideas about bein' an Indian lover," Armstrong added, "I'd better give you the details on why Silver Pigeon requested you for sub-agent."

"Why did he?"

Armstrong seemed to enjoy answering.

"We gave him his choice for sub-agent. Colonel Johnson or me. He didn't want Johnson because Johnson is too honorable. Indians like him. Gets concessions too easily. Silver Pigeon knows that if Johnson is sub-agent he can't keep his hold over the Weas, Senecas, Delawares, Chippewas and Shawanees. Johnson could work on them separately. And The Pigeon is another confederation builder. Thinks he's a second Tecumseh."

"Why didn't he want you?"

Armstrong laughed. "I'm too mean. I hate 'em and The Pigeon knows it. He asked for you."

Blair's laugh was dry. Armstrong had just held up a brutal mirror that reflected a Blair who was just man enough to sign the papers, not man enough to cause Silver Pigeon any trouble.

He looked beyond Armstrong to the men across the common who were drifting closer to the blockhouse door, and he wondered what he could do.

Armstrong laughed. "Just thought I ought to let you know who you're up against, Blair. He's a cute one. Awful cute!"

Young Bolding stepped through the cabin door. "Judge Pease says he can't recess any longer, Mr. Blair. The men all decided the judges had enough time to make up their minds."

Blair sighed. He reached into his chest pocket and pulled out a scrap of paper containing four names. He handed it to Bolding. "Take a quick look around the settlement, Bolding. Any cabins that have new thin-scraped buckskin windows, mark the names here and bring the list to me in the blockhouse."

"Just what legal instruction should I draw from this, Mr. Blair?"

"More than you think. Just get the list. And hurry!"

Blair walked across to the blockhouse.

Armstrong said, "Good luck. Don't forget I tried to help."

From the doorway of the blockhouse men watched the law man come. Blair saw the strong, braided, leather thong that looped down from Amos Exeter's hand. They gave way enough to let the lawyer in. It was hot inside. He wondered why the judges had such a big fire.

Stuttgart fell in alongside him as he walked up to front the judges.

"Blair," he said softly, "I never would have got 'em so curled up if I'd known how hot they was on the subject up here."

Blair nodded.

Judge Pease looked at Blair, giving him all the time he wanted.

Blair planted himself sideways between Captain Michael and the rows of seats. He stood so he could see both the judges and the crowd, his feet broad-based. He could not tell whether Captain Michael was nervous.

He nodded to the judge.

Judge Pease wrapped gently with the gavel. Blair felt the men lean forward for the judges' decision. He also detected a surprising change in the judge's delivery. Calvin Pease usually bit off his words briskly and loud. But now, though his eyes were alert, playing back and forth across the people, his voice seemed deliberately languid and monotonous as he very slowly discussed the issues influencing his and Judge Brown's decision. It seemed he was forever leading up to the decision, which must surely come in the next phrase, but didn't.

Bolding returned with the list of new buckskin windows in the village. He handed it to Blair while Calvin Pease was still warming up to his decision.

In preface to his decision Judge Pease found it pertinent to explain the structure of the newly formed judicial system of Ohio. That the Supreme Court consisted of four judges who split into two teams, two judges traveling over each circuit.

Brute Christofferson who had been hunched forward with his elbows on his knees now leaned back against the back wall.

In monotonous monotone Calvin Pease explained that when Ohio needed a Supreme Court the two circuits joined together and the four circuit judges then became a Supreme Court, sitting in banc.

Brute Christofferson's head sagged forward in the stuffy room made hot by the fire and dry by the judge's talk.

Calvin Pease, with voluminous parenthetical explanations, deviations and ramifications, defined the limits of common-pleas jurisdiction.

Sam Hosmer leaned heavily on his rifle.

Asa Buttrick's head nodded in the hot room, then recovered.

Calvin Pease explained the status of the specific Indian tribes in the Northwest Territory as foreign powers.

Asa Buttrick's head dropped to his chest and stayed.

Quietly, without change of pace or inflection, Calvin Pease announced that the case was dismissed.

There were a few moments of quiet. Nodding heads snapped alert. The Kentucky counsel remained quiet during the puzzled silence.

Just as Blair was privately congratulating the judge for diluting the wrath of a township beyond the action point, he saw Hope Emerson rise from her bench halfway back in the blockhouse.

"It's plain to see, sir, that you know the law extra fine. That's what we need, sir. But does that all add up to: my brother doesn't get his money back and that red devil gets to keep it?"

Calvin Pease nodded.

Brute Christofferson yelled from the back, "Beg your pardon, sir, but no he don't. Not in this town!" Christofferson surged forward toward the dock. Amos Exeter fell in beside him with the leather thong and there was a general rising in the back of the room.

Jonathan Blair reached in his pocket and pulled out his scrap of paper. He nodded to Judge Pease who now rapped sharply on the bench, arresting the movement.

Blair grabbed that instant of silence and yelled, "Hope, the money system is all wrong. But it's no worse for your brother than for Captain Michael."

"I don't take you, Jonathan," she said evenly. "The Indian knew what he was doing."

Blair clamped his lips and brought the paper up to the level of his eyes. "I mean, Hope, that I have here the list of men who gave Captain Michael those wildcat dollars which he gave your brother. They were given to Captain Michael in payment for the last twenty packboards of thin-scraped buckskins he brought down here, the buckskins which are now the windows in your cabins. Shall I read the list of names, Hope?"

Exeter scratched his chin and glanced down at his buck shirt. Stanley Slasher looked down at his buckskin leggins. The others just looked down. Hope Emerson looked around at the men, finding no eyes to meet hers as they shifted and hawed.

"No, Jonathan." The spark went out of her. "I reckon that won't help."

Hope Emerson turned to the door of the blockhouse and her shoulders sagged as she walked out, as did those of most men who had just seen it proved that even the law was no escape from a money system which was daily turning men's life-work savings into piles of laughing colored paper.

Blair forced himself to join the perimeter of the crowd in front of Hosmer's store. He felt it was his place, though no one apparently thought so. He did not look at Hope Emerson.

In addition to the feeling of duty, though, he had a yearning admiration for the young man whom they all watched. Blair raised to his tiptoes to see the young Irving face over the crowd as he climbed to the seat of his wagon and took the reins from his wife. Hope Emerson's brother was like Hope herself. He did not discuss a given project and confer and plan and compare alternatives. He just commenced.

He had no money now to take land of his own here, nor to raise his Merinos with Hope's flock. And since he refused to go shares with any man, they directed him west to a certain Slover Navarre who had on occasion been of service to those who needed land and had no money. Navarre had become legendary among the squatters in a vast triangle from Pittsburgh to Louisville to Vincennes to Detroit.

Irving's matched pair leaned into their collars.

Gavagan's big voice yelled, "There may be more Indians out there, Irving! But anyways there'll be a dang sight less lawyers!"

The crowd laughed. Some glanced for Blair's reaction. The laugh swelled way beyond the due of Gavagan's joke as Mesopotamia released the strength they'd saved up for a hanging.

Hope Emerson's brother pushed west by south for the Illinois Territory. As the crowd splintered into small groups to watch the receding wagon, Blair found himself alone. Hope Emerson walked toward him, but when she noticed it she deflected her course. Blair walked toward his cabin. He forced himself to walk slowly under the gaze of Hosmer Village or Mesopotamia, as it was now officially listed on the Western circuit of the court.

There was one in the crowd, Emanuel Ault by name, who leaned close to Justin Bolding and said, "Don't smile, Sonny. He can still teach you a lot."

"Huh?"

"He bought that Indian's life for the price of that laugh."

"Was that such a bargain?" Bolding smiled. "It's the going price, isn't it?"

"You fool," said Ault. "A hung Indian today would have cost us three million acres tomorrow at Blair's treaty meetin'. May anyhow. Even unhung."

Chapter 3: THE CONTRACT

WHEN THE lights in Hosmer Village went out, one yet burned in the cabin of Jonathan Blair. His head, bent over the table, was silhouetted and framed in the small greased buckskin window, a target for whatever any man felt about Jonathan Blair.

Blair himself was reading one of the pages of the treaty. On the bunk young Justin Bolding sat copying another page. To his preceptor's back he said, "If I were you, after what happened today and what's likely to happen tomorrow, I wouldn't sit with my head in that window, Blair."

Blair stiffened at the bald use of his last name by his pupil. A preceptor was due some respect from his student. Blair let it pass, and regretted it immediately because Bolding said, "I'll turn in now, and copy the rest of this treaty tomorrow."

"It's got to be finished tonight, Bolding."

"The idea of my coming up here was to read law under you, not to practice penmanship and to be your clerk."

"The idea? Whose idea?"

"Mine," Bolding said. "Whose else?"

"Well, I happen to need a copy of the treaty. But it's as good a way as any to teach you the language and content of a treaty. You wouldn't have learned that under your eastern preceptors."

Bolding grinned at Blair's back. "As a lawyer, how many treaties will I be called upon to write?"

Blair turned abruptly to erase Bolding's grin. "All right, Mr. Bolding, repeat to me the content and purpose of Article Six."

Bolding was bright and he grinned smugly, "Article Six. In addition to the 150,000 acres reserved for the use of the Wyandots, the United States are to grant in fee simple 640 acres each to Doanquod, Rontondee, Tauyau, Honornu, Captain Michael, Anthony Shane, and about ten others as a reward for—well, anyhow, it's a bribe to a few special Indians and half-whites to make the treaty go smooth."

"It's payment for services," corrected Blair, "with General Harrison in the war."

"Maybe, but that isn't what Major Armstrong and Schaacht said the night they planned this treaty at Schaacht's house in Cincinnati."

Blair burned under the fact that his student knew more of affairs at first hand than he knew himself.

"Never mind that," he said. "What's Article Fourteen?"

"The United States reserves the right," Bolding answered with irritating promptness, "to build roads even through the part they leave to the Indians."

"Article Eighteen?" snapped Blair.

"The Delawares also cede all their lands in the Western Reserve and between Cincinnati and Vincennes."

"Article Ten?"

"The United States agrees to build a sawmill and a gristmill for the Wyandots and to furnish and maintain two white blacksmiths, one for the Wyandots and one for the Senecas."

"Article Nineteen?"

"Treaty becomes effective and binding on both parties when ratified by the great white Congress," said Bolding. "And it's your job to make it stick and I don't envy you."

"Well, finish copying it, because you're going to help me make it stick, and when we meet the Indians, you'd better know it by heart. They will."

Bolding finished copying it and suddenly he was on his feet, reaching for his pistol, for the door began to open slowly. But he relaxed when he saw Hope Emerson's short rifle open the door. And he sat down as she stepped into the cabin. Jonathan Blair stood up.

And in the sitting down of Bolding and the standing up of Blair was the story of Hope Emerson. When you had not known her long you would sit down, and when you had known her long you stood up.

She leaned her rifle against the wall, ran her small brown hand through her light, swept-back hair and sat down.

From her breast pocket she drew two pieces of paper covered with leather against the weather. Without referring to the events of this afternoon she said, "Jonathan, I need you to write me two letters."

She handed him the paper. "Don't make any mistakes. I bought only two sheets of paper from Mr. Hosmer."

Blair sat down and took the quill and the ink from Bolding.

"First one is to Mr. Thomas Rotch. Write on the envelope that he lives on Big Sippo Creek, a mile east of Tuscarawas River somewheres in Stark County. Write 'Dear Mr. Rotch: On the two pairs of imported Merino white sheep you agreed to sell to me for my brother, we have run into financial trouble.' "

Blair said, "Hope, I feel that I ——"

" 'He has lost his money,' " continued Hope. " 'However, I wish you to hold them for me, as I have some money owing to me from the Wyandots at Upper Sandusky. This money will be in good currency and will make a good down payment. I will then get a loan from the Mesopotamia Hog & Trust for the balance. This part will be in Mesopotamia Hog & Trust notes which, though not so good as the United States Bank notes or Piatt Bank notes, are in very fair acceptance most places north of Columbus.' "

There were some other details about the transfer of the rare Merino sheep. Blair had Hope make a mark for a signature and he folded the paper so that it became its own envelope. He waxed it.

He took the other sheet of paper and Hope said, "On this one you won't have to write so small. It's short. Mark it for Reverend Seth Gershom, Indian Mission, Upper Sandusky, and make it say, 'Dear Reverend Gershom: You had agreed to make a special trip down to Hosmer's Village to publish the last of the three banns of marriage between myself and Jonathan Blair. This is to tell you it will not be needed' "—Blair stopped writing. But Hope continued—" 'and save you a trip during the time when the trails will be bad. Hope Emerson.' "

Blair rose, "Hope!"

Hope's placid brown eyes were neither kind nor mean.

"No talk to be done, Jonathan, and no bad feelings."

"Hope, what I did about your brother I did because ——"

"I understand about that part, I guess. But lately there's no way of knowin' what side you're on, Jonathan. I don't mind a man bein' against me or for me, just so I can tell which. But the way things are shaping up about the Indian lands and about the money, looks like you'll likely be somewhere's in between all the time. That's all right for a smart man and a law man like you. But I'd not be able to hop about so light-footed with you, Jonathan."

"Hope!"

"There's changes here, anybody can see. Isn't like when we first came out here. 'Twas plain what a man had to do . . . or a woman. Cut the trees. Get seed in. Keep a clean rifle against the red devils. Different now. Instead of shootin' Indians we treaty with 'em and go to law with them. And instead of trustin' a man for sheep, now you got to look at the color of his money and who signed it. It's time now for somebody like you that works with writs and writin' and words. But I got to stay with the old kind, Jonathan. I belong with the Hosmers, the Stikes, the Hawkinses and . . . like that. Good night, Jonathan."

When she left there was a hole in the room. Blair looked over at Bolding. But Bolding got busy copying, his head down. Blair found himself noticing that she had not said she belonged with Christofferson. She had named Hosmer, Stikes, Hawkins.

When Jonathan Blair stepped into the blockhouse on the 12th day of December 18 and 17, it was quickly apparent to him that the blockhouse had become the center of two concentric circles.

Scattered over the common in apparently casual groups were the Indian delegates who were not to be actually inside the treaty room. To Bolding's glance they were just isolated groups of two's and three's. But Blair saw that the little groups formed a rough circle around the blockhouse.

Inside this vague circle, lounging around the outside of the blockhouse on all sides in casual attitudes was a ring of Hosmer Village settlers. They leaned against the walls, idly talking and cleaning their rifles.

Inside the blockhouse Jonathan Blair sat opposite old Captain Michael. Behind Captain Michael on the puncheon benches sat the sachems of the Weas, Chippewas, Ottawas, Delawares, Shawanees and Silver Pigeon, the Wyandot. Behind Blair sat Bolding, impressed for once.

Blair's remarks had to be addressed to Old Captain Michael, nominal chief of the Wyandots. But they had to be especially designed for the ears of the much younger man who sat behind Captain Michael, his son, Silver Pigeon, one of the smartest men in the Northwest, bar none . . . white, red or half-breed.

At a time when every town in the Northwest considered its many eighth and quarterbloods to be white men, Silver Pigeon, with more white blood than red, called himself Indian.

When the long introductions demanded by the older Indians were complete, Jonathan Blair smiled, "Captain Michael, I have good news for you. The United States Congress has ratified this treaty exactly as you made it with Generals Cass and McArthur. They have not changed a single word."

Captain Michael did not raise his eyes from the parchment in front of Blair. "You have brought the treaty money?" he asked.

"Yes, Captain Michael. I have the annuity money."

"Good, Mr. Blair."

Blair looked up, for this last comment came not from Captain Michael but from Silver Pigeon who continued whittling a point onto a maple shoot with his long knife.

"We are glad you have brought the money, Mr. Blair. It is a sign of good faith. However, I have some bad news for you. You tell us that your Congress has ratified the treaty. Unfortunately, however, *my* Congress has not ratified the treaty."

"*Your* Congress?"

"Yes. These." Silver Pigeon rotated his knife around to include the half-circle of Indians, who grinned. "Black Hoof, the Shawanee, has pointed out to me that while your Congress has been ratifying the treaty, we have been joined by fifty-seven wandering Mohawks and we have had more children, and the white men have become even more anxious to move into our lands. It means we must have more than the 150,000 acres you assigned us and we must have larger payments. Also, the damages your government agreed to pay for burning our huts in 1813 are too small."

Silver Pigeon shoved a piece of paper onto the table and resumed whittling. "We will need this in addition to what the present treaty allows."

It was in the handwriting of Reverend Seth Gershom of the Indian mission. No wonder Armstrong thought Pigeon could write. Blair read it:

100,000 *acres*

$500 *more in annual annuities to the Wyandots above the present* $4,000.

"You would have me ask for this much more, having no idea if you would then obey the terms of the treaty?" Blair asked.

"I have already done more to obey the treaty than you. We have already withdrawn most of our people up to Upper Sandusky, as we agreed."

"But we see your men occupying the same ground as before the treaty, every day."

"That does not violate the treaty. Read again Article Twelve which I insisted upon."

Bolding handed Blair the treaty.

"Article Twelve: The Wyandots shall be permitted to hunt upon the lands herein ceded even though it becomes the property of the United States."

Silver Pigeon grinned. "They are hunting," he said.

"But there are not just a few," Blair protested. "There are several bands of twenty-five and thirty men."

"They are hunting."

"But they put up huts and they occupy every bit as much ground as before the treaty."

"Hunting," said Silver Pigeon.

"But they have their women with them, and their dogs and children and ponies."

"Hunting equipment."

The English-speaking Indians in the room suddenly wore broad, wary grins.

The vibration of Mike Stikes' grumbling voice came through the blockhouse walls to Blair's ears.

"How long will they hunt?" asked Blair.

"Until we see some acts of yours to keep the treaty, such as money. Since there is not trust, Mr. Blair, the treaty must be gradual. You pay part. We withdraw some. You pay more, we withdraw more. Until we can trust . . . which I doubt."

"If we pay part of the annuities, then will the so-called hunting stop?"

"Not so many will hunt."

"Well, how can I be sure that you ——"

It was a different Silver Pigeon who looked up this time. He stalked to the table, stabbed his knife into the treaty. Bolding jumped.

"How can *you* be sure? Yes! That is my question! Can *I* be sure?

Seventeen ninety-five it was the Greenville Line . . . forever! No more cessions. But in 1805 . . . it was 'just a little piece more off the east and . . . and that's all forever!' Eighteen seven you push us out of the Miami Valley . . . but no more cessions you say 'that's all, . . . forever!' Eighteen nine and 1810 . . . you treaty with the Miamis when we Wyandots are not looking. You treaty with the Delawares. You sign treaties with little chiefs I never heard of. Then you say 'that's all . . . forever'! Forever is always only two years with you! Now my people have their backs to Lake Erie. On two sides of us already, white men. My people look to me and they ask. They ask. They ask. And I cannot help. I cannot stop the 'forever' treatying. Always smaller ground, and I cannot help. God damn you, Blair, have you ever been in such a place . . . where you cannot help your own people! That is the day you will know something, Blair . . . when you cannot help your own! That is when I want to see you!"

He spit on the treaty.

"Yes, Mr. Blair, there will be hunting."

Blair reached under the table. He brought up his leather pouch.

"Silver Pigeon, I will see about the extra land and I will see about the increased damages money. These appraisals on your burned cabins *were* too low in my opinion."

Blair opened the pouch.

"Article Four. The United States agrees to pay to the Wyandot nation annually and forever the sum of four thousand dollars."

Blair spread out the four thousand dollars in good United States Bank notes.

"I want you to see that I really have the money, Silver Pigeon. I will pay you half of it right now . . . two thousand dollars. Then we will watch the hunting for a month. If you have withdrawn all your people to your seven and one-half townships, then we will pay the other half in installments."

Blair stood up and stretched out one hand with the pen, the other for a handshake.

Silver Pigeon declined the shake, but he took the pen. He quickly scratched his eaglelike pigeon to the Wyandot receipt, threw down the quill and motioned Captain Michael to put the money in the deerskin sack. He wouldn't touch it himself.

"Mr. Blair, I do not rush to take the handshake. I think you try. But I need to know first if you *can* keep your word."

"If I *can* keep it?"

"Yes. Can you keep your people off our reserve? Already I see white surveyors up there. Can you keep your Congress and your Governor from asking more and more?"

"This treaty is now the law of the land," said Blair.

Pigeon looked old. "Yes. Yes. The law. We will see, Mr. Blair."

From behind Blair's back, Bolding stared at the great Indian.

Silver Pigeon motioned to the Indians who now slung their rifles and followed The Pigeon to the door. The young chief reached for the door handle. Suddenly he yelled in pain. The door smashed open against his fingers and into his face.

The blockhouse was quickly full of Mesopotamians who leveled rifles at the crowd. Silver Pigeon looked at Blair for an explanation. The injury on his face reduced Blair to a traitor. Joe Hussong yelled, "Stand still!"

When the commotion settled, Sam Hosmer walked in slowly, unarmed. He held a list in his hand.

Mike Stikes walked to each Indian and removed the rifles gently from clinging hands. The Indian faces recovered from astonishment to hatred.

Sam Hosmer spoke quietly, "Can't any of us figure the way ye been doin' us lately, Blair. But somehow your law talk works us around in the wrong. But ye'll understand how we can't stand by and see them red skonks take good money off a settler and get away unhurt. So ye'll please to have Captain Michael throw that bag of money on the table there so's I can reach it."

Blair looked at Hosmer, astonished.

"Sam, I didn't expect you'd go to robbery."

"Not robbery, Blair. Collectin' a debt, call it. Have Captain Michael throw the money on the table."

"Sam, that money is owed them by the Republic. I'm commissioned sub-Indian agent for Wyandots, responsible for their welfare. You touch that money, I got to take you to law."

"We'll only take what's comin' to us."

"Coming to you?"

"Yeah." Hosmer threw down his piece of paper in front of Blair. "Seems to me Article Twenty-two in that treaty says upon execution of the contract all Indian debts to white settlers will be paid."

Blair looked at the paper:

Owing to Michael Stikes for shoeing horses of the people of Chiefs Doanquod, Howoner, Rontondee, Monocue, Silver Pigeon, Captain Michael, Anthony Shane, Tauyaudautauson, Cherokee Boy, John Van Meter $200
Owing to Samuel Hosmer for gray wool blankets $160
Owing to Hope Emerson for sheep $200
Owing to Amos Exeter for 8 tierces whisky, 336 gallons @ 36¢ $120.96

The list went on, totaling $1400. Justin Bolding opened up the treaty to Article Twenty-two. Blair wrinkled up Sam's list and threw it down.

"Sam, you can't do this. These prices were figured on ordinary paper dollars. This money here is in good United States Bank notes."

Hosmer picked up the list.

"Like you said yesterday, Blair. A dollar is a dollar. Isn't our fault what kind of dollars they got."

"Sam, you'll defeat the treaty. You want them off the land, don't you? Then let them take their money and get out of here."

Joe Hussong walked over and put his hand on Captain Michael's buckskin money bag. Captain Michael backed off. Hussong moved after him. Michael twisted the bag away from Hussong and then brought it back so that it reported against Hussong's face and turned his nose and chin red. Hussong grabbed the old Indian by his leather shirt.

But he let go suddenly as the iron fingers of Mike Stikes dug into the muscle behind his collarbone.

Through the open door Blair could see the other Wyandots approaching the blockhouse swiftly.

Stikes snatched the bag from Michael and threw it on the table. Sam Hosmer grabbed it. Blair reached to take it from Hosmer. But before he touched the bag he was restrained by the long arm of Silver Pigeon.

This was still a different Silver Pigeon now. The wrath was gone from his face, or seemed to be. His voice was deep and controlled, almost pleasant. "No, Mr. Blair. Mr. Hosmer is right. We will pay the money . . . give it to me."

Blair was amazed. "Don't use *that* money to pay with!" he warned.

But Pigeon took the bag from an astonished Hosmer, and then he

continued with smooth, rich tones. "We pay. But we ask one favor."
Pigeon tucked the bag securely under his arm. "Each man comes to
our town above the Greenville Line at Upper Sandusky, and collect
his money in person. Would that be too much for you to do for us?"

A Wyandot from outside stepped into the blockhouse and the white
men came on guard. But Pigeon waved the Indian off. The men with
Hosmer relaxed. Hussong set the butt of his rifle on the floor.

Hosmer asked, "Why should we trek all the way up the trace just to
collect what's due us! And maybe lose our hair doin' it?"

Pigeon's face, dark for a white man, light for an Indian, was a bland
mask. "Would you not give me the chance to let my people actually
see the money, to show that your Congress has kept its word? It will
be easier to get them to obey the treaty. Also, it will teach my people
thrift, that they must pay for what they buy."

"I can see that," said Hosmer. "But suppose you run off with the
purse?"

"You can send guards with me to watch the money. Is that not good?"

Hosmer pondered Pigeon's speech. Stikes lowered his rifle. Flannerty
said, "Hell, he's right! And little enough to ask . . . for honest to God
United States Bank notes!"

Stanley-the-Slasher said, "Besides, if them red devils don't actually
see the money, they'll never believe they got paid. Then we'll have the
bastards on us again."

Jonathan Blair noticed the breadth of Silver Pigeon's back blot out
the light as he went through the door with the money. The lawyer
had the strong feeling that he and Mesopotamia had just lost out to
one of the cleverest men in the Northwest.

Well north of the old Greenville Indian boundary at the place once
called Fort Ferree and now more often called Upper Sandusky, the
Reverend Seth Gershom strode back and forth across the front room
of his hut, trying to make his answer come out civil, befitting the
White Father.

The man who sat opposite him calmly whittling a point onto a
hickory stick was his match in every way. Silver Pigeon was as tall and
lanky as the reverend. And at least in this argument he was somewhat
ahead in strategy.

Gershom's rage was the greater because Silver Pigeon's obvious disbelief that the Maker could have sent such a one as Gershom was the very same disbelief which kept haunting Gershom himself. Apparently it was also the same one which prompted the Methodist-Episcopal conference to pass over him eight times for appointment to a regular eastern church, and relief from this Godforsak——from this miserable mission a hundred miles north of mankind.

But Gershom finally stopped his pacing in front of Silver Pigeon and he said, "No! You shall not use the mission tent for that purpose . . . or for any other purpose until you join the mission and bring in the rest of the Wyandots!"

"I only want a place big enough for all my people to watch while we pay our debts to your white brothers." Pigeon's shavings landed on the reverend's new black bombazine pants. "The council house is not big enough. That is part of your teaching, Reverend, to pay our debts."

Gershom brushed off the shavings. "But your purpose is to stir them up. Haven't we had enough bush fighting?"

"But I will use your mission tent for the Christian purpose of paying our debts."

"Then if you have Christian purposes, why will you not join my mission and bring in your anti-Christian party?"

"You know better, Reverend. If this Great White Spirit of yours meant it to be for all men, why did he not appear among us Wyandots? Why did he not cause that Book to be written in Wyandot language?"

"He did. What do you think I am doing up here? Look!" Gershom held up four sheets of parchment on which he was laboriously translating the Bible into Wyandot.

Pigeon pointed to him with the knife, "He sent *you*?"

Gershom sucked air over parted teeth. But he held his tongue, for at that instant Fawn came in from one of the two back rooms of the hut bringing Gershom's supper. Those who loved him saw him only as he wished to be seen.

She put the trencher down and left.

"Your sister, Fawn, has joined the church," said Gershom.

"Fawn wants to believe something is good, Reverend. It is hard for an Indian to believe anything is."

Pigeon resumed his carving.

"I was prepared to help you, Reverend." Pigeon always said "Reverend." It made Gershom uneasy the way he said it. Yet he was glad the Indian chief used the title in front of the other Indians, for whatever reason.

"I am adding a few more requests to the treaty." Pigeon interrupted his whittling to hand the Ottawa copy to Gershom. "I was going to ask you to read Article Sixteen and write out one like that for us Wyandots."

Gershom read: "ARTICLE SIXTEEN:

> Some Ottawas, Chippewas, Potawatomies, being attached to the Catholic religion and wanting their children educated, the United States does grant the rector of St. Ann's at the place called Detroit three sections of land for the financing of a school."

The Indian detected the concentration and envy on the reverend's face and pushed his advantage. "When you write it," said Pigeon, "do not ask for land. Ask for money for the support of your mission. Make it a reasonable annual sum. Mr. Blair is a reasonable man . . . to a fault."

Pigeon recovered the treaty from the lax claw of Seth Gershom.

"I suppose you won't mind now if I happen to be the tomahawk for getting your mission, since you say your White Spirit 'works in wond'rous ways.' And it will be all right now if I use your mission tent to pay our debts to the settlers of Mesopotamia when they arrive?"

Silver Pigeon was out the door.

Seth Gershom sat to his supper, eating slowly, and very little.

On the day of the paying of the debts of the clans of the Wyandots to the men of Mesopotamia at the place called Upper Sandusky, a great and fearful respect came to the white men for the mentality of the Indian, Silver Pigeon.

And as Sam Hosmer walked to the table to receive his money from the hand of Captain Michael, he was made to feel small by the austere height of Silver Pigeon who stood behind Captain Michael.

Silver Pigeon stayed Captain Michael's hand so he would count the money out slowly and with more show.

As Hosmer walked away from the table with his money there was a stirring and a mumbling among the Indians who sat in the mission tent watching. After Hosmer came Hope Emerson and then Stikes and Exeter and the others and with each the murmur grew louder.

Blair moved toward the open end of the tent where the other settlers stood. They might want to be leaving in a great hurry.

Silver Pigeon would have to do no talking to his people after today. With their own eyes they saw the white men come and they saw the white man take away. And to them there was no difference between the Great White President of the United States and Sam Hosmer of Hosmer's Village.

Even Joe Hussong knew that the white men had lost something here today. But he had no idea how much.

When all the debts were paid Silver Pigeon turned to Blair. His voice was gentle, for he could afford it. "Mr. Blair, this leaves us very little as you can see. Would you change our remaining money into smaller bills? You can see to stretch this money over all these people, we would need very small bills."

Blair looked at the money in Hosmer's hands. He said, "Silver Pigeon there are no small bills in these United States Bank notes. Only small bills we would have with us would be Mesopotamia Hog & Trust notes. And we're frank to say they're not as good."

To Blair's surprise, Silver Pigeon said, "That will be all right, Mr. Blair. We will accept them. And perhaps you could compensate us for the difference in exchange by giving us more of your Hog & Trust notes."

With the extra willingness of the guilty, Hosmer Village emptied its pockets and pooled its common currency to change the Indians' money. There was still not enough. Hosmer wrote out a draft to be presented to the Mesopotamia Bank for the balance.

Captain Michael reached for the small bills from Silver Pigeon, to pass them out to the Wyandots. But Silver Pigeon did not yield them up. He sorted them slowly and stuffed them into a snakeskin case.

"No, Captain Michael. We have other uses for these. They would not be much good to our people anyway."

He nodded. And Mesopotamia felt itself dismissed. They were glad to leave the silent tent.

Many now knew what Jonathan Blair had felt from the first, that the sudden and purposeful courtesy of Chief Silver Pigeon would somehow cost them.

Chapter 4: MADE IN PITTSBURGH

JONATHAN BLAIR slashed lines through the columns of figures and threw down the pen. Three times he got three different totals for the cost estimate of supplies called for under the Wyandot Treaty, each higher than the amount the government had furnished.

Blair could not concentrate, and as he looked out through his glass window, he knew why. It was so quiet.

The stultifying silence which had hushed the big woods all the way from the blockhouse in Mesopotamia down through the settlement at Boxford's Cabin . . . on down the river to the Borough of Columbus and south through Chillicothe to Cincinnati and the Ohio River waterfront . . . was epitomized right now by the abysmal absence of sound that arched across the common from Stikes' forge.

The quietness was in Amos Exeter's tavern which could not even draw customers for three-cent whisky. The quietness was at Hosmer's store where the usual crowd was diminished by the number of Sam Hosmer's ashamed debtors. Hussong's herd of hogs didn't thunder in over the west road for the droving south twice a month.

But when the clangor of iron ceased from Mike Stikes' forge, then the silence became deafening.

Blair watched the lanky Stikes pace around in his shop, wiping off the foot treadle to the giant bellows, greasing the rust off idle chisels. But there was no one to wipe the rust off Stikes, who now idled against the triple-width doorway to his forge, staring across toward the Blair cabin.

Lately Mesopotamia's idle stares all converged on the Blair cabin. Blair moved out of his window.

Stikes, who lived by bending iron, could not understand how a man like Blair lived by sitting on a stool, scrivening upon parchments. In fact, few settlers in Hosmer Village had ever understood this.

As Blair watched, Stikes moved. Without dropping the small iron

54

rasp which hung from his right hand, he strode now toward the Blair cabin.

When he pulled Blair's door to behind him, he raised and lowered the iron latch several times, listening critically to the way it seated. Absently, he twisted it onto its side and pulled it out through the hole in the door.

He dropped onto the edge of Blair's bunk and began filing a small indentation in the latch at the point where it contacted the latch bar.

Without looking up he said, "Blair, it's two months now since I gave you my land grant."

"Haven't got the Indians out yet, Mike."

"Don't look like you will either. Slasher was out marking black-walnut timbers. Said them red devils are still all over the land."

"He's right."

Stikes replaced the latch in the door, worked it twice, removed it, continued filing.

"You law fellows don't have to work to very close measurements, do you?"

"Don't get you, Mike."

"The treaty says the Indians are supposed to be out of there. You're the one supposed to see to it. But for all those papers and talking and all, the Indians are still there. I got a paper says I can have a piece of that land. But I can't get it till you get the Indians out. But I guess law don't measure so close as iron work and the like."

Stikes stopped filing.

"Blair, will you give me back my land grant and I'll go down to County and try one of those fifty-dollar lawyers."

Blair reached in his leather pouch and tossed Stikes' land grant over onto the bunk.

"Sure, Mike. But nobody can get your land for you until I get the Indians off."

Stikes pocketed his land grant and fit the latch back into the door. He worked it up and down.

"I see," he said. "Blair, I can get a loan for part of my next payment from the bank. But I doubt the government'll accept a part payment only. I was bankin' on you gettin' my new land for me by the time I get kicked off this place here."

Stikes walked out. The repaired latch slid noiselessly into place

behind him. Things were dead wrong when a man with Stikes' genius
for iron couldn't make out.

Blair opened the door. "Mike, come here."

When Stikes was reseated and cleaning the filings out of his file
with his fingernail, Blair explained how Article Twenty-three of the
Wyandots' treaty bound the United States to deliver a list of hard
goods which were catalogued:

823	saws	10	draw knives
3,292	horseshoes, assorted	823	axes W/3½ foot helves
3	bbls. iron nails	24	scythes
20	hammers	5	frows
50	bbls. salt per year	5	grubbing hoes
50	gimlets	20	sets of horse gears
50	augurs	200	yards Russian tent sheeting

"You mean in addition to the money we got to give them red devils
all that stuff!" Stikes asked.

"It might solve your problem, Mike. A contract must be let to furnish these items to the Wyandots."

"Some Pittsburgh iron monger will get a nice job of work."

"Why Pittsburgh?"

"Be the natural place for them high gover'mint men to buy any kind
of iron work."

"The sub-agent buys the supplies called for in this treaty."

"You?" Stikes looked surprised.

"Point is, why couldn't *you* make some of this stuff, Mike?"

Stikes snatched the treaty and ran his blue-black fingernail down the
list.

"The horseshoes, I could make. And the nails. Couldn't make the
gimlets, nor the augurs. But axes! If Yellow Creek Furnace 'ud give
me credit on black plate iron I can make axes better than Pittsburgh!"

Stikes' long bony claw stung Blair's shoulder and he headed for the
door.

"But wait, Mike. There's a problem."

Stikes turned back.

"I want to get one contractor to supply the whole list called for in
the treaty. So it'll be Buttrick you'll be dealin' with, not me. And whoever takes on the whole contract will have to guarantee all goods."

Stikes' blue eyes searched Blair. "Could you speak plainer, Blair? What you sayin'?"

"I mean the government won't replace anything. The contractor will have to replace any defectives the Indians complain of. So he'll look them over close."

Stikes was wounded.

"Mike, I only meant it should have that 'store' look to it . . . like Pittsburgh."

"Blair, these'll be axes like . . . never bit timber this side of the Allegheny Ridges."

Blair was gone from Mesopotamia the better part of four weeks. He caught up with the circuit court and tried a case on Big Darby Creek. Then he traveled to negotiate with a small group of Delawares and Shawanees at Wapahkonetta, and he rode to Piqua to appraise the value of Shawanee, Delaware and Seneca improvements at that place, for they now insisted on the same compensation for their improvements as Silver Pigeon's Wyandots.

When he rode back into Mesopotamia late at night the place was silent except for a wonderful clangor that came from Stikes' forge. The settlement was dark except for a garish orange from Stikes' place. The glow reflected wet and shiny from the sweaty back of Stikes whose long, corded arm swung the hammer down against an orange fragment of plate iron. Orange sparks splayed off the anvil, bounced off Stikes' leather apron onto the floor, framing Stikes in a flickering ring of sparkles.

The sight of Stikes caused Blair to ride over to the big double cabin of Asa Buttrick. Buttrick had clear Pittsburgh glass in his windows and through the front one Blair could see the agent-trader sitting at the table with a ledger in front of him.

When they sat down at the table Blair shoved the last page of the treaty in front of Buttrick.

Buttrick leaned back, read the list of hard goods to be furnished to the Wyandots.

There were few things Buttrick, the trader, understood, but he knew, everything there was to know about a trade. He threw the treaty back on the table and hooked his thumbs over his straining belt.

"Yes, Jonathan?"

"I'm offering you a chance to bid on supplying this treaty, Asa."

Buttrick's head snapped forward so that his jowls bulged his ears out from his head. "Jonathan, do you think I'd touch this contract?"

"Why not? It's business, and there's mighty little of that around."

"Think a minute, Jonathan."

"Of what?"

"Where do you suppose I get my loans for trade goods?"

"Gideon Schaacht."

"That's right, Jonathan."

"What's he have to do with your bidding on this contract?"

"Think it out yourself, Jonathan. Don't you suppose every dock agent and merchant down on the Cincinnati wharf read that treaty in the Scioto *Gazette?* Don't you know times are so bad a man would ride five hundred miles to get an order like this? Didn't you ever wonder why nobody came to ask you for the trade? A firm named Fleming handles all Indian cession contracts."

"Yes?"

"And Schaacht handles Fleming."

Blair left Buttrick's door open behind him. He led his bay slowly across the common toward the orange glow of Stikes' forge. Stopping just outside the circle of light from Stikes' open-sided shop, Blair wrapped the bay's bridle around a hitch post, and framed his speech to Stikes.

Stikes shoved the long tongs into the forge and pulled out a chunk of incandescence which he plunged into a tub of water, ducking back from the steam which leaped to the loft.

Blair's eyes probed the corner of the shop. In the shadows there, he saw Stanley-the-Slasher polishing an axe helve vigorously with a leather strop.

Blair stepped into the light. Stikes looked up. Sweat streamed down his neck onto his bare red chest, but exhilaration was in his voice.

"Blair!"

Stikes' arm dived into the tub of water for a blue-black hunk of hammered iron which he shoved into Blair's hand.

"How do you like that?"

Stikes snatched the blanked-out axe-head back out of Blair's hands and replaced it with another which was filed smooth and had a hole in it for the helve.

"Notice? Hole tapers to the inside. When them red dogs swing, it'll only drive the head on tighter."

Stikes snatched that one away and replaced it with another, which was by comparison a polished jewel. He dropped the narrow end of one of slasher's polished helves through the hole in the shining axe head, and handed it to Blair.

"Six-pound head. Yankee pattern. Single-bitted," he bragged.

The shaft felt like velvet in Blair's hand, the head gleamed black. With one hand Stikes trailed a horse tail hair across the blade. Half of it drifted to the floor.

"Too good for them red devils," Stikes claimed, "but you said quality."

Blair put the axe down. "Mike, I don't think we . . ."

"Oh, don't worry about quantity either. We got sixteen already," Stikes said.

"Yes, but it looks like we might not . . . that is, I didn't think you'd get started so fast," Blair said. "There may be a change in . . ."

"Hah! We're ahead of ya on that, too, Jonathan," said Stikes. "We didn't think them three-and-a-half-foot axe handles would swing right. Slasher's makin' 'em all four foot. Heft this one."

Blair swung the axe up onto the anvil and left it there.

"Mike, I'm worried about the contract that I said . . ."

Stikes clamped a bony claw on Blair's shoulder.

"Jonathan," he promised earnestly, "don't you worry. After what you're doin', we'll stand behind every damned axe, even if we got to make 'em all twice. You go get some sleep."

But Jonathan Blair could not sleep against the ringing of Mike Stikes' anvil through the big woods all night.

The only fact Blair had to go on was one: Asa Buttrick was afraid to bid on the Wyandot contract. Why?

But the ceaseless pounding of Mike Stikes' hammer left no time for thinking. And Blair did know one other fact about Asa Buttrick. Buttrick had for twenty years jealously fought off all competitors. He procured better prices on the Cinci wharf for the produce of the big woods than any other agent. And he supplied the settlers with cheaper imports than any other agent.

Between Buttrick's fear of the Wyandot contract . . . and his long record of combative competitiveness, Blair decided to bank on the latter. He went over to Hosmer's store and asked for the names of some other agents besides Buttrick.

Hosmer answered the questions and then squinted Blair into sharp focus.

"Ye're not bargaining to cut Buttrick out of the contract are ye, Blair?"

"Buttrick doesn't want it."

Blair left Sam pulling his right ear and he went back to his own cabin. He began filling four separate sheets of paper with numbers which struck close to the estimates Sam Hosmer had given him. He varied the handwriting so that each sheet looked different.

Blair rose as Hope Emerson entered his cabin. Her entering admitted the pounding from Stikes' forge, but it also brought with it a quiet that drifted into the room with her pine soap fragrance.

The time between the end of chores and the sunset was always a time when Hope Emerson seemed different to Blair. You could see the comb marks in her light hair, pulling it back to uncover in the evenings a halolike outline of untanned skin around her forehead and face. In the evenings, too, Hope's face relaxed from its squinting against the sun's reflection off the backs of her flock, and the twinkle lines off the corners of her eyes were white and untanned, giving a translucence to her face that encouraged Blair to think this was not a work visit.

But her voice was business.

"Jonathan, I got an answer from Rotch. Will you read it to me?"

Thomas Rotch wrote that so many farmers had found that pure white Merino wool was the only hard money crop in the West that he was pressed to fill the demand. His price for a pair of pure Merinos remained $1,500. He would guarantee them for eight months of good health after inspecting the adequacy of her shelters and her pasturage. Payment must be in notes which were in good standing as far east as Steubenville and Pittsburgh.

Hope said, "Before I buy I got to decide if Government Land Office will take a partial payment on my land. If not, I'd be better off to keep my common sheep and use my money to buy a new piece up where you're clearing out the Indians. Be no use to have a new pair of Merinos if I lose my land here. How soon you going to get the Indians out, Jonathan?"

"Not until I deliver the bill of hard goods the treaty guarantees to them."

"What's holding that up?"

"Buttrick won't bid on the contract."

"Looks like you got *other* bids there, Jonathan."

Although perhaps absurd, Blair was not the only one who attributed an all-knowingness to the quiet grey eyes of Hope Emerson. So he explained Buttrick's fear that Schaacht wanted no bidders, and that these were decoy bids for Buttrick's benefit.

Hope rose. "You'll likely outscheme yourself, Jonathan. Seems awful roundabout."

Blair didn't answer. He stared at the bids.

"Also," said Hope, "you'll feel pretty darnation small in the sight of Asa Buttrick."

"I'll feel worse in the sight of Mike Stikes. Listen."

Hope listened to the hammering from Stikes' forge.

Blair paced back and forth. "Day and night he's been goin' like that. Makin' axes for the Wyandot contract. My doing. I got him started."

"I see."

Blair paced.

"Still 'n all," said Hope, "you're not goin' at it right."

"How then?"

"Why not butt right into it?"

"Butt right into Gideon Schaacht?" Blair smiled and sat down. "How?"

"'Pears to me you got to sometime. Put a notice in that Scioto *Gazette* for bids. Then let him do whatever he's going to do. Then you'll know. This way you're fightin' what you can't even see."

Blair smiled at Hope's beautiful naivety.

"Trouble with you, Jonathan, you've not found out yet, that's what we've all been doin' out here all along. When old man Hosmer first moved in here, he butted right away against Rontondee and Captain Michael."

"But Rontondee drove him out twice. And I can't afford to lose this one, Hope."

"You got to be willin' to lose. If you don't dare lose, then you always got to settle for half or less."

"You don't understand, Hope, Gideon Schaacht is the only man in the West who can help anybody. He has the power to lend. And that is also the power to take away."

"Then it seems to me you may be the *one* man he can't beat."

"How do you mean?"

Hope looked around at the nearly empty cabin. Then she looked at Jonathan's worn boots and followed up his linsey trousers to his soiled white shirt. She looked up at the empty loft. There was not insult, just a question of fact.

"What could he take away from *you*?" she asked. Hope left.

Blair looked across the common toward the orange glow of Stikes' forge. The clanging of Stikes' hammer drummed out Hope's last question, "What could he take away from *you* . . . that would be worth anything?"

Blair sat to his table. He wrote:

> "*Bids are now accepted at the cabin of Indian Sub-agent Jonathan Blair in the town of Mesopotamia, known as Hosmer Village north and west of the Towne of Columbus on the old Harrison War Road, for a bill of materials in satisfaction of the Wyandot Indian Treaty as follows:*
>
> 823 AXES
> *etc."*

In eight days the advertisement brought results. From the front of Hosmer's store Mesopotamia watched the Blair cabin with a new-found awe and respect.

Outside the Blair cabin was an enormous black stallion with a light tan saddle. It was flanked by two smaller ones. Matt Gavagan said, "Maybe you'll have a new look at Mr. Blair now ya see the kind of visitors he's got."

Hosmer said, "But are ye sure, Gavagan? Can't figure *him* comin' t'see Blair in person."

Gavagan bawled out, "Guess there'd be a lot of crow eat around here if it turned out Blair got Schaacht to come up and loan good United States Bank notes to our bank."

They all looked at Sam Hosmer who in turn studied the black stallion. "I'm hungry to eat it," the old man said. "Raw and unsalted, feathers included."

The knock on Blair's door demanded answering, but gave no time to answer. A tall man bent his head and shoved into the cabin.

"Hello, Blair. Gideon Schaacht."

He did not wait for acknowledgment nor introduce the two men who entered with him.

"Sorry I forgot to tell you the procedure on these Indian cession contracts," said Schaacht. "I saw your advertisement."

The back of Schaacht's big hand waggled toward Blair's table. In instant response the short heavy-set assistant plunked the Scioto *Gazette* on the table where Schaacht indicated.

"I brought up the contractor who handles all these. Meet Fleming. Cincinnati."

Blair looked at Fleming, but he was obviously not the one to talk to.

"Mr. Fleming is free to bid on the contract," said Blair.

Schaacht brushed this aside.

"Blair, Fleming handles *all* these contracts. We can't take any chance on poor goods or comebacks from the Indians. Got to be a supplier that can stand back of his goods. Government can't guarantee the stuff."

"I'll see that my contractor backs his goods," Blair said.

"Blair, I didn't come up here for discussion. Fleming handles the bill of materials. We put you in as Indian sub-agent to dispatch this matter. Not to delay it."

Blair looked surprised.

"*You* put me in?"

"Does that surprise you? Cass and McArthur and I decided on you. You're supposed to be an attorney and you know Silver Pigeon and that preacher up there, Gershom." Schaacht's eyes fixed on the lawyer. "What are you grinning at, Blair?"

"At myself," said Blair as he sat down. "I'm appointed sub-agent and then I find out it's because Silver Pigeon wants me. After that I find out Hosmer Village people want me for sub-agent. They figure it will advantage them in getting Indian lands after the removals. Now I find out I'm Indian agent because *you* want me to be. What do *you* want out of it?"

The two assistants were obviously nervous for Blair. Schaacht's voice stabbed, "Blair, it is not too late to make new appointments. Colonel Armstrong is still available."

"That still doesn't explain your concern over Indian affairs, Mr. Schaacht."

"My concern and my authority seem natural enough since my assignment from Mr. Monroe and the Treasurer is to stabilize Western fiscal affairs. I would be seriously remiss to let one sub-agent interfere."

Blair sat slack at his table.

Schaacht said, "Well?"

Blair reached for the Wyandot Treaty. With a carefulness exasperating to Schaacht, Blair rolled it up and tied a leather thong around it.

He held it out to Schaacht. Schaacht did not move to touch it. And in that instant Jonathan Blair experienced something of the power of a man who can decline a job, a man who can afford to lose.

"Blair, the War Department expects sub-agents to execute their duties."

Blair continued to proffer the treaty.

"And for gross negligence or dilatory execution there are material disciplinary measures."

Blair straightened his elbow pushing the treaty closer to Schaacht's massive, brass belt buckle. He looked around his own cabin. Schaacht's eyes followed Blair's in an inspection of the worthless contents of the cabin. He looked back at the treaty which Blair held out to him. Gideon Schaacht, for the first time in his economic-political career, was looking at an opponent who had nothing to lose.

Schaacht turned to his two assistants. "Step out and find water for the horses."

He sat down across the table from the lawyer. "All right, Blair, just what is your interest in placing the contract for this treaty?"

The ringing of Mike Stikes' anvil penetrated the walls of the lawyer's cabin, and Jonathan Blair drove a hard bargain this day on the contract-letting prerogatives of the Indian sub-agent for Wyandots above the old Greenville Line north and west of Hosmer Village.

It must be said for the bigness of Gideon Schaacht that when he lost the main point he had no desire to salvage the niggardly scraps often reserved for the loser. He gave it all. A great grin broke over the long sharp face. He slapped the table and rose, relaxed.

"Very well, Blair. My only interest is in seeing the contract responsibly placed. You can give out the contract. But get the Indians out of there and quick!"

Schaacht walked to the door and reached for the handle.

Blair could see how men became devoted to the giant. His manner now attracted one's good wishes. Blair wished to talk no more business. But the ringing of Stikes' hammer was still in his ears and he said,

"One more thing, Mr. Schaacht. You say you're extremely interested in hastening the removal of the Indians, though I don't see its connection with the United States Bank."

"With the Indians gone, Blair, we open up that whole rich forest to settlement. Eastern settlers bring in good eastern money."

"Don't know as it'll work out that way. But assume you're right. The quickest way to get the Indian cession executed is for us whites up here to treat the Wyandots decent."

"Sure. You've got to get your people to stop annoying them."

"*You've* got to do that," said Blair.

"Me?"

"You."

"How?"

"By relieving the financial pressure that makes the whites around here keep pushing Silver Pigeon."

Schaacht relinquished the door handle and his geniality. Blair felt Schaacht's mind snap closed, but he also heard Stikes' hammer and he said, "You've got to give Sam Hosmer's bank here a United States Bank loan."

Schaacht looked shocked. "You've had more than one man's share of telling me what I've got to do today, Mr. Blair."

Schaacht turned and opened the door. But as he did so, he stepped right into the inquisitive and admiring face of Mesopotamia. The crowd had moved over from Hosmer's store to look at the extra-large black stallion and to admire the light tan saddle and to ask Schaacht's two assistants about the status of the dollar down in Chillicothe and Cincinnati.

Schaacht closed the door and turned to Blair in annoyance.

But Blair said, "As long as most of them are assembled, Mr. Schaacht, I'd like you to tell them what you decided about the contract. Strengthen my effectiveness if it looks like you're on my side."

Schaacht studied Blair a moment. "Very shrewd, Blair. And a good idea."

As Schaacht spoke to the men of Mesopotamia from the stoop in front of the lawyer's cabin, Jonathan Blair knew that he was watching an extremely capable man at work. A less perceptive man might have affected plainness of speech "suitable" for a group of settlers this far north who still wore leather and no chest linen. Schaacht made no such error.

He spoke of the overall economic welfare of the entire territory. And to men who were starved for a confident giant to take a firm grip on the miserable Western wildcat currency, Gideon Schaacht looked extremely adequate.

He did more than that. The tools of Gideon Schaacht were men, and he knew enough to keep his tools sharpened. He placed a hand on Blair's shoulder in closing and he said, "Jonathan and I feel that in this instance it would be best for him to place the Wyandot contract where he sees fit. This is not usual but Jonathan pointed out to me the advantages of doing it this way . . . this time."

Blair could see Sam Hosmer reappraising him as he stood there obviously in the confidence of the great man. And despite himself Blair felt his own face flush with a pleasure which made his intentions seem traitorous. But he could also hear Mike's sledge ringing imperiously.

Schaacht stepped down to his stallion, but he never got his foot to the stirrup. Jonathan Blair chose that instant to address the crowd.

"You remember they told us the United States Bank was only worrying about Cincinnati and Chillicothe and Vincennes and didn't have sense to know the north counties need decent currency, too?"

The crowd inched closer and nodded. Schaacht whirled on Blair. Blair didn't meet his eyes. Stikes' hammer was loud in his ears. "Well, Mr. Schaacht has come up to make an appraisal of our properties to see if it's feasible to make a United States Bank loan to the Mesopotamia Hog & Trust Company."

A commotion broke out in the crowd. Matt Gavagan yelled, "By God! Let's give a whoop for Mr. Schaacht and for Blair!"

Blair saw the shock on the faces of the two assistants of Gideon Schaacht and as he turned away from the crowd he could feel Schaacht's eyes boring through his back. The lawyer did not know how he would pay for this.

But the appraisals began on Monday.

Asa Buttrick could smell the balance of a trade.

The instant he stepped into Hosmer's store on the fifteenth of July he knew that he was unusually welcome. And this despite the fact that Sam Hosmer was long practiced in the art of the frontier dicker.

Blair noticed that Buttrick armored himself behind a vast, sluggish lethargy of his great body. Blair had seen Buttrick when every ounce of his two hundred odd pounds was alive and vibrant, like the time he had brought in the first small load of Pittsburgh window glass for sale on the frontier. But today he was a sleepy-eyed hulk, civil enough, but wearing the reserved tolerance of a man who thinks he is being imposed upon.

While Sam Hosmer pointed out to him the keenness of the blade of a grey-iron axe which he dandled temptingly, Buttrick refused to reach for it. Instead he picked up a roll of harness leather and studied it indifferently.

Blair noticed with alarm that the axe Hosmer was handling was not one of the Stikes axes, but an axe which had been in his store without takers for several months. Blair privately damned an old man's carelessness.

Buttrick said, "Sam, after all these years you wouldn't try to unload back inventory on me, just because it's a government contract."

"Only reason this lot of axes has been here so long, Asa, as ye know well enough, is nobody is buying much these days. I can give ye a price on them . . . so ye can make a profit."

Buttrick absently unrolled the harness leather. Indifferently he said, "Yeah, Sam, but I need eight hundred twenty-three of them. How many can you furnish?"

"Got twenty-five in the store, but I can get more. The firm closed down, but they got more in stock."

Buttrick sunk a thumbnail into the leather harness. "If the firm's out of business I can't use 'em. You know how the government holds you to a contract. I got to have somebody to go back to in case of faulty issue. If these axes hone down to nothing, who would I go to?"

Blair wished old Sam were a match for Buttrick.

Buttrick expected an answer. The absence of an answer from old man Hosmer forced Buttrick's head up to attention. And when he looked up this time Hosmer was not standing there with the grey-iron axe. Instead he had eased back two steps, and in place of the grey-iron axe he held this time across his two palms a sparkling jointure of black iron and gleaming yellow hickory. Hosmer let it lie lightly on his two wrinkled palms in a way that changed the axe into a necklace on a purple velvet pillow. The sun flashed off the black iron and Buttrick involuntarily grabbed the axe.

Quickly he turned it on each side, then he tossed it, caught it, swung it down to his side. He hoisted it up, ran his thumb over the cutting edge.

"Where did you get these!"

He looked up for an answer. But Hosmer had moved away. He was rewinding the harness leather with great concentration.

Blair mentally apologized to Hosmer; and suddenly he felt a little sorry for Buttrick.

"Where'd you get 'em?" Buttrick asked.

Hosmer hung the coil of harness on a twelve-inch peg and bound the coil with a thong. Buttrick said, "Where'd you . . ."

But Hosmer had moved back farther in the store. He was rearranging the harness stock, looking up only often enough to catch Buttrick in deep absorption over the axe. Buttrick hoisted it up to look at the butt of the helve. He ripped off a corner of the Scioto *Gazette* and sliced it neatly without even holding the paper taut.

Hosmer strolled back.

"Six pound head," he said slowly. "Yankee pattern. Single bit."

"I can see that. But who made it?"

"Helve is polished hickory. It'll wear out ten Wyandots."

"How many can you get?"

"Might be able to get enough to fill your order."

"Who makes 'em? There's no mark."

Hosmer's wrinkles realigned themselves into a grin.

"Asa, when I told you who made the rope you went and bought it direct. Didn't give me the trade."

Buttrick brought the axe to his nose and smelled it.

"You're in the right, Sam. Every man's privileged to keep his own source. I like the axe. Can I come back on you for defections?"

"Yeah."

"But can *you* go back on the *maker*?"

"That's not your problem. I'll stand back of it."

"Price?"

"What kind of money?"

"Say John Piatt Bank notes."

"Four dollars a piece."

"How about if my money was Bank of Chillicothe notes?"

"Three dollars, seventy-five cents."

"How about Mechanics Bank of Cincinnati notes?" Buttrick kept his head bent to the axe, but he raised his eyes to search Hosmer. Hosmer reached for a copy of the Scioto *Gazette*, studied it a moment, made a few calculations with a charcoal stick and he said, "Three dollars even, I guess."

Buttrick grinned. "You know your paper pretty good, Sam. How about if it was Mesopotamia Hog & Trust notes?"

Hosmer was torn between good business and good faith to Mesopotamia. He said, "Two ninety-five."

Buttrick smiled. "You got more guts than sense, Sam; but it's still too high. How about if I paid in United States Bank notes?"

"One dollar apiece if you pay in United States Bank notes, Asa."

"And how about if I pay in silver?"

Hosmer slipped a little in his eagerness. "Fifty cents a piece," he snapped, "for silver."

Buttrick caught Hosmer's hand before he could withdraw. "I'll take half at fifty cents each in silver. Half at one dollar each in United States Bank notes . . . if I can get 'em."

The two men exhaled like tired fighters. Hosmer sat down. Buttrick opened his coat. Blair moved about freely. Buttrick swung the axe about, twirling it so it sparkled in the sun.

"Just one more thing, Sam," he said, relaxed. "I'm not going to get stuck to the government on this contract. I'll buy from you. But I got to be satisfied who makes 'em."

"Best iron mongery in the trade."

"Who's that?"

Hosmer hesitated. "Mike Stikes," he said.

Buttrick dropped the axe.

"Who?"

"Mike Stikes."

Buttrick stood there a moment staring at Hosmer then he buttoned his coat with finality and started for the door. He laughed. "Hosmer! Are you crazy? Mike Stikes!" He laughed. "No contract, Sam."

Hosmer was up. "You can't buy an axe that good."

Buttrick laughed. "But you said 'an established mongery.' "

"What's wrong with Stikes? Everybody here knows his work. That makes him established."

"Mike is fine. None better. But . . . but he's just old Mike. Heck, everybody knows good old Mike. Fine man. But he's just good old Mike, that's all."

"What difference so long as he makes good axes?"

"Well, I know, but . . . but he can't be the best in the . . . why Mike Stikes is just one of *us*. We all know Mike."

Buttrick laughed; and he left.

Hosmer sat dejected, but not surprised. Blair, however, was still stupefied when he heard footsteps from the rear of the store. A voice approaching from behind the harnesses said, "I saw him come in, Sam. Couldn't wait. I came over to listen."

"Mike!"

"Yeah, I heard what he said."

Hosmer looked at the hanging arms of his friend Stikes.

"Then ye heard how it is, Mike. Home folks just aren't experts, it seems. They're just people you know all your life."

"I'll take the axes back," said Stikes. "Won't have you stuck with 'em."

"No, ye don't Mike. I was gonna take a profit. The losses go with the profits."

"No, Sam." Stikes hauled the axes out from under the counter and piled them up carefully.

"Put 'em back," said Hosmer.

"No. You'll never unload all these."

"Put 'em back."

"Can't have you stuck, Sam . . . for a bunch of red bastards anyways."

"I won't be stuck," said Hosmer. "There ain't axes like them this side of the Alleghenies . . . in fact this side of England."

"I know it," said Stikes as he hoisted them. "But that don't count."

But Hosmer shoved them back to the floor.

"Yes it does. I'll sell 'em. Take a long time. But when this fouled up currency of ours is settled, there'll be settlers coming in again . . . in bunches. There'll be somebody along from out of town."

Stikes' claw stroked his chin. "From out of town," he repeated reflectively. "Somebody from out of town."

Mike dived for the axes. "Sam! You just now put me back in business. I'll be back." Stikes swung the axes up to his shoulder and strode out the front door, leaving Hosmer and Blair uninformed.

Throughout the next week Blair wondered at the hammering that went on at the Stikes' forge. He couldn't see what Stikes was doing because he had closed the big sliding door that usually left the whole of the shop open to view. Slasher kept going in and out of the forge, too.

Blair joined the circuit court again when it got up as far as the town of Columbus. He tried a case of escapement of apprentice against Stuttgart, a case of bank-note forgery against Wembly, and a case of assault against Stuttgart on behalf of a quarter-breed Shawanee living in the town of Columbus. He won both actions against Stuttgart, lost against Wembly.

The Shawanee quarterblood asked Blair how the Wyandot treaty was coming along and mentioned that he had seen Silver Pigeon in the town of Columbus a week before. This disturbed Blair for two reasons. When Silver Pigeon was not with his Wyandots at Upper Sandusky, discipline disintegrated. Captain Michael could not control the tribe. Gershom could control the Christians, but they were outnumbered two to one by the others who in Silver Pigeon's absence looked to Rontondee. Rontondee's leadership usually meant sporadic bush fighting and various murders, both white and Indian.

The second of Blair's misgivings was that Silver Pigeon had only one reason for living . . . that was the Wyandots. When he was *with* them he was laboring for the Wyandots. When he was *away* from them he was still laboring for the Wyandots.

Further, Silver Pigeon had long since given up the physical resistance. Resistance in Silver Pigeon had gone under the skin . . . into a smoldering, scheming obstructionist policy which could not be combated on one front. It pervaded every phase of relationship. Defeated on one encounter, it diverted to another effort.

It would seem that Silver Pigeon had been defeated in the payment of the debts to white settlers, and so Jonathan Blair wondered earnestly where he was and what he was planning.

Blair had ridden back north to within ten miles of Hosmer Village when he saw ahead of him the wagon of Matt Gavagan. It was unusual for Gavagan to have the canvas up. It indicated a weather-damageable cargo, like flour. It was still more unusual to be able to overtake Gavagan's wagon, for Gavagan drove with a flair. But Blair soon saw that the wagon was stopped. Blair dismounted.

"Trouble, Matt?"

"No, Blair. But how far behind you is Buttrick?"

"Didn't know he was behind."

"Yeah. S'posed to be comin' up today. I want him to overtake me."

"Why?"

"He always snoops around to see what I got on. Today I *want* him to see."

"Why?"

"I promised Hosmer to keep it secret. Be best if you weren't standin' here when Buttrick comes."

When Gavagan's wagon pulled into Hosmer Village, Blair started over to the store. Buttrick splashed his mount across the ford and tied up behind Gavagan's wagon. Hosmer came out.

"Get everything, Gavagan?"

"Yeah."

Gavagan leaped down from the seat and pulled off his gloves with a little more of a flourish than usual because there was a little more of a crowd than usual. It was a rare thing now when a new cargo came into Hosmer Village, and Gavagan pulled the tail-gate pin with a jerk that banged the gate down loud against the body. The axes were tied in bundles and he handed the first to Hosmer and the rest to bystanders to carry into the store.

Blair moved inside.

Hosmer knifed the rope on his bundle and absently handed one axe to Buttrick. Then he went out for more.

When Hosmer returned Buttrick was examining the blade six inches from his eyes. Then he swung it alternately in each hand. He grabbed it just under the head, swung it out in an arc letting the helve slip through his hand until the butt ridge stopped against the heel of his hand.

The onlookers also grabbed axes and fondled them. Hosmer yelled from across the store, "What you think of 'em, Asa? They got some of the features you admired on the others."

"Don't see much difference," said Buttrick.

"Isn't much. Oh, there's a little ring carved around the butt of the helve on each one, and a hole punched in for runnin' a thong through . . . so y'can hang it on a wagon. 'Bout the same."

"Who makes 'em?"

"Turn it over. It's chisel-stamped on the head."

Buttrick turned it over, carried it closer to the window. "H-m-m," he read. "Pittsburgh Small Iron Works." Buttrick held the axe off a ways. "Hah! Now *t-h-e-r-e-'s* an axe!"

Hosmer remained busy storing the other bundles of axes. The others in the store stopped handling the axes and watched Buttrick. The older settlers looked away from him, though, and some of them grinned.

Buttrick walked away from the crowd, back to where Hosmer worked. He lowered his voice some. "What's the price of this axe?" he asked, ". . . to me. Same quantity as before?"

A mask of vast indifference faded over Hosmer's face. "Well, this one'll cost you a little more. Seventy-five cents each in silver or a dollar and a half in United States Bank notes."

"That's all right. 'Long as I know there's a good name back of it, it's worth it, right, Sam?" Buttrick chuckled and inspected the axe head again. "Pittsburgh Small Iron Works. Hah! Good house, Sam?"

Hosmer scribbled in his credit book. "Yeah, the best," he said. "Sign here, Asa."

Buttrick signed the book and Sam Hosmer yelled up to the front of the store. "Gavagan! Don't bring any more in! Take 'em all over to Buttrick's place!"

It was late that night when Mike Stikes shoved open Blair's cabin door. He laid his land grant on the edge of Blair's table and he said, "Jonathan, wouldn't surprise me if you was too busy to handle it." He nudged the land grant closer to Blair. "But if you thought you'd have time, I'd take it as a favor if you'd handle the grant for me."

These were the events which taught Jonathan Blair, among others, that an expert is a man from another town, and these were the events which explained how the Pittsburgh Iron Works came to be located in the Ohio Country.

Chapter 5: A BARREL OF SILVER

MATT GAVAGAN remained seated on the high box of his wagon where he could look down on the excited Wyandots who swarmed around his team.

But his disgust was not so much for the Indians as for Jonathan

Blair. Gavagan had slurried the wagon into the center of the Indian town of Upper Sandusky with an ostentatious dust-churning worthy of the Trans-Allegheny stage downstate. It brought the red men out, running. Gavagan had set the stage for Blair to deliver the axes with an impressive flourish.

But instead the lawyer was down there unloading the axes with his own hands, brushing the trail dust off the heads, laying them on the ground, making sure all the blades faced the same way so that they made a gleaming display. If you didn't know that Blair couldn't even shoe a horse without pounding his thumb, you'd think he had made the axes himself.

Justin Bolding watched also. With his arms folded, the young man reflected that his preceptor was losing the show. Instead of sending for Silver Pigeon and turning over the supplies with an upper hand, he was losing the occasion to Silver Pigeon, and perhaps a few million acres of the Northwest as well.

Silver Pigeon arrived last, tall and austere. Blair held up one of the axes for him to feel, like a merchant trying for a sale. The Pigeon ran a finger over the edge and nodded. He said, "And how have you succeeded about getting the damages-money for our improvements?"

"War Department has disallowed the amount as too high."

"Then how about the money for the church mission?" Pigeon persisted.

"What do you care about the mission?"

"Not much, but the Great White Spirit keeps order in my town. So I want it."

"I think we may get that. Five hundred dollars. But it takes time."

James Pointer and a few of the English-speaking Christian Wyandots alerted at this good news and started to ask Blair questions about the mission. But Silver Pigeon had learned to belittle each favor or concession with another and larger demand. He had learned it from General Duncan McArthur and Major Armstrong and Cass and Worthington. He cut off his people's enthusiasm with a question, "Then what about the additional fifty thousand acres I asked for the reserve here in Upper Sandusky?"

"We'll talk more about that when your men stop hunting on that land. For now, notice, we're doing well holding up *our* end of the treaty."

"For such a treaty you should."

Pigeon turned and walked away, and the question of when and if the whites would be able to occupy the reaches north and west of the Greenville Line was still very vague.

Blair went over to see Reverend Gershom and Fawn, the sister of Silver Pigeon. He took her a three-inch-square mirror which he had bought at Columbus. He stopped to say hello to Mudeater. And then he went back to Matt's wagon.

Returning south to Mesopotamia, Blair sat on the box with Gavagan. Bolding stood in the wagon bed behind them and between them. He said, "If you'll excuse the observation, Blair, you're letting that Indian fly too high. They're going to go one way or another, sooner or later. Nobody's going to thank Jonathan Blair if he makes it easier on them."

Blair studied the ears of Gavagan's team.

Later he said, "Bolding, I'm going down to circuit court. While I'm gone, see to renewing Exeter's ferry license, make out a voucher for Buttrick's payment from the War Department and read Wood's Institutes through covenants, damages, detinue and dower."

"I'm already up to that."

"Then read through executors, extortion and felony," snapped Blair.

"Yes, sir," said Bolding. "And when do I get bar membership?"

"When I say you're ready."

"My God, are you trying to get me ready for the Philadelphia courts?"

"You're ready for them now. But out here you've got to know something."

"That explains your outstanding success no doubt, Blair."

"And you'll do me the courtesy to call me Mr. Blair."

"Courtesy is important out here?"

"More than in Philadelphia. Out here it keeps you alive."

At the store the conversation stopped when Blair entered. Stikes and Hussong and Hope Emerson and Exeter and a few others were there.

Hosmer asked, "Well, Blair, them red devils agree to stay on the reserve when ye delivered the stuff?"

"Not yet. But they will."

"When?"

"Soon as I can get the damages money for them. And the extra acreage. And the mission they want."

"Hunh. Ye sure got the patience of a saint, Blair, when ye're dealin' with our enemies."

"They're entitled to the damages money."

"What proof they'll move if ye get it for 'em?"

"No proof. But I think they will."

"Hunh. Think! You better *know*! Looks like we're gonna need that land ourselves when we get kicked off here." Hosmer put his hand on a large leather bag. "Riddle was up here," he said.

"Riddle! Then we got the loan?"

"We got *a* loan."

"Then we can make the land payments," said Blair with pleasure. "Let's see the money."

Hosmer spilled the bills out onto the counter. Blair looked at them. "Where are the United States Bank notes?"

"They ain't," said Hosmer.

Hosmer let Blair stare at the pile of regular Western paper dollars. There were Zanesville Bank notes, Owl Creek Bank notes, Cincinnati Farmers & Mechanics notes, a few Detroit notes, some on the Bank of Vincennes, Louisville and Muskingum Bank. It was a collection of the regular Western wildcat bank notes.

"New policy," Hosmer said. "Riddle told us 'It's money.' Now that the United States Bank is backing it up, it'll circulate, he said."

"Like hell it will," said Gavagan. "I turned down that Muskingum paper from old man Boxford just yesterday."

Hosmer explained. "Riddle says it'll be different now . . . with the United States Bank here. He says the United States Bank accepted this stuff on deposit from the United States Land Office. No reason it shouldn't be used just like any other monies on deposit at the United States Bank."

Hosmer stuffed the money back in the bag as if he were sweeping up sawdust. He looked at Blair.

"So what's it gonna be, Blair? Ye gonna get them Indians off that ground so we can get on it? Or are ye gonna go see this Schaacht and get him to loan us some *decent* money? It's your turn."

Blair started to object. How in God's name did they call one man to account for the failure of all Western currency! But he remembered

Hosmer had not asked how one man was to lick the Wyandots; he had built a blockhouse. Buttrick had not asked how one man was to feed a village during the famine; he had gone out and brought back corn.

"I'll go see Schaacht," Blair said.

On the way to Chillicothe, Blair stopped a week at the Borough of Columbus for the sittings of the circuit court in that town. On the last day of the sittings he had only one case. And, like every law case these days, it was about money. Since the legislature was not sitting, and since there were a lot of auditors, Calvin Pease and Judge Brown were holding the court in the incompleted Hall of Representatives on the first floor.

The important thing about the trial was that among the auditors Blair was disconcerted to see the face of Silver Pigeon. He was curious and concerned. The Pigeon never ventured south of the Greenville Line without a purpose. The purpose was never trivial.

But Blair had to concentrate for the moment on defending Jarvis Pike against "Citizens of Columbus." Stuttgart was making the most of the pride of the citizens in the new statehouse and their jealousy of the contractor, Jarvis Pike. Blair heard him telling the judges, "Jarvis Pike seems to feel that because he constructed the statehouse he owns it. Look out the side windows of this Hall of Representatives toward Broad Street right now. What do you see? You see Jarvis Pike's corn growing on the statehouse grounds. Look out the back door into the wood yard, what do you see? Jarvis Pike's four cows! Look beyond the wood yard. Jarvis Pike's wheat! And by what right? As you know, sir, Mr. Monroe promised to visit the Ohio Legislature this summer. At that time our Governor and our legislature plans to ask his consideration for more generous loans from the United States Bank. When he sees Jarvis Pike's steers in the statehouse wood yard . . . is he going to think we are running this state in a businesslike manner? Should Jarvis Pike's cows decide the credit rating of the West?"

Stuttgart sat down.

Pike reared up. "I got the cows in the back! Not the front!"

Blair pulled Pike's sleeve. The contractor sat.

Blair addressed Stuttgart first, "I assure you, Mr. Stuttgart, I am extremely concerned with Western credit, and any possible help from President Monroe." Then he addressed the bench. "But Mr. Stuttgart asked by what right does Mr. Pike use the statehouse lots for his

cattle and corn and wheat? I am about to show you. Judge Brown
and Judge Pease, will you notice that Jarvis Pike honored his contract?
The statehouse is a full seventy-five feet long and full fifty feet wide
according to contract. Notice that though the contract calls for common plain brick around the foundation, Pike used smooth-faced brick
for which he paid in good United States specie. Notice he used black-
walnut shingles on the roof for which he paid in good Virginia pounds
one year ago."

Judge Pease looked annoyed. "Mr. Blair, the question of Mr. Pike's
execution of contract is not in suit. Is this pertinent?"

"It will be, sir."

Blair concentrated on Judge Brown.

"Notice in the halls, Pike has put wooden columns for which he
paid in New Jersey silver pounds."

Pease's fingers began to tap the bench impatiently.

Blair came to the point quicker than he had planned. "All these
bills Jarvis Pike paid in good currency twelve months ago. But when
the state of Ohio came to pay Jarvis Pike for his good work, they
paid him in the currency of the Cincinnati Farmers & Mechanics
Bank, the Zanesville Bank and the Bank of Muskingum. And because
of the current rate of distrust now discounted against this paper,
Jarvis Pike's pay amounts in reality to only 56 per cent of his contract price. Would you then prevent him from attempting to recover
something from the statehouse property by planting a little corn?"

Pease did not raise his head or his voice. Smoothing his rough thumbnail with a small knife he monotoned, "Mr. Blair, are you saying
that any of us who receive shaved money should plant corn on the
statehouse lands? Or on the lands of the payer?"

There had been scant legal case to start with. But the judge's incise
question shattered it.

Blair looked out the window to measure the height of Jarvis Pike's
corn. It looked a little better than knee high and this was the fifteenth
of July. Blair asked, "Sirs, when do you sit *en banc* as Supreme Court?
That is, an appeal filed today would come up about when?"

A tired-looking Judge Pease now turned his grey head to the window to examine Jarvis Pike's corn critically. He pursed his lower lip.

Blair said, "It's Kentucky White, sir."

"Means about a hundred-twenty-day growing season," the judge reflected aloud. "Yes. You'd get it harvested all right."

Blair said, "The defense rests."

The crowd laughed. But the laugh was quenched by the unlaughing face of Judge Calvin Pease.

As he walked with the crowd toward the tavern across High Street, Blair heard a deep voice say, "Now if you can get some more time for *us*, like you did for Pike, it will be good."

Blair turned to look into the grin of Silver Pigeon.

"What are you doing here?"

"You judge Silver Pigeon by yourself. Always you have a reason to be some place. Come. We will eat."

"Your men stop hunting yet since we delivered the treaty goods?"

"We will eat and talk. Come."

Blair noticed several strange things about Silver Pigeon's actions. The Pigeon said they would talk. But he insisted on sitting at one of the four large common boards where private talk was impossible. Pigeon hated whites, but he was winningly polite at table. His presence there caused much interest among the others, not only because of his commanding appearance, but because it was known that he led the Wyandots and that Blair was in charge of removing the Wyandots to a small reserve.

Pigeon customarily refused to adopt the clown role which was forced upon any Indian who mixed his company, yet today he grinned and ate his food with his hands.

Pigeon could speak English nearly as well as any at the table. Yet today Blair noticed that he spoke Indian English, which is the way settlers liked their Indians.

The men gave Silver Pigeon a long irregular Conestoga cigar and enjoyed his wonderment at it and his difficulty at sucking on it. The more they laughed, the more Pigeon played up his difficulties. More whisky was called over. The lawyer observed that Silver Pigeon was becoming the center of the group, and apparently on purpose.

The cigar went out many times, and the relighting of it each time drew gales of guffaws.

However, the time when Pigeon called loudest for a light, it seemed to Blair the cigar was not extinguished. But a long burning stick from the hearth was proffered from the far and opposite end of the table. Pigeon leaned laboriously to touch his cigar to the coal. It was especially comical as he did not support the cigar with his hands, and it jutted from his mouth like some misshapen drum stick. The Indian waggled his head in dissatisfaction with the coal and then he made a small motion which Blair suddenly knew had been planned weeks.

Silver Pigeon reached into his leather breeches and pulled out a dollar bill. He held it against the coal until it flashed into flame. With this he lighted his cigar. There were some chuckles.

Apparently he did not get a good light. He pulled out another dollar and lighted it also, applying it to his cigar. This also failed. The Indian reached still another bill toward the coal for ignition.

But this time the coal was withdrawn. Silence sobered the table. Pigeon, with his mouth full of cigar, beckoned impatiently for the ember to come back to his outstretched dollar bill. But there was no response this time.

A few benches scraped back from the table. A few men rose slowly.

A harsh voice cut the silence.

"What's a damned Indian doin' with so much money he lights cigars with it!"

Pigeon looked bewildered, but to Blair he didn't look bewildered enough.

A big fist snatched the bill out of Pigeon's hand and examined it.

"Are you crazy, Indian?"

Pigeon looked wounded. He reached quickly into his pocket now and brought out a handful of the bills. "Why crazy?" He shrugged and slathered them the length of the table. "No good. No good wampum. No buy nothing. Cigar light only."

He picked up two bills, tore them in half and shrugged innocently to the crowd. "This kind no good."

"What currency is that, Indian?"

Silver Pigeon raised and lowered his shoulders and turned up his palms.

Blair reached slowly for one of the bills. He found himself staring at the signature of Samuel Hosmer under the words:

ONE DOLLAR
Redeemable in specie,
Mesopotamia Hog & Trust Company

The gruff-voiced one at the end of the table snatched a leather folder from his own pocket and examined his own money. He rushed out of the tavern. Another did likewise.

Blair yelled, "Come back! This money is good!"

But in seconds the table was empty as men scrambled out to divest themselves of Mesopotamia Hog & Trust notes, to go home to examine their money for Mespo notes and to warn friends of this latest failure in the dwindling number of respectable banks.

Across an empty table Jonathan Blair now looked over expecting a clowning leer on the face of Silver Pigeon. But instead he looked into a suddenly resolute, sober, smooth-skinned mask. This was no fumbling clown. This was Silver Pigeon, son of Captain Michael, grim and ingenious chief of the Wyandots and leader of the six major tribes . . . capable, formidable . . . brilliant. Blair remembered now the day Hosmer Village had collected its debt from the Wyandots and he knew how long was the memory of the Pigeon, and how patient.

The Indian's voice was vindicative. "And I am only begun, Blair. Only begun."

"Pigeon! For God's sake do you know what you have done!"

"Yes. And you could have stopped it!"

"How?"

"Get us that other fifty thousand acres and the damages money, and the mission."

"I can't work any faster!"

"You better learn how."

Blair grabbed his hat. "I may be able to stop your damage though." He started for the door.

"You're too late, Blair!"

Blair turned. "What do you mean? This is the first place you've done this, isn't it?"

Pigeon shook his head. "The last place. I started in Piqua. Worked north."

Blair bolted out of the tavern.

Blair raked the bay's belly with his heels, and headed north up the old Harrison War Road. But he knew he was racing against the fastest runner in the West . . . a bank rumor.

At Boxford's Cabin he dismounted. The bay was steaming. Blair watered and rationed his mount and himself, and when he handed his dollar to old man Boxford he knew he had lost the race this far. Boxford did not reach for the bill.

"I tell you it's a lie!" Blair yelled. "The money is as good as ever! It's a deliberate attempt to . . ."

But Boxford only spread his fingers and rotated them fanwise in front of Blair. "Whatever you say, Mister. But have ya got any silver?" Blair laid a silver dollar on the block. Boxford placed the chisel on it twice and hammered twice, neatly excising a pie-shaped tenth of a dollar. He handed the nine tenths of a disk back to Blair.

Blair rode north at a gallop despite the darkness and the water sloshing in the bay's belly.

He was glad that he was approaching the settlement at night. They wouldn't gather round to get the news as they always did when anyone came up from the south and civilization. He would be able to work quietly without getting everyone excited.

First thing to do would be to get a list of all the Land Office payments due from each settler. Then he'd get Sam to sub-loan the United States Bank loan money to the settlers. He'd collect the money from each of them, borrow a new horse, get Bolding and a couple others to ride with him as guards for the money. If they rode day and night for the Land Office at Chillicothe they might get the payments across the counter and receipts in hand before Silver Pigeon's rumor reached the Land Office and caused them to reject Mesopotamia notes.

It must have been midnight when he reached Mesopotamia. So he was surprised to see by the mounts at the rail and the silhouettes against the skin window that Hosmer's store was crowded with settlers. He wrapped the bay's lines loosely around the rail and entered.

A few heads turned to Blair, but most of them continued to stare at the slouching figure of Joe Hussong seated on the bench under the harness rack. His usually dark face was drained pale. Camelia Flannerty wrapped a long belt of white linsey around his upper arm, but every time she brought it around it turned red at the back of Hussong's arm.

Some of the settlers stared where Hussong stared, at the shrunken frame of Samuel Hosmer who stood between the stocks of two rifles which lay across the counter, pointing toward the crowd. Wisps of smoke still drained out the muzzle of the one on the left. The one on the right had the flint pulled back to half-cock. Hosmer's left hand was only an instant away from it. He said, "It'll kill me to do it, Joe. But I'll fire again if I have to. I told ye the silver stays in the barrel."

Amos Exeter said, "But, Sam, Joe's right. They're saying Mesopotamia notes aren't worth . . ."

"I don't care what the babblemongers are sayin! It'll pass. The notes are as good as ever! Don't let them ruin us with talk like they did the Shawaneetown Bank. Don't ye know it's only the damn barrel of silver that's kept ye're money good as it is. Don't ye know if I was to pass that silver out t'night a lot of ye will be holdin' waste paper by mornin'!"

Flannerty said, "Sure, Sam. But it's our land payments we got to make. Redeem at least *part* of our notes in silver and let us go pay the . . ."

"I'll protect ye're damn money *despite* ye if I have to! I didn't hang onto this silver this long to have ye panic now and give it all out, and leave us with nothin'."

For the first time Blair noticed that Hosmer's big-knuckled hands shook as an old man's hands shake. "Ye're arm pain ye, Joe?" His eyes were lonesome and disappointed as an old man is disappointed in his children. But his mouth was straight across and he said, "Blair, it's good ye're back. We got work to do, quick. I loaned out that hodge-podge of currency Gideon Schaacht sent up as a loan. But it didn't go round . . . not enough to each man to make his land payments . . . not the way they'll discount that stuff at Land Office. We'll make up the difference to each man in Mesopotamia Hog & Trust notes."

"Make it up in silver, Sam!" Exeter pleaded. Hosmer ignored him.

"We don't have enough Mespo notes, but we'll write 'em out now. Schaacht promised he'd hold up the value of Mespo notes by publishing 'em at the top of the list in the Scioto *Gazette* . . . that's how guilty he felt about not sendin' us United States Bank notes for this loan."

Hosmer pulled a sheet of printed but unsigned Mesopotamia Hog & Trust dollar certificates from a pigeon hole. He kept his left hand near the stock of the left rifle. With his right he began signing the notes. Elizabeth Hosmer held the money from twisting under Hosmer's quill. As he signed them, Elizabeth tore them off.

Blair said, "Sam, you can't just sign more notes unless they're backed up."

"I still got the barrel, remember, Blair." Hosmer continued signing. "Anyways, we only need a few more. Ain't like the Owl Creek Bank where they got a paper circulation of near ten thousand, and I know he ain't holdin' enough bullion to back a third of it."

For the next hour Jonathan Blair was busy amid a sullenness brought about by the presence of a barrel of silver in the midst of men who thirsted for silver. But no one else moved toward the barrel, a gentlemanliness insured by the two rifles within six inches of Sam Hosmer's hands.

Mesopotamia watched the lawyer at work in silence. It was a strange sight to see Blair work at something with such sureness. Blair set Bolding to computing the difference which each man had to make up in Mesopotamia notes. He and Bolding then took the Mesopotamia notes as Hosmer signed them, and distributed them in the proper amounts to each man so that each could cover his Land Office payment.

Blair guided Hank Flannerty's hand in signing his name to a promissory note to Hosmer's Bank. "Don't press down so hard on the quill, Hank."

He told Mrs. Shane to sign both her first and last names.

He sent Brute Christofferson to borrow horses and relief horses for the ride to Chillicothe.

Blair worked fast because he knew that while they worked here in the store, Silver Pigeon's rumor would be traveling by word of mouth through the taverns along the road toward the Land Office. Men would be paying for their whisky and saying, "By the way, don't get caught with any Mespo dollars. They're lightin' cigars with 'em."

Blair showed Denaro how to fill in the phrase "lands and chattels shall be forfeited." That meant he had to answer Denaro's question.

"That's right, Denaro. Means that if you can't pay back the loan the bank takes your acreage."

And as Denaro's brown eyes turned full on him, Blair understood as never before the full weight of the burden which had been carried these last twenty years by Sam Hosmer. For Denaro asked, "Blair, it's gonna be all right, yes? The Land Office gonna take this paper and give the receipt, yes?"

"If we hurry, Denaro!"

"But I got now the new grapes on this land."

"If you lose the land you lose the grapes, too."

"But you gonna fix it all right, yes? That's why you do this."

Blair was impatient, for in the time it took Denaro to trace the letters of his name, a bank rumor could travel five miles even through solid forest.

Blair saw Bolding holding the corner of Hope Emerson's note, waiting impatiently for her to sign it, and Hope sitting there studying it before she signed, as if she could read it. Blair said, "I'll get hers, Bolding."

Blair read it to her quietly, gently.

"Sounds like I'm signing away my life, Jonathan, but if you say it's proper . . ." She made her mark. "You figure it's going to be all right, don't you, Jonathan?"

Brute Christofferson loomed through the door to report that the horses were ready. Blair was stuffing bills into his leather saddle bag. Each group of bills was tied with a leather thong, and a piece of paper on each told whose money it was and against which piece of ground it was to be applied at the Land Office.

But Blair suddenly stopped filling his bag. A deep familiar voice outside the door said, "Thank you for guiding us up here. We won't need you now."

Another familiar voice answered. A voice which could speak better English than it did, "Not go yet. You said show Indian how comes silver for these paper notes."

"Oh, yes . . . come in. We'll get that handled."

The door scraped open harshly and Gideon Schaacht stood in the opening, whipping the rain water off his hat. Behind him stood Silver Pigeon. Behind Silver Pigeon stood two soldiers. Their faded blue uniforms were dark blue on the shoulders from rain. Dark blue under the arms, from hot riding.

Schaacht walked to the counter where Blair was packing his saddle bag. He picked up one of the bundles, inspected it. Then he picked up several others, read the names, put them down.

"Land Office payments?"

"Yeah."

Schaacht circled over in front of the iron grill. He seemed to ignore Hosmer, but he looked in at the cask.

"Silver's still there," he observed.

He continued his circle of the store by walking over to where Joe Hussong sat. He stuck out a long finger and touched the red on Hussong's bandage. He examined the end of his wet finger and turned his head back to Hosmer. Then his eyes lowered to the rifles lying on the counter on each side of Hosmer. He wiped his finger on a handkerchief and walked back to the doorway where he stood facing Sam Hosmer.

"Hosmer, we hear a rumor that Mesopotamia notes are . . ."

"It's a damned lie!" snapped Hosmer, too quickly.

Blair saw Bolding look quickly at Schaacht expecting some severe reaction. But admirably Gideon Schaacht softened a fraction even as Hosmer continued.

"There's the barr'l of silver that backs up them notes and it's still sittin' there. And what's more it's gonna keep on sittin' there . . . as every cuss in this room now understands, I hope."

Hosmer looked over at Hussong.

Schaacht said, "Good. I'm glad to hear it's only a rumor."

He turned to the men in the room. "You'll all do well to follow the advice of your Mr. Hosmer. Rumors are sometimes deliberately started by inferior banks who want to buy up good currency cheap to stabilize their own position. Happened just two weeks ago over in Vincennes and also in Dayton. Don't rush to believe the worst."

This man Schaacht was a leader. The men in the room grew strong under his voice. And his faith in Hosmer reinstated their own faith in the founder of Mesopotamia. It was pitiful to see the relief on the old warrior when for once he had a little support on his side.

Schaacht said, "But Mr. Hosmer, before this rumor spreads, it is necessary to fight it. It is important to redeem a few Mesopotamia notes in silver, so that the word gets around that you're sound."

The old man snapped back on guard.

"I have come up to count your gold and silver," continued Schaacht.

"Now wait a minute, Mr. Banker," said Hosmer, warily. "Ye talked yer way right back around to the other side. The silver's there. You can see it fine from just where ye're standin'. None goes out."

Schaacht held his hand out to Silver Pigeon. Pigeon placed in it a handful of Mesopotamia notes.

Schaacht walked over to within ten feet of Hosmer and threw a few on the counter. "Hosmer, we've got to redeem a few of these to show the territory that you're redeeming in silver like it says on the face of these notes, 'payable in silver on demand.'"

Hosmer picked up the notes and counted them. Twenty dollars worth. "If ye set such a store by appearances," he grudged, "I'll redeem this money. No more."

Hosmer placed his left hand on his rifle and kept his eye on Schaacht. With his right he handed the key to Elizabeth Hosmer. She opened the grill and went to the barrel. She counted twenty silver dollars out of it and handed them to Hosmer who stacked them in front of Schaacht.

Schaacht counted out the rest of the bills.

"A few more, Hosmer."

Hosmer counted the dollar bills. Twenty-two. He handed the key to Elizabeth, who brought out twenty-two more.

"That satisfy you?" Hosmer challenged, pocketing the key.

"That'll help some," said Schaacht. "I don't ask you to distribute any more. But I do insist on personally counting the rest of the silver and gold in your cask. That's my right as principal creditor of your bank and my duty as the United States Bank."

"Your *right?*"

"If your notes are good I'll see they're accepted at the United States Land Office. If they're bad it's my duty to protect the government."

It was unfair for an old man like Hosmer to have to argue with a giant to whom the President of the United States of America was only "Mr. Monroe." But Sam Hosmer had never been in a fair fight. He pulled from his pocket the only watch north of the town of Columbus.

"It's after two o'clock in the morning, Mr. Schaacht. You can count the specie in this bank, but not until banking hours. That's tomorrow. I never open before end of morning chores."

Schaacht smiled and beckoned to one of the soldiers. The crowd noticed for the first time now that one of them was Major Armstrong. He walked over to the counter and placed a paper in front of Hosmer. Hosmer read it, not all of it, but enough.

"Huh. Ye went to some trouble I see. A warrant. Blair! You're our law man. Read this and come out with some law talk that proves he can't come in here and count silver in the middle of the night."

Blair studied the warrant.

"Hell, tell him!"

Blair reread the warrant.

"Well, what you waitin' on, lawyer?"

"The warrant is drawn right, Sam," Blair said reluctantly. "He can count our silver now. No use to try to stop him."

He handed it back, but Hope Emerson snatched it and returned it to Blair. "Read it again, Jonathan," she said. "And find somethin' wrong with it. If Sam Hosmer don't want the silver counted tonight it's for good reason."

Blair said, "Hope, the instrument is sound. There's no harm to let him count it."

Schaacht said, "Major Armstrong, shoot off the lock."

Armstrong backed up to the door and poured priming powder in the channel of his sidearm. He raised it shoulder high and pulled back the flint.

Sam Hosmer shoved his wife out of the way and stepped sideways to stand in front of the lock.

Blair looked at Hope. But Hope looked at Brute Christofferson. She said, "Brute!"

And Brute Christofferson walked over and stood beside Hosmer. Seeing Hosmer and Christofferson standing there in front of the lock, Mike Stikes also walked over, as did Hope Emerson. Mesopotamia closed ranks against an outsider.

Blair looked at Schaacht. And he walked over to stand by Hope Emerson. Schaacht said, "Blair, you should be proud of the people you represent. But I have a job to do."

Schaacht turned to Armstrong and snapped, "Major, the barrel."

Armstrong traversed his aim from the shielded lock to the barrel of silver.

The explosion dinned in the store and the smoke hung in the moist air. The ball from Armstrong's gun did not even completely smash one of the staves in the barrel. But it was enough to snap the rawhide hoop and separate the bottoms of the staves from each other and from the bottom barrel head. The barrel remained upright, though slanting.

The crowd surged close to the counter. The silver dollars from the top of the barrel had jumped onto the floor and some were still rolling. But through the gap between the staves and the bottom of the barrel there spewed out onto the floor in front of the settlers, not silver nor bullion, but a cask full of half-penny horseshoe nails.

With his back to the iron grill Sam Hosmer spread himself between the settlers and the cask, his hands clinging to the iron grill behind him. But their faces told him they had already seen.

The left side of Hosmer's face contorted in rage. But the right side of his face was ghastly with lack of expression. His right hand grip fell limp from the iron and the arm swung down in front of him. His head dropped on his chest and his body swayed forward yanking loose from the rough iron grill his left hand which scraped off some rust and left a red stain on the grill. Hosmer's body sagged down and his forehead thumped the floor.

Speechless, the settlers watched one of the silver dollars roll out under the iron grill. It dropped off the slight elevation and rolled over to the iron-grey head of Samuel Hosmer where it circled onto its side, spun, shimmered violently against the floor, and was still.

Chapter 6: THE RIDERS

JONATHAN BLAIR learned in a matter of seconds what a formidable force is the life-time reputation of a good man. And at this moment the good name of Samuel Hosmer worked against Mesopotamia as powerfully as it had ever worked for it.

In the presence of the crumpled grey-haired frame on the floor the settlers forgot what had caused it to crumple. They forgot that the lands and chattles of Mesopotamia depended upon the acceptability in the Chillicothe Land Office of the paper dollars signed by Samuel Hosmer, which dollars Blair was now stuffing into his saddle bag. They forgot that this acceptability depended up until a moment ago upon the weight of silver in Sam Hosmer's barrel. The silver had suddenly turned to rusting iron. And as soon as that word traveled through two hundred trail miles of woods to the Land Office in Chillicothe, the Mesopotamia Hog & Trust notes would become rifle wadding.

Dazed, they forgot also that Gideon Schaacht was standing in the store; that it would be his first interest to get this word to the Land Office. Because if the money once went into the United States Land Office, it would next be deposited in the United States Bank which was the federal depository. Schaacht's bank could refuse to accept it, but Mr. Monroe would not be pleased about that. He might not even allow it.

Blair saw Schaacht move for the door. Although Schaacht's head turned to stare at the crumpled man on the floor, his right hand held the tunic of Major Armstrong, and his left forefinger stabbed at the chest of Silver Pigeon. Both listened intently, Schaacht's lips were moving rapidly. Over the mounting confusion Blair caught a few phrases from Schaacht's instructions.

"Horses ready . . . no stops except water and food . . . utmost importance."

The crowd's confusion drowned out Schaacht's next few words, but Blair then heard a snatch . . . "Old Harrison War Road to Chillicothe."

Blair heard Silver Pigeon say, "No, too long. Shorter way. Shawanee Trace."

"You know the way?" asked Schaacht.

"Day or night," said Pigeon. "Shorter."

Blair threw a thong around the bulging saddle bag and yanked it tight. He noticed Justin Bolding walk over to Schaacht to say something. Then he saw Schaacht shake his head imperatively negative and push Bolding away. Blair could not listen any longer for Hope Emerson tugged at his arm.

"Jonathan! Help lift Sam into Gavagan's wagon! He's still breathing!"

Blair shook his head and knotted the thong around the money. "Get somebody else!" Hope seemed not to believe him.

"You got to go with the wagon, Jonathan, up to that doctor at Fort Tawa! You know him. Nobody else knows him. You got to see to it he fixes Sam!"

"Hope! Somebody else! I've got to get to Chillicothe . . . now!"

"Jonathan!"

"I've got to, Hope! Everybody's land payments! Matter of hours. Schaacht will . . ."

But she wasn't listening. Her hand caught hold of one of the wooden buttons at her breast and she backed away from him, with amazed distaste.

"Hope, don't you see?"

Her voice was hate. "I see Sam Hosmer lying on the floor," she said. "I see you leaving. That's all I need to see, Jonathan."

Without taking her eyes off Blair she called, "Brute!"

Her voice was not loud, but Brutus Christofferson was beside her in an instant. She continued staring at Blair, but she said, "Brute, put Sam in Gavagan's wagon. Get to Fort Tawa as soon as you can. See the doctor does right."

Blair grabbed Christofferson's wrist.

"Brute, you're goin' with *me*! You got the horses ready? We'll need Tyng, too!"

Christofferson shook his arm, snapping Blair's grip so that a bow string twanged up the inside of the lawyer's forearm.

"Hope, for God's sake, can't you see!" Blair pleaded.

"I already said I see, Jonathan," she said. "You'd better go."

Blair noticed that most of those not directly helping to lift Sam Hosmer were watching him. He looked around the store, meeting the cold face of Mesopotamia. Each face reminded him who had been the one to sanction the opening of Sam Hosmer's barrel of silver. Each face indicted him.

One face, however, seemed only to be amused. Justin Bolding stood contemplating him with academic interest which infuriated the lawyer and he said, "Come on, Bolding. It's you and I, I guess."

The doorway was blocked by Major Armstrong who kept his eyes on Blair while handing his discharged pistol to the sergeant to be cleaned. He lifted the other from his belt. Armstrong pulled back the flint and shook the weapon to level the powder train. He looked to Schaacht for instructions. Schaacht said, "Leave your sergeant here to hold Blair and Bolding while we get down to Chillicothe."

The sergeant unslung his own rifle and stepped over behind Blair and Bolding. Blair said, "Schaacht, you make a mistake if you spread this word to the Land Office."

"Hard to see how that would be a mistake, Blair."

"This was one of the *good* local banks. Destroy this one and you'll find out how hollow the others are. But if you let it ride along on faith awhile, the banks can all get back on their feet. You should be trying to hold them up . . . like Hosmer did . . . with his bare hands and a barrel of nails."

"Just how, pray, can I put horseshoe-nail banks on their feet?"

"Help the men get title to their land."

"How does this save the bank, Blair?"

"If they could be sure of title they'll some day fill that Scioto with barges of Slasher's black-walnut shakes, Hussong's pork, Hope Emerson's Merino wool, rifles, whisky, flax. That's the same as money."

"I'd have trouble explaining that to Mr. Monroe, Blair. You and I have a different understanding of money, Mr. Blair. Hold him here, Sergeant."

Schaacht surged for the door, but he stopped when Silver Pigeon said, "Wait!"

Schaacht turned impatiently on the Indian. The Indian said calmly, "Better the sergeant comes with us. Need men to make bridge at stream. Nobody catches us the way we go."

Pigeon looked over at Blair and Bolding. "Besides," he grinned, "the law man does not ride the horse very good." The Indian sobered. "And also the law man is smart in the head. Soon your sergeant will be the prisoner of Blair."

Schaacht snorted. "When the sergeant has a gun?"

"I have had more advantage over Blair before than a gun and lost it. I had 1,500 guns. I do not wish to lose this one. Come."

Schaacht looked at Bolding. "All right," he said.

Which is how the race began that night.

By the time Blair had gotten his rifle and rations, by the time he had wiped the grit and dust out from under his saddle and padded a couple of raw spots on the bay's flanks, Schaacht's party was a quarter of an hour south.

Blair and Bolding plunged south over the old Harrison War Road, single file, Blair in the lead. The wind whipping his eyes reminded Blair now how tired he was. The bay's gait was labored and his great chest dinned with the metallic breathing of fatigue.

Yet Blair rode with a leaning-forward impatience that matched the churning in his stomach. The picture of Hosmer, limp on the floor, rode with him. Also, the open-eyed reproach of Hope Emerson. It became necessary for Jonathan Blair to lay at her feet the signed receipts for the land payments of Hosmer Village, and to say, "There, Hope. Now do you see? Do you understand now, Hope?" Blair's heels gouged the bay.

One thing else disturbed and puzzled Blair. Pigeon had remarked, 'the law man does not ride the horse very good.' Blair had always been a good rider, but in following the circuit court these last few years he had become a superior rider, and he believed Silver Pigeon knew this. And the Pigeon usually put thought behind every sentence. Blair could find no reason for this statement. Further, Blair knew that the old Shawanee Trail pretty much paralleled the Harrison War Road. It was straighter, of course, because the Harrison Road followed the curves of the Scioto. But at night it would seem to Blair to be slower, especially for a party of four. Pigeon's choice puzzled Blair. And to be ignorant of what Pigeon was thinking was to be caught with wet gun powder.

Coming out of the tunnel of oak at the Boxford Clearing the horses left the moist forest footing to clatter across the hard-packed opening, and Blair slowed slightly in surprise at the sight of light in Boxford's cabin. Boxford's stocky shadow suddenly stood in the patch of light and called, "Hey! How's the old man?"

Blair pulled up. "How'd you know anything was wrong?"

"They just went through. Schaacht and the Indian and them two soldiers."

"How long ago?"

"Quarter to half an hour. Said the old man was dyin'. How is he?"

"Don't know for sure," said Blair. "What else did they tell you?"

"They said he got an awful shock."

"They say from what?"

"Said it turned out he had just had a little coverin' of silver over that barrel. Rest of it was nothin' but nails. Said it liked to kill the old man when everybody saw."

Bolding was catching up from behind, with the spare mount in tow. Blair leaned down to Boxford. "That's a lie, Boxford. You understand? Anybody asks you, it's a lie!"

Boxford was amazed at the strength in the fingers of the lawyer which now clutched the muscle behind his collar bone.

"You understand that, Boxford?"

"Yeah. Yeah, Blair. Least I can do. Far as I know the barrel was full of silver."

Bolding pulled up in time to hear that. Boxford asked, "*Did* he die?"

"Not yet," said Bolding. "But most likely will."

They resumed south. The trail remained wide and Bolding pulled up abreast of Blair. Over the breathing and thumping of the horses he called, "You mean to perpetuate that lie, Mr. Blair?"

"That's right."

"Do a lot of harm. Think of the people who can get cheated."

"You think of them. I'm thinking of these." Blair slapped his saddle bag containing the land payments of the Hosmer Village settlers.

"They didn't seem to be thankin' you any for worryin' about them last I saw."

"They will."

"They think you ran out on Hosmer when he needed you. 'Fact they think you killed him."

Blair didn't answer.

" 'Fact you did."

Blair grazed the bay's flank with his heel, but Bolding kept up. "Being a lawyer, Mr. Blair, you're fostering this lie with full knowledge and aforethought."

"You just ride," Blair yelled.

"And even if you get receipts before the Land Office finds out that money's no good, I wouldn't want to defend your part in court."

"I'll worry about the law, Mr. Bolding. You ride."

The trail narrowed and Blair pulled ahead. But the back of his neck burned as he could feel the younger lawyer studying his back in the dark. Blair turned in his saddle.

"Your horse is fresher! Ride ahead and wake up the ferryman at Shawanee Crossing!"

The relief which the lawyer felt when his apprentice was in front of him instead of behind him was a chilling revelation to Blair. He went back over the conversation he'd just had with Bolding. He remembered now that glancing instant in the store when he had seen Bolding go over to talk to Schaacht. He remembered Schaacht shaking his head. He had not heard Schaacht's words. But it seemed now to Blair that he could imagine the words that should have accompanied that shaking of the head and the way Schaacht had pushed Bolding away. "Stay with Blair," the gestures seemed to say.

And now as Blair squinted ahead on the dark trail he seemed occasionally to see a faint blur of white above the rumps of Bolding's two horses, as though Bolding were turning his face to look backward frequently. Blair wondered if Bolding were also uncomfortable riding in front.

When Blair pulled up at Shawanee Crossing Bolding was dismounted, talking to the ferryman. Ferryman stood shivering in the cold morning darkness. He wore a leather shirt, the bottom half of which was wet. His legs were naked and his leather trousers were hanging over a small spit, dripping water into the small fire below which sputtered, as did the ferryman.

"What in damnation is all the commotion tonight! They paid me at the other side of the creek and then that big major cut the rope so's I couldn't pull the ferry back. I started to pole her back and that big giant with the eagle beak had 'em hitch their horses to my ferry and pull her up on the south shore. I had to wade back. So you're out of luck."

Blair snapped, "How long ago they go through, Ferryman?"

"A half hour. Say, what about that old man, Sam Hosmer? He die?"

"Will the Shawanee Trace branch off to the west of the Harrison Road just across this creek?" asked Blair.

"Always has. What about that old man? I always set a store by that cussed old buzzard."

Blair turned the bay down the bank toward the creek. "Keep your rifle high, Bolding. We'll ford it. Go ahead."

Blair gestured to the path, giving Bolding the right of way.

It could have been Bolding's nervous horse. But Blair noticed it when Bolding's horse skittered sideways, making it logical for Blair to go down first.

The noise of the horses floated out in the still air over the water with eerie crispness. At the water's edge, Blair said, "Bolding."

He looked up and down the creek and across it.

"What?"

"We make a mistake to cross here."

"Why?"

The short syllables reverberated clearly over the water.

"Armstrong never leaves a trailblock without leaving it covered. He learned that from Navarre."

"Schaacht will be running that party, not Armstrong."

"Maybe."

"And the Indian said they'd want all their men with them."

"Nevertheless."

Blair looked downstream, examining the crossing possibilities below.

"You're slowing us up, Mr. Blair."

"I thought *I* was the one that was in a hurry. Are you in a hurry, too, Bolding? Why?"

"Seems to me you're getting awful cunning in the last few hours, Mr. Blair. You never were so careful before."

"Never had so much reason."

Blair swung downstream along the shore. But he turned back when he heard the splashing as Bolding rode impatiently across the stream. In Blair's distraught frame of mind it seemed that Bolding was trying to get a lead, to get ahead of him.

Blair brought the bay around and crossed behind Bolding. The water came over the bay's shoulders. The saddle bag got wet. Bolding's mount strained up the opposite bank and was silhouetted a moment against the sky. Suddenly Blair yelled, "Bolding!"

But by the time Blair had seen the flash at the top of the bank the explosion was echoing up and down the creek, and Bolding's horse had doubled and was sliding back down into the creek.

They left Bolding's horse lying half in the creek, half out; and they came up the bank downstream aways.

Back on the Harrison trail Bolding was shaken. He rode the spare and he said, "Thanks for yelling."

"It's all right. Hurry up."

"We going to take the Shawanee Trace or the old Harrison Road?" asked Bolding.

"Which do you think could be better, Bolding?"

"I'd say the Shawanee Trace, judging by the Indian's talk."

"Then, we'll stick to the Harrison Road," Blair said.

When dawn broke they could tell that Schaacht's party had definitely not taken the Harrison Road. They went through the Columbus settlement when the sun was nearly straight overhead. Bolding wanted to stop to eat. But Blair allowed only time to water the horses.

"First you say I'm too fast," said Bolding. "Then, too slow."

The horses were knock-kneed with fatigue and they did not make good time throughout the day. Evening brought them into the settlement of Circleville on the east bank of the Scioto. They were only twenty-five trail miles from Chillicothe. Bolding urged that they put up there for half the night. They were at the moment outside the blacksmith shop.

"No. We'll get to within a mile or two of the Land Office before we rest," Blair said. "When it opens in the morning we'll be first inside."

"Then I can do better than that for you," Bolding offered. "I know where the land agent's cabin is. We could go right to his house before he goes to the Land Office. Beat everybody."

Blair thought about this. "No." He wondered why the all-fired rush. "I'll be satisfied to be first in line."

"Then we'd be better off to get a few hours sleep here and rest the horses," Bolding said.

Blair thought a minute while he uncinched his saddle and then he said, "All right. You get half a night's sleep. Might be a good idea. I'll push on closer to Chillicothe. Meet you there."

Bolding removed his own saddle and leveled a pair of red-rimmed eyes at his preceptor. "No, Mr. Blair, I couldn't let you do that. With all that money in your saddlebag you might run into trouble. We'll both go."

"Sure worry about me, don't you, Mr. Bolding?"

They studied each other for a moment, causing a slight grin to flicker around Bolding's mouth. The smith examined the animals' hooves.

Pointedly Blair paid the smith with a Mesopotamia dollar note. He watched the smith's face intently.

Bolding also watched. The smith examined the note very carefully and then accepted it without challenge. He gave change. Blair said triumphantly, "It looks as if we're ahead of Schaacht this far anyway. Mount up, Mr. Bolding!"

To Jonathan Blair, waiting in Chillicothe, it seemed to take hours for the town to wake up. The sun already had a little warmth to it, but it did not reach down into the damp defile beside the road from where Blair stood watching the front door of the United States Land Office an eighth of a mile down the road. He hoped the land agent appeared before Schaacht's party. Or maybe they were already too late.

Bolding sprawled asleep on the ground. The two horses stood drowsily. Blair took off his leather shirt. Before he broke the surface of the sluggish brook, it reflected to him his thick beard, reminding him how long since he'd washed, slept or shaved. Reminded him, too, that in the Land Office that face must not reflect panic or anxiety. He must lay the money on the counter and ask for receipts in a routine manner. The beard would help him conceal his apprehension. He would keep his hands below the counter while the agent made out the receipts. Keep the voice low and steady, relaxed.

The agent would ask how the money got so wet. Blair would say the ferry at Shawanee Crossing was washed downstream. No. That would cause the agent to ask, "How come?" there being no rain lately. Blair would have to think of something better. But he distrusted his tired brain.

Blair picked up his fringed buckskin shirt and brushed it with his hand. The dust and grass and debris remained, so he raised it overhead and snapped it like a blanket. The report brought Bolding to his feet grabbing for his bridle leather.

"It's all right," Blair grinned. "I'm not going anywhere without you."
Bolding looked sheepish.

"Go back to sleep. No need both of us watching."

"*You* go to sleep," said Bolding. "I'll watch."

Both stayed awake.

They saw a rider dismount in front of the Land Office and sit on the steps. He did not go in. They did not recognize him.

"Just a man waiting for it to open," said Blair. "I don't want to wait too long right outside the office."

"Chances for too many questions?" asked Bolding.

"That's right." The lawyer studied his student. "Don't forget, Bolding, I haven't signed your certificate to practice law."

"I could go up and watch for the land agent," Bolding suggested.

Blair thought this over a moment. But he said, "We'll just stay together."

Several other men arrived and sat on the steps beside the first man. A small knot of horses and wagons were now tied to the rail in front of the closed Land Office.

From the depths of his concentration Blair asked slowly, "Bolding, when you were down here with the bank was it usually like this?"

"Like what?"

"A crowd outside the Land Office so early in the morning."

"Sometimes."

"Such as when?"

"Such as four or five days before and after a payment comes due on a large area which was sold pretty much all at once. Or if a new area is being opened up for purchase, after cession of Indian lands."

Blair continued to study the crowd, somewhat relieved.

The bay, who had been nuzzling the leather oats bag, suddenly lifted his big head in a high arc and flicked his ears. Blair whirled to find himself looking into the muzzle of a short rifle. It was hip high in the brown hands of Silver Pigeon.

The Indian was calm. He said, "You start for the Land Office now, you arrive just ahead of the agent who just now leaves his cabin. Could go to head of the line without much notice."

"Pigeon!"

The Pigeon smiled and lowered his rifle. Bolding got up from the ground slowly and with amazement.

"How did you know we were here?" he asked.

"I have known since daylight. Pigeon did not wish the lawyer sleep through the opening. Go now."

Blair reached for his hat, but he hesitated. "That means we'll walk into Schaacht and Armstrong?"

Pigeon smiled. "No."

"If you are here, they are."

"No."

"Why?" asked Blair.

"Pigeon leaves them at crossing southwest of here and directs them west. One crossing of trails looks much like another in moonlight."

"What is this change of heart?" asked Blair. "Remorse?"

"No."

"You break the bank of Mesopotamia and now you want to fix it?"

"No."

"What then?"

"Blair, my people always make this mistake. Wyandots and Delaware raid *one* of your settlements. While we do this, your other towns rise up and circle us. We fight always your little finger, never do we cut off the head. But this Schaacht shows the Pigeon a chance to cut off the head."

"*He* told you?"

"In the store, remember?" The Pigeon shrugged. "This Schaacht said he comes to protect the *big* bank from your bad dollars. So I send him for long horseback ride. Better to poison the stream at the spring with bad money."

Young Bolding's jaw hinged open, hearing this from an Indian. Blair said, "Y'see, Bolding, how you could learn a thing or two from studying an Indian treaty?" And the lawyer added, "Pigeon, you are smarter than Satan."

"No. Indians are not smart. Would we have signed this treaty, and the one before that, and the one before that if we were smart?"

The Indian nodded toward the Land Office. "You better finish your business."

"My business or yours?"

"Ours," the Pigeon grinned.

Blair tried to look as if he were sauntering up the steps to the Land Office, while taking them two at a time. Part of the crowd surged in the door ahead of him, but Blair worked himself toward the head of the line. He recognized two men from Columbus in the middle of the line. He knew they might ask him questions about what happened in the tavern in Columbus, or perhaps somehow they had heard about Samuel Hosmer's barrel of silver.

"Jonathan!"

Blair shouldered through the door.

Justin Bolding crowded through behind him and grabbed him by the arm, "Stuttgart's calling you, Blair."

"Never mind that. You stand here by the door. If Schaacht or Armstrong or that sergeant should by any chance come up those steps, you do anything to keep them from getting in. Anything. Understand? Remember your law certificate."

"Jonathan!"

"He's still calling you."

"Never mind. Get by the door."

Bolding let go. Blair was fifth in line at the land agent's counter. The first two men were making simple second payments. The agent examined their money, checked their acreage in the Doomsday book, accepted the money and gave them receipts.

The third man Blair recognized as the Piqua settler who had helped him before in Chillicothe. The settler stepped briskly up to the agent, placed a list of names on the counter.

"Garth," he said, "I'm payin' for this list of freeholders. You'll find 'em all in the fourth range, fourth and fifth townships, Delaware Indian Cession Tract."

While the agent ran his quill over the map onto the Delaware Cession and down the fourth range line, Garth studied him. And Blair studied Garth.

The lawyer felt that Garth was not so much at peace with the world as he looked.

The agent checked off the names against the map and he said, "Uhm-hmmm. Yes, sir. And you brought their payments?"

The agent held out his hand to receive. But Garth said, "They asked you'd be sure to mark them paid on the map."

"Uhm-hmmm. We'll take care of that in due time. The money?"

"I was to watch with my own eyes while you marked the map."

"Um-hmm," the agent bristled like clerks the world over. "You shall watch . . . as soon as we count the money."

"All right." Garth plunked down a leather bag carelessly enough so the agent could see money was no problem, but carefully enough so he could hear some hard money ring against the counter. He half-turned away, taking out his pipe. "You'll find it all there."

The agent began counting. The specie was only a small pile compared to the paper money.

With the air of a man whose business is done, Garth said, "Hope the rain holds off till I get back."

The agent's only reply was his thumb slicking across his tongue and thumping against the counter with each bill. Blair noticed the agent counted the paper money into two piles. The large pile he pushed forward toward Garth. Garth ignored it, scraping out his pipe.

"Mr. Garth."

Garth examined the inside of his pipe closely.

"Mr. Garth."

Garth knocked his pipe against his boot heel. The agent reached across the counter and tapped him on the shoulder. Garth looked up, as if surprised.

"Mr. Garth, I'm sorry. But these bills on Bank of Urbana are no good here."

The clerk was already looking up at the fourth man in the line, but Garth did not move away from the counter. He looked incredulous.

"What!"

"I'm sorry," the agent said.

"But we're tradin' in these notes every day of our lives," Garth protested.

"If you'd been a week earlier, I could have taken them. But not now."

The agent held out a list for Garth to examine. "See. They were crossed off the acceptable list just a week ago. Overissue." Blair craned at the list, but couldn't read it.

"Aw, now. What do you mean overissue?" asked Garth.

The agent fingered the bills, bending them so they crackled. "Come, Mr. Garth. Everyone of these bills is cracking brand new. Be honest. These bills haven't traded hands once. They came fresh out of the Urbana Bank, signed just special so you could bring them here."

Blair hoped the Mesopotamia notes in his saddle bag were soaked enough to give them a circulated look.

Garth gathered up his money and left the counter in quick admis-

sion. There was no apology on his face, just concession. He stood facing the line. He grinned, wishing them better luck than he had had.
Three others fell out of the line behind Blair when they saw what happened to Garth. They obviously held Urbana Bank notes also. The
three joined Garth.

Garth spied Blair. His face lighted with pleasure and he advanced
with outstretched hand.

"Blair! Were you able to get holt of some good . . ." But Garth took
a quick look at the agent and curbed his question. "See you outside
later, Blair."

The fourth man in the line stepped up to the agent and placed his
money on the counter. Blair craned his neck to see what kind of money
the fourth man held. He saw some Bank of Lancaster notes, some Virginia pounds, some Muskingum Bank notes and there were some
strange brown ones. Before Blair could make them out he responded
to a tug on his sleeve. It was Stuttgart.

Stuttgart was the most objective lawyer Blair had ever met on the
Western court circuit. Though they opposed each other violently at
every step of the traveling court between the Scioto and the Miami
Rivers, Stuttgart greeted him with genuine Kentucky cordiality.

"*Thought* I saw yuh, Blair. But that beard threw me off. What happened afta that day in the tavern with that Indian and all? And you
dashin' off north like a scalded gobbler?"

"Nothing. The Indian was drunk."

"But I heard that the bank notes he was . . ."

"What brings you down here, Stuttgart?" Blair asked quickly, glancing at the agent.

"I'm payin' some land payments for a group of cli'nts north of Cincinnati. But what's this we been hearin' about Hosmer and . . ."

Stuttgart found himself being abruptly ushered toward the door by
Blair who held him just above the elbow in the friendly manner of
colleagues, but with such amazing pressure upon the bone of the upper
arm that Stuttgart sucked air. Blair wore a fiercely broad smile on his
face. But through grim, smiling lips that hardly moved he said quietly,
"Stuttgart, get back in the line. Stay there. And don't talk to me until I
get out of here."

Blair retrieved his place in line. The man ahead of him completed
his transaction and Blair stepped to the counter. He said as little as
possible. But the ink had run on some of the slips which told which

packets of money belonged to which settler. It was necessary to name these men for the agent.

The small bundles of money were lined up neatly in front of the agent. Each bundle had on the outside of it a few bills of either the strong Marietta Bank or the respected Cincinnati Bank, which may have been the reason the agent immediately got out the receipts and filled in the men's names on the receipts. There was a receipt in front of each bundle of money. The agent was a methodical man.

"Now, then, how did it get so wet, sir?"

"Wading through a stream," said Blair.

"Um-hmm," with a vapid upswing on the second syllable just as though everything in this life was just fine.

Methodically the agent counted the first bundle.

"I see you figured the Dayton Bank notes at fifteen per cent under face value. Just right."

The agent counted the next three bundles and signed the receipts with an upflourish of the wrist and the voice.

"Um-hm."

Blair reached for the receipts. But the agent said, "Wait'll I sign 'em all. Then I'll double check and we'll be all set. Um-hm."

Blair's fingers yearned for the receipts, but he rested them on the counter. The agent untied and counted the next three bundles and signed the next three receipts; eight or ten inches from Blair's hands they were.

"Um-hm."

Blair pressed his hands hard against the counter to hold them still. The agent counted the next three bundles and signed three more receipts.

"Those were correct. Unusual. Um-hm."

The clerk untied the next three bundles. The veins in the backs of Blair's hands stood out from the pressure against the counter. Blair put them in his pockets. The agent counted all the bundles, carefully, skillfully, quickly; but it seemed forever. He was meticulous about flourishes in his signature. He spoiled one and made it over, just as if his name were important. Blair burned, because it *was* important. This man's signature changed debtors to owners, it separated peace from frustration, pride from shame. The agent collected the receipts, "Um-hm," and he presented them towards Blair whose hands flashed out of his pockets.

But suddenly, almost as if Blair's quick motion had scared him, the agent withdrew the receipts.

A voice behind Blair said, "Hold these receipts! I represent Gideon Schaacht. Mesopotamia Hog & Trust notes are no longer acceptable at the United States Bank."

A cold shiver raced under Jonathan Blair's scalp tingling the base of every hair on his head. He snatched for the receipts which withdrew just enough to let his hand bang the counter. In a rage he snatched again, leaping half over the counter. But the agent stepped back still more. Blair turned to the voice behind him.

"Bolding! You *bastard!*" he said.

Chapter 7: *PAYABLE ON DEMAND*

THE TURNKEY looked at Blair with some admiration.

"They said you was a gentle one where you come from," he said. "Huh! I'm glad I'm not from there. How's your hands today? Pain yet?"

Blair looked down at the bundles of blue linsey which contained his throbbing hands. He twisted his body painfully on the bunk to look out through the bars at the grinning jailkeeper.

"They say that young Bolding looks a sight. Say it took five of them to stop yuh. At least there's five assault charges on yuh. You was like a blooming wildcat they said. Fists was flying like the spokes on the Cincinnati stage they said. How's your nose? Tell if it's broke yet?"

Blair rose painfully and rolled his shoulders back to shrug off the coat. The sun was up long enough to warm the jail.

"Come over by the bars and I'll help yuh."

The jailkeep pulled the coat sleeves off over the large bundles of hands. Blair winced.

"They was some said you was losin' your mind. Then there was one said you was just findin' it."

Blair lay back slowly on the bunk, testing each move for new pain. He closed blue-black lids down against the shiny blue and yellow puff which swelled under his eyes. Never before had Blair thrown every muscle of his body blindly at other men with the enraged prayerful intention of hurting. Even during the late English war against Tecumseh and Proctor he'd not experienced the armored immunity of a wrath which felt no pain until later. That insane red instant in the Land Office had been his first such experience. And now that the anesthetic anger had gone, pain came.

"Here comes the young buck now," the jailer said.

Blair let his eyes idle up a solid pair of new black boots, on up a pair of rich white wool breeches that covered straight young legs to a white ruffled shirt that showed between the lapels of fine-weave forktail coat. Only the face was familiar. For Justin Bolding had changed his clothes.

He was also well barbered, except for a little patch of whiskers at the corner of his mouth where the lip was split and too tender to shave.

He obviously expected Blair to begin. But Blair left the burden of speech on Bolding.

"Blair, I'm not interested in your opinion of me. I just point out your self-righteousness is somewhat ridiculous. What you jumped me for was protecting the system against a bagful of worthless dollars. Is this a bad thing to do?"

Blair gave no defense.

"What you jumped me for was for doing a job for my employer."

"Your employer!" Blair raised his head until the pain stopped him.

"Yes. Schaacht sent me up to read law under you."

Blair rolled his head to look up at the roof rafters.

"What do you want here?" Blair asked.

Bolding reached in his breeches pocket and pulled out folded money. In the manner of capable young men handling large money carelessly to bristle their elders, Bolding counted five wrinkled United States twenties into the jailer's palm.

"Let Mr. Blair out," he said. "I believe bail is set at one hundred."

"I don't come out on your money, Bolding."

"Very well." Bolding pocketed the bills without arranging them.

From his coat pocket he took a paper. "Then you can sign it in here."
The jailer unlocked the gate and brought the paper in.

> *"I, Jonathan Blair, having been preceptor to Justin Bolding, do hereby affirm that said student has completed a course of study under my direction which has given him a sound grasp of legal practice, fitting him for membership at the bar in any court in the states and territories North and West of the Ohio River.*
> SIGNED:————"

Blair did not take the paper from the jailer.

"You don't need *my* signature, Bolding. Go get some of your Jacob Burnets or your Longworths or your Worthingtons or Ewings or Chases to sign it for you."

"I studied your damned out-of-date books. I listened to your wood-smoke version of the law. I kept your damned briefs. *You*'ll sign it."

"You're not qualified."

"Not qualified! *You* say I'm not *qualified?*"

"That's right."

"Examine me."

Blair thought a minute.

"All right. What is a dollar? Legally speaking, of course."

"Why, a dollar is a piece of paper which is backed up with 371 grains of silver or 25 grains of bullion."

"There isn't a dollar in the territory backed up with that much metal. So who says when a piece of paper becomes a dollar?"

"Why, the . . ." Bolding fingered a bill from his pocket. "Why, the . . . now wait a minute, Blair!"

"Are *you* the one that says what is a dollar and what is not?"

"Of course not, but . . ."

"Well you said it in the Land Office the other morning. All by yourself, you decided." Blair tapped his saddle bag. "You changed these from dollars to paper. Are you the one that says, Bolding?"

"That question has no bearing on my law certificate, Blair."

"It will, Bolding. When you get the answer I'll sign your certificate. What is a dollar?"

Bolding stomped out of the jail.

A sudden quiet in the jail was pronounced enough to cause Blair to look up. It heralded the commanding arrival of Gideon Schaacht who stepped between his two aides, Riddle and Fleming, to approach Blair's cell.

"Blair."

Blair caught himself rising at the imperative address of the banker. But he saw that the pause was expressly for this purpose and he lay back against his rolled up shortcoat.

"Blair, you were right."

Blair folded his arms over his chest.

"I perhaps have made a mistake," said Schaacht. "Perhaps I should have listened to you."

Blair sat up.

"At least Mesopotamia has opened my eyes. When I saw how hollow the Mesopotamia Bank was, I made a few other examinations. Sent men to nearby banks to count the specie in their vaults. My findings are beyond belief. Or rather, what I am *not* finding. It will be necessary for me to check every debtor bank in the territory."

Blair stood up.

"I told you so, Schaacht. You should have let well enough alone until they could get on their feet!"

"Never mind that, Blair. We have work to do."

Schaacht handed some bills to the jailer who unlocked the gate. "Come on out of here. We've got to get you some clothes and get busy."

Schaacht was three steps toward the outside door before he felt that Blair was not following. He turned back.

"Come on, Blair. This is serious. We'll get you some decent clothes."

"What for?"

"You'll hear all about it."

Blair closed the cell gate against his own exit.

"What for?" he asked.

"Because you're going to work for me. For the bank. Salary will be eighteen hundred dollars a year in United States Bank stock."

"Eighteen hundred a year for what?"

"All right, Blair. Make it two thousand, but hurry."

"Two thousand a year for what?"

"You're a lawyer, aren't you? I need a lawyer and I need a good one. I happen to know your ability."

"*You* know *my* ability!" Blair laughed.

Schaacht never took his eyes off Blair as he reached behind him toward Riddle. "I also knew you'd not believe that I know, Blair. Let me show you something."

Riddle placed a folded paper in Schaacht's hand. Schaacht consulted it.

"Last spring you argued Woodbridge vs. Boxford, Gardner vs. Wright, Irving vs. Captain Michael, Mesopotamia vs. County, and some others I have listed here."

Blair rose to the unmistakable compliment of Schaacht's thorough investigation. But then he caught himself. "Then you must also have noticed how many I lost."

"I did. I also observed how impossible were the propositions you defended, and how remote were your chances in the cases you won."

Despite reason Blair warmed to this detailed study of his work.

"Furthermore," continued Schaacht, "you are just right for what I need done. You retain enough polish to have the respect of bankers. Yet you've become crusted enough with territorial woods smoke so you'll smell good to the local judges. You've got enough age on you for the gravity of what we must do, yet you're young enough to stand the pace."

"What pace?"

"Four out of the six banks that we've hastily examined are practically without silver. Some have assets to back one-sixth of their printed money. I expect that proportion pertains throughout the Territory. I will have to demand payment of all United States Bank loans in specie immediately. And in order to get it, I shall use the courts. You'll need stamina."

"Schaacht, you're a fool!" Blair laughed. "Do you think you can sue banks that are broke!"

Schaacht had worked at being patient. The effort wore out. "I've been called a fool by many smart men, Blair. But I've always reversed the greeting in the end. Are you coming?"

The jailer opened the gate again.

"You walk out that gate and you'll have a future, Blair. Stay inside it, you'll see what you'll have."

For answer, Blair swung the gate. The puzzled jailkeep pulled his hand out of the way. The latch tongue scranched over the rusty riser and clanked into the slot with finality. The director of the United States Bank stomped out, followed by Riddle and Fleming who each by turns stole glances back at the man who had thus spoken to Gideon Schaacht. Blair found himself being studied by the open-mouthed jail-keep. Jonathan Blair was just beginning to know what he had chosen.

As the dusk thickened Blair became aware of a cessation of footsteps outside his window . . . a small, light pair of boots, they sounded like, and for a moment he had a sensation of being watched. He rose to the window, but he could see nothing in the gloom.

The footsteps turned around and receded. And then shortly they were coming down the center aisle of the jail. The jailer brought a candle and handed it to the visitor, who then proceeded towards Blair. The candle reflected a billowing expanse of gold-threaded white, a skirt.

She stood looking at Blair, Gideon Schaacht's daughter. And she was unreal. Blair was accustomed to women who wore their address, history, and number of children on their person. Faith Hawkins had a wedge of bright new cloth that expanded the waist of her faded linen church dress, marking the day she changed from a bride to a mother. Hope had soft, smooth hands from the yolk of the sheep. But this woman had no marks . . . unless it would be care like Gavagan gave his team before a trip to Cincinnati. But she looked as though she'd be the same even if she were born into any other house.

They studied each other like a swan in the water meeting a dog on the shore. She had the advantage, though, because Blair couldn't look direct for long before he began to feel like the dog on the shore.

She handed in a long thin cigar. Blair took it between his linsey mitts. She held in the candle. Blair worked a thumb loose and lit the cigar.

"Well, have you seen enough?" he asked.

"Enough to know you won't do it."

"What?"

"Sign Bolding's certificate."

"Huh. That's important to you?"

"Well . . . yes."

"You look like you could have a hundred others. Is he so great?"

"No. But I've had a hand in the making of him."

"Then if it's a comfort to you, your Papa Schaacht will have no trouble getting half a dozen better lawyers than me to sign his certificate. They'll examine him. But he would pass. He can get it signed."

"I know. And he probably will. But I thought if he did something on his own, it would be . . . I guess it doesn't matter who signs it." She was cold as ice, but something in Blair wanted to follow her out.

In the middle of the night Silver Pigeon spoke softly so as not to wake the jailkeep who slept slouched on a bench in the aisle of the lockup.

"Hurry up, Blair!"

Blair sat up sleepily. "Why do *you* want me out so bad?"

"You got work to finish." Silver Pigeon stood outside the cell and spoke through the bars. "The damages money and the mission money and annuity. And most of all the fifty thousand acres you promised so long to get for us."

"Huh. You said I was too slow."

"You are. But there is nobody else."

"That's a tough order, Pigeon. It'll be a man-sized job."

"Yah. But you gonna be a man yet."

Blair's head snapped up. But the Indian had grin dents in his cheeks. He said, "Come, Blair."

Blair watched in surprise as the Indian put the key to the lock and opened it. He watched him lift the gate a half-inch, rub a piece of candle wax under the hinges and swing the gate silently open. The lawyer grinned, but did not move.

"Can't come that way, Pigeon. Put the keys back in the constable's pocket."

Silver Pigeon looked puzzled.

"If I broke jail now," Blair explained, "they could arrest me."

"Arrest?"

"Hold me until court sits. Put the keys back."

Pigeon shrugged. He walked over and kicked the jailkeep's outstretched boots.

The jailer scrambled awake. By reflex he grabbed his pocket for the keys. Pigeon dangled the keys toward him. The jailer snatched them.

"What are you doing here?"

Pigeon took a roll of bank notes from his pocket. He counted ten bills into the jailer's lap.

"Let the lawyer out," he said before the jailer was oriented.

"I can't do anything until I talk to the judge or Mr. Schaacht."

"Let him out now," the Indian said.

"I can't do anything."

"You don't need to."

Silver Pigeon looked at Blair who walked out of the unlocked cell. The jailer stared at the gate, then at the keys, then at the Indian and Blair. But not for long, for they were gone.

Blair entered Mesopotamia at night in the rain. There was a light in Hosmer's store, and he headed the bay there. That is, he intended to go to the store, but his hand apparently compelled the rein more northerly. He arrived at the burying yard.

Squinting into the dark Blair brought the grave markers into focus. He was relieved to see no fresh-cut headstone shining out newer than the others.

But as he remounted Jonathan Blair's left boot did not slide easily into the stirrup. Fresh turned earth on his boot sole clogged it. He dismounted.

The mound of mud was six inches high. The stone was dark-colored, but newly chipped flecks of mica caught the moon. Blair put his face within five inches of the stone. A silver dollar shone back at him, recessed in the rock, sealed in apparently with melted glass. Blair's squint could not bring out the chiseled letters below. But his fingers had no trouble, for they already knew what shapes they would trace.

SAMUEL HOSMER
1737—1817
A MAN, BY GOD

Blair led the bay to the hitching rail outside the store. With his hand on the door he paused. Though the wind played a great 'Amen' through the high tops of the giant oaks, the voices of arguing men came from the store in Mesopotamia. Blair expected Mesopotamia would look and sound different if Sam Hosmer ever went. It was a shock to hear Joe Hussong's voice inside the store, sounding as it had always sounded, like a rain barrel on a hog caller's porch.

"All right then! The rest of ya can do as ya please! But I know *my* mind! When they come to take my place they're gonna walk out dead, because I'm gonna shoot. And Adams and Mitchell agreed to do the same. And what about you, Gavagan?"

Blair heard no answer. It must have been a nod of the head.

"And you, Denaro?"

There must have been another nod.

"That's five of us. And I can get more, too. Navarre was through here again this week. He's just in from the Illinois Territory and the Indiana Country, and he says there's plenty more gonna do the same. And I mean I'm gonna shoot even if it's *you* come up my path, Ault. So when you come to my place, state your business quick enough so's you don't catch your death of lead."

There was a silence against which Hussong defended himself.

"All right, look at me if y' want! But the most of ya know well enough that's just what the Old Man would say, too . . . if he was still around to say. If your Indian-lovin' law man hadn't as much as kilt him."

"Yes! I said 'kilt.' And for what! Now we find out Blair didn't even make it to Chillicothe in time anyhow. He let the word get out. United States Bank won't accept our notes from the Land Office so the Land Office won't accept 'em from us. Now Ault tells us we still owe for our land. On top of that we owe Ault the money we borrowed from Hosmer that Blair's got somewheres."

Blair heard Stikes' voice say, "Hussong, you forgettin' you're the one started agitatin' to open that barrel of nails? Besides, we don't know for sure that our money is no good!"

"Ault says it ain't."

"Ault's word's never been law here before," said Stikes.

"Is now," said Hussong. "He's the new president of your bank. I don't get how the United States Bank can appoint him president of our bank just because we owe them money. But you let 'em do it. And Ault says our money's no good."

"That doesn't make me believe it," said Stikes.

"All right, Mr. Stikes," Hussong said slowly. "Let's just see what you *do* believe. Here's the thirty-two dollars I owe ya for my rifle and my wagon wheels. Will you take it?"

The dead silence told Blair how they all waited to see if Stikes would pick up the Mesopotamia dollars. Blair listened to hear what Stikes would do. The whole West seemed to listen.

"Ha! That's what I thought!" It was Hussong. "You know well as I do what these are good for. This!"

Blair could hear footsteps approaching the door. He stepped aside as the door opened. A fistful of paper dollars plummeted out the door and fluttered to the wet ground. Some went aloft in the wind. The door slammed shut.

Blair was reaching for the door latch but he stopped because there now drifted out to him the voice of Hope Emerson.

"Not like us to be doin' like this till we hear from Jonathan. Sam would say wait for Jonathan. He set out to make our land payments. So it's likely he did."

"Huh."

"Are you forgettin', Joe, that Blair's the one fixed it so the Indian contract money came to Mesopotamia? You forgetting Blair's the one got Schaacht to come up here and give us a loan? If Blair said he'd make our payments he likely did. And if our money has gone as bad as everyone says, we'd have heard it from Jonathan first off."

"Hope, you just talking?" asked Hussong. "Or are you sure that's right?"

"Sure enough that I'll go get those bills you just threw out, and you can consider you paid me thirty-two dollars on account for the lambs."

Blair heard Hope's small boots approach the door. By the light from the door which opened suddenly, Mesopotamia found Blair stooping to gather up the bills which had not blown away.

He straightened up and stepped inside the store slowly. Hope gave way before him.

Blair looked at the circle of faces around the inside of the store and he saw that the pinched, anxious face of Mesopotamia was like all the faces he'd seen on the way up the Scioto. Their question was in their eyes as they stared at the bills in Blair's right hand. It was soon answered.

Hope stepped forward and grasped the wet bills that Blair held. But he did not let go. He looked around behind him until he found Joe Hussong. The lawyer silently handed the bills to the hog farmer.

Hussong crushed the bills and flung them to the floor.

"That's what I thought," he said.

Only Joe Hussong paid Blair the compliment of hating him. The others merely insulted him with well-meaning forgiveness, admitting the money trouble was too big for a woods lawyer.

In Stikes' forge Blair cried out against their ignorance.

"Don't you see, Stikes! *Nobody* could have done anything!"

Stikes finished screwing a brass shoulder-plate on the stock of a rifle which he lined up with three others. He stroked the barrels of the rifles. "Don't you worry, Blair. We'll take care of it." He hoisted one of the rifles and squinted critically down the sights. "Like we always did before," he added. "Old Sam would have said to do it this way if we could get no other help."

At the mention of Sam Hosmer there was no more talk for a moment until Stikes said, "Oh, you're not to feel bad about Old Sam. They would have found out Sam's barrel was empty sometime anyhow. Same thing would have happened. You just chanced to be the one that . . ." Stikes laid a piece of rifle iron, orange from the forge, on the anvil and hammered it harder than necessary. "Sure could use him around here now, though," he said.

Stikes began to beat an octagonal shape into the bar of iron. Then he said, "Hope wants you to come out to her place about somethin'."

Blair found Hope in back of the shed. She was standing by while Brute Christofferson shoveled the last of the dirt on top of a dead lamb. From her hand old Aaron, sire of most of her flock, nibbled at the clover she held for him. Blair pointed to the dead one, "What killed it?"

"We did," Hope said.

"You?"

"Got the tremors. We can't get any tonic. Had to kill it before the others get it."

Blair looked back at Christofferson who was smoothing off the mound of earth.

"Why no tonic?"

"Money," Hope said. "Nobody's giving out sheep tonic except for silver or gold." She patted the head of old Aaron who nibbled at the clover. "That's the way it is, Jonathan, you got to kill a few to save the rest. Can't be friends to all of them. A softhearted shepherd can be the meanest. Got to set yourself for it."

She faced him to see if he heard.

"Old Aaron here goes next," she said. "He doesn't know it."

Christofferson came over to Hope. Giving his back to Blair he reached down to take hold of Aaron. "You better go in the cabin, Miss Hope, while I . . . uh . . . take care of this one."

"No. He started the whole flock. Least I can do is be here with him in the end. Go ahead, Brute." But Christofferson straightened up and looked beyond her to the trail. Hope looked where Brute looked, and suddenly she put her hand on Brute Christofferson's bare arm. "No, Brute! You'll only make it worse. You go up and see to the flock."

Hope's small hands quickly pivoted Christofferson and pushed him away. Old Aaron sulked at being deprived of the clover.

Blair looked toward the trail and the source of the trouble. Emanuel Ault approached.

"That's what I called you for, Jonathan," Hope said. "He came out here writing down things in that book of his. Brute threw him off the place. But he's back, like he said. Can he do that?"

Emanuel Ault had a formidable kind of courage. He could forego the good wishes of men. Nor was it any detraction from his physical strength or courage that Christofferson had thrown him off Hope Emerson's farm, for there were few men walking in the world who could match Brutus Christofferson's strength. But here was Ault back again.

Ault was not a farmer settler. He had been a surveyor in the West for Shuldane. He had a contempt for the land as anything but a product to be measured, bought and sold. Unerringly, Schaacht had picked this man to head the Mesopotamia Bank during the foreclosures.

There was a certain honesty in Emanuel Ault. His hair was hacked short and it jutted forward. There was no attempt to comb it.

Observant, too, he looked Blair over and he said, "Blair, you're leaner."

Blair said, "What brings you out here?"

"And your nose is broken," Ault noticed. "And your hands are scarred up. Beginning to look like you belong here." He grinned.

"What's your purpose, Ault?"

Ault brought out his small black book and a charcoal pencil. "Tabulating property. Miss Hope, there's four improvements on your property, counting the shed, right? And there's a spring and a hundred acres, right? Now, how many animals have you got?"

Hope turned to Blair. "Jonathan, can he come on my place and count things and give a list to Schaacht?"

In the argument which followed, Blair said, "Ault, you don't actually believe Schaacht can go through with closures against all banks which owe the United States Bank? Do you know how many there will be?"

"I'm concerned with only one, Blair, this one."

"Schaacht is too smart to attempt such a thing."

"How many sheep, Mrs. Emerson?"

Blair said, "Look, Ault. Hold off on this survey. I will go to Schaacht and explain to him that if he will hold off until after harvest, the people might have a chance to make a payment. He will understand that."

"All right," said Ault. "You just do that. How many sheep, Mrs. Emerson?"

On Thursday, Blair bent to lift Aaron into Gavagan's wagon, but before he had caught hold of the ram, Brute Christofferson possessively scooped the ram up in his arms. He hoisted him easily and jealously, and Blair had the irrelevant vision of Christofferson lifting Hope just as easily. Brute set the animal on the bed of Gavagan's wagon and closed the tailgate.

Hope said, "Just as soon as you get the tonic, Jonathan, give it to him. And whenever his head hangs down, give him some more."

Blair tied his bay to the tailgate of the wagon and he started to climb up to the seat beside Gavagan. That's when Hope said to Christofferson, "Did you give him the shirt, Brute?"

Brute colored and stood mute.

"Did you give it to him, Brute?"

Christofferson gestured a huge hand toward Blair. "The rest of him is all dirt and woodsmoke, Miss Hope. It ain't gonna make him more impressive to this banker if he had only a clean shirt and the rest of him is all . . . well, look at him."

"Give it to him, Brute."

Christofferson reached inside his shirt and pulled out a package wrapped in the Scioto *Gazette*. He handed the package to Blair. But before he let go he said, "This here's a shirt Miss Hope says you're to wear while you're talkin' to this bank man."

Blair took the package and Brute added, "But you're to take it off right after. Bring it back to Miss Hope when you're done with the banker. She has it for a purpose."

Gavagan slapped the lines and they rolled south.

At Columbus Blair inquired who had sheep tonic. In The Swan tavern Jarvis Pike told him to see R. Taskin.

As Blair was leaving, taverner Pike stopped him. "Blair, you remember that Indian that was in here with you? He really started something."

Blair knew this, of course, but he wondered why Pike should remark on it.

"I'm thinkin' that red skunk isn't so dumb as he acts." He pointed to the corner of the tap room where he kept all the newspapers that drifted into Columbus in the pockets of travelers. Gavagan went to see R. Taskin about tonic. Blair went for the newspapers. He devoured them hungrily, going through each in a matter of seconds, picking up a new one before he'd finished the first, impatient that his eyes could not absorb the type as fast as his mind could take in the unbelievable catastrophe he read there.

Gideon Schaacht had acted swiftly, and with incredible fierceness and presumption.

The *Scioto Gazette* said: "Colonel Gideon Schaacht has announced that the United States Branch Bank at Chillicothe is immediately calling for the balance due it from all the independent banks at a rate of 20 per cent per month. He has said that payments must be in specie, that is gold, silver or United States Bank notes. Only six banks are excepted from this rule, being those whose currency is still respected and which pay specie regularly upon demand."

The *Cincinnati Liberty Hall* said: "Cincinnati banks are attempting to contract their own debts to pay the severe demand of the United States Bank. But borrowers have neither specie nor United States notes nor notes of the six acceptable banks. In attempts to satisfy the local banks property is thrown on the market here in the most reckless manner. Good eastern horses are for sale at five dollars gold."

The *Indiana Herald* printed: "The United States Bank has now unbelievably demanded that payment be made in silver or gold coin or bullion, none of which has been seen in this country for three months in any quantity. Petition is now open for signing in this office by all subscribers who wish President Monroe's notice called to the fact that the bank he sent out here to save our currency now intends to go into our vaults and rob our last gold pistareen, leaving our worthless paper more worthless than before."

The *Vincennes Western Sun* shouted: "It has long been predicted that the Republic of the United States would divide at the Alleghenies, forming two separate countries. That hour has now arrived. Colonel Gideon Schaacht, director of United States Bank at Chillicothe, has bankrupted the West. Exchange papers here show that thirteen banks in Ohio have closed, six in the Indiana Country. The Illinois Territorial Bank at Shawaneetown has reported that compliance with the United States Bank order is impossible. They await United States Bank action."

There were more papers, more figures. But it added up to the fact that almost every citizen in the West was now ultimately the debtor of the United States Bank. Schaacht must be crazy to expect payment.

Gavagan came back to say that R. Taskin was selling no tonic except for gold or silver. They pushed south toward Chillicothe.

At Circleville, Blair made for the tavern and the newspapers. The unbelievable act of Gideon Schaacht was written into all of the papers there, too.

Gavagan could not understand how a newspaper could swell the veins in Blair's temple, "The thing's too big to get mad about, Blair. Your bank man demands gold. There is no gold. So he won't get gold. He's too crazy to worry about."

Blair rolled the *Lebanon Western Star* into a club. "That's the trouble, Gavagan. He's not crazy. He is smarter than the devil himself. He's got a box seat at hell's peek hole."

Gavagan shrugged.

Blair said, "Let's try to get the tonic for the ram here."

But they could not get it for paper money.

As Gavagan's wagon approached Chillicothe, Blair carefully removed the newspaper wrapping from the shirt Hope had sent with him. As the wagon rolled along Blair removed his own shirt which was ripped in several vertical slits up the front from the fight in the Land Office.

Gavagan watched idly, his elbows on his knees. He said, "Darnation, Blair. You're down to muscle. Not eatin' reg'lar or what?" But there was some admiration and surprise in Gavagan's voice. For in truth Blair's recent months of activity and anxiety and haphazard eating and sleeping had leaned him down to a hard statue of muscle and nerves. His face was thinner and changed some in appearance because of the broken nose. And actually Blair was finding this not to his disadvantage in moving through the big woods. His more rugged appearance, coupled with a certain recent impatience of manner brought him quicker answers from tavern keepers and stable boys. He caught people studying him, but they paid attention to his business.

Blair unrolled the shirt Hope had sent. The whiteness of it showed him how dirty his hands were. It was made from Tyng's flax, and though it didn't have the bone buttons of a Cincinnati shirt, it had seams as straight as the Philadelphia shirts of Justin Bolding. The ruffles on the chest of it were a bit too large, but it was a work of patience that surprised Blair coming from Hope Emerson. He wondered why she had made it.

Gavagan's laugh surprised the team into a jog. "Darnation, Blair! Two of you could get in it!"

It was true. The shoulders of the shirt overlapped Blair's own excellent shoulders by two inches.

Blair took it off in bewilderment. He folded it up.

"Was Hope's late husband a big man, Gavagan?"

"Hell, no! Well, he was big, yes, but not *that* big. Besides that shirt is new. Nobody's wore it yet."

"Couldn't be for her brother," Blair thought out loud. "We saw *him*."

"Blair, it looks like Hope's set her cap for a big . . ." He let it hang there because both of them had the same thought.

"Aw, it couldn't be," Gavagan said. "First place Christofferson never wears a white shirt."

But as Blair wrapped the shirt up in the newspaper, he said, "Everybody wears a white shirt at his own wedding."

Inside the front part of the United States Bank at Chillicothe Justin Bolding stared at the soiled and shredded shirt of Jonathan Blair with appraisal so candid that it caused Blair to wear it like a flag.

Blair had come direct to the bank. Gavagan had gone for the sheep tonic.

"I want to see Schaacht."

"He's talking to a couple of men. Be free in a minute."

Bolding reached under some papers and shoved his legal preceptor certificate in front of Blair. He also handed him the quill. Blair shook his head.

"Why not, Blair? I did the work. I know the law. I know it as well as you. More, in fact."

"Get one of Schaacht's friends to sign it for you. A man who can break every bank in Ohio wouldn't have any trouble getting a little certificate signed."

"I know that," bristled Bolding. "But you're the one should sign it."

"You find out what a dollar is yet?"

Bolding took Blair down the hall and up the stairs to Schaacht's office.

There were two men seated in the office and Gideon Schaacht stood looking out the window. He turned only long enough to see that it was Blair and that he was sweating in the face and hotter still inside. Gideon Schaacht was wise enough in the ways of arguments to know the advantage held by a hot, sweaty man.

"Schaacht!"

But the banker also knew how to drain the momentum out of angry men; and he left Blair only his broad back, an unsatisfactory target for wrath.

"Schaacht!"

The two men in the room looked at Blair quizzically.

"Schaacht, turn around and listen to me!"

But when Schaacht did turn around he had organized himself to steal the heat from Blair's argument. He said patiently, "Why should I listen, Blair? First, you're going to say, 'Are you crazy!' Then you'll say, 'Can you demand gold from banks that have so little of it that it's buried in the ground?' "

"Well, can you?"

"I not only can, but I *have*. There *is* the machinery for due process of law here, you know, even if it is crude."

"Do you mean . . ."

"I mean I am putting in suit next week every debtor bank and individual in the West. And I *will* recover the balances due here." He stabbed a long skinny finger at the ledger in front of him.

"You're crazier than I thought, Schaacht."

"You've lost the right to call me crazy, Blair. I asked for your help and you refused. I've had to go and get my own. Mr. Cutler here is from the mother bank at Philadelphia and Mr. Strock is here representing a group of eastern land investors. There are more coming to my house this evening."

As Schaacht talked, a righteous indignation grew in his voice which turned Blair's anger some by its logic.

"You stand there and criticize me!" Schaacht continued. "But if you know a better way, you can sit in this chair. You want it?"

Schaacht stood up and waved an open palm to his chair. "Well, do you have a better way or don't you?"

"Yes," Blair said. "Give us until after the harvest. Some might be able to pay. If not, at least you'll foreclose on corn that's in the barns. What good is it to you standing in the field?"

Schaacht's fist hit the table. "No! After this harvest you'd say, 'wait till next harvest.' If it's going to work, it's going to work *now*."

"Then it isn't going to work, Schaacht. You don't seem to understand the money trouble is really land trouble. Suppose the bank ends up owning half of Ohio, Indiana, Illinois Territory and Michigan Territory. You still won't have your money."

But even as he said it Blair had already begun to see and, in truth, to admire Schaacht's solution. He half-turned to look at the Mr. Strock. And he knew he was looking at Schaacht's answer.

"You're mistaken," said Schaacht. "This can be the beginning of the real growth for the West. You men came in and knocked down the trees. Now there are men in the East willing to come in and buy your improvements and advance from there. The bank *will* recoup."

"What about the original settlers?"

"There are more trees to the west to knock down," Schaacht offered.

"And more Indians."

Blair was speechless as he visualized thousands of settlers . . . not young ones . . . moving west now to more misery, to wear out thousands more axe handles, to wear out more wives.

"Don't look at *me*, Blair. I didn't make the situations."

And Blair had to admit this. He turned and walked down the stairs and out onto the hot dusty road that came from somewhere in the east and went to somewhere west of Shawaneetown, Illinois. And he wondered what was out there. And by the three shiny black carriages tied to the rail in front of the bank he realized that already the West no longer belonged to the Sam Hosmers nor to the Joe Hussongs . . . nor the Jonathan Blairs. But then it never had belonged to Blair.

Blair had been waiting in the Cross Keys tavern for Gavagan two hours. When the first lamp was lit, Blair asked the keeper, "You seen a teamster, name of Gavagan? Drives a hundred-hundred with a new slat in the tailgate?"

"The one with that pure-bred Merino in the back?"

"That's the one."

"Yeah, he left a message for a man named Blair. That you?"

"Yes. What?"

"Said to tell you he couldn't get tonic at the first place. But he heard of two more sheep farmers. He was going to see them. Said the 'Rino was gettin' awful feeble."

A customer sitting one bench over from Blair came over, a fairly well-dressed man. He said to Blair, "Pardon me, did I hear you say you owned that Merino that was in the wagon?"

"No," Blair said. "I brought it down for a friend."

"To sell?"

Blair studied the stranger. He had money, Blair noticed, because he was drinking the sour-mash whisky in the small mugs instead of the corn in the big tankards. He might be one of Schaacht's eastern investors. He talked like Bostoners. The stranger gestured to his two friends who came over.

"To sell?" he repeated.

"Not exactly," said Blair.

When the two men came over they asked what ram was sire and who was dam for this Merino. The sharp interest of these men made Blair think how wonderful it would be to take back hard money to Hope in exchange for a ram she expected to lose to the tremors. To cover his ignorance, Blair shortened his answers.

"He's registered out of Adam Rotch's flock," he said.

"You positive about that?"

"Positive."

"You got a letter or anything from Rotch that says so?"

"No. But this one is Number 34 by Rotch's first ram."

"You interested in selling? Or is your friend?"

"We were just going to look around. Not in any hurry."

"Are there more? Does your friend have more?"

"Yes."

"How old is this ram?"

Others in the tavern hearing the magic word "Merino" came over to listen to the dicker. The tavern keeper hovered near, interested. Blair said the ram was four.

The stranger said, "If you'll let me examine that ram, I'm prepared to make you an offer if he's the pure white fleece."

"My friend is interested only in metal money."

"If you can prove sire and dam, I'll offer two hundred, gold."

Blair didn't know Merino prices. But he had watched Hosmer and Buttrick. He said, "We'd need three hundred twenty-five in silver or three hundred in gold."

The stranger said, "How's his health?"

"Good."

The interested barkeep almost dropped the tankards which he now waved toward Blair, "But you said you brought that ram down here to get him some . . ."

"Another whisky!" said Blair, loud.

"You ain't finished what you got," the keeper protested.

"Fill it up anyway!" Blair said.

The stranger said, "If the animal looks sound, and if you can name the sire and dam, I'll offer two hundred seventy-five gold, cash."

The barkeep clanked the whisky reproachfully in front of Blair so it sloshed out. The tavern door opened. Matt Gavagan's square silhouette filled the doorway and started toward Blair.

"Blair, this is the damnedest town of Shylocks I ever been in. It's no wonder they moved the state capital out of here. The money pinchin' sons-of ——"

"Glad you're back, Matt," said Blair loudly, rising.

"You won't be when you see the ——"

"Did you get it?"

"Naw, they got some but they won't part with it for nothin' short of blood . . . silver."

"Well, he's had good rations. A few days on common clover won't hurt him," Blair said.

"Who's talking about clover, I'm talkin' about ——"

"Oh, alfalfa? Well, that's all right, too."

"Alfalfa? Who said anything about ——"

"Matt, these gentlemen have made us an offer for the ram. If you think $275 will be satisfactory to Emerson, perhaps we'll sell him right now."

Gavagan's laugh filled the tavern.

"Two seventy-five! For that!"

"What's funny?" There was a flatness in Blair's voice which jolted Gavagan's quick Irish wit.

"Funny? Why . . . why, the idea of two seventy-five is funny. You know Emerson would expect four hundred for Aaron."

The stranger snapped at the name.

"Did you say Aaron?"

"I did," said Gavagan.

"Is that *the* Aaron out of Rotch's flock?"

"How many Aaron's could there be?" asked Blair. And they went out to the wagon.

They stood the ram in the dirt road in front of the tavern in Chillicothe. Gavagan's big hand held Aaron's chin aloft so that his wet, orange nose quivered. His other hand held up Aaron's haunches in a haughty stance.

The stranger said, "Let go of him a minute."

Gavagan ignored that and pointed out the length of the fleece. One of the men brought a lantern from the tavern. The stranger ran a thumb under Aaron's gums and lifted the black-orange lips. He pulled down the wool away from the eye.

"Eyes, a little cloudy," he complained.

"That's because of the lantern light," Gavagan explained.

"Let go of him," said the stranger.

"Notice the thickness of the wool on the chest," Gavagan said. "His offspring'll shear about twenty to twenty-five pounds and only 30 per cent shrinkage at the mill."

"Let go," the stranger repeated.

Blair said, "Let go, Matt, so he can look."

"Look how far down the wool comes on the shank," Matt said, still holding the ram.

But the stranger brushed away Gavagan's hands. When he did so Aaron's head drooped. The stranger watched this critically. But as he watched, the ram's forelegs buckled and dropped his chest to the dirt. The rear legs remained firm, but the haunch wavered and then flopped onto the right flank. Aaron's tongue came out of his mouth.

The stranger rose and slowly wiped his hands, not in self-congratulation, but in genuine disappointment.

"I'm sorry," he said. "A shame. He was prime. Had style, too."

Gavagan rose and flattened his lips, unsurprised.

Blair dropped to his knees. His hand went to the animal's chest. Then quickly he rolled Aaron over and put his ear to the chest. He heard neither heart nor breath.

"You're sorry," Blair said from his knees. "*You're* sorry!"

Matt Gavagan had never seen wet rage and disappointment on the surface of Blair's eyes, like he now saw reflected from the lantern light. Nor had he ever seen such swift motion on Blair's part, like suddenly the gentility was gone from the lawyer. Strength was there too, for he lifted the large ram as though it were a rag and draped it around his neck. He pushed himself to his feet and walked across the road toward the United States Bank. Gavagan followed in wonderment.

Virginia Schaacht walked down the steps of the bank on the arm of Justin Bolding. They stopped and stared at Blair. The girl's hand went to her mouth. Bolding said, "Blair, what's that?"

Blair pushed past them, walking east, rapidly. Gavagan stretched his pace to match Blair's.

"Blair, what you doing?"

Blair walked east past five houses.

"Blair, listen. What the hell you gonna do with a dead . . . ?"

Blair turned the corner and walked up a short lane. In the lane were five carriages tied to posts in front of a house with glass windows as tall as a man. Blair turned up the walk.

"Blair! You can't go in there with that!"

The double door was a massive barricade. Where the latch should have been there were two iron rings. The ram's front and rear legs crossed over Blair's chest. With one hand Blair held all four shanks while his other reached for one of the iron rings. Gavagan grabbed the lawyer's wrist. He was surprised at the strength with which Blair shook him off. Blair banged the ring up and down viciously.

"Blair!"

But Blair continued to hammer. A colored man in white stockings and shiny low black shoes opened the door, but stood blocking it. There was braid on his chest that reminded Gavagan of the time he'd seen General Harrison close-up at Fort Washington in 18 and 14. Gavagan backed off. He could see Bolding and Virginia Schaacht coming up the walk behind them. But he was surprised to see Blair move into the doorway. The door opener stood fast until he got a mouthful of wool as Blair hunched forward and pushed right through. The houseman grabbed at Blair's back, but the material ripped leaving him with a handful of shirt which he examined in amazed disdain. He started after Blair who receded inside the house. Gavagan followed cautiously with open mouth.

Blair marched straight on down the hall ahead of the white-stockinged braid. He stepped down two steps into a sunken dining room.

He was a stark figure standing there under a dazzling candelabra staring at the diners, who likewise stared back. Gavagan's amazement at Blair turned to amusement. He followed. He noticed the food was gone from the table. There was a small glass of something in front of each of the dozen well-dressed male diners who stared back at Blair, speechless. Gavagan noticed the cigars were straight ones, no twists. The braided colored man stood behind Blair and in front of Gavagan, absently holding more of these cigars. Gavagan took one out of his hand and passed it under his nose.

In the center of the gleaming table was a map. Gideon Schaacht, at the head of the table, was arrested with his arm and finger outstretched, pointing to a place on the map.

Blair walked to the head of the table.

"Present for you, Schaacht!"

He hoisted the ram up over his head and dropped it in front of Gideon Schaacht, splashing his brandy, and his cigar onto the white cloth and pinning his arm to the table.

Slowly Schaacht shook his stupefaction. He withdrew his arm from under the ram and brushed his sleeve. He motioned the colored man to pick his brandy-soaked cigar off the tablecloth and he rose to his towering height to look down on Blair.

"What, may I ask, Blair?"

"A present for you," Blair said. "As dead as the Northwest. It's dead for lack of two dollars gold. See if you can sue the life back into it. Get a judge to order it to breathe. Take it to court!"

Schaacht threw his napkin on the table and reached for a new cigar. "All right, Blair. I intend to. You think I won't. But I will. These men are here to revive the West. You'll see the economy spring to life with money they bring. I'll foreclose against indebted property and they will buy it."

Blair stared around the room at the twelve men, who were silent with surprise.

Schaacht said, "And further, Blair, I will begin with Mesopotamia, for a good reason now. You have twice made that place the leader against the bank. And I don't underrate you. You force me to demonstrate my intentions there first. The others will see, and that way we won't have any rebellion on our hands." Schaacht leaned towards Blair. "Oh, yes, you see I'm well aware of *that* threat."

Schaacht turned his cigar to the candle held by the servant. Then he pointed to the sheep. "And thanks, Blair. You have just shown me the way. Sheep it shall be. It's one of the few things of immediate cash value up there. I noticed these Merinos listed as loan security. And Mr. Bolding has explained to me about . . . uh . . . about your concern for Mrs. Emerson. You have thrown her sheep on my table and challenged me to turn it to gold. I *will*."

Schaacht raised his glance to Bolding who stood behind Blair on the steps. "Bolding, tomorrow kindly advise these gentlemen of the recent excellent market in Merino wool. Give them the prices. I'm sure several of them will find Merinos an exciting investment. Our Mr. Ault will receive proposals concerning Mrs. Emerson's Merinos."

Blair's cheeks quivered with rage and it must be admitted, with fear; for he understood the new pointedness of the contest.

Schaacht put his hand on the ram. His voice was gentle. "Jonathan, I asked you to join me in my mission which is important. I thought you were big enough to see it as a national effort. You refused me." Schaacht's eyes burned into Blair. "So I will do you the honor of directing my poor abilities against you personally. You left me no choice."

Blair went cold in the knees and hot in the face. "Schaacht, you won't get the chance because I will drive you and your damned United States Bank out of the Northwest."

Schaacht's head went back, and his mouth opened in a silent laugh. The men around the room smiled with him.

"Not *that* important you aren't, Blair! Don't take me wrong."

The volume in Blair's answer wavered the cigar smoke in the room. "Don't take *me* wrong, Schaacht. Every day and every night that I have left will be spent to drive your damned government bank out. *And I will do it! By God,* I will do it!"

Jonathan Blair shoved the dead ram of Hope Emerson of Mesopotamia into the face of Gideon Schaacht and pushed the ram and the banker to the chair so that the chair skidded backwards over the stone floor with a screech which might echo all the way east to Philadelphia and west to Shawaneetown, Illinois.

Chapter 8: THE HONORABLE BODY

"HE CAN'T do it, Gavagan. Can't."

Gavagan drove the team silently with new respect for the law man who rode beside him.

"Can't do it," Blair repeated. "And even if he could, he won't get the chance. I'll run that bank out of this state. And I'll start right now, while he still doesn't believe me. Before he expects it. Understand that, Gavagan?"

Gavagan noticed Blair trying to lean the wagon forward faster, and he flicked the lead rein.

"My plan is clear," Blair said. "Straight forward and simple. Nothing he can do to stop it. And he won't expect it so soon. Understand, Gavagan?"

"Yeah."

"What do you understand?"

"You've just been telling me you're scair't stiff."

"No! I've been telling you . . . yeah . . . scared stiff."

After a half mile of jogging over the dark trail Gavagan said with some disappointment, "But you don't act any more like the man that just threw a dead ram in Schaacht's face and told him off. What in tarnation you so worried about? I don't see what *you* got to lose."

"You don't?"

"No."

"Then if you were me where would you stand when they take Hope's sheep away?"

They jogged a few hundred yards in silence. "Yeah," Gavagan said. "I see what ya mean. And the rest of them, too."

Gavagan unconsciously moved over a little from Blair and dropped into a silence, giving Blair a foretaste of the reaction he could expect from all his neighbors from now on.

Later Blair said, "I'll unhitch my bay from the back at Columbus and you go on back to Mesopotamia alone."

"What'll I tell Hope? About the ram, I mean?"
After a half-mile Blair said, "With Hope you tell the truth."
"Yeah."

Jonathan Blair walked through the muddy roads of the newly
styled Borough of Columbus, looking at the taverns. He was not examining the kind of accommodations. He was looking for the best
place to stand from which to fight the first man he had ever truly hated
and feared.

In front of the Red Lion, Blair recognized the horses of Judge Calvin
Pease and Judge Ethan Allen Brown. He went in and found Calvin
Pease eating, surrounded by the lawyers who had cases coming up in
his court. The judge was one to finish his discourse or finish his chew-
ing before he acknowledged any remark sent to him. But the ripped
shirt and the new-found directness and impatience of Blair's address
stopped a bite of pork halfway to the best judicial maw in the West.

"Judge Pease, I want to get a law passed this session. Where do the
representatives put up usually?"

Pease lowered the pork.

"Wouldn't it be better to sit still your first session and listen, Blair?
Get the hang of the assembly?"

"Don't have time, Judge."

"I see. Then put up at The Swan. That's where most of them stay.
Both the House and the Senate. You know anybody?"

"No."

"Then The Swan is especially good for you. Jarvis Pike is proprietor.
He knows all the assembly men. He ought to be especially obliging
to *you*, after your brilliant defense of his corn in the statehouse yard."

The lawyers around the table laughed. The judge ate. Blair left.

At The Swan, Jarvis Pike said, "Yeah, Blair. I'll give you the front
corner on the second floor. That way you can watch the street and see
who's going to caucus with who, and who's coalitioning with who else.
Usually save that room for Duncan McArthur; but he's a director of
that United States Bank and he's leadin' that all-righteous Chillicothe
Cabal, so to hell with him."

Blair was glad Pike was against the bank. Pike took him to the
entrance of the common room where men were eating.

"Now here's some you'd oughta know," Pike said. "There's Micajah
Williams out of Hamilton County. He's pluggin' for a road bill. That

ugly lookin' one is Bela Hult out of Coshocton County. Good man.
And he's from far enough north to be on your side. There's William
Moore, Muskingum County."

Jarvis Pike named a lot of them. Many of the names were somewhat
familiar to Blair. "For the most part," Pike explained, "them fancy
lookin' ones with the chest linen that ask for shavin' water every day
are from down around the Cincinnati counties. Them wooly lookin'
ones are from up in the woods, the woolier the norther. And they
don't carry much weight in this assembly."

Blair looked down at his own doeskin trousers and he put on his
buckskin jacket to cover the tattered shirt.

"You want anything," Pike said, "you see me."

For the next two days Blair attended every minute of every session.
None of the legislation was of much interest or pertinence to Hosmer
Village. But it gave him a measure of the men. He was able to observe that the massive Bela Hult from Coshocton County concerned
himself with the important bills: an act reorganizing the militia, an
act creating a northwest road. Blair also noticed with relief that the
handsome impressive representative named Tremaine from down in
Washington County was actually a lightweight who was backing a
wide program of such matters as an act to buy a bell for the cupola
of the statehouse, an act to designate the north boundary of Ohio,
which couldn't be more theoretical since Silver Pigeon was very effectively determining the actual north boundary of white territory.

Blair was delighted to see that he did know a few. One was Jackson
Garth who was here from near the Indiana Country. He was concerned
with a couple of Indian matters and a law on the handling of estrays.
And his very presence gave Blair confidence, for Garth was not a com-
plex individual. He approached the crude gods of this assembly with
his hat on, spoke loud, matter-of-fact and with an unabashed courage.
His obvious ignorance of procedure and party and coalition lines did
not reflect badly on him, but rather belittled the artificial boundaries
which he crossed and recrossed as though they did not exist. You might
chuckle at his ingenuous trampling upon the alliances and traditions,
but you wouldn't point them out to him. Every line in his square-cut
body and face naively wished all men well, and presumed a like return. Without belligerence he tolerated no infringement on his own
rights or dignity. Blair marked him for a friend.

Blair noticed also that this was an extremely young assembly. With the exception of a few like Garth and Bela Hult and Duncan McArthur, who was acting speaker of the house, the members seemed to be about twenty-six years old. Competent, confident and aggressive young men. They made Blair see how much he had paid for his isolation up on the frontier these past many years. He felt backward, sluggish, ignorant. But he kept in front of him the vision of Gideon Schaacht and Hope Emerson's sheep.

And each night in his room at The Swan he worked on framing the law which had begun in anger and refined in determination, aimed at the head of Gideon Schaacht. On the sixth night he copied it onto clean parchment.

PREAMBLE:

Whereas the president and directors of the Bank of the United States have established two offices of discount and deposit in this territory at which they transact banking business by loaning money and issuing bills in violation of the laws of this state and by trading notes and bill:

Therefore,

Sec. 1 *Be it enacted by the general assembly,* That if after the first day of September next, the United States Bank shall continue to transact business within this state, it shall be subject to a tax of $100,000 per annum.

Sec. 2 *Be it further enacted,* That the auditor of state shall make out his warrant under his seal of office directed to any person whom he shall appoint, commanding him to collect the amount of tax in said warrant from the Bank of the United States.

Sec. 3 *Be it further enacted,* That the person so appointed shall enter the Bank of the United States and demand payment of the amount; and if payment be not made such person shall forcibly levy upon any money, bank notes, or other goods and chattels the property of the bank.

Sec. 4 *Be it further enacted,* That the person entering the bank, after demand and refusal of the payment of the tax aforesaid, if he cannot find in the banking room any money or goods, chattels, etc., it shall be lawful and it is hereby made his duty to go into each and any other room or vault and every closet, chest, box, drawer to open and search and

seize any money, bank notes, etc. or so much as will satisfy
the aforesaid tax.

Sec. 5 The person appointed to execute the auditor's warrant
shall, when the money is paid or seized, receive for his compensation 2 per cent upon the amount paid or seized.

The tax Blair proposed was ruinous, prohibitive and confiscatory,
which it was meant to be.

Blair folded the parchment carefully and carried it up to the Red
Lion where he laid it in front of Judge Pease who sat late before the
fire instructing the lawyers clustered about him. The judge read Blair's
proposed law through twice. He rose and walked back and forth in
front of the Red Lion hearth as Blair had seen him do at the bench.
He had the parchment rolled in his fist behind his back. The surrounding lawyers were obviously interested in the judge's interest.
Stuttgart said, "Has Mistah Blayah discovud a new way to make
dollahs, Judge?"

Judge Pease stopped pacing: "Blair! Are you suddenly trying to
attract a lot of attention to yourself?"

"No, sir."

"Are you trying to split this country in half at Pittsburgh? Under
some provincial delusion or other?"

"No, sir. But I might hold it together."

"That what you think you're doing . . . all by yourself?"

"I didn't say that, sir."

"Then just what *are* you trying to do, Blair?"

The judge's questions keened the lounging group of lawyer's curiosity about Blair's bill. They waited for Blair's answer.

"Let's say I'm just trying to save a woman's sheep for her," Blair
said.

"Huh. Long way around to fix a simple chattel mortgage."

"I want it fixed for good."

"Huh!" The judge slapped the rolled parchment against his palm.
"You just might fix the whole territory while you're at it. But don't
you find it just a mite presumptuous, Mr. Blair, for a lawyer from
Hosmer Village to take upon himself the economics of the Territory?"

The circuit lawyers laughed. But the judge whirled at Stuttgart.
"What are *you* laughing at? Why don't *you* get presumptuous once?"

The judge turned back to Blair and looked him up and down as though he wished he saw a better man but would have to make do with this one. "You know it's unconstitutional, of course, Blair."

"I do not, sir."

"You know at least then I trust that old John Marshall . . . uh . . . the Chief Justice of this Republic has spent the last ten years of his life trying to make the general government supreme over the states . . . that he has it by now well established that the states do not tell the Federal Government what to do . . . or *tax* it."

"But the Federalist party is nearly dead, sir."

"John Marshall, you'll find, is far from dead, sir."

Blair said, "Judge, I don't come to argue the Constitution. I come to drive a sheep plague out of the West."

"How long can you stay this mad?" asked the judge.

"Long as it takes."

The judge started toward the writing table in the Red Lion. "Then you've got to get a lot smarter in a big hurry. Come here."

The group of lawyers watched Blair follow the judge to the writing table where the two wore out three quills and many sheets of foolscap.

The judge added ten sections to Blair's law.

When the clerk of the house started the first reading of the bill, Blair was disappointed to see the members of the House of Representatives were mostly looking up at the newly plastered ceiling, many of them seeing real ceiling plaster for the first time since they had left the East, and the younger ones, for the first time in their lives. This plaster did more to prove that the Ohio Country had really become a state than did the pompous presence of Duncan McArthur in the Speaker's chair.

But by the time the clerk had read down to the second section of Blair's bill, there was not a single eye on the ceiling. The honorable representatives bolted upright in their chairs. They looked at each other to see if they heard right. They looked at Blair to see what kind of man would write such a bill; and then they looked at McArthur to see him choke. Grins flickered here and there in the chamber. The clerk, obviously enjoying the shock power of what he was reading, enunciated and paused and inflected, abandoning the usual singsong.

Jackson Garth slapped the flat of his hand on his table and he bawled out, "By God, that's tellin' them! Let's get to the votin'!"

Duncan McArthur rapped the unpainted gavel on the unpainted rostrum, "Out of order, Mr. Garth."

McArthur did a noticeable thing then. He assigned the bill to a committee for study and he said, "Gentlemen, I must leave the chair immediately on a matter of urgency. Will Thomas Kirker please take the gavel?"

Kirker gavelled the house to order, as some of the house members craned their necks to watch the exit of Duncan McArthur, those who knew that General Duncan McArthur was a member of the Board of Directors of the Bank of the United States.

Jonathan Blair rose and followed McArthur out. He followed him at some distance to The Swan. But McArthur did not enter the building. The general went directly to the barn behind the inn. When he came out Blair watched an odd sight from a distance of fifty yards. The general was accustomed to having the horsekeepers help him to his saddle. But this time the general was helping the horsekeeper. There were a few emphatic instructions from the general.

The commotion brought Jarvis Pike out the front door of The Swan in time to see his horsekeeper southbound like a Kentucky cavalryman. Pike remonstrated with the general, but McArthur walked back to the statehouse.

Blair let enough time pass and then he walked into The Swan and asked Pike, "Could I get the keeper to shoe my bay?"

"You could if I had a keeper."

"There was one here last night."

"Yeah, but that highhanded McArthur went in and sent my keeper on an errand."

"Oh? Be gone long?"

"Don't know. He sent him to Chillicothe."

The Borough of Columbus stayed up late that night. The place had a mischievous relaxation like on the night General Harrison sent the British prisoners of war back here in 1813. Knots of men talked in The Swan and The Red Lion with shriller voices and easier laughs. Both places sold more whisky that night. Blair's proposed law seemed to remove a kind of film from the eyes of other representatives who now thought they saw an obvious way out of their troubles.

Young representatives looked up at Blair when he walked through The Swan, and when he had passed, they renewed their conversation with increased vigor. These glances had in them a certain respect, but no envy. They were glad someone had done it. They seemed to be appraising him to see if he would go through with it, reserving judgment.

The position was uncomfortable for Blair who was not accustomed to being the cause of men looking up from their whisky. As he was mounting the steps he overheard Jarvis Pike remonstrating in the hall around the corner with Duncan McArthur.

Pike said, "There was no call for a gallery to be built in the representatives chamber. I lost money as it is."

"We'll pay extra for it, Pike."

"Well, there's no room for a gallery. Besides anybody wants to watch they can just walk in the door. Who's comin' that we got to have a gallery?"

"Build it over the doorway."

"Well, I'll put up four uprights, six by sixes, and I'll take and run a little platform, say four by twelve. That's all. And a ladder to get up to it with."

McArthur said, "uh . . . better make it a closed stairway."

"A closed stairway!"

"Yes . . . uh . . . might be . . . uh . . . a lady want to watch."

"A lady!"

So it was no surprise to Blair that the second reading of his bill was accompanied by the pounding of Jarvis Pike's axes.

Nor was it a surprise on the third reading of his bill to see the representatives craning their necks to the back of the room. The platform filled the room with the smell of new-hewn oak. But from the same direction also came the faintest trace of perfume, which increased the turning of the heads of the members.

However, what filled the room more than anything else, inspiring new pomposity in the Speaker and new decorum in the room, was the commanding presence on the rear platform of . . . Gideon Schaacht.

To many he had been only a legend, and they stole quick glances at him, and longer ones at his daughter. Quick, because it was the peculiar ability of the banker that even in a large crowd he could make each man feel that the sharp eyes of Gideon Schaacht were upon him in particular. Even Blair now felt most uncomfortable in the overlarge shirt that Hope had sent and which he had to wear, his other being unpresentable. So strong was the aura of Schaacht that it seemed to turn the room around. What was formerly the back felt as if it should be the front, and it was as if there were two Speaker's rostrums in the chamber . . . one where McArthur sat, the other where Schaacht sat.

The session adjourned for eating and resumed in the afternoon. Blair noticed a lot of fresh shaves in the chamber for the afternoon session.

Blair thanked the world for creating Jackson Garth. He was on his feet early and he said, "Seems to me we took a little jog in the road here somewheres. We were doing fine with the bank-tax bill. Now suddenly we're slowed up. The bill is out of committee. Let's put the ayes and nays on it right now."

"The phrase," said McArthur, from the Speaker's rostrum, "is 'I call for the question.' "

"Well, whatever it is, I do it," Garth challenged.

But before Blair could second the motion McArthur said, "There being no proper motion before the house, it has been recommended to the chair that this bill go back into committee in fairness to the bank to let the director . . . uh . . . fill in the other side of the question."

Bela Hult labored his hulk to his feet on the floor. He half-turned to face Gideon Schaacht, but he spoke to McArthur, "Mr. Speaker, one hearing by the committee has been adequate on all previous bills in the session. I see no reason for exception."

McArthur said, "Since we've moved the statehouse way up here in the woods we will frequently have to depart from procedure to give fair representation to the bulk of the populace which remains down along the river and at Cincinnati."

And with great swiftness matters moved from that point to the place where the brocaded Tremaine was on his feet with a motion to put Blair's bill back in committee.

Bela Hult heaved himself up then and said if it was the desire of this honorable body to put the bill back in committee, he favored enlarging the committee and he personally would like a place on the committee.

Blair thanked the world also for creating the massive Bela Hult. But at the same moment he witnessed another demonstration of the power of Gideon Schaacht who rose now to thank Mr. Hult.

Schaacht wore such great ease and authority that it would have marked a man as very small indeed to point out that Schaacht had no right to speak in this meeting.

His great height coupled with his deep voice shrank the room from the chamber of the House of Representatives to just a group of men conferring in a hallway. And he took the group into his confidence so much that they were honored. He said, "So the larger the committee the better I would like it, as I think that when you have a look at the monetary problems of our Western states and territories, you will be able to help us solve them. I would appreciate any attention you could give us."

Having invited them in, Schaacht then proceeded to drop in enough technical money talk to shut them back out. Obviously this was a matter for experts, not for muddy-booted circuit lawyers out of places like Hosmer Village. When he was finished he did not sit down, but instead assisted his daughter down the stairway and out the door in an exit which adjourned the meeting more effectively than the Speaker's anticlimactic gavel.

Gideon Schaacht was formidable.

Jonathan Blair was about to find out exactly how formidable. When he left the assembly this time he was not surrounded by a group of representatives all asking questions and slapping his back. Jackson Garth was on his right. Bela Hult hulked along on his left. The others as they left the two-story statehouse skirted wide to the left and right of the trio.

Hult said, "Let's see what intelligence is being nailed up on The Red Lion over there."

They walked across the ruts to The Red Lion, but the crowd around the sign was thick and Garth said, "There's another one going up over there on the tree, Blair. And isn't that that satin-pantsed bank clerk that kept us waiting in the hall at Chillicothe?"

Blair turned to see Justin Bolding leaving the tree with a hammer in his hand. The sign he had tacked up said:

A U C T I O N
Fine Herd of
MERINOS
Quarter Bloods
Rams   Ewes   Wethers
at the place called
MESOPOTAMIA
(Foreclosure)

At the bottom it told which trail to take and the average travel time.

Garth said, "Why that son of a bitch!"

Bela Hult said, "He's going to fight from the flanks, Blair. And rough."

"If you only knew how rough, Mr. Hult."

"Why? They *your* sheep?"

"No. Uh . . . a friend of mine."

"O-o-o-h."

Blair was not on the committee to consider the bill, but he could tell by the attitudes of the men who came out of the meetings that Gideon Schaacht was not wasting time. Bela Hult was on the committee and he was gradually emerging as the bulwark for Blair's bill. He had a great bull-like voice and courage to match, as well as wit. He had the further advantage that he had been a colonel of militia under Harrison during the late war, and having recruited two battalions he had a wide acquaintanceship in the northern areas. It also gave him leave to exchange insults with Duncan McArthur on a more or less even rank.

But among the smoother skinned members Schaacht's velvet talk and his rock-hard fist were telling. None missed the big club implicit in the auction advertisement whereby Blair's township was to suffer.

On the evening of his tenth day in Columbus Blair walked slowly back to The Swan. The loungers there seemed to be taking a greater than usual interest in him, which he understood when he felt the light touch on his sleeve. Virginia Schaacht, like her father, had that quality of being extremely present. She could never hide in a crowd. Waves of aliveness seemed to radiate from her so that even at a distance of three feet she seemed surroundingly close to a man. Life in her was so close to the surface that Blair could see the pulse throbbing in her white throat. And everything about her was so washed or brushed or burnished that as she moved or turned or breathed, twilight caught part of her and sparkled off with refreshing newness that a man never saw in Mesopotamia except in some new piece of iron work off Stikes' forge, which would glitter only until the air and the rain and mud got to it.

"Jonathan."

His first name coming out of a throat and lips like hers was as if she had stooped to wash his old socks, and he said, "Yes, Miss Schaacht."

"I wondered if you would sign this."

He stared at the certificate. It was Bolding's law certificate, but he did not take it. Instead he stared at the blue-veined hands which held it so surely, and he wondered how Bolding held such devotion from such a lovely creature.

"No," he said.

She didn't fold it up, but continued to hold it out.

"No?"

"No."

"It would be only a matter of signing your name," she urged. "Only take a moment."

The gold choker seemed too heavy a thing to press down on such a throat and it twinkled as she faced slightly away from Blair.

"I thought your idea was for him to do it himself," Blair said. "Looks like *you're* trying to do it for him."

It was apparently a new experience for Miss Schaacht to beg, but she smiled doggedly. "I was prepared to offer a bargain, Mr. Blair," she said.

"A bargain?"

"Meaning no offense, and thinking it could be very important to you in the assembly, I thought if you'd sign this I could get that shirt cut down to fit you right."

Blair looked down at the shirt which furled too loose above his wrists. He reefed the billowing waist under his belt. And as he looked down to see how much he had soiled the borrowed shirt lent to him by Hope Emerson, the full extent of his desecration came to him, for in the dust of the road under the fine-booted toe of Virginia Schaacht was a fragment of an advertisement for the Merino auction in Mesopotamia. The lawyer knew that he must go there in a hurry.

"The sides could be taken in," Miss Schaacht said. "And the sleeves shortened."

"No thanks," Blair said. "I'll grow up to it."

He left her standing between the ruts which were called High Street.

Chapter 9: THE LANDS AND CHATTELS

BELA HULT barged into The Red Lion common room with his loosely braided grey queue flopping nearly in the face of Jackson Garth who followed.

Bolding and Virginia Schaacht saw him stop in front of Calvin Pease. "He's gone, isn't he? Just when the attack gets hot?"

"Use your head, Bela," Pease said. "Where will it be tougher for him to be, here in the assembly? Or up watchin' 'em foreclose the sheep of his neighbors?" Pease addressed Hult, but he looked at Bolding. "Be mighty damned lonesome up there for Jonathan Blair."

"Oh, y-e-s," Hult remembered. "A woman's sheep, aren't they?"

The drums beat again in the old colonel from Coshocton County. He shoved a .60 caliber forefinger in the smooth-shaved face of Justin Bolding. "Then by God we'll hold his lines for him while he's gone. And you can report that upstairs to your fancy banker friend, Mr. *Bold*ing!"

"Yes, sir!" Bolding threw a mock salute. But his grin clouded upon the approach of Gideon Schaacht who stood erect with his arms hanging down to his sides. Schaacht said, "Mr. Bolding, I presume it was in good nature, but I suggest you don't use the military salute in such a flip manner to a veteran of two wars, particularly one of Colonel Hult's stature. Hult raised a pair of battalions for Harrison from Coshocton County and West."

"But he just said . . ."

"The more he's to be respected for the honorable opposition he is giving us in the general assembly. But I came to tell you to go up to Mesopotamia to give service and counsel to our guest investors who are attending that auction. And I want you to take a message to Emanuel Ault."

"You said Riddle was going to Mesopotamia."

"You'll have to go instead. Major Armstrong is already up there."

"But I know those people. Riddle could be more . . . uh . . . effective up there," Bolding said.

"Riddle is leaving in another direction on other business of the
same kind."

"Where?"

Schaacht did not look at Bela Hult, whom he knew to be listening
closely anyway.

"Coshocton County," he said.

Bela Hult's massive bull neck swelled even more, pumping blood
into his brown ears, turning them dark red.

Up north of the Borough of Columbus on the fringe of white settlement in the place called Hosmer Village, shock and disbelief converged on the porch of Hosmer's store.

Beyond the unbelievable fact that the auction had actually begun,
the shock was compounded for these people by the fact that Major
Armstrong had actually given the order to fire, and his sergeant had
actually discharged his rifle, even though a wild shot. It was further
compounded by the realization of each settler in the crowd that he
was actually standing there looking on without interfering while Hope
Emerson's prime breeding rams were led onto the porch of Hosmer's
store for the appraisal of a group of strange easterners.

Emanuel Ault stood on the porch with his black ledger on a flour
keg. Hope Emerson sat beside him. Her arms were folded in her lap,
except when she would raise them to signal the dog, Boss. There was
a sag to her shoulders which no settler had ever seen before.

She spared the settlers by not looking directly at them. She looked
at the strangers who stood in a half-circle, close around Ault. But
when her eyes would chance to the outer rim of settlers, Mike Stikes
would look down at the ground. Amos Exeter would bend down to
brush off his pants. William Tyng would look away.

Brutus Christofferson turned his head to Jonathan Blair and he
said, "You fixed it good, Blair."

Joe Hussong added, "Yeah, real good, Blair. You like it?"

Hope Emerson had to handle the rams as Ault called their names
out because Christofferson refused. In this work she did not have to
move around much because the dog, Boss, was long accustomed to
cutting a particular sheep from the pack and nudging him into position for shearing or bleeding or breeding.

That it should be a woman whose property went under the hammer
was the more degrading to Hosmer Village.

In a settlement more southerly and easterly than this the auction might have been impossible. The tempers of the settlers might have overpowered the platoon of Federals under Major Armstrong. But these men had lived on the red-white fringe through the Wayne campaigns, through the late English War and through the Indian bush fights which continued still. They were more familiar than most men, and more recently, with the shiny red underside of human flesh and the bright whiteness of fractured bone. And they were also familiar with the blind depth of Major John Armstrong's ambition. They knew he had ordered a set of silver shoulder oak leaves out of Philadelphia three years ago, and they knew his contempt for the militia veterans and their everlasting pension claims.

He bawled out, "I'm not up here to kill any man. But you may as well know I haven't got thirty-four years in this consarned army to blow it up now over a damned platoon of sheep. Go ahead, Ault."

Ault continued, "And this ram here, gentlemen, is Galahad out of Adam Rotch's flock sired by Aaron."

Galahad walked on the porch like a stage. He headed for Hope, but he was nudged back by Boss. His hooves stabbed the planks in a tattoo as he tried to skirt Boss. His curled horns tipped and scraped at Boss and then he saw the unfamiliar crowd and turned an aristocratic orange-black nose to beat at the buyers from above a chestful of the most expensive wool in the country.

One of the easterners bid $125 gold. The ram bleated.

Gavagan laughed.

The easterner who was called Ruoff, and who was obviously some experienced in stock, said, "One-fifty."

Another bid $155, and Ruoff said, "Turn the ram around so we can see the chest."

He looked at the three great folds of chest wool, then he asked, "How many hanks to the fleece?"

Ault turned to Hope. Hope said, "Forty to sixty depending if you shear once or twice a year."

Ruoff nodded and bid $200. Another buyer bid $225. Then in quick succession Ruoff asked, "How old? How many ewes has he served? Let me see a hank of the britch wool."

Hope cut off a hank from the inside thigh. Ruoff fingered it and bid $250.

Christofferson cussed loud enough for Blair to hear it. Ault started to knock the ram down for $250 gold when an accented voice from the back of the crowd called, "Please do not be so foolish!"

Hope Emerson's face lighted as she saw the newcomer shoulder through the buyers to the porch of the store. It was Adam Rotch, plainly dressed but well, except for trail-spattered boots. He carried a fork-tailed coat over his arm. He bowed slightly to Hope.

"Mrs. Emerson, I heard about this, and I came. I cannot claim that I came to help. I cannot buy your sheep and give them back to you. But some facts to these gentlemen I can explain."

The Dutchman turned to the crowd of buyers.

"Gentlemen, you are very foolish. Fine Merino wool-breeding lambs you bid on like mutton sheep. Twenty men in this territory only can raise the Merino. Mrs. Emerson is one of them."

Rotch ignored the smiles. "You are bidding your gold on animals you know nothing about. One man only here I heard who talks familiar with them. And to bid so low he knows better. I helped bring this strain into this territory. I do not intend it should fall into the hands of cattle and hog farmers. Do you know about the tremors? Do you know in four days you can lose a whole flock you were two years building? Do you know how to breed them and raise them so the wool comes not cotted and kempy and chaffy? Do you know how to breed for clothing wool instead of combing wool?" He looked over the crowd. "Therefore, I say you, if you wish the investment, invest your money in the wool mill, or buy Mrs. Emerson's fleeces *after* shearing; these things will not die or change. But a Merino you cannot raise like a milk cow."

Hope watched the faces of the crowd. Some of them were affected by Rotch's speech. But Ruoff snapped, "Very well, Mister. But if we can buy the sheep we can also buy the shepherds. My bid stands."

"Then I add only this, sir, that Adam Rotch can let no Merino ram which was born of Adam Rotch's flock go for $250. For the ram on the stand now I bid $350."

The crowd swallowed breath.

Then Ruoff said, "Three hundred and seventy-five dollars, gold."

And the bidding blossomed.

When dusk set in, Ruoff said he refused to bid on any more sheep in the poor light, and bidding was postponed until the following day. As the crowd broke up Hope said, "Brute, would you tag the ones that are sold?"

That's when the crowd turned back to face the porch for they heard Christofferson rumble out distinctly, "No, Ma'am!"

Hope looked surprised. The crowd looked at Christofferson.

"But I'll see that somebody does tag 'em," he added.

Blair's left shoulder sagged under the massive grip of Christofferson. "Blair, you . . . you lawyer! You'll tag 'em! It's *your* handiwork!"

Before Blair could catch his breath Christofferson was yanking at his shirt front, stripping off the garment. "And before you start you'll take off this shirt you were told not to wear!"

Boss drove the Merinos back out the east road through the dusk. Blair followed. Christofferson followed Blair. Blair noticed that the dog carried himself with the self-possession of those who know their work well and the importance of it. Though the sheep were many and the dog was a single being, he moved so strategically that he seemed to be numerous. When Galahad approached the Emerson farm and headed for the range, Boss leaped up on top of the flock and ran lightly over their backs to the head of the column in time to deflect Galahad into the shed runway. Not satisfied, the dog looked back toward town and then turned into a rippling, furry mass, as he flew after a yearling which was then disappearing into the undergrowth.

Blair turned to watch. But Christofferson prodded, "Don't worry. He'll do *his* job. Come on."

The lawyer trudged through the gate.

In the shed Hope stood beside Christofferson who held the lantern, throwing his own huge shadow against the wall, so that it bent at the roof line and projected his torso against the ceiling.

Blair bent his bare back to the sheep work. The tagging of the sheep was simple, but he performed it with the immense and ridiculous care of a man trying to atone for the unatonable.

As he moved from one animal to another he did not look up. But even as carefully as he worked, his inexperienced handling of the animals burned Christofferson. And the lawyer's humility robbed Christofferson of satisfaction.

"It's no good!" he roared as he brushed Blair aside and grabbed the sheep. "Get out! Get out! You can't help . . . even at this!"

But the big man straightened up obediently as Hope touched his arm.

"No use to blame Blair, Brute," she said.

"A-a-h! If he hadn't trifled with the damned bank!"

"If he only trifled with it, he wouldn't have caused all this. And if he more than trifled with it, then he must know more about it than we do. Best go bring in the common sheep off the range, Brute, while we all cool down."

Christofferson handed Hope the lantern and left with Boss running ahead of him.

The door swung shut leaving the widow and the lawyer as strangers inside the shed.

She came closer and lowered the lantern so he could see his work. Without looking up he tagged two ewes and moved to another. He did not look up, but he was aware of her soft, doeskin skirt flowing over to bring the light to him. In mute and desperate apology Blair bent closer to his work.

Even above the peevish complaints of the old ewe, Guinevere, Blair thought he could hear Hope breathing, and he wondered what expression she wore on her face; what he would find there if he stood up.

With his eyes on the toes of her small boots which showed beneath the fringe of her skirt he began to straighten up. The boots did not move away and he looked into her face, his hands out to his sides, palms up.

"Hope, I . . ."

She was Hope. She was young, she was old. The unflinching eyes made her your daughter. The relaxed squint lines made her your great-grandmother. The full mouth and bosom made her your woman. But you had to decide which you deserved, and prove it.

She stood slightly shorter than Blair, straight, but without effort. The lantern lighted the bottom of her chin which lifted slightly as she returned his gaze, and it lighted the underside of her light hair which was swept back from her ears and throat.

"Hope, I . . ."

"If you'd do the same again, Jonathan, don't apologize."

He squinted through the gloom to see what she meant.

"And if you wouldn't do the same again," she charged "don't relieve your mind on those that paid for it."

He reached for the lantern and held it up so that he could see her face better.

He hung the lantern on a peg overhead and he put his arm around her waist and pulled her linen blouse against him. She was soft against his chest and under his mouth. But then she stiffened in his arm.

"No, Jonathan. I'm traveling Hosmer's road. You're going some other way where I'm not . . . not at comfort."

"Hope, you're the only . . . the only . . ."

She pushed away from him and the shed door opened. Christofferson stepped in. He looked at Hope's blouse where the moisture of Blair's chest had darkened it.

"Blair, I'll mark the rest of the sheep!"

On the second day of the auction of the chattels of Hope Emerson under the contract with the Mesopotamia Hog & Trust and the latter's contract with the Bank of the United States, Justin Bolding arrived. His arrival was of some assistance to Major John Armstrong because it diluted the hatred with surprise; not only surprise and expectancy that Justin Bolding should dare to step into this place, but wonder at the beauty of the woman who came with him . . . Virginia Schaacht.

Her velvet and broadcloth presence was first a thrill and second a wound. First, it gloriously reminded the linsey and leather-clad women settlers what a wonderful thing a woman was. Second, it sent their hands flying to tuck under frayed cuffs and loose curls, and their glances to reprimand men who had brought them to these log walls and full cradles . . . and the full burying yard.

From the pulled-back corners of deerskin windows they devoured the dove grey skirt that moved in long soft folds and the blue-black velvet bodice that changed hue with the light. The women speculated on what silks and lace might be underneath. The men just speculated.

They wondered where such a person would sleep in such a place as this, and what would she eat, and where would she hang up those clothes in this town while she slept.

Faith Hawkins, to the embarrassment of her husband, offered Miss Schaacht to stay at their cabin. They had moved out to the old Woodbridge place which had the only rain gutters north of Columbus.

To Miss Schaacht, Faith Hawkins explained, "This does us nicely until we can build another."

To the townswomen, Faith overexplained, "Well, the girl must sleep somewhere, and since we have the room . . . and besides, maybe she'll get Gideon Schaacht to . . . anyway, it's not her doing."

Virginia Schaacht had the wisdom not to attend the auction. The bidding remained firm even though the sheep offered this second day were poorer. None of the ewes sold had any record of producing twins or triplets. And a few culls were rejected by the buyers. A black ram and two black ewes found no takers and reverted to Hope Emerson.

Blair did notice a strange thing when the black ewes were displayed. Brute Christofferson suddenly walked over to take Asa Buttrick by the elbow and the two walked quickly toward the back of the store.

Major Armstrong noticed this, too, and he came over to Blair, accompanied by his sergeant. "What's fixin', Blair?"

"What do you mean? Looks quiet to me."

"Too quiet."

Armstrong looked over the crowd. "Your people are too easy in the face," he said. "Not mad, like yesterday."

Blair now observed for himself.

Joe Hussong was cheerfully cutting his fingernails with an eight-inch blade. Amos Exeter stood with his arms folded, his tobacco in his cheek and his head cocked with interest toward the lambs on sale. Blair knew enough of his people to know that he was on the outside of something. But he said, "They can't fight your guns, Armstrong."

"No, but they're not even sulkin'. Sergeant, walk over to the tavern and then to the blockhouse. Look around."

At the end, Ruoff said, "Mrs. Emerson, could we leave the sheep in your shed overnight and pay you for feed?" Hope was about answering when Major Armstrong cut in, "Like hell! You'll get those sheep out of this town tonight or I'll not answer for you gettin' 'em at all."

"Sir?"

"I said take 'em out *tonight!* You think you can come into a town like this and foreclose the only money crop in it and them not figure a way to get it back? I only got twelve men here, y'know."

Ruoff turned to Gavagan and said, "Then can we contract with you to haul them out tonight?"

"No, sir. Not in *my* wagon tonight or any night."

"Why not?"

"You got yourself in here," Gavagan looked over at Hope proudly. "Now get yourself out."

But Hope said, "They'll just get somebody else to haul 'em, Matt. You might as well have the drayage money."

Christofferson had returned. He said, "And better put up the canvas on your wagon, Matt. Looks like rain."

"You mean you actually *want* me to haul for these . . ."

Gavagan turned the wagon toward the forge. Christofferson pulled a rag from his pocket to wipe some flour meal off his hands. He said, "I'll go round up the sheep and get them loaded, Miss Hope, and I'll put up a barrel of feed to send along."

Blair was surprised at Christofferson's cooperation. Apparently Armstrong was, too, because Blair heard him turn to his sergeant and order, "Two of our men instead of one go with that wagon. Have 'em well mounted and carry sidearms. Put Corporal Mulvane in charge, and tell him his stripes are ridin' on those sheep."

Ruoff made his arrangements, too; he sent two of the eastern buyers along with the wagon when it pulled out.

Amos Exeter had taken over the old Shuldane house on the common and made it into a tavern. The easterners stayed in the upstairs. However, on this night they sat late in the taproom downstairs congratulating themselves on their purchases and drinking Exeter's corn whisky, joking about the way it scorched the throat.

The inside of Blair's cabin was dust-laden from his long absence, but he did not clean it up. It was mildewed, too. Blair also went to Exeter's tavern. He sat alone, which was not a new experience for him.

He noticed William Tyng and Stikes watching him from another table, also Exeter from behind his tapboard. Then he saw it was because Major Armstrong was approaching his table. In Mesopotamia men walked to Exeter's tap, paid for their whisky and then carried it to the table, if they wished to sit. The major, though, made no stop at the tap. He pulled out a bench and sat to Blair's table, freeing his sidearm from the bench and looking around. "Why don't they go to bed, Blair?"

"Be natural for them to stay up . . . considering what happened. Considering also there's the most strangers in the place at one time since Harrison's troops went through."

Hussong walked into the tavern. Tonight the dark-skinned, thick-necked young hog farmer was quiet, friendly. He joined in easily with Stikes and Dolk who accepted this junior on their own level by now. But it made Armstrong sit up.

"What's *he* doin' in here?"

"Came in for drink and talk," said Blair. "Why?"

"He's too relaxed. That one I expected somethin' cussed from. Didn't expect him to take it sittin'."

"What can he do?"

Armstrong's sergeant came in. But before he could ask his question, Armstrong said, "Any activity on the east road, Sergeant?"

"No, sir."

"West road?"

"Nope. Cabins dark."

"Keep the men walking around the town."

"Yes, sir."

"And especially around the Emerson place."

"Yes, sir."

"And what arrangements have you made to watch out for these buyers?" Armstrong gestured to the smooth-cloth backs of the easterners. "And their horses?"

"We'll have adequate guard, sir, if the major would advise them not to go walking around, but stay close to their quarters."

"They've been told."

"Very good, sir."

The sergeant turned. Armstrong called him back with an afterthought. "What'd you want to see me about, sergeant?"

"The major has covered everything, sir." The leather-faced soldier backed one step before turning, shutting the major out with that elaborate observance of military form with which old and competent sergeants reprimand heavy-handed officers.

It left the major more unsettled and he said, "Blair, look here! What's going on?"

"Don't know, Armstrong."

"You know your people well enough to know *some*thing is itchin' this town tonight."

"Yes. But I don't know where to scratch it. They don't tell me everything."

"No, but they're watching you."

"That's because you're with me, Major."

"Look here, Blair. Before you get through with the Wyandot business you're going to be needin' me. I don't envy you the job and I'm not goin' out of my way to make it tougher than it is. But there's one thing you better understand. Keepin' the peace up here during this auction business happens to be v-e-r-y important to me, and if you don't help me, I'll sink you lower than the bottom of Schaacht's boots."

"Peace in Mesopotamia is that important to you?"

"I don't give a damn about Mesopotamia. But Schaacht is gonna do this same thing in maybe fifty towns before he's through. If Mespo acts up they'll all act up. If Mespo takes it quiet, they'll all take it quiet. I only got half of a half-strength battalion and that's spread from Coshocton County to Shawaneetown in the Illinois Country. What the hell could *they* do if the whole West starts actin' up?"

"Nothing. So why don't you relax?"

Armstrong shoved a hungry face close to Blair. "Because when they pick the commander for the new western regiment, I don't want Schaacht saying to Monroe that I couldn't keep order. That job's going to be mine. That clear?"

Blair wiped the whisky from his mouth, but he couldn't wipe the grin. "Very clear," he said. "But I can't help you."

"But the Emerson woman would tell you what's up. This is her fight mostly."

"Yes, but she didn't ask me to help."

Armstrong smiled. "And that kind of stabs you, don't it? Especially with that big galoot sleepin' so handy in her shed."

"What do you mean, Armstrong!"

Armstrong was on his feet. As he rose his sergeant came back in. "Sergeant, check the Emerson farm. See what Christofferson is doing."

Armstrong noticed the heads in the tavern snap around when he mentioned Christofferson. Some half-rose from their seats. The sergeant said, "That's what I started to tell you, sir. He's gone."

"Gone where?"

"Don't know, sir."

Armstrong exploded. "Mount up three men. Hurry up!"

In the back of the canvas-covered wagon of Matt Gavagan, Brutus Christofferson's huge, cramped body worked fast in the darkness. Only three of his large fingers would squeeze through the handle loops of the big shears, and it was hard to get enough pressure with three fingers to trim the wool quickly. He tried to get four fingers through the shear grip by removing the ring on his little finger, but the finger was too big; the ring would not come off.

With great effort and speed he snipped at the fleece, changing the shape of Galahad. He cut about two inches of wool off the great rolls of wool on Galahad's triple chest, so that the front was no longer rolled, but flat. He trimmed the dock and the pasterns, so the dew claw showed, as on common sheep. He took a half-inch off the withers and crooped both flanks lightly. He ran his big hands lightly all over the animal and decided that he had sculptured Galahad successfully into an ordinary ram, except for the horns.

He felt along the dark wagon-bed for the saw and he pulled Galahad's large magnificent curly horn down on his knee, sawing just short of the curl. Galahad bayed and bleated and bucked up with such surprising force that Christofferson landed on his back on top of the nervous ewes who pranced around so much that Gavagan shoved his head back through the canvas.

"Quiet, Christofferson! That corporal's no more'n twenty-five yards ahead of us. And the one in back has been riding closer, too."

A voice from way ahead called back, "Anything wrong, Gavagan?"

"Naw," answered Gavagan. "Talkin' to the hosses."

Christofferson decided the horns would have to stay.

He said softly to Boss, "Guinevere next."

Boss crawled over the sheep and dropped down between two of them that were next the tailgate. Christofferson wedged his way on his hands and knees through the sheep to Boss. Boss had Guinevere located. Christofferson trimmed her majestic wool down as he had done with Galahad.

Quickly he worked the shears over all the sheep. Fibers of wool floated around inside the wagon irritating Christofferson's sweaty face and tickling his mouth and the inside of his nose. He sneezed. The front canvas opened.

"For God's sake!" hissed Gavagan, "Quiet! How near you done?"

Christofferson edged up close to Gavagan. "Think I'll make it before we get to Boxford's Cabin. How far we got to go yet?"

"Less'n ten miles."

"Slow down. Need more time," said Christofferson.

The big man now crawled to the left-front corner of the wagon and pulled a deerskin bag from under a protesting ewe. He reached inside it and pulled out a handful of whiteness. Methodically, carefully, now he rubbed a bleached flour meal over the wool of the sheep, hoping to lighten their color. Merino sheep appeared darker than common sheep because the richer yolk from Merinos picked up more dust. He could not see what shade of white he made each sheep. But he rubbed his hands repeatedly over every part of every sheep and through the hanks of wool, spreading the white dust, hoping that he was turning them to the white grey, typical of ordinary territory sheep.

Suddenly he stood very still on his knees with his whitened hands motionless out in front of him. The wagon had stopped. He heard the corporal say, "Can't you go any faster, Gavagan?"

"Load's pretty heavy, Mister," Gavagan said.

"Not that heavy."

"Not if my right-front wheel wasn't binding," Gavagan said.

"Oh. Bad?"

"Yeah."

"Let's light a lantern and jam some ham fat or tallow in there."

"Naw," Gavagan said. "Won't do. But when we get to Boxford's cabin, he's got a wheel puller. Won't take me long."

The flour dust and the wool were in Christofferson's nose forming up an almighty sneeze in his head. He grabbed his nose with his right hand and opened his mouth, freezing his face in an agonizing grimace. He breathed through his mouth in short, panting breaths.

"All right," he heard the corporal say.

But a crescendo of pressure built up in Christofferson's nose. He buried his face in the side of a sheep which deadened the blast some. But he heard the corporal ask, "What was that?"

"Pretty chilly for them sheep," Gavagan explained.

"Sounded like a sneeze."

"That's what I say. It's chilly."

"Aw-w-w. A sheep?"

"For God's sake!" exploded Gavagan. "You never heard a sheep sneeze?"

"A sheep?"

"Well, where in hell were you raised that you never heard sheep sneeze?" charged Gavagan. He reached for the canvas. "Come here. Look."

But the corporal said, "All right. All right. They sneeze then. Get it rolling."

As the wagon began to roll and jounce over the rutted and root-ribbed south trail, Christofferson crawled back to the tailgate. He picked up one of the smallest ewes. He held her out over the tailgate using the sheep's body to push the tail canvas back from the tailgate. He anchored the heels of his boots under the gunnels which projected

into the top of the wagon bed and he leaned way out over the tail-
gate, lowering the ewe as close as he could to the ruts in the road.
He hardened his stomach, but the tailgate cut into it unmercifully.
When the ewe's hooves were two feet from the ground he dropped her.
She fell to her knees when she landed in the dark. But she got up.

Christofferson lifted the canvas so he could watch her as the wagon
left her behind. He was not certain himself how the sheep would act.
Would she stand there in the middle of the road so that the buyer
and the soldier behind would come upon her? Or would she move
off the road into the brush and trees?

He lost her in the dark. But he waited there with the canvas lifted
until he judged the wagon had traveled five or six perches. He heard
no activity back there. He waited until the wagon had covered about
five more perches. That would give the riders back there a chance, if
they found the ewe, to overtake the wagon and ask any questions they
might want. But nothing happened.

Christofferson grabbed a lamb and dropped her over the tailgate
in the same manner. Again he waited while the wagon covered about
ten perches. There was no result. Now he began putting others over
the tailgate, dropping them silently to the ground in the blackness.
He dropped the lambs first, but interspersed an older ewe about every
third one. He held back the rams so that Boss would have the rams to
use as leaders when it came time to round them back up and head
back north.

After dropping each sheep over the tailgate, Christofferson waited
awhile.

That way they couldn't bunch up right away. Also, it gave him a
chance to see if the riders following were noticing anything. Since he
heard nothing from the rear he decided that each sheep as it was
dropped must be moving off to the side of the road, or maybe it was
too dark to notice them in the road.

Boss did not understand this procedure, and he paced anxiously
from the headboard to the tailgate, sticking his head over to watch
after each drop and whimpering his disapproval at Christofferson.

"It's all right, Boss. It's going to be all right."

When he came to the heavier ewes and the rams, Christofferson's ribs
and stomach pained him from leaning over the iron-edged tailgate. He
devised a rope sling in which to lower the animals. When their hooves
touched the ground, he let go one end and pulled the rope out from

under them. Sometimes they fell on the rope and Christofferson had to yank the rope, rolling the sheep over.

Chistofferson was just fixing the sling on Galahad, the last animal, when Gavagan's head shoved through the front canvas.

"Christofferson!"

"Yeah." Brute crawled forward.

"We're coming into Boxford's clearing. You got 'em all out yet?"

"One to go . . . and the dog."

"Well, hurry up. And then get yourself out. There's lights in Boxford's clearing. Somethin's up down there. Might cut us off. Hurry up."

Christofferson lifted Galahad with great difficulty because of his fatigue. He lowered the sling. When the reduced tension on the rope told him that Galahad had touched the ground, Christofferson let go the rope and let it slide out. Gavagan hissed through the front canvas, "Couple men riding back towards us. Don't look like the corporal or the buyer. Came from Boxford's."

And suddenly Christofferson was listening to talk between one of the riders and Gavagan, who kept the wagon moving so that the men had to ride along abreast to talk.

"Major Armstrong sent me down by the other trail to see if everything was all right."

"Well, didn't your Corporal Mulvane tell you everything is all right?"

"Yes. But I'll just have a look in the wagon. One thing Armstrong taught us is when you make an inspection, make it in person."

"All right. All right," yelled Gavagan with sweeping disgust. "When we pull in up ahead at Boxford's Cabin, you'll have light and you can crawl in and count each one of their little noses if you want."

Christofferson pulled Boss to him and inched back to the tailgate. He held the dog firmly with his right arm, and wrapped his left hand around his muzzle. He put his mouth close to the dog's ear and to compensate for the fact that his whisper was even fainter than breathing, he repeated it.

"Boss . . . round up and home. Round up and home. Understand that, Boss? Round up and home. Round up. Home. Good Boss."

The man's big hand patted the dog and kneaded his loose pelt over his ribs. Then he tightened his grip as if trying to compel the animal's intelligence.

"Round up! Home! Good Boss."

He pressed the canvas flap back very slowly, taking advantage of every noisy jounce and wheel squeak to push it back a little farther. He held Boss over the gate with both hands, leaned down as close to the ground as he could and let the dog drop silently to the trail. The wagon moved on so that the canvas cut off his view of Boss; but as he put his own foot over the tailgate he saw very clearly the four hooves of the sergeant's horses who was dropping back to follow the wagon into Boxford's Cabin.

Christofferson pulled his foot back inside and lay down in the bottom of the wagon bed. There was a canvas up by the headboard. Christofferson crawled under it and lay still.

The wrath of Major John Armstrong in front of Hosmer's Store in Hosmer Village the next morning was the special vinegar of a man who is laughed at in public.

The major had no humor in his soul to lighten his heavy touch of destiny. And his mind so directly related the present dilemma to his chances for commanding the new western regiment that Corporal Mulvane's faded blue sleeve already displayed two large inverted V's of contrastingly unfaded material which conspicuously marked his demotion. Broken threads around the edges of the unfaded area told late arrivals of the abruptness of the demotion. The chevrons themselves lay in the dust near the corporal's feet.

The major roared, "Will you, damn it Mulvane, explain again how you could lose a whole wagonload of sheep right out from under your damn nose?"

"We were with the wagon every step of the way, sir."

"Well, you take that Gavagan up in that blockhouse and you and the sergeant stay there with him until you can come back here and tell me where to go find those animals! And I don't care how! Just find out!"

The ex-corporal reached to take Gavagan first. But Gavagan yanked his arm away.

Blair said, "Major, you are empowered to enforce order in this country during emergency, but you are not given power to arrest or detain any of our men for driving a wagon."

"Well, you just heard the corporal say that he . . ."

"I just heard the corporal say he didn't know. You can arrest the sheep, but not Gavagan for driving his own wagon."

Hosmer Village crossed its arms and smiled and watched. More of them assembled as the argument wore on. The major fumed. It was easy to enforce an auction. There the men got mad and violated the rules. You could protect it by firearms if necessary. But how do you fight a whole town full of men who only stand and smile?

The buyers were all assembled now, and from across the common Virginia Schaacht made her way east on foot to join the crowd.

Armstrong started to work on the buyers who had accompanied the wagon. What had they seen? How many times did the wagon stop? Where was each man when the wagon stopped?

The argument was interrupted by a slight commotion from the south where the roadway climbed up out of the little dip at the river ford and came toward the store.

As Hosmer Village watched, a small column of ordinary common sheep faltered up the grade. The lead ram wavered at the crest of the rise, but not long, for Boss came flying up the slope and nudged him east, out toward the Emerson place.

"There they are now!" said Armstrong.

But his joy vanished. Amos Exeter said, "You're seein' things, Major. Them ain't 'rinos. Just plain old sheep."

Armstrong turned to Hope. "Are those your sheep, Mrs. Emerson?"

Hope studied them awhile. "Likely are," she said slowly. "Most all the sheep in this place *are* mine."

"What are they doing this far west of your place?"

Hope didn't answer. The major lowered his face into hers. "I said what are they doing so far west of your place?"

Before she could answer, Christofferson said, "Miss Hope, those are the ones I took over to graze on William Tyng's place. I had Tyng's boy round 'em up and send 'em back by Boss."

Armstrong turned to Tyng. "That right, Tyng?"

"That's right, Armstrong."

Armstrong walked over close to Christofferson, "Why? Why should you all of a damnit sudden decide to bring 'em back?"

It was Armstrong's habit on the offensive to step so close that his adversary must necessarily take a step backward to reply in comfort. But Christofferson stood still. He said, "Well, now that you sold her 'rinos, she's got more than enough range to graze her own common critters. That right, Miss Hope?"

Armstrong kept his eyes on Christofferson as he turned away.

Ruoff said, "Armstrong, you're wasting time. A child can see those aren't Merinos. Too white. Let's get busy."

As Boss worked the flock up the East Road they caught Virginia Schaacht just as she was crossing the road. She started to turn back but part of the flock were behind her. They brushed by her on both sides forcing her to stand still.

This attracted Mesopotamia's attention back to the sheep. But it was plain to see that these sheep were not shaped like Merinos. They did not have the big fluffy chests and straight backs.

Hope said, "Brute, you better go open the shed door so they can get in."

But Brute answered, "What's the difference with those miserable sheep, Miss Hope, if they stand outside or get lost . . . now that the 'rinos are gone?"

"Still I think you better, Brute," she said. "They may not be much, but they're all we've got."

"All right, Miss Hope," he said. He turned to Gavagan. "Can I borrow your wagon, Matt? Be quicker."

Brute left the crowd.

When the flock had gone by, all the women of Mesopotamia noticed with both dismay and a touch of delight, that the sheep had soiled the striking black velvet skirt of Virginia Schaacht. They watched her bend to examine the great smirch across it. She lifted it with one hand and brushed it with the other, but it only smudged, and she continued across to join the crowd.

Involuntarily Mesopotamia made wide room for this self-possessed young lady who walked among them. The young women marveled at a girl who obviously wore not a single piece of homemade cloth. Their hands went to their hair as they looked at the smooth, finished outline of Miss Schaacht's brunette head.

The younger women also felt a strong desire to go and wipe off the great light streaks on the velvet skirt, only because it seemed to them sinful to treat such a skirt so. She must have many such skirts, they thought.

Faith Hawkins, however, did express concern for Miss Schaacht's skirt.

The older women folded their arms in silence or directed their attention elaborately away from Miss Schaacht to the more important and more pertinent discussion of the men. But in this they were in error;

for Miss Schaacht answered with fine graciousness, "Please don't worry about the skirt, Mrs. Hawkins."

She bent to brush the velvet. "You see, it comes off with brushing . . . just as easily, in fact, as it came off the sheep. I thought perhaps it was some white powder you folks put on the animals to prevent disease or something."

Smiles in the crowd faded.

The buyers came alert and Major Armstrong moved over to Miss Schaacht. "Would you mind if I inspected that, Miss Schaacht?"

Bowing with enough stiffness to keep the inspection official, the major bent to examine the skirt, which she belled out with her knee so he could see it in various lights.

Hope Emerson said, "All sheep are like that. The yolk in the wool attracts dust and holds it."

Without straightening, Armstrong looked up from the skirt to Hope Emerson. "I see," he said, very politely. The crowd began to break up. But the major said to Miss Schaacht, "Pardon me, Miss Schaacht." And he reached out his hand toward the skirt. Blair noticed the major pick a few small fibers off Miss Schaacht's skirt, which he twirled between his fingertips, thoughtfully studying the crimps.

Finally, the major straightened up, still observing the fiber in his fingers. "I see," he said.

And as he said it, Jonathan Blair thought he also saw.

Major Armstrong walked slowly away from the crowd, motioning the ex-corporal to follow. While the crowd dispersed, Blair watched the two soldiers walking toward the blockhouse where the rest of the troops were quartered.

He saw the major reach down into the dirt and grab a pair of chevrons. He handed them to the ex-corporal, who grasped them quickly. But the major did not let go. He put them in his pocket.

But Blair noticed the ex-corporal listened intently to whatever the major was saying. Intently and hopefully, Blair thought.

The lawyer noticed that Hope Emerson moved swiftly to her light wagon.

He also noticed from the porch of Hosmer's store that shortly after the major entered the blockhouse, the corporal came out again and sauntered to the hitching rail there for his mount, which he rode off slowly to the east.

The lawyer remained there quietly with Amos Exeter and Jim

Dolk on the porch, and in the space of a quarter-hour he observed that six more soldiers came out of the blockhouse and saddled up. He observed that they moved off independently and aimlessly . . . but all east.

He also observed Emanuel Ault and the buyer called Ruoff moving swiftly and independently toward the blockhouse.

Without taking his eyes off the blockhouse, Blair said, "Jim."

"Yeah."

"You've not had much occasion to use it, but you remember we elected you Justice of the Peace of this place?"

"Yeah."

"You remember I gave you a little book that showed how to write out the various writs and summonses?"

"Yeah," Jim Dolk said, "but so far nobody wants any."

"I know, but you know the one about when you want to search a man's place?"

"Yeah, but nobody ever remembers about that until they already looked."

"Yeah. But the point is, if anybody asks you for a writ of search, you write real slow. Understand?"

"Yeah."

"*Real* slow."

The last of the soldiers to saunter his mount out toward the East Road was the major himself, accompanied by the sergeant.

Blair called out, "Major, don't forget to get a search writ first."

"For what?"

"For whatever you got in mind."

"And if I don't, you'll do something about it?"

"Everything I possibly can."

Armstrong laughed, "Is that liable to be much?"

"Remember that's what you said before I let the Wyandot contract for hard goods, Armstrong."

Armstrong studied him. He did remember the Wyandot contract, and he had observed some strange purposefulness in this lawyer of late. He said to his sergeant, "Ride ahead and tell Mulvane to wait until I get there with a warrant." He turned to Blair, "I'm gonna do this so damn legal, Blair, that you'll be sorry." He turned to Dolk and said, "Hurry up, Dolk. I want a search warrant. Quick!"

Dolk lit his pipe. "I'll have to go mix up some ink, Major," he said. "I have a pencil!"

"All writs got to be writ with ink!"

Chapter 10: THE VICE

THE LAWYER put down his whisky, unfinished.

The ears of Jonathan Blair were finely enough tuned to the motives of his townsmen so that the sound of tortured iron from Stike's forge in the middle of the night jolted him to his feet. Blair left the tavern. The long sliding door to the forge was closed, but through the cracks in the door slabs he saw Mike Stikes grinding a length of hexagonal bar iron. Stikes stopped and fitted the bar of iron into a piece of maple. There were seven other hexagonal bars and seven other pieces of maple.

That became Blair's calendar. Roughly, he judged he had seven weeks till those rifles would be ready.

The next morning his calendar and his suspicions were verified in Hosmer's Store, which was now run by Asa Buttrick. He overheard that Buttrick was expecting a shipment of special fine-grain black powder in about two months. That matched.

Blair walked up Slasher's Creek to Slasher's place, where he found the ground was covered with new chips. Down in the creek were several sets of enormous boulders. Blair could see the great levers with which Slasher each day moved the wing boulders back a little, bending the ash strips into half circles.

"Got orders for wagons, Slasher?"

"Man's got to keep busy at what he knows, Blair. Orders or not."

In the afternoon Blair went out the East Road toward the Emerson farm. There were a number of horses there and two wagons. When he approached, the conversation died. Then the big voice of Matt Gavagan, too loud even for Gavagan, said "Hope, if I were you I'd clear another five acres."

"Hope, I advise against it," Blair said.

"Against clearing another five acres?"

"No. Against what you're really planning to do."

"And what is it that we plan to do, Jonathan?" she asked.

"Obviously some of you are going to pull out of here and move up into the Indian lands about seven weeks from now."

Several men now looked at each other accusingly.

"No. Nobody gave you away," Blair said. "Stikes is building rifles. Slasher is building wagons. Buttrick has ordered powder. I advise against it, Hope."

"If you can put that together, Jonathan, I guess you can also put together that I got some sheep walkin' around up in there that I can't very well bring back . . . what with Armstrong workin' for the bank and Ault workin' for the bank . . . and you . . . well . . ."

"I still say stay out of the Indian country."

Gavagan cut in with a grin, "I guess you can put it together also, Jonathan, that she's got a pretty good man up there lookin' out for her interests already . . ."

"But the Wyandots are still spread out," Blair said. "And The Pigeon is spoiling for a fight. You'll upset the treaty."

Hope said, "We know better how to fight Wyandots than how to fight bad money, Jonathan. We've got to go."

"I'm only asking you to wait until we get the Wyandots paid off and moved back into Upper Sandusky, Hope."

"We counted on you havin' that done long time ago. Now it's too late."

A circle of grins invited Blair to answer that one.

Blair rode into the village thinking, reaching for a leverage to apply against Silver Pigeon to hasten the withdrawal to Upper Sandusky. He stabled the bay and stepped into his cabin. As soon as he let go of the door, it slammed shut behind him.

"Silver Pigeon!"

Blair studied him in surprise. For this was a more Indianlike Silver Pigeon than Blair had seen since '14. The Pigeon carried a rifle, which was unusual. He wore no hat. He wore no cloth. All deerskin.

The upslanted rays from the hearth lighted a different set of planes around The Pigeon's cheekbones and the undersides of his eye caverns. He looked Indian.

Blair sat on the bunk. Pigeon walked to Blair's small clay crock.

"Let us have one last whisky together, Blair."

"One *last*?"

The Indian tipped the crock and handed it to Blair who did the same.

"The Pigeon wishes to say you are not a bad man, Blair. Almost you could be an Indian."

"I'm glad you think so," Blair answered, "because I was going to talk to you about . . ."

"But that is the last good thing I have to say, Blair." The Indian sat opposite Blair with the rifle across his knees. "I want you to remember I said it because after this drink tonight there will be nothing between us but . . ." The Indian drew his finger across his throat.

"I wish it could happen to someone else," the Indian said. "But it is only because it is you that it will work."

"Will work?"

"Yes. You will get the extra Wyandot annuity money and the land and the mission money. The Pigeon waits no more."

"I'm trying. Pull back to Upper Sandusky," Blair said, "and I will keep trying to get the money."

"Yes. You *will* get it. For The Pigeon is now in what your Chief Harrison says 'strategic position.' Never again it will happen like this. But it happens this one time. And the Pigeon will turn the screw tighter and tighter and he will never let go. This is the only chance to turn the screw."

"Turn the screw?"

"Yah. The big white-haired one that makes the guns and the shoes for the horse, he has the big screw that he turns?"

"You mean Mike Stikes' vice?"

"Yah. Pigeon also has the vice. And Pigeon will turn the handle tight and tight more. In the middle . . . you."

As Blair listened to the Indian he knew that he listened to a statesman, a general. The Pigeon explained that he knew of the preparations of the group of whites to move up into the Indian country. He had already seen them moving through the woods, marking trees, cutting trees. He had seen the wagons Slasher was building. His men watched every exit to the north of Hosmer Village.

"And when they come, Blair, when they come, they will come into . . ." The Indian held out his two strong, slender-fingered hands, palms up. Then he turned them over in a gesture like wringing a neck.

"And this is the vice?" Blair laughed. "You think I care enough about what happens to the settlers who go up there to get you your extra annuity?"

"Yah. Not think. Know. The Pigeon will do like the Schaacht. The Schaacht fights the lawyer by fighting a woman. The woman saved the sheep from the Schaacht. But now she drives them to the Pigeon. The sheep are up there now . . . in the woods . . . with the giant. The woman will follow the sheep. And the Pigeon will wait for the woman. That is the vice. She will live as long as the lawyer gets the money. No money, no woman. No sheep also. That is the vice."

Blair already felt the screw tightening. There were no words low enough.

"Damn you, I'm doing everything I know how to do!"

"Yah. But more still you must do."

Blair's face lighted. "It would be easy enough for you to know that Christofferson was up there with some sheep. But that doesn't mean you know *where* he is up there."

For answer the Indian pulled something out of his belt and stood up. The hearth highlighted the bottom of his sharp jaw so that Blair could see an eerie replica of the great Tecumseh.

Pigeon grabbed hold of one of Blair's hands and placed the soft object in it.

Silver Pigeon walked out of the cabin, leaving the door open. Blair walked to the hearth and unfolded his hand. It contained a fine-grained hank of soft wool . . . Merino.

Hope Emerson fingered the wool. "Can't help it, Jonathan. I'd chance the sheep against the Wyandots quicker than against bank auctions."

"But it isn't only sheep."

She looked at him quizzically.

"It's lives."

Hope handed the wool back to him. "Always has been, Jonathan. That's what Hosmer knew. Maybe you're just finding it out." She took a pot of hot lead off the hearth.

"I mean especially *your* life, Hope."

For answer she poured the molten lead into the shot mold and closed the cover.

"Then as sub-agent for the Wyandots, Hope, I've got to order you to stay out of Indian country until the treaty has been executed."

She rose, and the base of her throat colored. "*Order* me?"

"Order."

"Thank you. Thank you, Jonathan." Her color and breathing deepened in a way to make Blair resent that a Wyandot should even set eyes on her. "You've had me off and on mixed-witted about you," she said. "But now you've picked your side."

She opened the middle cover of the mold and poured six shiny lead balls onto the hearth.

At dusk on the third day after Pigeon's visit, Blair went to the tavern where he knew Armstrong would soon arrive. Major Armstrong was a hard man to ask for favors, but it had to be done. It was a poor choice of a meeting place as it turned out. Because when the major entered the tavern the settlers followed him with their eyes. Their faces were straight, but their eyes were laughing at a United States Army major, regular army at that, sent on a sheep hunt by a civilian banker.

As the major fished out three cents for three fingers of Exeter's whisky, Blair observed ex-Corporal Mulvane's chevrons mixed with his coins, indicating that the major had not found the sheep.

The major drank it down in time to catch the receding Exeter for another one.

"A damnit sheep hunt," he said to Blair. "Assignment not even fit for the damnit militia. Why in the name of hell is Schaacht pickin' on this miserable town?" He elbowed Blair with his whisky arm. "By God, it's *you* he's aimin' at, Blair! You and your damnit meddlin' down to statehouses."

"Maybe. That's what I want to see you about, Major. I want more money to pay the extra annuities and damage money to the Wyandots and five hundred dollars for the mission and the fifty thousand extra acres for the reserve."

"Why tell *me*?"

"As major in command of troops in this area, I want you to recommend it to War Department."

Armstrong's head went back in a silent laugh. "Me? How's that gonna look after I've been recommending we just ride the red skunks to hell out of the place?"

"There's plenty of logic to it," Blair said. "The white settlers are preparing to move in. The Wyandots will resist. You have only two squads here. There are seven hundred Wyandots. Eight hundred Shawanees will throw in with them, 232 Ottawas counting kids, and enough Senecas and Mohawks and odd lots to cut you down. Spell that out to War Department. They'll give you the money. Save you a bad record."

"Got it all figured haven't you, Lawyer?" But the major was not laughing.

"You'd better make the recommendation just as soon as you can send a messenger to Cincinnati. There's not much time."

"No," Armstrong mused. Then he snapped, "But you think I'm crazy, Blair? When they go to pick the regimental commander I can see Monroe reading the report on me. 'Good officer. Good record. But lacks firmness in gaining Indians cessions. Found it necessary to recommend increased annuities for Wyandots.' Then there would be one in there by Schaacht. It would say, 'Good troop commander, but lacks understanding of civil necessities of peace time.' Just because I can't find his sheep. Sheep! Blair, where are those consarned sheep!"

"Don't know."

But Armstrong's eyes narrowed. "It's your mess. It's your town. And it's even your damned woman! Blair, where are those sheep?"

"Don't know."

"All right, Lawyer, put it this way. You tell me where to find the sheep, and I might tell the department you need more Wyandot money."

Ex-Corporal Mulvane approached the major. He carried a roll of deerskin in his left fist. "We just found this on the old Wyandot that hangs around once in a while. The one who calls himself Captain Michael."

"Anything about sheep?"

"In a way, sir. He said it was a message from The Pigeon to this here lawyer, sir."

"Then give it to him. As you were. Give it to me."

Armstrong flopped the buckskin lightly on the bar. But to Blair's ears it clanked like the handle of Mike Stikes' vice. When it unrolled Armstrong said to Mulvane, "Tell the sergeant to mount a fresh patrol . . . now!" Then he shoved his face into the lawyer's, "So you don't know where the sheep are huh, Lawyer!"

"No."

"Then what does this message mean?"

"It means The Pigeon has turned the screw tighter," Blair said.

On the unrolled buckskin in front of him lay the short, stubby ear of a sheep . . . Merino.

At a creek bed which he estimated to be thirty miles above the Greenville Treaty Line, Brutus Christofferson held the head of Galahad down close to the water and scooped handfuls of water over it just ahead of the horns where flies had found the coagulating blood where the ear should be. Christofferson did this absently. For his gaze was attempting to pierce the big woods. But the woods only laughed back and trees murmured to each other overhead. Christofferson would quickly look behind him and then back to the front. He had seen or heard no Indians, yet here was Galahad's ear gone, clean as a scalp. Christofferson looked to the rear again. To be watched and not see the watcher is panic.

Christofferson looked north. It was likely they had come from there. But if he turned south he'd get fouled in Armstrong's hunt. Armstrong would probably comb through the woods on a thin, broad front, same as he used to flush out Tecumseh's pickets under Harrison.

He corralled the sheep and walked them north up the stream bed, looking to the left and to the right, and holding his rifle alert across his chest, changing it so the muzzle faced first the left bank, then the right.

Armstrong had always taught them back in '14, "There are places where one rifle can hold off a battalion, if you search out a defile with a narrow enough neck."

Christofferson searched.

Jonathan Blair rode south. He hated to be away from the settlement where he could keep track of Armstrong and Silver Pigeon and Hope. But he had to see Gideon Schaacht. Staying in Mesopotamia he could not get funds for the Wyandots. And until he did, the Silver Pigeon's vice would screw tighter and tighter. Schaacht would do no favors for Blair's sake, nor for Silver Pigeon's, but he might for Ruoff's sake. He had brought Ruoff and the others out here to make them prosperous on foreclosed property. Their first investment had taken to its hooves and run away. Blair thought he held a forcing hand.

Blair was surprised as he rode into Boxford's Clearing to find Schaacht's great black hunter tied up outside Boxford's big double-cabin. There were others, too. Blair found the big man inside. He talked plain and quickly under the pressure of Pigeon's vice.

"Schaacht, I want something."

"Hello, Blair. If you're headed for Columbus, I can save you a trip. Your bank-tax bill was remaindered till next session. Your supporters dwindled considerably. And I was able to point out to the remaining legislators the punitive nature of your tax."

"Later, Schaacht. Right now I want something, quick."

The skin of Schaacht's cheeks was thin over his teeth and Blair could see the outlines of them as they shattered Mrs. Boxford's bread crusts. "What do you want bad enough to ask me?"

"More money for the Wyandots."

"You paid them what the treaty called for."

"It wasn't enough. Silver Pigeon knows what the Blue Jacket Shawanees got and what the Lower Miamis got. He demands the same."

"Why come to me? I'm a banker, not Indian Affairs Commissioner."

"No. But Duncan McArthur made the treaty and has certain discretionary powers where Indian cessions are concerned."

"Not the power to grant larger annuities," said Schaacht.

"No, but he has the power to authorize the same arrangement that was granted to the Shawanees."

"What was that?"

"They let the sub-agent auction off the Indian lands to be ceded to the whites and gave part of that money to the Shawanees."

"Then see McArthur. Why me?"

"Because McArthur's on your bank board and I've observed that men around you do what you want. You tell him to do this."

Schaacht shoved back from the table, crossed his legs, licked his teeth clean and asked, "Why should I?"

"Because if I don't get the Wyandots paid, they're going to butcher the Merinos your investors bought. And if you can't keep the investors happy, you've just got a handful of mortgage paper that isn't worth anything. I figure Mr. Monroe isn't going to think you're doing so well."

Schaacht's big mouth laughed, but his eyes didn't, "Blair, you'll have to do better. I have a few words for Mr. Armstrong that I dare say will hasten the recovery of the sheep. As for Ruoff, I can get others. You'll have to do better."

"I plan to," Blair said. "And here it is. Your investors want good land, cheap. And you also expressed interest in that northwest land. It's good. It's valuable. If you let me auction it off, there's a chance for your investors to get hold of it before the bounty warrant holders move in and take the best of it."

Schaacht munched the idea like a nut and covered his thinking with a draught from his mug.

"You're very shrewd, Mr. Blair," he said finally. "I do have to keep those investors happy. Also I want a piece of that land, personally. A big piece. But you are too modest, Mr. Blair. You overlooked a bigger threat to me and the bank."

"What's that?"

Schaacht wiped his mouth.

"You, Blair."

Blair met the black eyes.

"If I can get rid of you, Blair, I don't have to worry about the Ruoffs nor the Silver Pigeons. And, Mr. Blair, I plan to do just that. It would surprise a lot of people, even on my own staff, Blair, but my first job is to break you down, publicly and finally. Everything that's close to you, I'll have to smash . . . and every person."

Schaacht leaned his axe-sharp face close to Blair's. "So there is only one way I will help you get money for the Wyandots, Blair."

"What's that?"

"Withdraw your bill from the legislature." He leaned back in victory. "If you want your land auction, that's the price."

Blair felt a draining sensation somewhere above the roof of his mouth. His head bent to the palm of his hand which gripped his forehead.

"What about it Blair?"

A white spot of hate appeared on each of Blair's cheeks.

Bolding said, "Mr. Schaacht, would you step outside for a moment. Private business."

They went outside and Blair crushed his knees against his elbows.

Boxford said, "That's twice Schaacht's going up to Hosmer Village now. What in tarnation brings a big man like that up to a little place like that?"

Blair did not answer.

Schaacht and Bolding returned. Schaacht stretched out his boots in front of him. "Mr. Bolding has just pointed out some advantages to your plan which have a great weight with me," he said to Blair. Then he turned to his young assistant, "Bolding, you get from Blair the wording he wants in the land-auction authorization from McArthur. Ride directly to Columbus and catch McArthur."

"And I'll need surveyors," Blair interjected with rising spirits. "Tell Jarvis Pike to send me surveyors. Tell him pay will be in United States Bank notes."

Bolding said to Schaacht, "McArthur will probably say he doesn't have authority to do this."

Schaacht said, "Tell him authority is not something you're given. Authority is something you take."

Blair handed Bolding a paper and said, "When you get to Columbus have them run a notice of this auction in *Freeman's Chronicle*, and have him send word of it to *Vincennes Western Sun, The Pittsburgh Gazette*, and *The Centinal* at Cincinnati. Say the auction will be on November 20."

Schaacht added, "Send word to Ruoff and our other friends, Bolding."

Bolding left, and Schaacht said, "Shall we proceed to Mesopotamia, Mr. Blair? I have to see about a matter of some sheep."

The day of the land auction on the twentieth of November brought more strangers into Hosmer Village, or Mesopotamia as it was increasingly called, than had ever been there before. And more vinegar.

The settlers, those who were planning to move up into the Indian lands and squat, had waited for Blair's auction in the hope that they would have a chance at the bidding, that they might, at least, have enough good money to make down payment. It would be better to use their good money as down payment on new land than to apply it to their debts which were large. But now for three days they had seen the town fill with cloth-coated Easterners who paid for their whisky at Exeter's Tavern in bigger coins than Amos could make change for.

And as Blair walked slowly through the blockhouse toward the front where the big map of the Indian lands had been set up, he listened to snatches of the deep-souled grumble of Mesopotamia.

He heard Culpepper's drawl, "Looks odd this here Blair should take and worry so much about gettin' money for his red devils while his own kind are losin' property for lack of it."

Blair saw Exeter muttering to Denaro, "Tells us to wait for the auction. Then he fills the place up with money men that carry fortunes in their pants pockets. Lot of biddin' *we* can do here!"

He saw a group standing around Hope Emerson's relaxed straight figure. Hope Emerson had come to stand for a way for settlers to continue to get along without the moneymen and the lawmen. In fact, in a way she had come to stand for Samuel Hosmer. And she stood straight.

There'd been a lot of times in the past few years when the figure of Hope Emerson was an affront to a man. That is, her damn soft figure and her damn soft voice and soft skin and swishing skirt made a man want to take her around the waist and lead her gently and do for her. But about the time a man was thinking like that she'd catch him at it and beat him in a trade, or heft her own staples into her own wagon, leaving him to wonder if he were man enough to do her any good.

But there were things you could do for her now, and you wanted to join with her in this fight. Blair would like to have her touch him on the arm like she was doing right now to William Tyng as she talked to him.

But on Blair's arm as he walked to the front of the blockhouse there was instead the thick grip of Joe Hussong, "Blair, you acceptin' John Piatt Bank notes at this auction?"

"Can't. Treaty says the Wyandots got to be paid in specie or equivalent."

"Be a pity if your precious Indians had to lose out like us, huh, Blair?"

As he approached the map, Blair found Schaacht pointing out a parcel to Emanuel Ault.

"I want these two here, Ault. And if they go cheap enough, I want the whole township. But above all I want this place where the stream curves between these steep banks, a perfect mill site. But mind you don't bid more than . . ." Schaacht saw Blair, so he concluded, "And I presume you understand what I expect from you, Ault, and what you have at stake."

As Blair prepared to open the auction he was puzzled by a change in the chatter in the blockhouse.

Gideon Schaacht passed among the easterners talking briefly to small groups. As he left one cluster to go to another Blair saw the men grin, and some would slap others on the back and wink.

Blair hammered the side of the empty barrel.

"You've studied the plat, gentlemen." Blair pointed to the plat. "Township One in Range One in the Indian lands. Does any man wish to bid on the entire township?"

The silence that came back to him seemed organized.

"All right. We'll start bidding on sections. Begin with Section One, Township One, Range One. Who wants to open?"

Ruoff yelled up from the floor, "If you're sure the damned thing won't walk off and disappear like sheep, I'll open the bidding!"

The easterners laughed. The settlers even laughed at Ruoff's good nature.

"Seventy cents an acre!" Ruoff said.

A chuckle rippled through the blockhouse.

"That bid is not acceptable, Mr. Ruoff. It is below the government minimum."

"What is the government minimum?"

"Government Land Office has said no part of the public domain shall be sold for less than one dollar and twenty-five cents per acre. But we're not talking about minimum-grade ground. This range here is covered with black-walnut timber. It's well watered. And squatters have built a few cabins. What is your opening bid?"

"One dollar, twenty-five cents an acre," said Ruoff.

The chuckle broke into a laugh over in Gavagan's corner.

Blair was afraid he could see what was happening. But he said, "All right. Start at one twenty-five the acre. Next bid?"

The blockhouse was silent.

"What's the next bid?"

Stikes looked up at the rafters. Exeter looked down at his shoes.

"Hussong?"

No one spoke.

"Buttrick?"

Buttrick nodded negative.

"Fitchburgh?"

Fitchburgh crossed his arms.

"Ault?"

Blair went over to the map and put a check mark on Section One,

Township One. "All right," he said, "we'll put this section aside for now. What do you bid for Section Two?"

Blair was relieved to see Ault's hand go up.

"One dollar and twenty-five cents the acre for Section Two."

The grins came back.

Blair said, "Next bid?"

Silence.

"William Tyng, you always wanted a piece up in here. What is your bid?"

William Tyng had no bid.

"Culpepper, you always wanted the Indians out of here. What's your bid to furnish the money to move the Indians out?"

Silence.

"Next bidder?" Blair asked.

But there was no next bidder.

Blair was licked. This explained Gideon Schaact's cooperation in the auction. The lawyer looked out across the crowd to Bolding. "I congratulate you, Mr. Bolding. Your little plan has been carefully worked out."

Bolding mock-bowed.

"However, at these rates you obviously give me no help in raising funds to complete the Wyandot cession treaty." He closed the surveyor's field-notebook. "I find it necessary to close the sale."

The room came alive with buzzing.

Bolding called out, "You can't do that, Blair! An auction's an auction. Section Two goes to Ault for a dollar, twenty-five cents an acre!"

Schaacht's voice boomed over the crowd. "The auction is begun, Blair! By what authority do you stop it?"

Blair pulled out Duncan McArthur's letter and read,

". . . *and it will be the sub-agent's responsibility to see that sufficient funds are gained from the sale to achieve these ends or to cancel the auction.*

Very Obt. Srvt.
DUNCAN MCARTHUR"

Schaacht turned to the assembled buyers, particularly Ruoff. "I advise you to remain in this town a few days. We will see Mr.

McArthur and have this situation changed. The bank apologizes for this delay. But you will find it worth-while."

Blair worked with the Land Office man until well after dusk. Then he walked across the village to his cabin in the dark. As he stepped over the sill he tripped over some soft object. He recovered his balance, and felt for the floor. The object was soft and warm, and his fingers came away wet and sticky.

Blair quickly lighted a candle from the fire pit. As the flame climbed he found on his doorsill a large Merino ewe. Its throat poured blood onto the floor of the hut.

Blair called out, "Silver Pigeon!"

But there was no answer.

The heart of Silver Pigeon's vice was Hope Emerson. Blair saddled and mounted.

The Emerson place was dark. The rifle was gone from over the hearth.

Blair knocked on the closed door to the other room. There was no answer. Blair had never been in Hope's sleeping room, not even through the doorway. Nobody had, as far as he knew. He pushed the door open.

Though she was not in the room it was on this night that Jonathan Blair met Hope. That is, he had not expected such a room in Hope's cabin.

There was not a bunk as Blair had pictured with grey-wool army blankets. There was a bed with white cloth sheets. There was a pillow with a case. And the case had a lacelike fringe. There was a small table, and covering the table was a white-bleached sheep fleece. On the fleece was a wooden comb, one of the kind Slover Navarre used to make. On a shelf by the window was a cut-glass dish containing a bar of lavender eastern store-soap. And beside the soap dish was a copper jewelry box.

Blair rode back into the village.

A cluster of shadows milled around near his cabin, some mounted, some standing beside mounts. When Blair approached he saw there were only six persons. But he heard Hope saying to Hank Flannerty: "Be sure to bring them in well before sundown every night. And count them before you leave the range and count them again when you shed them, and keep your rifle with you."

"Yes, Miss Hope," Hank said.

Blair dismounted. "This means you're going?"

"Yes, Jonathan. We waited for your auction. It didn't work."

"It's going to work yet, Hope."

Hussong cut in. "Don't look like it to us, Blair. We're leaving."

"You'll lead Armstrong right to the sheep."

"He'll find us tough to follow," Hussong said.

"Even if you've got Armstrong handled," Blair said, "the minute you cross the line Silver Pigeon will be watching you as he is right now watching Christofferson."

"How would you be knowing all this, law man?"

"I had a message from The Pigeon."

Hussong laughed. "Where is it?"

"Just walk over behind my cabin," Blair said. "You'll see it."

Hussong and William Tyng walked rapidly out behind Blair's cabin. They returned slowly.

Hussong said, "I'm convinced. But what in the damn hell are you going to do to stop it?"

Blair saw Tyng lead Hope Emerson back behind the shed. But he said to Hussong, "I need some help from you to get the land auction to produce money for the Wyandots."

"That's a dead issue after this afternoon, isn't it?"

"Not if you'll help."

"All right! All right! But what!"

Blair singled out Hussong and Slasher and Tyng and he gave his instructions.

Up in the Indian country at the bend in the creek in the newly surveyed Township Two, the sting in the voice of Jonathan Blair was born of pressure, "No, Hussong! Don't put the marker on the side of the tree. Cut a post and set it on the boundary and trim the brush around it so anybody can see it."

The hog farmer moved sullenly to cut a post. "Blair, if I could see how this was savin' Hope's sheep, or helpin' the rest of us, it would be one thing. But what good it does to resurvey a piece of ground you couldn't even sell above gov'ment minimum, I'm damned if I can see."

"I'm not asking you to see. Cut the post."

"If I could even see how the Silver Pigeon might think this was gonna get his money for him, I wouldn't worry so much, but . . ."

"You'll see soon enough," Blair said.

Hussong and Slasher carried the new survey north. Blair stayed behind as he had done for the last six miles, always looking backwards, down the line. But this time as he walked north and looked south, he was rewarded.

Following the line up from the south, leading his horse with one hand, fighting the branches aside with the other, came Emanuel Ault. Blair remained motionless behind good cover as he watched Ault come up to the last survey post beside the steep bank of the creek.

Ault first looked at the post. Then he sighted across the top of the post to the opposite bank. A shrewd land-spier's eye like Ault's would notice the priceless constriction in the creek at that juncture, the steep high banks. He would quickly calculate the perfection of this as a mill dam-site and he would quickly convert that to a new meaning in dollars and cents.

Blair watched Ault stoop to pick up one of the axe chips and put it to his nose. He would find it fresh, very fresh.

Ault walked over to where the three horses were tied. He would recognize Blair's bay.

Ault took a small black book out of his pocket and made a notation. He would be drawing a map of the stream bed and writing down the survey marks on the post. Then Ault turned and mounted his horse and rode south.

At that moment Blair yelled for Slasher and Hussong, "We're done! Come on back!"

Slasher shoved his hat back and put his hands on his hips, but Blair did not wait to answer the question. He was not sure enough of the answer. He led his horse south through the thickest part, leaving Slasher and Hussong to round up the three protective troops and come on in themselves.

When Blair rode into the clearing at Mesopotamia he slowed down and looked composed. But his stomach churned.

Out of the side of his eye he saw Denaro come out of his front door to watch. Exeter came out the front door of his tavern and stood there watching. Buttrick drifted out onto the front porch of Hosmer's store. But Blair rode directly to the blockhouse which was being used to billet Armstrong's troops. He walked into the small enclosure which had been erected to partition the major's bunk from his men.

"Major, one of your men said the pay for your men was expected today. Did it come?"

"What's that to you?"

"I want to borrow that money for three hours tonight," Blair said.

"What!"

"Want to borrow that money for three hours tonight."

"You're crazy, lawyer. If you're down to schemin' to give my men's money to your Indians, that means you're desperate."

"Yes, I'm desperate. But I'm not going to give your money away. Just to borrow it for three hours. Just want to count it. You can have your men there to watch me count it."

"Why?"

"Can't tell you, Armstrong. But I promise nothing will happen to it."

"If you can't tell me what you want to do with my money, you can whistle for it."

Time was running out for Jonathan Blair. He didn't want to read about any more dead Merinos in Hope's face.

The lawyer walked to the tavern slowly enough for all to see. He bought his whisky and seated himself at the large table near the mug rack so that Ault could approach him without seeming to seek him out. He made it easy for Ault.

The tavern filled quickly, as he hoped it would, with men who thought they appeared to saunter.

The only one who moved fast was Mike Stikes who had other concerns. He walked up to Adams in considerable agitation. Blair heard him ask, "You the one that borrowed my . . ." But the rest of the conversation was drowned out in the tavern noise. Adams shook his head and turned up his palms. Stikes went from one man to another, apparently asking the same question. But Blair noticed that Ault was now seated at the far end of his table. Blair wanted to start proceedings so he yelled to Stikes, "Mike!"

Stikes broke off the questioning and turned to Blair who said, "Mike do you have the makings for another set of wooden millwheel gears like you made before?"

"Yeah, if I can ever find one of my tools."

"Man wants me to have you get started on a set."

"Who?"

"Tell you all that later. But he wanted you to get started."

From the far end of the table Emanuel Ault asked, "Somebody buildin' a mill around here, Blair?"

"Not around here."

"Where? And who's buildin' it?"

"Not at liberty to say."

"Seems if you're brokerin' some kind of a mill sale you'd let your neighbors in on it, those that wanted in."

"You had your chance and weren't interested, Ault, beyond a dollar and a quarter an acre."

This talk brought the loose crowd close around the table. Blair was aware of Ruoff to his left, but didn't look at him. Armstrong had come over. Schaacht's easterners were all here. Hope Emerson had come in.

Ault drank from his mug and said casually, "You trying to lead us to believe you sold some of that land up on the survey?"

"Nope," Blair said. "Just sitting here, unthirsting myself."

Ault's sensitive bargaining soul told him he had stepped into one. He backed off and was silent. Blair baited the trap a little, though.

"But I did think I saw you up there looking around, Ault, where we were running a few new lines."

"Couldn't've been me, Blair."

But Ruoff pointed at Ault. "But it *was* you, Mr. Ault."

Ault half-rose. "Oh? And just how did you know this, Ruoff?"

Ruoff turned to Blair. "Yes, I was there. So were some others. Look here, Mr. Blair. Just what's going on up there with those new posts you put in and all? Who did you sell it to?"

"Don't think I have to say," Blair winked very slightly at Ault. "Do I, Ault?"

The wink angered Ault. "Look here, Blair, don't try to get me . . ."

But Ruoff also saw the wink, and he said, "Ault, did you go make a deal with Blair for that land?"

Blair let the argument flare for a while until Ault said, "Ruoff, he's got no buyer. Where would he get a buyer from?"

"Just the same," Ruoff said, "I'm changing my bid. I bid two dollars an acre for a piece of that Township Number One."

"Isn't for sale, Mr. Ruoff," Blair said. "We had to close up the auction, remember? You gentlemen weren't interested."

"I'm interested now . . . at two dollars the acre."

Attention was diverted as one of Armstrong's men entered with a message. Blair was trying to keep the conversation at the table alive, so he did not hear all that went on between the major and the soldier. Except he did hear the major say, "Well, if it's meant to be a message for Blair, it's the strongest language I ever read. Give it to him."

Then he was aware that the soldier had placed an oddly folded piece of heavy tea-wrapper paper beside him and he was saying, "That old Indian was hanging around outside, Mr. Blair. Said this was a message for you."

Blair moved it to one side so the conversation would keep going. But the major said, "The message is for you, Blair."

Blair's tightened lips told the major to keep quiet. "I know, Blair. But this is one you better read."

Blair unfolded the tea wrapper so the others couldn't see whatever would be written here.

He unfolded the last flap, but then suddenly he folded it back up again. A wave of whiteness drained the color from under his dark skin as though a vice had cut off his blood.

Blair walked toward the door. Armstrong followed. Hope also. Outside the tavern Armstrong said, "Judging by the size it's . . ."

"Yeah," Blair said, "It's his."

Hope asked, "Sheep?"

"No. Not about sheep, Hope."

"Then what?" She reached for the tea wrapper. Blair moved his hand, but hers struck his. The wrapper flew, and suddenly among their three pairs of boots there lay in the dust of the clearing called Hosmer Village a wide-band gold ring. And through the ring might as well have been a finger. For this was the ring that Brutus Christofferson had never been able to get off over his great work-widened knuckle.

Hope's two hands went almost to her mouth. Then she kneeled to pick up the ring and turned back to the east. Blair grabbed her wrist and held her.

"Let go. I'm going to him, if he's still . . ." She jerked her arm. Blair held on. "You're the one that did this, Jonathan!"

"I suppose. But you're the one that told me to butt Schaacht head on."

"I didn't say to butt back with *my* husband."

Blair dropped her arm absently. "Your *what?*"

"That's right. Starting now." She put the ring of Brutus Christoffer-son on her finger. "If he's alive."

"But you never said you . . ."

"Loved him? No. But I guess he's saying plain enough how he feels about *me,* and what he's willing to do about it. And I guess maybe that's what love is all about. I'll be going now to tell him so."

Blair no longer had hold of her wrist, but he didn't need to. He said, "You can't now, Hope. You go now, you'll lead Armstrong right to the Merinos, and it's already cost your man considerable to keep them hid."

She looked from Blair to Armstrong . . . empty.

Blair said, " 'Course I know now you'll try to slip out later. So I'll have to have Armstrong put you under arrest, Hope."

"Arrest me?"

Armstrong reached for her arms.

"Yes. I've got blood enough on my hands now," Blair said, "without letting you trespass on Indian lands to stir up more."

"Is that why you're doing it?" she asked.

"Won't prove anything to you if I answer that."

Blair went back into the tavern.

Ault said, "Blair, we've come back to our senses. You couldn't pos-sibly have sold those lands to anybody except somebody in this tavern right now."

"I didn't say otherwise," the lawyer said.

"And we know you didn't do that. Nobody here bought."

As their confidence returned, the lawyer's case crumbled at the table.

Two of the easterners left the tavern. Jim Hawkins went home.

That's when Major Armstrong entered the tavern carrying a leather pouch. He clanked it on the table in front of the lawyer.

"Blair, that money was delivered this afternoon like it was arranged. But you'll have to look out for it yourself. I can't look out for it for you."

Blair's wits were dulled by the events of the evening and he turned a questioning stare at Armstrong who stood behind his left shoulder. Armstrong rubbed two fingers down the length of his nose and Blair came awake.

"Good, Major. Is it all there?"

"Is it all . . . ? Oh, I don't know, didn't count it."

The lawyer spilled the bag onto the table and began to count the gold coins first.

Ault was on his feet pointing to Ruoff, "Ruoff! You dog!"

"It's not mine, Ault. I think it's——"

But Ault was already addressing the lawyer. "Blair, I'll give you two dollars and a quarter per acre right now for the township with the mill site on it!"

"Two-fifty!" snapped Ruoff.

"Two-seventy-five," said Ault.

"And you understand," Blair said, "that I want cash, metal money or United States Bank notes. And I want it now."

"Two-ninety!" Ault snapped. But Ruoff was already consulting a small piece of paper in his pocket and he said, "Two-ninety-five, Blair!"

Jonathan Blair unrolled the survey plat, which ever so conveniently happened to be with him. In the excitement none noticed the long soul-deep breath that came out of the lawyer.

Out in the blockhouse the northwest bastion served for a jail in this part of the country; and ex-Corporal Mulvane closed the wooden gate behind Hope Emerson. The woman did not look at him, nor did he touch her. She walked to the northwest firing port and looked out into the darkness, giving him her back. The ex-corporal stood outside the wooden grill running his right hand reflectively over his right sleeve where the chevrons used to be, slowly getting an idea.

The private assigned to stand guard on the rifle parapet outside Hope Emerson's cell arrived.

"All right. I'm here, Mulvane."

Mulvane turned to the newcomer, "Won't be necessary for you to stand watch here, Gardner," he said. "I'll stand your turn."

Gardner looked over at the woman in the cell and then back at Mulvane. "I see," he grinned, "seniority still has its privileges, huh?"

The private left. Ex-Corporal Mulvane adjusted the chain, but he did not lock the lock. He sat on the parapet with his back against the grill, but not so that it interfered with the swinging of the gate. His rifle he held upright between his knees.

As minutes passed ex-Corporal Mulvane permitted his head to sag, snap up and then sag even farther. His rifle was seen by the prisoner to sag likewise.

Ex-Corporal Mulvane felt a tentative, exploratory tug on his sleeve. But his head lowered even more.

Some minutes later he was aware of a delicate tug on his rifle. He left the weight of his hands on the rifle, but no strength. He felt the rifle ferrule slide out of his hands. The rifle was deftly twisted then so that the frizzen evaded his thumb and was gone.

The ex-corporal remained in his slumped-forward attitude while he counted twenty-two, being four more counts than the number of steps to the descending ladder. He then sprang silently to his feet and followed her.

Back in the tavern the survey plat was now covered with black marks and names written in charcoal. There were still a few blank spaces on it, and for one of these Emanuel Ault was bidding angrily against Ruoff. He consulted his little black book. "Four dollars an acre for Section Fourteen! And that's my last word!"

Ruoff, with infuriating quietness, said, "Four-fifty."

"Ruoff, don't you see we're just cutting each other's throats!"

"Then why don't you stop bidding?"

"Because the man I represent . . . four-seventy-five, damn it!"

"Five dollars," said Ruoff.

Blair said quietly, "Gentlemen, I remind you that this is the section just upstream from the mill site which is already marked out. Whoever controls riparian rights here will control the amount of water downstream at the mill site."

"Five-fifty," snapped Ault, with finality.

"Five-seventy-five," drawled Ruoff.

Hosmer Village stood awed as the easterners bid on the land. But they were also impressed by the calm and the effectiveness of Jonathan Blair. While Blair listened to the bidding with one ear he was thinking of the ring in the dust and how hard Pigeon had turned the screw.

Ex-Corporal Mulvane was neither tender nor squeamish. Yet the preparations he now witnessed set up a queasy writhing in his stomach and a pounding in his chest and temples. This was not related to the throbbing in his wrists where the leather thongs cut into the blood flow.

Neither was ex-Corporal Mulvane any less brave than others. But he had grown hard to kill in six years service by not underestimating the fury of a vengeful Indian. Mulvane had seen the empty sleeves of troops who had survived the River Raisin massacre. He'd helped bury the parts after the Copus Massacre at Greentown so he knew as he watched Silver Pigeon direct the preparations that he was in the hands of a bitter Indian.

But from his position kneeling on the dirt floor with his wrists bound behind him to his ankles, ex-Corporal Mulvane did not know what to do.

He was glad the woman's eyes were bound. Not that it was his fault that she was here; yet it was, too. They had her trussed to an upright, her arms over her head and lashed to the timber, in a vulnerable, helpless position. Her mouth was bound with a strip of deerskin, her eyes with another.

They had removed the eye bindings from Mulvane, apparently so he could watch. They were in an abandoned squatter hut. Mulvane had no idea which direction they had been taken after the capture. There were weeds and tree-sprouts growing up inside the hut, but it could have been any one of several abandoned squatter huts north of Hosmer Village. Mulvane could not tell which one.

It was a horrible waste of a well-made woman, Mulvane thought, as he watched the four red devils busy around her. As they tied the knots they grinned in silence both at the woman and at The Pigeon. When they tied too tight, she winced. They grinned and slacked off the tension on the thongs. But apparently they liked to see her tighten up and hear the muffled exclamation from under the deerskin. One short, heavily muscled Indian spied the wide gold ring on her finger. To reach up for it he had to stand on tiptoes and crush his odorous self against her. He removed the ring with insulting gentleness from her finger.

But The Pigeon yelled, "*Sa cati arin ga!*"

The short Indian roughly jammed the ring back on her finger. Next he picked up the woman's doeskin jacket and put it on, preening himself in it.

He then walked over to her and felt the cloth of her blouse with admiration. He grabbed a handful of it and tugged lightly, experimentally, to get it for himself. But The Pigeon looked up from a contraption he had and snapped, "*Sa cati arin ga!*"

The short Indian let go.

The Pigeon came forward out of the gloomy corner of the hut. That's when Mulvane sucked his breath, for in the chief's hands Mulvane now recognized the huge wooden vice from Stikes' forge.

The Indians stood back and watched The Pigeon walk up to the woman. He unscrewed the vice to its greatest width, placed one jaw of the vice behind the post, rotated the other jaw around until it enclosed the lower ribs. He pressed his fingers against the lower part of his own chest, working them lower and lower until he had found the rib he wanted. Then he pressed his fingers again against the woman's chest, locating the same rib. He lowered the vice accordingly and turned the handle. As he turned he watched her face. The short Indian giggled in juvenile glee.

When the woman exhaled with a moan, The Pigeon stopped turning and loosened it some.

The blood pounded to Mulvane's head. He yelled, "Stop! Damn you!"

The Pigeon tightened the screw just a little to show Mulvane what damage his talk could do. The pressure straightened the woman up painfully. It reformed Mulvane instantly. The Indian released the pressure, and Mulvane exhaled.

"Money!" Mulvane said, seeking some way to arrest The Pigeon.

"Money, what?" asked Pigeon.

"Money . . . you. Blair get money . . . you," Mulvane said.

The Pigeon grinned. He let go of the vice, leaving just enough pressure on the screw so that it held itself up. He walked over to stand close to Mulvane, looking down at him with his hands on his hips. "You don't need Indian talk for me, soldier. I am the Silver Pigeon. The Silver Pigeon understands. The Pigeon also understands better about the money. That is why all this." He gestured to the woman.

The intelligence encouraged Mulvane. "Then if you're so damned smart, use civilized methods to get it!"

"Tried that," the Indian said. "No good. Try Indian ways now."

"Stinking savages!"

Pigeon walked back to the vice. "Yes, stinking savage. Better Pigeon does not forget he is a stinking savage."

He said, "*Owa he!*" The short Indian stepped forward with a willing grin. Pigeon pushed him back and called forward a tall Indian. The Pigeon turned the handle over to him and said, "*Yan da squa.*"

The tall Indian turned the screw a little. The woman winced and breathed hard. The Pigeon reached over and slacked off the handle and handed it back to the tall Indian, *"Yan da squa."*

The Indian turned the screw again, but this time, more gently. They practiced several times and then the Pigeon said to him, *"Scat timendi quas waugh sunt ya an des hra. Yan da squa."* He then held up one finger in front of the tall one's eyes repeating, *"Scat."*

The Pigeon then turned to Mulvane and said, "And for the ears of the soldier, 'One turn of the screw every day at sunset.' "

The Pigeon picked up his rifle and ordered his men to bind Mulvane's eyes and unbind his feet. "Now we will see how fast Mr. Blair can act," he said.

Mulvane's ribs ached as he thought of the woman. He felt a bursting in his chest like the cracking of ribs. They led him out of the hut, blindfolded.

In later years there was much criticism of what came to be known as the Second Wyandot Treaty, subsequent examiners stating that the annuities paid to the Wyandots by the sub-agent were too high as compared with the standard set with the Miamis, Delawares and parts of the Shawanees. This Wyandot settlement gave grounds for later discontent among the other tribes when it became generally known.

Principal complaint was that the sub-agent paid over the money too quickly, without holding out sufficient funds as security to insure that the Wyandots did in fact withdraw to Upper Sandusky as stipulated. It was also claimed that the sub-agent allowed himself to be outmaneuvered in the final settlement so that he was forced to settle with undue and improper haste, certain matters of procedure being entirely overlooked.

However, as the story was passed down through the years by the descendants of the aforementioned Stikes, Amos Exeter, and a certain Major Armstrong who were present at the meeting, the sub-agent conducted the transaction along conventional lines, absolutely refusing to believe the Indian's story about the fact and manner of holding Mrs. Emerson hostage, until such time as a certain Corporal Mulvane was brought into the place wildly yelling, "Two turns of the screw already. For God's sake don't let it be three!"

At which time the sub-agent rose and went quickly across the common to Stikes' forge to inspect it. Finding the vice missing, he returned immediately. Stikes followed him. The sub-agent's face was drained white, being normally toward the dark side, and he stood there with his lips drawn against his teeth as though he could see the beloved form of the woman stretched taut against the post. It was said he felt of his own ribs with his left hand and his mouth opened and a look of terrible pain came over his face as if it were his own ribs that were hurting. It was said then that he hurled the leather bag of money into the Indian's breast bone, driving him back toward the wall. The sub-agent then grabbed him before he could fall to the wall and propelled him out the door onto a horse, and the entire group rode north in a plunge through the woods that drained the horses. At a certain small fork in the trail the Indian pointed to the right fork where there was an abandoned hut, himself plunging down the left fork with two Indians behind him, while the white riders clattered down on the hut.

Some days later upon the return of Gideon Schaacht to Hosmer Village, he was apprised by Mr. Ault of the fact that he was now the possessor of five thousand acres of Indian lands bought at a price of seven dollars per acre to which Mr. Schaacht was committed. Mr. Ault had purchased this land for Mr. Schaacht and seemed quite proud of his adroitness in the matter. When asked why he had been so precipitous in the purchase, Mr. Ault advised Mr. Schaacht that he was very lucky to get it as the sub-agent had had a buyer for it, and it was with difficulty that Ault was able to get it at all. Hearing this explanation, Mr. Schaacht turned to the sub-agent who was present and asked, "Just who was this buyer you had which drove the price up so damned far?"

They say that the sub-agent for Wyandots hesitated a moment and looked at Mr. Ault, studying him, as though he were loth to do him injury. But that he finally spoke quietly, saying, "I never said I had a buyer."

Ault leaped up from the table. "What about the survey! And the posts you drove in marking out the mill site! And the money!"

The sub-agent then said, again quietly, "Is there anything to prevent a man from driving a stake in the ground if he wishes . . . whether he has a buyer or not?"

The director of the United States Branch Bank, who was a man of very tall stature and lean face turned to the sub-agent and seemed to be speechless. But he looked at the sub-agent as though he had never seen such a man before.

And, indeed, most of Hosmer Village had a new regard for the sub-agent of the Wyandots. That is, he was no less a mystery to his neighbors, but it was noticed that Mrs. Hope Christofferson would occasionally stop by his cabin, when he was out, to instruct the Flannerty girl how better to clean it.

Ex-Corporal Mulvane was occasionally heard to criticize the sub-agent on the poor condition in which he kept his rifle. In fact, the corporal was seen to take the sub-agent's rifle once a week to the blockhouse and return it to the lawyer's cabin, cleaned. Whether he did this on his own volition or under instruction from the major was not certain.

Michael Stikes bolted his vice back onto his bench. But whenever newcomers came into his forge, one would usually ask, "Is this the vice? The one that did it?"

And Michael Stikes had the habit then of dropping his work and telling about the Second Treaty.

And up along the headwaters of the Sandusky River at Upper Sandusky and vicinity, the Reverend Seth Gershom in charge of the mission there heard Wyandots refer to their new grey wool blankets or new rifles or nails or axes and then say the words, "Mr. Blair."

BOOK II

Chapter 11: THE PARLIAMENTARIANS

IN THE winter of 18 and 19, Jonathan Blair rode into the Borough of Columbus, and perhaps never before had he really felt the power of Gideon Schaacht. Never had he seen a man put his mark on a town so swiftly.

It was a strange mark. A combination of fear and respect, and hope of favor. The mark of Gideon Schaacht was on the faces, in the voices. Blair found it first in the stable at The Swan. The horsekeeper said, "Not that stall, Mr. Blair. That's Schaacht's."

"Is he here?"

"No. But he might."

Blair found the mark of Gideon Schaacht even in Jarvis Pike's shame-faced reception in The Swan. Pike closed the register book.

"Sorry, Jonathan. But they got plenty of rooms over at The Red Lion."

One thing Blair had learned in the past few months, he had learned to wait and to listen. He did both now with a calmness which made Pike talk faster.

"I was just talking to Jeremiah Armstrong. Plenty of rooms."

Blair looked at the keys hanging up behind Pike. Pike said, "And Colette over at The Eagle has rooms. Say, did you know The Eagle is changed to The Globe?"

Blair had a way of studying a man lately that seemed to be born of disappointment. Pike said, "All right." He opened the book and shoved the quill and pot forward. "But havin' you here'll cost me."

Blair sighed.

"How d'ya mean?" he asked. "It'll cost you?"

"Well, maybe you didn't know that Coshocton County's pretty near ruin't, Blair. That's the thanks Bela Hult gets for carryin' your bill while you was away."

Blair looked around the public room of The Swan. He found that his arrival was noticed. Even men who had not been at the last session

seemed to know him, which meant that in the space of his walking
from the door to the registration book he had been pointed out to
them by older hands who now looked back to their food while the
newcomers stared at Blair.

"And the bank-tax bill?" Blair asked.

"Deader'n Tecumseh."

"Stuck in committee?"

"Hell no. Hauled it right out on the floor right away, and the
screamin' of the 'nays' was like crows landin' in my corn."

Blair met Gideon Schaacht's mark his first day in the statehouse.
He read it in the two empty seats on either side of him.

Blair voted aye on the bill to reorganize the militia; voted aye on
the bill to create new counties in the lands recently ceded by Silver
Pigeon. He proposed naming one of them Silver Pigeon County. This
was overruled.

Blair voted aye to the expenditure of $41 "for a reasonably accurate
map of the Republic of the United States." Aye for $8 for Jarvis
Pike for firewood for the legislature. Aye for $1,200 a year for the
governor's salary. He voted nay for fining any man "for swearing the
name of God, Jesus Christ or The Holy Ghost." Voted aye for fining
"any person who shall play bullets across a street or thoroughfare,"
voted aye on the four-dollar per head bounty on wolves.

He voted aye on the act "for financial relief of Simon Kenton in
reward for his services against the aborigines, he being presently
destitute and in bad health and without family."

He voted nay to the "act for the erection of a headstone on the grave
of Simon Girty, deceased and believed to be without family."

And then he met Gideon Schaacht's mark again. That is, Gideon
Schaacht had nothing to do with framing the law. But the act was
made necessary by Schaacht's action:

"AN ACT REGULATING PRISON BOUNDS

Whereas the increase in debtors has overwhelmed the capacity
of jails: Be it therefore enacted that every person imprisoned
for debt shall be permitted to remain outside the jail building.
But he shall remain in an area which shall be not more than
400 yards from the jail structure, the bounds of such area being
required to be plainly marked on the ground."

Blair was on his feet to propose the addition of a second article, specifying that the debtor's plaintiff pay the cost of maintaining the debtor in jail, or the debtor be released. The proposal was instantly popular on the floor.

But that's when Jonathan Blair saw the next mark of Gideon Schaacht. For the man who rose to answer his proposal was none other than Justin Bolding. And in this Bolding who rose from the opposite side of the chamber, Blair was struck by certain subtle, skillful improvements.

In the first place he used the parliamentary phraseology with the scrupulous accuracy of a newcomer, but in a tired, automatic manner which lent him the authority of an old Federalist.

But Blair noticed a difference in his clothes, which must have been carefully calculated for their political effect. He no longer wore the fine black fork-tail coat and the chestful of Philadelphia ruffles. Instead the grey tweed cloth of his suit was precisely tailored, but it was coarse. The tail of the coat was a short square-ended spade. The linen was good, but mostly covered up. It was a suit that would leave a man's politics incognito either in the common room of The Red Lion or in the tap room at The Swan.

And there was that skill in the young man's talk . . . you couldn't say it was the words or the tone . . . but it seemed to join sides with you and lay the cards out on the table so candidly that you did not notice they were face down.

His voice was not sharp, but it had the depth you like to find in the chest of a young man who seems unaware that he's young. He said, "Gentlemen, let's just take a look at that. Obviously Mr. Blair's idea is aimed at the United States Bank which is the biggest creditor. And I say that's probably fair enough. But let's not step in our own muskrat trap. Don't forget the bank is not the *only* creditor. You just might make it impossible that way for the small, harassed creditor to prosecute his debtors and thus gain funds with which to pay his own debts . . . say to the bank. I dare say half the men in this room are owed money by someone. Would you wish to pay your debtor's board and room?"

Bolding's reasonableness was powerful. But the young man had become all the more formidable because he had somewhere learned that a clear-cut victory is obnoxious to men. Immediately he gave some of it back. He said, "However, it would seem fair enough if we said that if neither the debtor nor the creditor can support a man in jail, we release him. That way creditors are encouraged to leave a man enough property to support *himself* in jail."

Bela Hult sat there like a molting owl. The Bank had a smart man in the statehouse.

Towards the end of the third day, Blair rose to resubmit his bill for taxing the United States Bank out of the state. Though every other eye in the room watched him walk forward to hand it to the clerk, the Speaker seemed only to see the upraised arm of Justin Bolding who promptly moved for adjournment. The motion was carried with such calculated alacrity that Blair found himself soon standing in a nearly empty chamber with Jackson Garth on his right and Bela Hult on his left.

Hult said, "You see how it is, Blair?"

"Yeah," Blair said. "I see how it is."

In the common room of The Swan, Blair waited for Virginia Schaacht to finish reading the newspapers over in the corner where Jarvis Pike kept the papers that people brought into Columbus. But she didn't finish, and after all it *was* the common room. He walked over. She nodded. He nodded. He grabbed the nearest paper.

He knew she was half-watching him as he read the papers. Most people watched Blair when he read papers. There was something compellingly gluttonous about the way Blair read papers at any time, especially tonight as he sought tools with which to whip Schaacht.

Blair thought he knew why these legislators acted as if they didn't hear when the bank bill was mentioned; why they left the room when a discussion of it came up; why they left unfinished meals at the table when he broached the subject. And he thought he knew how to beat it.

Blair's hungry eyes devoured three newspapers almost as fast as he could turn the pages. Then he found a paragraph in the *Western Herald and Steubenville Gazette* which slowed his pace.

THE GREATEST OPPRESSION

No government measure since the first settlement has hurt the West more than the Treasury Department order instructing the Land Office cashier to accept only such monies as are accept-

able to the United States Bank. Since the Bank will accept only
its own notes, or silver, or Pittsburgh Bank notes, Western men
are left with no way to pay for their lands. What makes Pittsburgh paper better than Ohio, Illinois, Michigan, Indiana
money? We separated from England for a much lesser oppres-
sion! What holds us back now?

Blair tore it out of the *Herald* with a ripping noise like secession
itself. It snapped Virginia Schaacht's eyes toward him. He jammed the
clipping into his pocket, and grabbed the *Vincennes Western Sun.*

TWO MORE BANKS UNDER

The Vincennes Bank, under the oppressive order to pay back
loans to the United States Bank at 20 per cent per month has
ceased to redeem its notes in silver, and has begun drastic foreclosures in an effort to comply with the United States Bank
order. The Shawaneetown Bank will follow.

Blair ripped this article out and jammed it in his side pocket also.
The Miami Herald said:

Two wagonloads of gold and silver have just been drained out of
the West and hauled to the United States Bank which forwarded
it to Philadelphia for safekeeping. How long will it be at this
rate before the western country is exhausted of all coinage? Already there is not enough metal money left here to conduct
business! Such is the blessed tendency of the United States Bank
branch which despoils us of our wealth under the guise of helping us!

Blair looked for more reports of this nature with which to impress
the members of the House that no special favors promised to a community by Schaacht could save them now.

He ignored the rest of the news except to notice that Illinois had
finally become a state. Cincinnati had now grown to 1,100 houses. St.
Louis had 3,000 people in it.

Blair smiled some at an article which said that "McArthur and
Major Armstrong had successfully closed a new treaty with Chief Captain Michael of the Wyandots, completing the Wyandot cessions.

"The negotiation was skillful upon the part of McArthur, leading to an uneventful and amicable withdrawal of the Wyandots to Upper Sandusky, and freeing some two million acres for white settlement."

Blair snatched the *Detroit Gazette* which said:

BEWARE

What money is good today may be bad tomorrow. Below you will find the currencies of the major Western banks classified as "Decent," "Middling," "Good for Nothing." However, this should be daily checked at this office.

Blair jammed his pockets full of more clippings which told of Western foreclosures and agony from Pittsburgh to St. Louis.

He yanked *The Indiana Herald* towards him, but it ripped in half. He looked up to find that the other corner of the Indiana paper was pinned under the velvet elbow of Virginia Schaacht. She did not give way, but smiled at him tolerantly.

"You're doing some research no doubt, Mr. Blair, about conditions?"

"I'm aware of conditions, Miss Schaacht. But I intend to make some others aware of them."

She lifted her elbow slowly as she watched him. He pulled the *Herald* and some others up the table. Her handbag was dragged along inside one of the papers. He returned this to her and moved to the far end of the table.

That's when he noticed that underneath the handbag there had also been a sheet of foolscap on which was some writing in a calculated, vertical hand.

He was about to return that to her, too, but the notations oddly compelled him to read:

"*Concerning dress:*

make sure cut and quality of the cloth is fine like Tremaine's, but throw them on the back quickly and neglectfully, like B——.
Colour: use the grey of the well-bred, but not slavishly nor on all occasions as is being done by the pretenders and imitators.
See that the boots are well shined when in

*Cincinnati and Chillicothe, but never shined
in Columbus.*

Speech:

> *with the authority of Gideon Schaacht. The
> only way most men will judge the truth of
> what you say, is how much you believe it. Say
> it as though it were the last word. Wherever
> possible speak from a saturation of knowl-
> edge like B——.*

Argumentation:

> *see editorial in January 15th Detroit* Gazette
> *for sound, logical support of United States
> Bank policies.*

Spirit:

> *like B——."*

The writing was firm and regular, and it marched across the page
like destiny . . . somebody's. It was a kind of plat for building a man
. . . a road map to power. In his absorption he had picked up the
paper. But he was aware of a swishing approach and suddenly the list
was snatched out of his hand, and he was measured by a cool pair of
grey eyes.

She folded the sheet into her handbag with a touch of petulance.

"There's nothing against it is there?" she defended.

"Nope."

Her compressed lips demanded more from him. He shrugged.

"Your clothes are specially made to your . . . uh . . . specifications,"
Blair said. "Your wagonette was built special for you. Even heard your
beautiful mare was bred specially for you."

"To what point you cite all this, Mr. Blair?"

Blair shrugged again. "Only natural you should design your own
man, too."

"So glad you approve."

"Wouldn't expect you to be suited with any old ready-made the
Maker happened to strew around here. But I'm a little surprised to
see you doing the manufacturing yourself. Can't you find anybody
around to do the hand work for you?"

"Matter of fact, I have, Mr. Blair. You."

"Sorry. I'm not in that business. Besides, I don't think the raw stock you picked will take an edge as fine as you want ground on it. If you mean Bolding."

"I think you'll be able to do it."

"Me?"

"You're going to be the grindstone," she said.

The velvet skirt which swished away from him was smooth over her hips and then fell into long active folds in the fullness of the cloth. They swirled a little now as she stopped and turned for an after thought.

"I know you'll figure it out," she said. "So I'll say it. The 'B——' in my notes was you, Mr. Blair. But don't make too much of that. You just happened to come to mind handily when I needed an example. I can find another if it makes any difference."

Blair grinned. Virginia Schaacht walked back to Betsy Deshler's house where she had a room.

Jonathan Blair found out what it was to be a whetstone. Daily the blade which Virginia Schaacht was fashioning ground against him as he tried to pass his law taxing the United States Bank out of the West. And daily the blade therefore grew sharper. Bolding became skillful, adroit, subtle. He blocked Blair's bank bill despite the powerful exhibit which was building up for Blair's side before the eyes of the legislators. Daily, word of new foreclosures thundered into Columbus, increasing debtors who lived in huts set up around the jail.

The reports of the financial devastation dominated the talk in both The Swan and The Red Lion. But the standard way to express the ultimate and the most shocking news was, "Yes, but have you seen Coshocton County?"

Gideon Schaacht's respect for the power of Bela Hult was expressed in the pressure he brought against Hult's county. But the more Schaacht bludgeoned Coshocton, the firmer Bela Hult stuck to Blair's bill. And it was the staunch bull-like support of Hult beside him that finally enabled Blair to overcome the terror of the representatives and build up support for his bill to the point where he could almost get it through. How close he was could be measured by the fact that Gideon Schaacht returned to Columbus.

But as fast as Blair was building support, Bolding's skill was increasing to the point where he walked into Blair's room at The Swan one night.

"Blair, you're very close to getting your bill through."

"Thanks."

"But you're so close that we're going to have to take a drastic step. You are smart enough to see that it will defeat you. I thought to save ourselves the trouble of going through with it, we would just tell you what we plan to do, and you will probably concede and save everybody the grief."

The sight of the self-possessed young Bolding strained Blair's self control. But he managed, "Go ahead."

"As we see it, Jonathan, if we can take five votes away from you, you're licked."

Blair knew it was closer than that, but he said, "Go ahead."

"We figure we know the five shakiest ones on your list."

"I suppose you do."

"We can go to those five and tell them that if they vote for your bill, well, it'll be like Coshocton County for them, back in their home areas."

"I think Schaacht is too smart to make such a brazen threat," Blair said.

"He's too smart to have the United States Bank taxed out of existence."

"And he's too smart to make such a bald proposal, I still say, Bolding."

"It won't be baldly stated, Blair."

Blair could see how it could be done. He could even hear Schaacht saying it, ever so gently. He could visualize the frightened faces of representatives seeing the economic havoc about to begin back in their home towns. He could see them beseeching for some alternative. He could see Gideon Schaacht furnishing that alternative. He could see five key votes who would not answer the roll call the day his bill came up.

"I see," Blair said.

"I thought you would, Jonathan."

Blair walked to the wall where he had pegged a map of the Northwest Territory on which he had crudely marked the Ohio counties. As he looked at it today it looked like a huge spider web, and he could see Gideon Schaacht, sitting in Chillicothe, manipulating the web, increasing the pressure here, letting up a little there . . . to influence the destiny of the West.

Bolding said, "So we've revealed our hand now, Jonathan. Shall we go ahead and play our cards or can we consider it a gentlemen's contract that you'll withdraw?"

"Huh." Blair's voice was parched. "Where would we get the gentlemen?"

Suddenly Blair grabbed a handful of Bolding's tweed chest and yanked him to his feet, backing him toward the door.

As he backpedaled Bolding said, "All right, but which are you going to do?"

Blair opened the door and shoved Bolding out.

"Go ask your two teachers which I'm going to do."

Blair wasted no time finding Bela Hult that night. Together they spent a busy four hours. A series of hasty meetings with key members persuaded them that they just might have a one vote majority, possibly three, if the vote were taken immediately. They decided it was a better risk than waiting for Schaacht to go into action.

And in the House of Representatives the next morning, Jonathan Blair tried to call for the question to be put to a vote on a special rule.

However, he could not get recognition from the chair. After repeated failures he looked at Bolding, and in the satisfied smile which came back to him he read the bad news that his plans had leaked out.

Bela Hult tried for recognition. But the opposition was apparently too busy arguing a new bill on the handling of estrayed livestock.

Jackson Garth likewise could not get the Speaker's attention. Blair's pulse throbbed in his neck as he sat there helplessly listening to talk about strayed animals. Through his head went pictures of Hope's Merinos banished from the town by the men who now stood here and babbled innocently about estrays.

A little before noon, though, he saw Adonijah Fallon walk into the chamber. Fallon doubled as a county surveyor and statehouse page. He walked directly to Justin Bolding and handed him a paper.

Bolding allowed a respectable number of minutes to pass. Then he was on his feet moving for an extra-early adjournment. Blair felt the doors slamming in his face.

But suddenly he was surprised to hear his own people voting down the adjournment. Under the surprise of this defeat the chair carelessly recognized a reticent and apparently harmless member who, upon gaining his feet, called the question of the bank tax to vote.

In the buzzing of voices the Speaker looked at Justin Bolding. Bolding turned around sheepishly and looked back to the gallery platform

in the rear where sat Gideon Schaacht. Schaacht passed his hand over
his face in fatigue and reproach, and he beckoned to Adonijah Fallon.
The count was about to begin when Blair saw Fallon walk up to
the Speaker's rostrum and hand up a note. The Speaker then said,
"Gentlemen, the Speaker must leave the chair on sudden emergency."
He held up the unpainted gavel. "I therefore appoint as chairman pro
tempore . . ." The Speaker's gaze ranged over the members as if he
were trying to decide. Then he said, "Mr. Jonathan Blair. Will you
take the chair, please, sir?"

This surprised Blair, but pleasantly. He walked forward to the
rostrum while the house buzzed with voices. The handle of the gavel
was sweaty and was dropped into his hand before he had a good grip
on it. The Speaker left hurriedly.

Blair looked to the rear of the hall where Virginia Schaacht sat.
He smiled, spread-eagling himself a bit. She smiled back, apparently
not begrudging him this slight victory.

Under cover of the buzzing Blair leaned over the rostrum and spoke
quietly to the clerk. "Mr. Clerk, what is the procedure for beginning
the voting?"

"You don't have to do much, sir. Just instruct me to call for the ayes
and nays alphabetically. Here's a copy of the rules."

The balloting began. In the beginning of the alphabet there were
more nays than ayes. But when Garth and Hult were called one after
the other, they both responded with such great booming "ayes" that
it seemed to influence a few others and the ayes began outnumbering
the nays. At the rostrum as the roll was called, Blair kept score of the
ayes and nays.

The clerk worked his way through the alphabet, and the replies
came back, "Aye!"

"Nay!"

"Nay!"

"N-a-y!" That was old Captain Vance, a Federalist who bragged of
serving with John Marshall in the Rebellion.

"Aye!"

"Nay!"

Blair seemed to stop breathing between votes, it seemed that close,
according to his tally sheet. He could count up quickly because he
marked the nays opposite the ayes.

But when the clerk came to Representative Zephias, the vote was done; and Blair was appalled to find that the balloting came out on dead center. While the clerk counted the votes slowly in a dead-still chamber, Blair counted his list again quickly. He had been right. One more vote would have made the bank tax law. One more vote would have driven Gideon Schaacht back to Philadelphia.

Then a great exhilaration swept up his throat. He leaned over to the clerk.

"Mr. Clerk, *I* vote 'aye.' "

The clerk looked surprised.

"I said, 'I vote aye'!" Blair repeated.

The clerk looked up at Blair blankly.

"I said . . ."

"I heard what the representative said, sir. But the chair traditionally casts *no* vote, sir."

"The chair casts . . ."

"No vote, sir."

"No vote!"

"If you'll look at these pages, sir," the clerk handed up the roll book for Blair's inspection, "you'll see the Speaker has not voted."

Bela Hult was shaking his head vigorously negative, but Tremaine of Cincinnati moved adjournment.

Jonathan Blair looked out over a chamber which swam before his eyes. The faces were blurs. On the gallery platform in rear he saw Gideon Schaacht rise and a feminine figure beside him rose. They turned and began to descend the ladder. In Blair's distorted vision the white blur on top of each pair of shoulders seemed to contain a great leering smile. A snapping noise near his stomach caused him to look down and find one half of the splintered gavel in each of his knotted fists. The chamber suddenly filled with laughter . . . laughter that would soon thunder from Pittsburgh to Mesopotamia to St. Louis.

Chapter 12: THE WOMEN

IN THE winter of '19 the settlers of Hosmer Village, as it was still called by the elders, anxiously gathered in Hosmer's store to hear the report of Matt Gavagan. They had asked Gavagan to stop at Columbus on his way back north to tell Blair of Schaacht's visit to Mesopotamia and his offer. Schaacht's talk had been statesmanlike, based on the economic good of the territory, but it added up to this: get Blair to call off the bank-tax effort in the legislature, and you will experience immediate relief from the pressure of foreclosures. Major Armstrong will ccase his search for the Merino sheep. Even a few loans may possibly be arranged to ease certain emergencies.

Schaacht had also been wise enough to give proof. Major Armstrong's platoon had immediately withdrawn from Mesopotamia following Schaacht's visit. The eastern purchasers left Mesopotamia and went to Coshocton County. Foreclosure proceedings instantly ceased against Hank Flannerty.

Matt Gavagan had taken a load of tan bark to the tannery at Chillicothe. Now he was back and enjoying the eagerness with which the settlers waited for news of Blair's decision.

"The smallpox has moved up from the river through Chillicothe. Chillicothe is better already. But it's stringin' up the Scioto to Circleville, creepin' north towards Columbus. Some say it's movin' faster than bad dollars."

Hussong snapped, "But what about Blair? You see him?"

"There's two taverns quarantined 'tween Circleville and Columbus a'ready. I almost got my team quarantined in Blue Jacket Town."

"Did you see *Blair?*" Hussong barked.

"Blair. Yeah, I saw Blair."

"He said . . . and he told me to say it just like he said it . . . he said to tell you please that he'd learned you can't fix it just for *one* town. To make things right for one town, you got to fix it right for all the towns in the territory. He said, 'tell Hussong it's like the hog cholera, you can't keep one hog well unless you keep the whole passel fit.' He said, 'tell them to trust me to do right.' "

"Hell! We trusted him overlong now!" Hussong roared. "We're goin' down there and bring him back. Who's comin'?"

Stikes said, "Wait a minute, Joe. You got to add it up a little different on Blair lately. He *did* get them red devils backed up on the reserve y'know. And he did get that land opened up so's, at least, we got a place to go now, if we have to. And none of us helpin' him none either."

Gavagan said, "And down at that Columbus, our Blair's a some'at different critter than what he is up here. While I was settin' with him, three of them white waistcoats came up and asked him questions, like he knew somethin'. Seemed he did, too. And there's some of 'em callin' him 'Mr. Blair,' and like that."

Hussong's face darkened, "I'm callin' him a damned meddlin' scribblin', book-readin' bandit. Who's comin' down there with me and git him back outa there before Schaacht sets them blasted moneybags back on us with their bargain-huntin' friends?"

Exeter moved over behind Hussong. Hawkins did the same. Elisha Adams said, "Count me in."

Mesopotamia divided out heavily on the side of Joe Hussong who said, "Gavagan, we usin' your wagon, or are you with the lawyer?"

Gavagan said, "I'm not exactly *with* him, Joe. But I'm not against him either."

"All right, Slasher, we use your wagon?"

Slasher fingered his chin and moved over to join Hussong.

Hope Christofferson stepped into the gap of floor space which about measured the difference of opinion in Mesopotamia.

"You forgettin', Joe, that Blair's got men from all over the state thinkin' his way now? You forgettin' how it's gonna look, you bargin' in there and yankin' him out and undoin' everything?"

"That's the idea of it! So's I can keep my hogs, and you can bring your 'rinos back down home like a man . . . uh, that is like a woman! We elected him. We can de-elect him, too!"

"You can drag him out all right," Hope said. "But then maybe we want to send him back again to ask for somethin' else; how's he going to go back down and ask for favors if we cut the horns off our own ram, right in front of everybody?"

Hussong backed up and folded his arms. "All right, Mrs. Christof-

ferson," he proposed. "You know a better way of gettin' him back here,
you do it."

Hope looked down at her doeskin skirt. "I'm not much of a one at
goin' in places like that," she said.

Hussong poked a finger at her. "You do it. Or we do it." He grinned.
"The lawyer always was kind of partial to your kind of handlin',
Hope. And I reckon his pretty curls wouldn't get so mussed up if you
was to . . ."

Christofferson took a step forward. Hussong protested, "I'm only
askin' are we gonna do it . . . or you?"

Hope turned to Christofferson, "Brute, have Hank Flannerty go up
and look after the 'rinos tomorrow."

She turned to Hussong, "I'll bring Blair back," she said.

The way it was at The Swan during court days or legislation days,
after the evening meal the men got up from table with full stomachs
and walked across into the common room.

In this supposedly unguarded, pleasant hour men walked slow and
thought fast. And though an observer from the upcounties would see
only a swapping of cigars over brandy, the real swapping that went on
here was allegiance. It was the most efficient vote-trading market because by watching that front door plus the small table in the corner
of the dining room, plus an occasional glance at the long bench in
front of the hearth, a man could about judge what would happen in
the chamber across the road tomorrow.

For this reason whenever the front door let in a February draft almost every head raised up briefly to see who came or went. But on
this night the heads stayed up, because almost every man in The Swan
was now looking at the largest man he had ever seen.

The man obviously was accustomed to stares. His sleeves ended just
below his elbows. His great cold-reddened left hand held a large fur
hat. The hand had only three fingers and a thumb. He stood by the
door, surveying the room. His companion invited stares, too. Any
woman was rare at The Swan, but this woman was striking in that by
her dress she must not have been at an inn often. Yet by her poise she
had been in one every day. She wore a doeskin jerkin with a hood
thrown back off her hair which was short and swept back and filled
with sparkles of snow. The hood of the jerkin was trimmed with fur
and lined with sheep fleece. She waited for the man to find the way.

The huge man led her to a chair in the hallway between the dining room and the commons. She sat, composed, while he strode to the register desk. After an exchange of talk, Jarvis Pike went up the stairs. The tavern watched to see who would be summoned. And presently Jonathan Blair came down.

After he had seen his guests Blair looked aggressively around the room, but relaxed. The curiosity was intense, but nowise disrespectful. The height and breadth of Christofferson had a way of making gentlemen out of any group.

Blair followed Christofferson to stand beside Hope. Christofferson said, "We don't come begging, Jonathan, but Hope has a matter to be talked out."

Hope said, "Brute, I'd be obliged you'd stand off aways. It'll be that hard, the talkin' I got to do with Jonathan."

"You want me to tell him, Hope?"

"No. Once I get it said, it'll be said."

Brutus Christofferson moved into the dining room where two men stepped back from the mug rack to make a place for him.

Hope said, "Jonathan, I guess you foreglimpse what I come about."

"I suppose so, Hope. I heard Schaacht was up to see you."

"I don't ask my favors light, Jonathan."

"I know that, Hope."

" 'Specially not from you, Jonathan, after what . . . now that it's not to be man and woman between you and me."

Blair knew she'd like to look down. But it was like her to do it the hard way. She looked him right in the eye, making it worse, because that way a man could see how much she was worth losing a finger for, or an arm, or most anything.

A man could see her being beside him in every kind of place and time, and what a difference it would make. A man wanted to lay that head in the crook of his shoulder and take the fight off her hands. But Christofferson had got her.

She said, "Point is, Jonathan, I guess you're doing pretty good with that law you're makin' to tax Mr. Schaacht's bank."

She looked around the commons at the men who stood in groups, mostly staring back at her and Jonathan.

"They say you got a lot of 'em down here to seeing your way of it. And though it's a sight of a jolt to everyone, they say you're getting pretty strong-handed down here and might have your way."

"Looks like it now, Hope. They voted me down once, but we have another chance."

"Schaacht was up to the village and had a thing or two to say that would make it so's we could bring the sheep down out of the woods, and take a lot of worries off people's minds if certain things happened."

"Hope, that's the way it would look at first."

"Anyhow, they're sayin' you got the reach on Schaacht, and I came down to ask you to . . ."

Blair interrupted. "Hope, remember you once told me 'butt right into them'?"

"Sounds like somethin' I'd say."

"Well, it seems to work."

"Uh-huh. Usually does."

"And . . . uh . . . remember when Aaron had the tremors you said, 'You can't be friends to all of them. A softhearted shepherd can be the meanest'?"

"It seemed right then," she said. " 'Course I could have been wrong."

"Then the time you said, 'A man's got to be willing to lose, or he can't win'?"

"Guess I said that, too. Sounds right."

"Then you told me . . ."

"I don't want to hear any more of my own words, Jonathan!" she snapped.

"Well, I've been kind of leanin' on those words, Hope."

"Uh-huh."

"Just thought you'd want to know I didn't forget, Hope."

"Uh-huh."

"Well, what did you come to tell me, Hope?"

She studied the big map of the Territory that hung up over the hearth in the common room. She looked at the men in the room from various parts of the country. She looked down at the fur gauntlet gloves in her lap.

"Well, we just came to tell you, Jonathan, that . . . uh . . . that we've got the flock up in the woods. Got cover over their heads. Got them pretty well hid. Flannerty and Brute go up there and see to them. Just wanted you to know that . . . uh . . . the sheep are all right. Thought you'd want to know, that's all."

Right there in front of everybody the men in The Swan saw a strange sight that night. Some thought maybe Jonathan Blair was putting on. Some thought it was too showy for out here in the Ohio Country. Of course, they couldn't see how he looked her deep in the eyes and said, very slowly and softly, "Thank you, Hope."

All they saw was how he bent way over, like it was Philadelphia or Boston, and took the woman's hand and put his mouth to it, slow and long, like she was some great countess or somebody.

In the dining room two men filled back in at the mug rack in the space which was left when Brutus Christofferson stepped away.

Friendly conversation between Justin Bolding and Jonathan Blair was extremely unbecoming in the eyes of those who loitered in the commons of The Swan. Justin Bolding's entrance into The Swan on the following evening therefore caused a longer than usual pause in the separate conversations in The Swan. Bolding's entrance reminded younger members of interesting thoughts about the daughter of Gideon Schaacht; and the older members wondered why Justin Bolding should come to The Swan to talk to Blair. Throughout The Swan chairs were yanked closer together.

Bolding walked directly to where Blair talked to Bela Hult and Jackson Garth.

Blair stepped a few paces over to listen to Bolding who said, "Jonathan, what is the existing law governing passage of currency from man to man in a smallpox quarantine area like, say, Circleville?"

"Bolding, why do you come all the way down here to The Swan to ask me that question?"

"Thought you wouldn't mind helping out an old student."

"At The Red Lion you could have asked Judge Pease or a half-dozen better lawyers."

"True, but lately you've studied a lot of law I've noticed. More likely you'd know."

Blair looked around the room. He saw how many were watching them.

"Wouldn't be you came here for some other reason would it, Bolding?"

"Like what?"

"Like making all these people here wonder what I'm doing talking to you?"

Bolding grinned but made no answer. As he left he said, louder than necessary, "Thanks very much, Jonathan."

Blair rejoined Garth and Hult. Hult studied the wet end of his cigar. "Jonathan, we heard your people from Mesopotamia came down to ask you to let up on the bank-tax law."

"Yeah."

"Then we saw that sheep-raising woman come down. Probably to ask you the same thing."

"She didn't ask it though."

Hult studied him. "But that's what she came for, didn't she?"

"Yes."

"Then we see Bolding coming over all the time to talk to you."

"You don't see me going to talk to *him*, though."

"I'm not quibblin' about details, Blair."

"What then, Bela?"

"Some of the men are commencin' to wonder if you're your own man any more, Jonathan."

Blair's head snapped up, "And what do *you* think, Bela?"

"Not sure." Hult didn't like what he was saying. But he bulled on through. "Everybody knows Schaacht is relievin' the pressure on a town here and a town there and it's bringin' him results. Three of our men swung over to oppose the tax last week. We're not sure who we got and who we haven't got any more. Schaacht's playin' this state like a piano. Pressin' hard here, lettin' up there. And it's known he offered to ease up in Mesopotamia."

"Bela, I started this law. I'm going to drive it through."

"Yeah, but your people ain't lost out by it as bad as some."

Jackson Garth said, "Bela you're overhet. Blair's on our side all the way. He started the whole thing."

"Yeah," Hult grunted. "But maybe he wants out."

"How could he get out?" Garth asked. "His bloomin' name is even on it. They're callin' it 'The Blair Crowbar Law.'"

"All right," Hult said. "But let's keep it clear where everybody stands . . . especially this week."

"Why do you say *this* week?" Blair asked. "Especially."

"That's what I wanted to tell you. Schaacht had Riddle bring up a shipment of gold. We saw them take it into the Franklin Bank. Figure it this way. For the next week or so the Franklin Bank will redeem its paper in specie. That's going to make it look as if everything is all right around here. It'll be the only specie-paying bank around. But it's the one the legislature'll see. To the shortsighted ones that makes our bill look unnecessary."

Garth whistled.

Blair ran his hand over his head.

"But I ain't through yet. We been underratin' that Bolding. He's got it rigged so the bill will come back out on the floor just a few days after the hard money gets good and circulated around town."

Garth whistled again.

Hult continued, "And they're gonna start redeemin' paper in gold the day the legislature gets paid."

Garth whistled again.

Hult added, "That's why everybody's got to see where you stand, Blair, good and plain."

But it was no clearer in the next week to Colonel Bela Hult where Blair stood. For the plan which was coming to Jonathan Blair was born of desperation. It would not stand much light of day nor any conversation. It would not appeal to the forthright Bela Hult. It did not appeal to Blair. It came from the long and lonesome study of the law. For years men had been trying unsuccessfully to disenfranchise their opponents. Jonathan Blair thought he had found the only way. It involved a woman. But it did not make good watching.

Those who watched saw Blair's first step. He moved out of The Swan. For quarters he selected an abandoned hut close to the river from which he could watch the comings and goings at The Swan.

Voting on the Crowbar Law was likely to come on the fifth of February. There were only four days left. And Jonathan Blair laid his plans now with the precision of Mike Stikes fitting the sear in a rifle lock, for he had to disenfranchise enough of the opposition to let his bill through, but still keep a quorum.

By the evening of the fourth of February it was quite well known around the borough that there would be a dinner that night at Sullivant's house across the Scioto. It was known too, that this dinner would be a kind of strategy meeting for action against the Crowbar Law in the chamber next day.

Blair had studied the route Virginia Schaacht took from the Deshler house to Sullivant's house on previous occasions. He knew that she might travel alone to the Sullivant's house, on foot or on horseback or in Deshler's light cart. He knew she might also come accompanied by Gideon Schaacht or by Justin Bolding or both. And for each of these possibilities he had an alternate plan.

The location he chose for his brash act was the side of the road opposite the entrance to The Swan. And he took up his position there, alone, about dusk. He was shaved so close that the cold air stung his face. But the nature of the task required a shave.

When men about the borough came by to enter The Swan, Blair waved to them, but he scrupulously avoided close contact with anyone.

Lights began to show through the glass windows of The Swan as dusk deepened. He hoped it would not get too dark, too quickly.

When she came, she came alone.

Blair was disappointed to see that she didn't drive the Deshlers' cart. He had planned to detain her by making something of some trouble with the cart. She rode her own horse, and she rode sidesaddle to protect the great crinkly skirt which blossomed out below a fitted fur jacket. She wore great fur gauntlet-gloves. On her head was what looked like a militia drum, made of fur with a fur apron down from the back of it protecting her ears and the back of her neck.

Since she was alone Blair knew he might have to use the most brazen of his alternatives. But that was not unpleasant.

She saw him standing there and she reined in.

"Mr. Blair."

"Evening, Miss Schaacht."

He came around on The Swan side of her horse and took the bridle. His other hand he held up to her as a dismount post. Her trusting weight on his hand made him feel guiltier.

"Well, tomorrow's the day, Mr. Blair."

"Yes. Tomorrow."

He looked around. There was no one watching from The Swan. He would have to drag out the conversation until witnesses came by. For in the opinion of Jonathan Blair it was important to him and to Mesopotamia and to the Northwest that he be seen at this particular time in front of The Swan with the daughter of Gideon Schaacht . . . and seen in a way that people could never forget. They must talk about it.

"I think he's outmatched you, Mr. Blair."

"Huh?" Blair watched The Swan and the road, searching, for people.

"I say I think Justin has lined up a three- or four-vote margin over you for tomorrow."

"You sound as proud of him as if you'd built the man from the shoes up."

Her quiet smile admitted as much. But her lips said, "I had a good model to mold him on. He's more you than you are, Mr. Blair."

"You love him, Miss Schaacht?"

"I will when I get him finished."

"Just where are you going to display this marionette when you get him finished."

"Washington."

"Uh-huh." Blair noticed that a couple men came out of The Swan and looked over and stood for a moment.

"Aren't you apt to be disappointed in him, Miss Schaacht? I mean, something you make yourself with your own two hands won't have much mystery to you, will it?"

Blair noticed that Mrs. Pike was walking east toward them. She would probably cross the road behind them and enter The Swan. And Mrs. Pike had a better circulation than *The Western Intelligencer*.

Miss Schaacht said, "What are you looking at, Mr. Blair?"

"Huh? Oh, nothing."

"Well, what were you doing standing here?"

"Matter of fact I was waiting for you."

"Me!"

Her face was white against the dark fur collar. Snow flakes clung in her eyelashes, melted, were replaced. Vapor from her breath spoke of warmth. A fleeting flicker of a dimple guaranteed it. Chuckling grey-green eyes denied it.

"Me?" she repeated.

"Yes."

As Mrs. Pike drew closer, Blair's old militia coat moved closer to the rippling fur jacket.

"You borrowed me for a model for your man, Miss Schaacht."

"Yes."

"I figured you're the kind of woman would want to pay back the loan."

"In what way?"

Mrs. Pike's footsteps came into hearing, then they stopped. Three men came out of The Swan. They watched.

Blair said, "I want to borrow you for a moment or so."

"Exactly how?" Her eyebrows arched. "I'm not exactly for hire, Mr. Blair."

"No time for details," Blair said. "But I promise it'll be quick." He put his bare hand on the fur of her sleeve. She looked down at his hand, but she stood still.

"Just how," she asked, "does this transaction take place between . . ." But she found out directly.

Blair's arm went around her waist prisoning her left arm and seizing her right wrist which he also pulled in against her waist.

Her lips parted in surprise as the breath was crushed out of her against the solid body of Jonathan Blair.

Although his grip around her body was harsh, his lips were gentle against hers. They could afford to be, for he had bent her so far back that she could not escape. His cold left hand was under the apron of her hat holding her neck, lest he bend it too far back.

She gasped for breath which he permitted her, but when the fur jacket had enough breath in it to yell, his coarse wool shoulder closed her mouth as he kissed her ear, and then her mouth.

He brought her back erect, but his left hand held her face buried against his coat in fuming silence.

He heard Mrs. Pike cough and resume her course across the road. The tail of a remark drifted over from in front of The Swan, ". . . but Schaacht pays in a damned pretty coin; I'll say that!"

The fur against Blair's chest surged in anger and he tightened his grip. Fragrance was squeezed out of her along with her breath. Even on these terms she was a wonderful thing to hold. Blair had nearly forgot how a woman that close seems the reason for living . . . how magically fine beyond anything.

Horse hooves crunched the snow, approaching from the west. Blair removed his hand from the back of her neck, but placed it quickly over her mouth. She bent her head back, but the hand followed until she could bend back no farther, being still pinioned around the waist.

"When I take my hand away," Blair said, "you can say what you want."

He watched the horseman's silhouette approaching. It was the crisp, well-tailored outline of Justin Bolding. The palm of Blair's hand grew warm from her mouth. He said softly, "When I take my hand off, you can still say what you want. But I'd advise you to look who's listening."

He released his grip on her waist and wrist just enough to feel if she was going to spring into action. She was. He tightened again.

"Easy," he said.

He released his grip slowly as the rider approached, but she still struggled vibrantly for freedom, so he tightened his grip again.

"E-a-s-y now," he whispered.

Slowly he released her, always ready to tighten again if she pranced. He timed it so that when she finally stood completely free, Justin Bolding looked down at her.

"Hello, Virginia. We'll ride together."

Her mouth ajar she looked up at him. Then at Blair. In charged silence she reached for her bridle and straightened the stirrup.

Blair laced the fingers of his two hands and placed them palm up on his knee for a mounting step. Her lips compressed against rage as she removed her glove and reached into her pocket. Into Blair's waiting palms she flicked a gold half-eagle.

"If I owe any more interest on that loan," she said with laborious control, "I'll pay in cash."

Blair examined the coin, flipped it in the air and caught it. Then he flagrantly examined Bolding from boots to hat, "Looking at the product," he chided, "I'd say you've got some change coming."

She mounted and cantered off. Bolding's stare questioned Blair. But then he heeled his horse to overtake the woman.

Jackson Garth moved out of the shadows. He did not approach Blair, but he stepped into the light in front of The Swan where Blair could see him. Blair waved. And Jackson Garth went into action.

By the time brandy was served that night in The Swan, Mrs. Pike had seen that the story had saturated the entire dining room and the tap. When the story reached the far corner of the dining room where Bela Hult sat, the big representative from Coshocton County threw his hand linen down on the table and rose. Jackson Garth reached out to stop him, saying, "Wait a minute, Bela!"

But Hult had heard enough. "If it's a woman he needs I could have got him one that wouldn't cost us our shirts!" Hult stamped out.

At The Red Lion, dinner was usually later than at The Swan, delayed by the late arrival of the Governor and Judge Pease and some of the busier state senators. So the story reached The Red Lion about the time Judge Pease got to his corn dodgers. The teller of the story added, "How could he do it, Judge?"

The maple syrup found the weak spots in the judge's teeth so he ate vigorously to shorten the pain. "Why not? The woman is soft and pretty. Blair is a long time without a woman. Lost *one* that I know of."

"But how could Schaacht's daughter be seen with Blair?"

"Blair's a fair piece of manhood. Stands 'bout nineteen hands high. Shaves. Strong handed. Good shoulders. Good head."

"Sure. But how can Blair break faith with Hult and those?"

The judge washed his teeth in a gulp from his mug.

"Break faith? How? Did Hult want to be kissed, too?" The informant started to laugh, but the judge's eyes nailed his laughter. "Wait till the testimony's all in, Mister!"

The judge turned to the others who had craned their necks over to hear his opinion. "That goes for the rest of you that call yourselves lawyers and senators!"

Across the Scioto at the Sullivant house the planners in favor of the Bank of the United States and against the Blair Crowbar Law relaxed. The score they totaled came to a three- or possibly a four-vote margin against the tax for tomorrow morning. There were about nine men present, and when Gideon Schaacht shoved his long, tight clad legs out in front of him and crossed his boots, it was plain to all that the business was over. Mr. Tremaine, representative from Hamilton County, asked if Miss Schaacht would play the pianoforte which he understood had been the second one hauled this side of the Alleghenies.

Justin Bolding adjusted the bench to it, but his mind was on Miss Schaacht and the silence which she maintained and the reason for it. In the course of which thinking he remembered how she was standing with Jonathan Blair earlier this evening and the strange talk that had gone on at that time.

Miss Schaacht was a good player of this instrument, so good that even her little experimental testing of the keyboard sounded like music.

But the soft experimental notes were in direct discord with a pounding which now came from outside.

Gideon Schaacht said, "Bolding! Go see what that racket is!"

However, Bolding was accompanied to the front door by three other men and Virginia Schaacht. Upon opening the door they found two men hammering a stake in front of the house through the snow into the frozen ground. To the top of the stake was fastened a small sign which faced the road.

When Bolding opened the front door, bathing the two men in light, the one who was pounding pointed to Bolding and said, "Stand right there! Do not come out until we are gone!"

He then gave one last quick blow to the stake and the two withdrew backwards to the gate. The loud-mouthed one lifted the gate latch, not with his hand, but with a long stick. The two backed out through the gate, careful not to touch their persons to any part of the gate. The speaker tossed the stick back inside the yard and called back to Bolding, "Sir, there will be an explanation along in the morning. My job was just to put the sign." He pointed to a sullen figure which they had not previously noticed out on the road. "Corporal Johanson and two others here from the Franklin Dragoons are posted here by Captain Vance to see nobody leaves this house."

Bolding went out to the sign, leaned down close to it but could not read it in the dark.

Corporal Johanson's voice cut through the black. "It's the quarantine, sir!"

It was moments before this sunk into Bolding. Then he said, "But nobody in this house . . ."

"No, sir. Not yet, sir. But you're tainted they say."

"Who's down with it?"

"Lawyer, name of Blair, sir."

"What's that to do with us?"

"Ask Miss Schaacht, sir."

The wind that whipped up suddenly off the river blew away the shouting that went back and forth that night in front of the Sullivant house.

In the chamber next morning the empty seats caused such a stir that it was difficult to bring the House to order. The buzzing grew and spread out into the hall until some members of the senate came downstairs to watch the confusion. The sergeant-at-arms came back into the chamber and reported behind his hand to the Speaker of the house that it was impossible to compel the absent members to attend, and he explained why.

Jackson Garth was on his feet demanding recognition from the chair. The chair was busy talking to some men who promptly left the chamber, bent on an urgent errand.

Meanwhile a great grin of realization was spreading over the massive

face of Bela Hult. Hult's voice soon roared out over the chamber, "Mr.
Speaker, I call for the question on the bank tax."

Presently the clerk was calling the roll for the voting. The Speaker's
eye was on the door. Then he leaned over to talk quietly to the clerk.
The clerk resumed calling the names, but noticeably slower. Frequently he asked a member to repeat his vote.

Bela Hult was on his feet roaring, "You're not hard of hearing,
Clerk! Get on with the vote."

The gavel rapped. The Speaker said, "I shall not hesitate to expel
the next member who causes disorder!"

Hult's chest swelled. Garth dragged the hulk down into a seat.

The Speaker kept his eye on the door as the vote continued slowly.

At The Red Lion, Judge Pease closed the book in front of him until
the excited representatives, attorneys and senators who crowded around
him obediently silenced under his stare. The judge then reopened the
book.

Stuttgart said, "Judge we won't bother you, but hurry! They'll be
getting to the M's soon and my client needs to get back to vote!"

Another said, "Judge, there's got to be an appeal from quarantine.
There's *no* form of confinement in which a man isn't entitled to a hearing. That's law!"

The judge closed the book. "Gentlemen, I shall give you an answer
on the point and if you're entitled to a hearing, I shall arrange it instantly. But I shall not lift a finger until this chamber quiets."

It was a measure of Pease's stature that even the public room of
The Red Lion did in fact become a "chamber" when Calvin Pease dis-
pensed justice there.

The crowd disciplined itself. The judge thumbed through his much-
worn book. He studied several different entries; then he said, "Ayeah."

"Ayeah, what?" begged Stuttgart.

"Quarantine may be imposed upon doctor's orders without appeal
or hearing of those confined."

"But, sir! It's not possible to take away a man's franchise or liberty
or right to hearing in this country."

"You're right, Stuttgart," the judge said. "Except in one single soli-
tary instance. Quarantine."

The leaning-forward crowd exhaled as a man and glared at Judge
Pease.

"Don't act so surprised, gentlemen," Pease said. "It's implicit in the nature of quarantine. Supposing a contaminated man were entitled to a hearing, where would you find a court who would hear him? Can you condemn a judge to the plague?"

But they were not listening. The group broke for the statehouse. Those last to leave suspected they saw a grin on the judge's face.

And back across the road in the lower chamber of the government of the new state of Ohio the vote rolled slowly but inexorably forward.

The Speaker did not seem to be listening. His eyes were on the door, waiting for some messenger. But the messenger did not come. The Speaker bent down to speak to the clerk, and the clerk thereafter pronounced the names still slower, but the name calling and the answering took on the irrevocable aspect of an eight-horse team topping a grade.

"Elton?"

"Aye, sir."

"Ellsworth?"

"Aye."

"Fallon?"

"Nay."

"Garth?"

"Aye, sir!"

"Goodridge?"

"Aye."

"Hult?"

"Aye! By God, sir, *aye!*"

As the vote rolled on a faint grin spread over the members of the House of Representatives of the State of Ohio. The grin widened and it spread out into the hall where the senators and some townsmen watched. The grin broadened and spread across the road to The Swan and The Red Lion, and then it was passed from rider to rider on the south road and the north road, and by sundown the grin had broken out into a chuckle which was already rippling as far south as Circleville and as far north as Boxford's Cabin. In the year 18 and 18 everyone understood that a tax of one hundred thousand dollars would close the doors of the branch of the United States Bank. Thus it was that a law was made as the long winter snow retreated into the fence corners and pulled back to hug the sides of cabins in the Territory north and west of the Ohio River.

Gideon Schaacht not being present in the hall, members pressed forward openly to shake the hands of Jackson Garth and Bela Hult whose eyes watered on this occasion.

Chapter 13: THE APPLICANT

HOSMER VILLAGE, or Mesopotamia as it was more often called lately, no longer knew how to treat its lawyer. There was a garbled story about him drifted up from Columbus Borough and it spawned mixed reactions. It caused Faith Hawkins to lift her skirts so they didn't touch the ground near Blair's cabin.

It caused Camelia Flannerty and Elizabeth Buttrick to stare from a distance into the Blair cabin to catch a new glimpse of the man who would kiss such a lady in the middle of Columbus.

The garbled version of the story widened the lips of Christian Kilgore to a painful grimace as if he had bitten into a wormy grape. It caused Matt Gavagan to throw back his head at the store in a great unguarded laugh, "I'm glad I didn't loan ya my wagon to haul him outa Columbus! He put it over all of 'em! Mark me now, that Blair's tough. They're findin' it out."

Hawkins said, "Aye, but usin' a woman like that . . . if what I heard was right!"

Gavagan grinned. "For Blair's sake I hope what you heard was only the half of it." He rapped Hawkins' chest. "I wouldn't mind finishin' that piece of work for him!"

Joe Hussong stared at the floor. "He's like to save us despite ourselves or break us . . . one. He's drove that bank out all by hisself."

Buttrick cleared his throat, "Uh . . . I have always said that Blair had a certain strength if he'd ever rise to it."

James Dolk shook his head, "Maybe. But it's against God the way he's risin'."

Emanuel Ault listened to everybody's comments. But he said, "We ought to be learned by now nobody goes against Schaacht. We'll find out now the hard way."

As if to support Ault, the village now saw the laboring heads of two horses come up out of the depression at the river ford like an extension of the long arm of Gideon Schaacht in the Northwest. One horse carried a woman, the other Justin Bolding.

It was another measure of Gideon Schaacht that those who worked close to him began to act and talk like him. In the store Bolding only said, "Where's Blair?"

They pointed across the common to Blair's cabin. Bolding started to leave. But Ault said, "The taint's still on it."

Bolding stopped.

"You mean he's still sick?"

"He don't say he is, but he don't say he ain't."

"Well, find out!"

Mesopotamia was sullen. Time was they'd show a man like this his place. But these days, the wrong word to Schaacht's men could put a hundred acres under the auction hammer.

Emanuel Ault said, "Who wants to go find out? You see that fence we run around his place? Nobody goes inside that. Flannerty's youngest boy takes eats up to the gate and sets 'em there. That's because the lawyer defended Flannerty in debtor court."

"How do you talk to the lawyer?" Bolding asked.

"We don't."

"But I came all the way up here to talk to him."

The men in the store looked at Virginia Schaacht, their eyes asking why she came.

Hussong said, "Go ahead. Go talk to him."

Ault said, "You could write him a message. Put it where Tim Flannerty puts the food."

You could see Gideon Schaacht in Bolding's gesture. He ordered, "Paper."

Ault produced it.

Virginia Schaacht surveyed the store, putting Mesopotamia on the defensive. Mike Stikes' young wife, Polly, defended, "We've bought trouble enough, Miss Schaacht, without the pox."

Miss Schaacht asked, "All that piled up by the gate? That's one day's food for him?"

"No," Polly said. "Three days."

At the old Shuldane house which had become Exeter's Tavern there was coarse laughter at Exeter's expense that night as they watched him scurry around to fit up an accommodation for a woman. They saw the Flannerty boy carry in a big bundle in a blanket. Hussong grabbed the boy's arm, "What you got there, boy?"

"They had me to fetch white sheets, Mr. Hussong."

"Where did you find any?"

"From Hope Emer . . . Christofferson's cabin."

Hussong hollered to Exeter, "Would I get white sheets if I was to put up here a night?"

There was laughter. The boy said, "Can you let go my arm now, Mr. Hussong?"

"One more thing, boy. When you left the lawyer's feed, what did Bolding's paper say that was there at the gate?"

"It was all law talk, sir. Beyond me."

Hussong looked at Hawkins and Adams. As one man they rose to leave the tavern.

But from the front of the tavern as they looked toward Blair's cabin, they saw a woman pick up the food which was there and Bolding's note. With a stick she opened the gate and walked toward the Blair cabin.

Hussong cupped his hands to his mouth. But Hawkins stayed his arm. "It's her funeral." He shrugged, "She knows."

Hussong dropped his hands, and they watched her walk toward the cabin. They saw her put the stick to the latch and push open the door. Presently they saw the dark deer-skin window of Blair's cabin flicker and glow orange in the dusk.

The lawyer continued shaving, his bare back to his visitor. The copper reflector behind the candle would not tell him if the dull knife was getting the whiskers. But it showed where the lather was. It also showed him the straight stiff woman who stood in his cabin.

She said, "You still have the pox?"

The only answer was his knife scraping against the grain of his whiskers.

"Or did you ever have it?" she asked.

The lawyer winced, either from the dullness of the blade or the sharpness of the woman.

"Well, do you have it still?" she asked. "Or did you ever?"

"You didn't get it," he said. "Doesn't that satisfy you?"

"Not completely."

"You're standing in my cabin, aren't you? The Schaachts are known to take good care of themselves. That must end the question."

"Not quite."

"Why?"

"A man who would wrack himself so much to save one woman's sheep wouldn't probably set out to give the pox to another woman. But a man that would push old Hosmer to his grave and let Christofferson lose a finger and then expose his home settlement to foreclosure . . . well, a man like that would do most anything to get a law passed."

"I didn't kill Hosmer! I'm not responsible for everything that happens!"

"What happened in front of The Swan that night, maybe was an accident, too?"

"You're a finely made woman. It was dark. It didn't cost you anything."

"That's why?"

"What does it matter now? Why did you come?"

She opened her handbag and brought out a small glass bottle. "I brought this," she said. "Called Jenner's Matter."

He turned and looked at the bottle of white liquid. But mostly he looked at the woman who held it. He had seen vaccine matter once before. But he was not sure now that he had ever really seen this woman before.

She said, "You don't need to stare as if it were poison. Five hundred have been vaccinated in Kentucky already. And Dr. Goforth in Cincinnati induced forty settlers there to try it. It's supposed to be done before, but . . ."

In unbelief the lawyer asked, "You brought that bottle up here for *me?*"

She backed away from his steady gaze. He took a step closer, she drew back more. Her withdrawal was interrupted by the bench which held Blair's saddle. She sat.

"You walked through that gate thinking that I have the . . . believing that . . . to bring that bottle to me? Why?"

It had been a long time since anyone had worried about the health of Jonathan Blair.

"Take it, and use it. It won't hurt. I've had it."

"Why did you bring it?"

"I suppose the same as a bootmaker takes good care of his pattern."
Blair took the bottle from her hand, but he set it aside. He leaned
over her. Her wide mouth and thrusting chin suddenly looked to
Blair strong and trusting. As she grew older the strong chin and straight
nose would probably crystallize into the eaglelike profile of Gideon
Schaacht. But for now they were lovely and compelling. She did not
withdraw when his mouth touched her forehead, for that was a kind
of admiration and gratitude. But presently he had drawn her to her
feet and to his chest, and that was something else again.

She let him have her lips for a moment and then her arm was free
and her forearm was against his chin. Her face was rouged with the
effort and her breath short.

Her voice was not as firm as her words, "But I don't intend to wear
the pattern," she said. "Only the boots."

He let her go. She straightened her waistband.

"But I guess I'm glad it happened this once in our lives."

"This once in our lives?"

"Yes." She took Bolding's note from her pocket and handed it to
him. "You see I think this will end it."

Blair looked at her. There was something very lovely and very adult
in her candid enjoyment of the moment just past. In fact as he looked
at her he made a private and presumptuous resolve which transcended
any plans she might have for "ending it."

But then he opened the note:

BLAIR:
You will be interested in the decision of Justice John Marshall
in the case of Mr. McCulloch vs. State of Maryland, in which Mr.
Marshall finds against the state. If I have studied well under you
this means that the states under no circumstances have the right
to tax any part of the Federal Government; and your tax against
the United States Bank branch in Ohio therefore becomes uncon-
stitutional and unenforceable.

Your resp't'ful student
JUSTIN BOLDING

Virginia Schaacht had seen men shatter before. She carried a mental
picture of the broad back of Gideon Schaacht walking away through
archways, leaving behind him human devastation, leaving others

to do the meaningless verbal picking up of pieces. In earlier days in Philadelphia she had stayed behind to help with this picking up. Then she had gone angrily to Schaacht.

"Virginia," he had said once, "the penalty of leadership is opposition. Is it kinder to pretend it's not a fight?"

And presently she understood the lonesome price Schaacht paid for his leadership, and she also began to leave these scenes without waiting to clean up, feeling as sorry for her father as for his victims.

About Blair, Schaacht had said, "Virginia, he fights so hard, that when he gives up it will be all at once . . . poof."

Gideon Schaacht's record of judgment was superior, and so Virginia Schaacht knew that today in Blair's cabin, she would see the . . . the poof.

But as she watched she was puzzled. If this were an explosion it was a grim one. This was a slow, bitter, smoldering kind of internal bleeding.

Blair's profile was towards her as he stared at the cabin door. The great muscular breastplate of his chest darkened in color. Then the neck, then the ears, and then she could even see the pounding in his temples. Lower on his chest there was a drumming under the ribs.

Absently his hand crushed Bolding's note into a small ball.

Then as Virginia Schaacht watched, it seemed to her she could see the color drain back out of Blair's face as though he had forced it out himself. He unrolled the note, reread it, and tossed it into the hearth. The motion was suddenly relaxed.

His voice was deep and relaxed, too. "All right," he said. "All right. I quit."

She sat, trying to read him. He even smiled faintly.

"You can go now, Virginia, and tell him he won."

And it seemed to Miss Schaacht that she had never heard such a menace.

Gideon Schaacht sat in the United States Bank in Chillicothe with his boots crossed on the desk at his own eye level, forming a front sight through which he squinted at Justin Bolding.

Being a young assistant worthy of larger responsibilities, Bolding did not trouble the great man with trivial details. "The job is finished, Gideon. There'll be no trouble from Blair. The Marshall decision crumpled him."

But the great man preferred to decide for himself what was trivial. "You just tell me what he said, Bolding."

"Why he said in effect that the Marshall decision of course ended the matter. That his bank tax was now unconstitutional."

"Never mind what he said in *effect*. What did he say *exactly?*"

"You mean the *exact* words?"

"I mean the exact words, *and* the tone of voice, *and* how loud, *and* how did he look?"

"Well really, sir, I didn't note every single . . ."

"Send in Virginia!"

Bolding colored, and left.

To Virginia Schaacht, Gideon said gently, "Virginia, what was your impression of the trip to Mesopotamia?"

"I think this will be it, father."

"Will be what?"

"Will be the biggest fight you ever had."

Gideon Schaacht's gaunt head rolled back and his mouth opened in a great rising basso laugh that thundered up a stairway of notes. But it didn't treble back down. It broke off unnaturally at the top step. His feet came off the desk. The face came on guard and the voice yelled, "Riddle! Bolding! Turner! Come in here!"

Up north of Columbus and north of Boxford's Cabin in the place called Mesopotamia in the hut of the lawyer a great shouldered man with only four fingers on the right hand sat down opposite Blair. His elbows went forward on his knees as he began his stiff-necked proposition.

"Jonathan, we all heard around the clearing how the trap you set for the bank got unsprung on you."

Blair smiled, "The Supreme Court says it's unconstitutional for a state to tax the Federal Government."

"That's what I mean," Brute said. "But we heard you don't plan to take that sittin' down."

"Our tax law is on the books, Brute. The auditor should collect the tax."

"That's what I said. But we hear the Federal is already givin' your law the horse laugh. Not even worried that you'll even try to collect. They got a prohibition out against the collection."

"An injunction."

"Yeah, that's what I said."

The big man unfolded a clipping from an old copy of the Scioto *Gazette.*

"Well, 'manuel Ault says he's got his instructions from Schaacht to start closin' down on Hope's place again. Seems he's fixed in his mind to make an example of her. That'll mean likely Armstrong'll be back with his soldiers combin' the woods to find those 'rinos."

Christofferson referred to the clipping. "Well, some of us notice in this law you got made that it says the auditor of state is supposed to appoint a man to walk into that United States Bank some day after next September fifteenth and collect the tax of one hundred thousand dollars owing to the State of Ohio."

"That's right, Brute."

"Then way down here in this Section Twenty it says: 'the person appointed to make this collection for the state shall, when the money is collected, receive for his compensation 2 per cent upon the amount.' "

"That's right, Brute."

"And 2 per cent of the tax reckons out at two thousand dollars?"

"Yes."

"Point is, Jonathan, with two thousand dollars I could square off all Hope's debt. And I could buy her another 'rino ram to replace Aaron, and a pair of seven-eighth or three-quarter bloods to boot."

Blair started to speak, but Christofferson said, "Point is, Jonathan, we saw that they listen to you down at Columbus Borough. If you'd see that Matt Gavagan and me got that job of collectin', we'd collect it for ya all right. Be somewhat justice for us to get the two thousand dollars after Schaacht keepin' Hope's flock runnin' from hollow to hollow up in the woods, losin' five pounds per head every fortnight."

Blair shook his head.

"You mean you won't?"

"No."

"Seems little enough to ask after the grief you caused us."

"That's the point, Brute. Some hold me for old Sam's passing. Others hold me for Hope's sheep having to run. Hope holds me for your finger. I'll not be held for any more grief."

"Grief?"

"Yes, Brute. You see, the collector is going to walk into that bank. But I don't know if he's going to walk out."

"You didn't worry about us before, Jonathan. Let us worry now."

Blair looked tired. He shook his head.

Christofferson stood up. His wrinkled forehead begged pardon for his defiant jaw, "All right, Jonathan. But nothin' says I can't go to Columbus and ask for myself."

"No. But I'll try to head you off."

In Washington and Philadelphia and Pittsburgh and perhaps even down at the Borough of Columbus the John Marshall decision against Maryland in the case of McCulloch vs. Maryland was coffee-house talk for lawyers between cases. Old John Marshall had hammered the last peg in to support the superiority of the Federal Government. The old man had spent a lifetime holding the Federation together.

But in Steubenville and Louisville and Coshocton and Cincinnati the great Chief Justice had just hammered a wedge into the middle of the Republic that split it apart at the Alleghenies.

In Mesopotamia Jonathan Blair saw the McCulloch vs. Maryland decision convert his people from land owners to squatters. That is, James Hawkins didn't know McCulloch from Maryland. But he did know it made Blair's bank tax illegal. He did know that the United States Bank was saved, and he was ruined . . . foreclosed.

He usually plowed an extra half-dozen furrows each spring, widening his field. This spring he plowed a half-dozen less.

"Put it this way, Blair. Why should I break new ground for the bank?"

Christian Kilgore usually grubbed out a few more stumps each spring as they rotted out. This year he plowed around them.

"I'll not bust my plow point, Blair, on stumps that will belong to the bank."

And Hussong had been breeding his Bedfords to Bedfords for years. Now he bred Bedfords to plain woods hogs. "They can take the trail better, Blair. And we'll be needin' stock that can travel."

The forest closed back in on the clearing at Mesopotamia. Second growth shoots filled in the clearings hungrily. When a man isn't clear who owns the land, the land lies idle.

Even Silver Pigeon noticed it when he came down out of Upper Sandusky.

"Men in the cabins, Blair? None in the fields."

Blair answered coldly, "What do you want, Pigeon?"

"Our people crowded in like whites. We got the white man's sickness. Kine pox. Takes a white man's medicine man. Pigeon wants one."

"I don't owe you anything else, Pigeon."

"True. The Pigeon asks only."

"It's not in the treaty, Pigeon."

"No. In The Book."

"What book?"

Pigeon grinned. "In white Father Gershom's Good Book."

"The Book was never anything to you."

"No. But it is your Book."

Blair had trouble enough. "You're on your own, Pigeon. Get your own doctor."

"I tried."

"Then why come to me?"

"It is the white man's sickness. We lost Tahwendah and Sootaie."

"How did they get it?" Blair was peevish. "Keep your people up where they belong!"

"I did. But you don't keep your whites down here."

Blair knew it was true. Settlers and trappers and traders trespassed the Indian reserve. Blair barked, "Throw them out!"

"You forget the treaty, Mr. Lawyer," Pigeon said with a bitter smile. "It says, 'If a white man crosses the Indian border he shall be unmolested, but Indians shall report him direct to the President of the United States.'" Pigeon shoved his face close to Blair. "How do I do this, Mr. Blair?"

Blair snapped, "Well, keep your men away from the whites!"

"It is not the men."

Blair looked up.

"The women. They want the white cheah-ha."

"Cheah-ha?"

"Babies."

Blair kicked a stump. "The doctors are all south, where it's worse. Way south."

"But you will get one."

"It would need money."

"The Pigeon will get the money. You will get the doctor." He added, "Father Gershom says so."

Emanuel Ault's thick legs slowed down as he saw the Indian talking to Blair. He approached nonetheless.

"Blair, I've got to start," he said.

"Start what?"

"Bolding brought word from Schaacht when he was up here. It'll go hard with the whole town if Schaacht doesn't see some signs of action against the borrowers. Hope's debt is the oldest. Logical place to start."

Blair was tired. Even the Pigeon could see it. He left. Blair just looked at Ault.

"I told Christofferson," Ault said. "He said see you. Said you knew how he might get some money. So? . . ."

Blair turned suddenly and hailed the Silver Pigeon who was already twenty rods north. The Indian turned. Blair yelled, "Tell Gershom to come down here to see me!"

"He will say 'what for?' "

"Tell him I want him to make a Christian," Blair looked at Ault. "Starting with nothing!" he added.

The Indian cupped his hands to his mouth. "And you will get the medicine doctor?"

"Send Gershom down!" Blair ordered.

Chapter 14: ST. GERSHOM

BEING THE two most misfit professions west of Pittsburgh and north of Chillicothe, the lawyer and the reverend should have been a comfort for each other in the year of 18 and 19. Instead the lawyer rasped, "It's your business, isn't it? If you can't make a Christian of Ault, how can you make Christians of Wyandots?"

"Because I don't have to undo the work of lawyers before I can start," the gaunt minister rumbled.

"Believe me, Gershom, if there were any recourse, I'd not beg like this. Will you do something with Ault, for God's sake?"

"For *God's* sake?"

"For mine."

"How exactly do you expect me to effect this instantaneous conversion, Mr. Blair?"

"Should I know *your* business, too?"

"I'm glad you put it on a business basis, Blair."

"Why? There's a fee?"

"A doctor for the Wyandots on the reserve. They prayed for a doctor. I told them prayers are answered."

"Gershom, I . . ."

"I know, you've got troubles. But I've got funerals."

"Contact your bishop."

Gershom's face blackened. Indeed, the bishop . . . the bishop who still thought the frontier was Pittsburgh, and never ventured west of it to see what Gershom had done.

The lawyer said, "You hold the bishop over us as a threat when you urge us to build a church building here; let the bishop demonstrate his power. Let him get a doctor for the Indians."

Gershom said, "Health and justice come high west of Pittsburgh. The bishop can afford neither. You get a doctor for my Wyandots."

Blair sighed. "Can't promise to deliver one."

The reverend's grin was grim. "Fair enough. I can't promise to deliver Ault."

The two men rose. The lawyer added, "And it's got to be quick, Reverend. A day or two."

A dry chuckle rattled the reverend's bony chest. "Please, I insist on a week."

"Maybe that'll do. You can stay here in my cabin. I'll fodder your mount. You take the bunk."

"I'll need accommodations for three Indians besides."

"What?"

"I will need Captain Michael and Stand-in-the-Water. The girl came because . . ."

"The girl?"

"Fawn. Silver Pigeon's sister. I need her because she can read. The other two can't."

Amos Exeter was outraged when Blair asked him if he could put the three Indians up in one of the back rooms of the tavern. But Blair whispered to him Gershom's mission in the settlement, and Exeter found room.

Blair was surprised to observe the forthright and daring manner in which the reverend began his work.

His presence in the settlement was welcome. There was the Culpepper babe to be baptized, a number of personal requests to The Maker which needed the reverend's special and official phraseology, and there were other clerical chores awaiting the reverend's saddlebag ministry.

But his long visit naturally brought the question, "Why?"

And Gershom did not tiptoe around the question. "Because," he always answered, "there is among you a certain one who has forgotten the last ten verses of Saint Matthew's great eighteenth chapter. I am here to save him."

Blair was amazed that the reverend so explicitly outlined his mission, leaving himself no face-saving retreat. But Gershom's great usefulness in the north was a brand of religion as direct as Slover Navarre's rifle. It was as productive as Slasher's double-bitted axe in a stand of hickory. It could be as bitter as Exeter's fresh-made whisky; and Gershom's relation to The Maker was obviously as direct as Blair's to Judge Pease. More important, his horse was fast enough and strong enough to stay abreast of sin in the Northwest.

Blair admitted to himself that Gershom's horse-borne religion, though it might not be for lawyers, did have enough power actually to spread relief over the faces of the settlers. Up here every man had to produce . . . including the preacher.

The purpose of Gershom's visit spread through the woods quickly. And it was definitely observable that grown men and women walked more like children, throwing off worry now that this grim parent had arrived.

It was natural for Emanuel Ault to hear about Gershom's expressed purpose. It was natural for him to notice how settlers looked at him with expectancy and anticipation. It was natural for him then to borrow a Bible from young Flannerty to look up privately the last ten verses of Matthew's eighteenth chapter.

And of course, having read them, he daily expected a visit from Gershom. He smiled. But to his own surprise he caught himself mentally framing the answers he would give to Gershom. "Now, look, Reverend, I see the parallel, but it's not quite that simple. Don't forget the *people* actually owned the Mesopotamia Hog & Trust. So I'm really only maintaining their own credit for them." The successor to Sam Hosmer found his answers so sound that he was even eager to deliver them to the Reverend Seth Gershom. He placed the benches in his house so that they would sit opposite each other when the encounter took place. He placed a slip of paper in the Bible at Matthew,

Chapter Eighteen, so that he could readily point out to the reverend a few inconsistencies in the economics. He was ready on Monday morning.

Monday came and went, and then Tuesday and Wednesday. But the reverend did not come.

On Thursday Ault cleaned his house some. He opened his Bible again to bolster his argument; and he was pleased to notice that he was right. "You see, Reverend, in the case of the master in this chapter, the ten thousand talents were owing to him and him alone. So he was free to act as he did. But the case here is different. It's public money, so to speak. What alternative do I have in the case of public money?"

It was when Ault's hound lifted his head to stare at him that Emanuel Ault caught himself talking aloud . . . to himself.

On Friday Ault saw the lank form of Seth Gershom approaching his house. Ault put some burned barley coffee on to boil. He got out two mugs. But the reverend veered off to the south toward the store.

On Saturday morning Ault studied the promissory notes of the people of Mesopotamia. But when he saw the long strides of Seth Gershom approaching he shoved the papers in his lock box. He opened the Bible and marked opposite the twenty-fourth verse for quick finding. "You see, Reverend Gershom, we're not talking about the same kind of money. Ten thousand talents figure out to about twenty million dollars. But all it would take Hope Christofferson to square up would be $1,800. Less, if you forgive the interest." Ault smiled in blank generosity, adding, "which I am quite willing to do."

But the Reverend Seth Gershom did not enter Ault's house. He veered off to the north.

On Saturday night Blair said, "The week's up, Reverend."

"I'll need two weeks, Blair."

"You even talked to him yet, Reverend?"

"No."

"Why not?"

Gershom was piqued. "Blair, I know my business, as you call it. See you keep *your* part of the bargain."

"Well, it's Saturday already, and you haven't even let him listen to you."

"Ault will listen to Ault. He'll only argue with Gershom."

"I don't see it, Reverend. But it's *your* job."

On Sunday Emanuel Ault attended the service in the blockhouse. Mesopotamia expected one of the public lashings at which the Reverend Seth Gershom was so expert. But there was none.

On Monday evening Ault fully expected a visit from Gershom. But Gershom didn't come. Ault had his case down to a fine point. Word for word he had studied the text, and word for word he could refute it.

But his rebuttal consumed much of his sleeping time. It seemed to Emanuel Ault that he heard noises in his house, below the loft. On Tuesday morning he was quite sure that he had heard them.

On Wednesday the village of Mesopotamia was alarmed at the arrival of Riddle and Colonel Armstrong.

"That's the sign it's going to start," Stikes said sadly.

"Yeah, looks like the reverend couldn't do us any good," Gavagan said.

And it was on Wednesday night that the lawyer said, "You're too late, Reverend. They'll start foreclosing now."

Gershom did not reply, and his long shapeless black-clothed figure kneeling at the bunk was now repugnant to Blair. "I said you can give up that prayin', Gershom. It's too late."

The kneeling figure remained motionless.

"You might as well go tomorrow," Blair said.

Gershom rose. His cavernous pock-marked face seemed composed. He said, "Blair, in the event they attempt a foreclosure against the Hope Emerson Christofferson lands and chattels this week, your part of it will be to examine the mortgage instrument."

"Examine it! Hell, Gershom, I can quote it to you."

"That would not interest me. Just examine it and see that it warrants any foreclosure action they may attempt."

"Warrants it? Of course it warrants it. I drew it up myself."

"Never mind that," Gershom said. "Just demand to see it if anything happens."

But strangely no action was taken by Riddle, though he followed Ault around constantly. No action was begun by Ault either.

On Sunday Mesopotamia was surprised at the arrangements the reverend had made in the blockhouse for the service. Though it was broad daylight, a candle burned on the puncheon platform at Gershom's feet.

The presence of Emanuel Ault in the front row of the blockhouse, when it was observed, started a hush of interest which smothered the chatter. The presence of Riddle on one side of Ault and Armstrong on the other quieted the place more.

Gershom stood erect, waiting for the room to come to that trigger-squeezing silence he required.

When the blockhouse was so quiet that the boys sitting on the rifle parapet stopped swinging their legs, the Reverend Gershom announced that he had come today to talk about money.

The reverend usually commenced with a loud pronouncement. But today he began in a low, modulated voice. He didn't have to talk loud. There was a compelling fierceness about the enormous face of Seth Gershom when he took the rostrum. Some watched him intently pondering how a man of such homeliness should become a minister. Some watched with admiration because such a face must surely be devoid of all vanity and must be a great strength in time of trouble. Children watched quietly because they sensed this must be the parent of their parents.

"And when the master had begun to reckon," Gershom began quietly, "one servant was brought before him who owed ten thousand talents."

Gershom's rumble increased slightly, "But forasmuch as he had naught to pay, his master commanded him to be sold, and his wife and children, and all that he had, and payment to be made."

Gershom's voice dropped. They leaned forward to catch his words, "The servant therefore fell down, and worshipped him, saying, 'Master, have patience with me and I will pay thee all.' "

Gershom dropped his voice still lower, "Then the master of that servant was moved with compassion and he . . ." Seth Gershom opened his great maw and he yelled, "WHAT DID HE DO? EMANUEL AULT!"

Ault was jolted. But he composed himself and sat silent.

"What did he do, Ault? You tell us the rest of the story!"

"I don't know it."

Gershom reached into his pocket and unfolded a paper. Quietly now he said, "I will help you remember the story, Emanuel. Come down front here and look at this document."

Ault walked slowly toward the minister. He looked at the document in Gershom's hands. He grabbed for it. Gershom withdrew it just out of his reach. He smiled, and his tone was gentle.

"Suppose this were the note for ten thousand talents, Ault, tell me what happened. Tell us the rest of the story . . . in the exact words."

"I don't know the story." Ault stared at the paper, which was the land and chattel mortgage of Hope Emerson Christofferson, somehow escaped from Ault's lock box. Gershom moved it slowly toward the candle which sat there.

"I tell you I don't know the story, Gershom!"

Gershom moved the paper closer to the candle.

"Don't, Reverend!"

"What is the rest of the story, Ault?"

"I don't know. I don't know!"

Gershom moved the note so close to the flame that one corner of it curled and turned brown.

"And forgave him the debt!" Ault yelled in panic, as he watched Gershom move the paper away from the flame. "But the same servant went out, and found one of his fellow servants which owed him a hundred pence." Ault breathed. "That's all I know." And Ault seemed truly surprised at himself that he had quoted that much.

Gershom moved the note closer to the candle. Ault gulped, and quickly gasped, "And he laid hands on him and took him by the throat, saying . . . saying . . . saying . . ."

Gershom moved the paper back toward the candle slowly.

"Stop. Stop! I'm trying to think! 'Saying pay me what thou owest. And his . . . his . . . the one that owed only about seventeen dollars . . . fell down at his feet and said, 'Have patience with me and I will pay all.' "

Gershom withdrew the paper from the candle.

Ault perspired. His face struggled to remember how the print looked on the page of The Book. "And he would not, but went and cast him into prison till he should pay the debt."

Ault struggled to remember the rest. Gershom moved the paper slowly toward the candle. The parish was puzzled to note that this simple act jerked Ault to his knees just as though Gershom had twisted his arm up behind his back. Ault's hands went to his head as if to ward off blows. But there were no blows, only the paper and the candle.

"I'm trying! Can't you see I'm trying! And then the bank . . . that is, the master came to the first servant and said, 'thou wicked . . . thou wicked . . . I forgave thee all that debt, should not thou also have compassion on thy fellow servant?' And the master was wroth . . .'"

"You left out something, Emanuel." Gershom moved the paper toward the candle.

"What? What?" Ault pounded his head. "What did I leave out?"

Gershom let the edge of the paper turn black and glow a little.

"I'm trying! Stop it!"

The glow broke into a small flame.

"And the master was wroth and delivered him to the tormentors till he should pay all that was due unto the master."

Gershom extinguished the flame on the paper.

Ault's head was down. "I'm thinking. I'm thinking. Wait! 'So shall my Heavenly Father do also unto you, if ye from your hearts forgive not every one his brother in their trespasses.' "

Ault sagged with relief.

Gershom stood staring at him. Without taking his eyes off Ault he said, "The congregation will kneel."

They did so.

Ault half-rose and reached for the paper. The minister moved the document toward the flame. "Kneel."

Ault dropped to his knees, head down.

At times Gershom found there was not time to pray to the Almighty for instructions. It was often necessary to issue instructions in His name, which could later be cleared with Him at leisure. This was such a moment. Gershom extended his great right claw over the parish, saying, "Be it understood in this community in the future, any man wishing to collect a debt of his brother by foreclosure shall first contact myself and explain the nature and amount of the claim. We will thus assist each other in living the teachings of Matthew. Should any man fail to do this, Saint Matthew shall cause the flames of the candle of justice to consume the notes of the creditor. The congregation will remain kneeling."

Gershom folded the document into his inside chest pocket and walked swiftly out of the blockhouse.

The congregation remained kneeling, puzzled; puzzled the more by the guttural Indian tones from outside, the slapping of leather on horse flesh and the sudden clatter of three horses leaving the village.

When the hoof beats faded in the distance, heads began to raise hesitantly. Only gradually did the spell of Seth Gershom lift.

Young Tim Flannerty walked out of the blockhouse beside Jonathan Blair. Blair looked in the direction of Gershom's retreat. Tim Flannerty said, "Mr. Blair, how would Saint Matthew know if somebody was going to foreclose somebody in this town, so he could get that candle out to . . . like Mr. Gershom said?"

Blair smiled. "If Saint Matthew slips up, Tim, Reverend Gershom has the makings in his pocket to handle it himself."

"You b'lieve Saint Matthew could do like Mr. Gershom says, Mr. Blair? I mean the flame burning and all that?"

"Ault seemed to believe it. Guess that's more important right now."

In the dimness of his cabin the lawyer exhaled and chuckled. "That rascal. The Book of Saint Gershom will be one to read."

He tossed his buckskin coat to the bunk, and he was halfway to the washstand when he sensed that he had not heard the coat hit the bunk.

It was in the hands of Fawn who was bending the leather between her hands. She smiled.

"Should soak. Too stiff."

"What the devil are you doing here?"

"Needs ash water," she smiled.

"What are you doing here?"

She moved to the hearth and scooped up some wood ashes into his small wash tub which had water in it. She then folded the buckskin into the tub, slowly, soaking it.

"Should come white."

The lawyer noticed as she worked that her own doeskin skirt was nearly white, and so pliant that it sculptured her. He noticed, too, that Fawn was the kind of Indian the land jobbers liked to send back east to demonstrate what fine neighbors the Indians made. He knew, too, as he watched her soft brown arms work, why it was that pack traders who went up into the Wyandot country were always so carefully supervised by Silver Pigeon, and given a hut next to his where they got more sleep than they really wanted, two Indians posted outside to see to it. Blair noticed the plaid-cloth blouse which she wore. He understood now why the two French pack traders northbound through Mesopotamia would not sell Faith Hawkins that blouse. He remembered, too, how on their way back down they had grinned at each other and told Faith they would have been better off to let her buy it after all.

"What are you doing here, Fawn?"

"Wait for the doctor. Take him north."

"The doctor?"

"Father Gershom says wait for the doctor. The lawyer will bring."

"Huh. He delivers promptly. But he collects promptly, too, huh?"

"What?"

"I say, they're mighty sure there will be a doctor."

"No. Pigeon sure. Father Gershom not sure. Big talk fight. Father Gershom say no doctor comes. Pigeon says yes. The Blair will get the doctor."

She smiled up at him.

"Fawn also says."

The Borough of Columbus was dead. The Governor had gone home to his farm, the legislature had gone home to theirs. Nothing was being bought, nothing sold. The lawyer had stabled his horse and walked inside The Swan. Jarvis Pike said, "Don't mind tellin' ya, Jonathan, we're sorry he licked ya."

Blair flared, "He?"

"Well don't curl up at *me*, Blair! You shoulda known . . . nobody fights Schaacht."

"Schaacht didn't lick us! It was John Marshall's Supreme Court made the decision."

"Sure," Pike said, wetting the end of a Conestoga cigar. "Sure."

"Well, wasn't it?"

"Sure."

"What could Schaacht have to say about that?"

"All right, the case before the Supreme Court was McCulloch vs. Maryland, wasn't it?"

"Yes."

"Not Maryland vs. McCulloch, but McCulloch vs. Maryland."

"All right. All right."

"Now Mr. McCulloch is who? He's cashier of the United States Bank branch in Maryland isn't he?"

Blair sat down, heavy.

Pike reached to the hearth for a coal for his cigar. He sucked fire through the Conestoga, but his eyes right-angled toward Blair. "Now I'm just a woods-born tavernkeep," he said. "But even I'd have sense enough, if I was in Schaacht's shoes, to get word to the mother bank at Philadelphia. I'd point out if Ohio can run the United States

Bank out of Ohio, every other state can run it out, too." Pike blew smoke. "Seems clear enough to me why Mr. McCulloch chooses to make a little test trial in front of old man Marshall just about now."

Blair didn't speak.

"Now you gonna tell me Schaacht didn't have anything to do with all this?" Pike asked.

"But that was just a little squabble over a matter of tax stamps to be pasted on bank bills. A very small tax. Pennies."

"Sure. That makes yours look all the more preposterous, don't it?"

Blair was silent.

"So preposterous in fact that Schaacht isn't even worryin' about your old tax any more. He knows the auditor won't dare to collect."

"How do you know?"

"I don't hear anything about the United States Bank packin' up or closin' down or hirin' wagons to haul itself back home."

And Blair knew it was true. There had been no sign that the bank was closing down. There were many signs that they were laughing at the tax law. It was uncollectable, unenforceable, and no threat at all.

"And y'see he's got it fixed now, Blair, so anything y'do, you're not just fightin' little old Schaacht any more, you're fightin' the whole bloomin' sixteen branches of the United States Bank, from Boston to Louisville. Schaacht plumb lifted the fight right out of your hands."

"How do you mean?"

Pike laughed, but he saw Blair was not joking. "Well, no offense meant, Blair, but isn't very likely, is it, that a little old woods lawyer like you is gonna take on the whole bloomin' general government?"

A brazen voice said, "I don't know as that 'ud be such an uneven match!"

The flat of a thick hand stung Blair's shoulders. It was Jackson Garth. It was great to see that wide-based stance of Garth, his broad, grinning face.

Garth and Bela Hult had agreed to meet here to talk to the Franklin Bank. Both their districts had been hit hard by Schaacht's foreclosures and they were seeking financial relief.

Schaacht's lash had marked Bela Hult's face. His Poland-China jowls now hung limp, more like the wattles of a turkey cock. He said, "Blair, how'd you happen to start this whole thing?"

It had been such a long road that Blair had to think back. "To save a flock of sheep," he finally said.

"For a client?"

"Not exactly a client."

In his mind Blair could see Hope Emerson Christofferson sitting on the porch of the store in Mesopotamia. He could see the sheep being led up onto the porch one at a time. He said, "And damn it, we've got the law passed, Bela, and we're going to make it work!"

"But we're findin' out a law isn't a law," Hult said, "until somebody tries to use it or break it. Until then it's just words. And the bank won't even have to break this law. It won't be enforced."

Blair was on his feet walking out of the tavern.

"Where you going, Blair?"

"To give them a chance to break it."

Blair found the auditor's office on the second floor of the long, shedlike building next to the statehouse. But he found himself looking at the back of a man seated at a desk, writing. Since he didn't recognize the man's back, he knocked. The seated one said, "Come in." And he continued to write, much in the manner Schaacht had with intruders. Blair walked in. When he came even with the desk the auditor rose to greet his caller. Blair looked at him full in the face.

"Bolding!"

"Yes, Jonathan." Bolding smiled and put his hands in his pants pockets, rocking back and forth from his toes to his heels, "I'm getting experience in all phases of government, you see. Won't you sit down?"

Blair stood.

After several moments of looking at each other Blair said, "I guess between you and me there's not much sense to waste time in talk. I've come to see if the auditor is preparing to collect the bank tax."

"Need I answer?"

"That's why I'm here."

"Blair, you know there's going to be no tax collected. You heard about the Marshall decision."

"Bolding, I don't know how you got to be auditor of this state. But you don't take your orders from John Marshall. You take 'em from the legislature. We ordered you to collect a tax of one hundred thousand dollars from the United States Bank if they haven't quit business by September 15. And I'm appointing myself a committee of one to see you do your duty."

"You don't think the Federal Government is going to stand by and let me collect that tax do you, Blair?"

"If the Federals stop you that's one thing. But just see it isn't *you* that stops you."

"Well, what do you want me to do, Mr. Blair?"

"I want to see some preparations going on here for collecting that the tax.' "

"Like what?"

"Like appointing a collector to collect the tax and instructing him in the provisions of Section five of the law."

"Blair, I confess the chances of collecting the tax are so farfetched that I haven't troubled myself with Section five of your bill."

Blair burned. "Section five says, 'the person appointed collector by the auditor shall enter the bank and demand immediate payment of the tax. Should he be refused, it becomes his duty to proceed by violence if necessary to levy upon all monies, goods or chattels present in the banking room. If he cannot find any monies present in the banking room it is hereby made his duty to go into each and every other room, vault, closet, chest, box or drawer to open and search and seize any monies, bank notes or specie or so much as will satisfy the tax.' "

Bolding chuckled. "Strong language."

"And explicit. You've got to collect the tax."

"In person?"

"No, you can hire a collector. We'll watch to see you appoint a good one."

"You'll be happy to know that I'm going through the motions, Blair. I've already appointed a collector."

"Who?"

"Very competent man. You'll be pleased."

"Who?"

"And very eager to have the job. His qualifications were excellent. And you'll be the first to agree that he needs the money."

"Who is it?"

"He asked me to keep it confidential."

"It's my bill, Bolding. Who is going to be collector?"

"Why do you want to know?"

"To give him some instructions. Naturally you won't take any but the minimum measures for collecting the tax."

"I may be understandably lax, Blair. But the man I have chosen is very acute. He has engaged his own assistant, and he has already taken the first measure for the success of the collection."

"What is that?"

"He made me promise to keep his identity secret." Bolding smiled. "Now I ask you, Blair, isn't that smarter than your course? If it is generally known who is to make the collection, would not the man be marked, not only by the bank and by the Federals, but by crowds of people who would follow him and watch for excitement? Perhaps, even bandits?"

Blair admitted, "You're right. The man uses good sense, thank goodness." He thought it over a moment, though. "But you could tell just me."

"He said especially not you."

"He knows me?"

"You find it hard to remember you're not just an upcounty lawyer any more, Blair. You and your Crowbar Law are no longer a secret in these woods."

"Why doesn't he want me to know who he is?"

"He knows that the friends who helped you put the law through will ask you who is to collect. He said it would be hard for you to refuse to tell."

"The man sounds good," Blair admitted. "But how come you would choose such a good man for the job?"

Bolding smiled. "Put it this way, Jonathan. The tax is not going to be collected anyhow. So I can afford to appoint a good man. Second, if I appointed an incompetent, your side would scream until I had to replace him, perhaps with a superior man."

"Uh-huh. But how come suddenly you keep your promise of secrecy to this man so scrupulously?"

Bolding smiled again, "Because, if by some chance or by some overt act, the tax *should* be collected . . ." Bolding shrugged his coat closed in front and buttoned it ". . . this is the man we'd most like to see jailed."

"Jailed! What says he'll be jailed?"

"Stealing a hundred thousand dollars is grand larceny in any man's court, isn't it, Jonathan?" Bolding smiled. "If you taught me correctly, and if I read John Marshall's decision correctly."

Before returning to Mesopotamia Blair rode south of Columbus a
way to knock on the door of a cabin belonging to a certain Saul Brooks.

Brooks turned out to be an abrupt blond youngish man with blue
eyes that asked your business as quickly as possible.

Blair asked him if he would come up to the Indian town at Upper
Sandusky to stop the pox there.

"No."

Blair said they would give him a square of land.

"I don't want land."

"What do you want? Maybe I have it or can get it."

"Money."

Blair's scorn must have shown through.

"Don't be too smug, Mister," the doctor defended. "You might want
money, too, if you'd been forced to practice medicine this far north
just because you didn't have a certificate from a medical college. That
takes money. I want it."

Blair was looking at a closed door. He shrugged. He had tried.

But as he rode into Mesopotamia he knew he hadn't tried hard
enough. In front of his cabin, The Pigeon waited with Gershom.

Chapter 15: THE MARKSMEN

IT WAS an effort for Blair to talk to Hope
nowadays. Because while she talked he was studying the curve of her
eyebrows and the composure in her eyes, the precise little groove which
ran from her nose to the center of her lip. He was thinking how
she would look in his cabin, and he was visualizing the giant
Christofferson moving around in the room in *her* cabin, the one with
the curtains and the rug and the mirror. At such times the lawyer's
gaze was larceny; and he felt somehow that Hope knew it, though she
made no sign.

"What did you say, Hope?"

"I said I know it's not your concern, Jonathan, but is Brute anyways mixed in your business about collecting the tax from the bank down in Chillicothe? He isn't, is he?"

"Why should you think so?" Blair was alert.

"No good reason, Jonathan. Except he's been up where those Federals are target practicing. Gave me notions. He says no, though."

"I'll go see what I make of it, Hope. Let you know."

Blair found Armstrong at the foot of the knoll where Stikes tested new rifles. But the strange sight was Armstrong standing beside Christofferson wholeheartedly explaining, "Now after you've taken the slack out of the trigger just hold that front sight on the target and squeeze the trigger. Don't hold your breath, but only squeeze while you breathe *out*."

They both looked up at Blair, questioning.

"Just seems like odd company, the two of you," Blair said.

Armstrong grinned. "Yeah. Looks that way. But Christofferson asked would we teach him a thing or two about shooting better. Why not? Better I get to know him, better chance I'll find where he's got those sheep hid."

Christofferson grinned. "You might as well give up, Major. You'll never find 'em."

The two men fired alternately. Both fired well. Armstrong slightly better.

Blair said, "What's all the special target practice for, Armstrong?"

Armstrong tossed his pistol to Mulvane to be cleaned and loaded.

"Just this, Blair. I've finally got a chance to get off this sheep hunt. You gave it to me. If an attempt is made by the State of Ohio to collect that tax of yours, I'm to stop it. We're going down to Chillicothe. And if we do this job right they tell me that I . . ." Armstrong looked down at the weathered major's leaves on his shoulder straps, "Well, don't worry, we will. There's nobody going to collect that tax."

Armstrong fired. Christofferson fired. Mulvane examined the target and called back that the major was on the bull, the sheep raiser was two fingers left.

Armstrong said, "Christofferson, you're turning your wrist as you squeeze off."

Blair asked, "Brute, you planning to be in Chillicothe anywhere near the middle of September?"

Christofferson studied Blair, then, "If I were . . . and if it was for what you're drivin' at, would I say so right here in front of the man assigned to stop me?"

"I suppose not. But I promised Hope you'd not be mixed in it."

"Jonathan, I been full-grown for quite a spell now."

The major laughed.

"Who did get the job then?" Blair asked.

"I don't know. I admit I tried. Thought you'd know."

"Did you ask who got it?"

"Said the man who took the job of collectin' the tax wanted it kept secret."

Blair studied Christofferson and his answer. So did Armstrong. Brute said, "Fire, Major."

Armstrong fired. Christofferson fired. Mulvane reported the major dead center. Christofferson a complete miss. Christofferson said, "I couldn't have missed."

The corporal insisted. Christofferson said, "Take your knife and dig out that top bullet. You'll find the major's ball right underneath mine."

Mulvane dug. He stood there with two battered bullets in his hand and amazement in his face.

Armstrong suddenly studied Christofferson who barely hid a grin under the labor of reloading. Armstrong reached over deliberately and shook the powder out of Brute's pistol and handed it back to him slowly. "That'll be all the practice you need for today, Christofferson," he said gravely.

Christofferson shrugged, belted his pistol and walked away. Armstrong said, "Wait!"

The big shepherd turned. Armstrong handed three half-dimes to Mulvane. "Put them up edgewise."

Keeping his eyes on Christofferson he gestured impatiently for three rifles. Mulvane stood back from the tree. The major had a way of swinging a rifle up so that it just seemed to fit right into the line which was already drawn from his eye to the target. He fired, kept his eye on the target, handed the rifle off, swung up the next one, fired, handed off the rifle, swung up the last one, fired. "Bring them back, Mulvane, and put them in Mr. Christofferson's hand."

Mulvane ran to the tree, wrenched out the three coins and brought them back. Into Christofferson's big palm he rolled three small coins, each encased in a blob of warm lead.

Christofferson clucked his tongue in admiration and handed them back.

"No. Keep them," Armstrong said, "as a reminder."

Christofferson started back toward the firing line as if to give a counter demonstration. But then he jogged the bullet-wrapped coins into his other hand, dropped them into his pocket. "I will, Major," he said.

It wasn't like Christofferson to consort with his enemies. He used to be less civilized and more honest than that. But there were other surprises about Christofferson. The next time Blair noticed it was when Christofferson came to his cabin accompanied by Slasher and Ault, who did the talking. Blair did not bother to cover his disdain for the groveling he witnessed. Ault handed him a piece of brown paper on which had been drawn a design for a railing, the kind of a railing you found in the Cincinnati courthouse or the Pennsylvania statehouse. The Mesopotamia banker said, "Jonathan, you think Schaacht would accept a thing like this as a gift from Mesopotamia?"

"Hah! Now we're going to crawl. That it?"

"We didn't come for your philosophy, Jonathan. Just your knowledge of Schaacht. You think he'd take it?"

"If you mean can you buy leniency with a fence? Answer is no."

Christofferson looked embarrassed. "That isn't exactly what we asked."

Blair looked at the sample of polished walnut Slasher brought along to show how it would be finished. The design on the paper was a handsome thing. It was a polished walnut railing to go across the inside of the bank to separate the customers from the desk where Blair had first met Bolding. It was even somewhat spectacular. There were four sections to the railing, one of which was a gate. There was a broad rail on the top, the kind men would lean on while asking permission to talk to Schaacht. There was a thinner rail a few inches from the floor. And in each of the four sections, demarked by posts, there was a round walnut medallion about twenty inches in diameter. They looked like huge walnut coins. Each of these big wooden disks were suspended in the centers of the sections by four chains which went out from the disks diagonally to hook into the corners of each section. And in the center of each walnut medallion was an eagle.

Around the circumference of each were the words, "Bank of the United States . . . Chillicothe."

"We can see you don't think much of the idea," Ault said, "but would he accept it for the bank?"

"He might do one of two things," Blair answered. "He might be delighted, and see in it a chance to make friends out of you. But more likely he'll throw you out as a bunch of snivelling bribers. But you might as well try your own way to save yourselves. He might like it. He's ordered a new bell for the front of the bank. A bigger one . . . louder."

Blair tossed the paper back to Ault. "Whose idea was this?"

"Christofferson's."

Christofferson colored under Blair's gaze.

"Brute!"

"The gift will be presented by Ault, though," Brute defended. "Gavagan agreed to haul it down."

When the lawyer next saw Hope, he said, "Don't worry about your husband being mixed in the collection of the bank tax. Don't worry at all."

When the thing was finished, it was a beautiful job. Slasher put it together so you couldn't find the joints and he polished it so the grain in the wood picked up lights in the sun and gleamed like glass under the rubbing. They loaded it on Gavagan's wagon, well-padded, and on the fifth of September they drove south.

On the seventh of September, Major Armstrong left a four-man garrison in Mesopotamia and pulled south with four men, mounted.

On the ninth of September Jonathan Blair was about leaving when Chief Silver Pigeon entered the town. Blair wore blue-cloth breeches and a leather short-coat. But he had in his saddle roll a pair of long grey stockings, a good pair of cloth pants, a white shirt and a white cravat. He had a saddle bag of papers. But before he had crossed the river to the south, the Silver Pigeon intercepted him and said, "Six Sundays we wait. No medicine doctor."

"I didn't promise you a doctor, Pigeon. I couldn't find one."

"I will go back and tell my women that. 'The lawyer tried, but he could not find one.' It will make them feel good about dying."

Blair dismounted. "How many?"

"Six more since I sent Fawn here. One fighter, two women, three cheata."

Blair stood thinking. Pigeon goaded. "Wait until it comes to your people, lawyer. Then you will find a doctor."

Blair flared. "Pigeon, you have brains! What is there to offer a doctor to come up and stay at the Indian towns? Why should he come?"

"It was you drove us up on the reserve. When we were spread out in the woods we did not get your pox."

"Past history won't help. Why should a doctor leave where he is and go up there?"

"We'll give him a square of land, a hundred chains on a side."

"That won't do it. Only thing I can think of would be money, and it would take a wagon load of it."

"Then get it, lawyer."

"Get it? Get it where?"

"From your great council."

"Pigeon, the government has paid all you have coming."

The Indian's voice hoarsened in hate, "Wait, lawyer. Wait for the day you can't help your own flesh. You will see."

Blair said, "There's only one way, Pigeon. Give me the smartest young brave you have. One that speaks good English. I will see if the government will send him to Transylvania in Kentucky to the lectures. Maybe that much I could do."

"How long . . . the lectures?"

"Three months to nine months."

"Three months! The pox is *now!* Three months they are dead!"

Blair stood in the glare of poison from the Indian's eyes. In frustration the Indian placed his hand on the lawyer's chest and shoved. It didn't satisfy. The Indian shoved again. And again, until Blair bounced off the hindquarters of his own startled mount.

Blair took it . . . in the name of his nation.

One hundred trail miles to the south of Mesopotamia lay sullen, regal, Chillicothe. It should have been called New Richmond, for here were the powerful, intelligent, self-righteous Virginians whose parlors had become the throne rooms of the Northwest. The Tiffins, Worthingtons, Nathaniel Massie, the Creightons, the Schaachts. As he rode south toward Chillicothe via Columbus, Blair reflected nervously how the Chillicothe Virginians still ran the West. In the beginning Chillicothe had been the center of settlement. But the Yankee Puritans had pushed in far enough to the north and west apparently to justify a center of government at Columbus. They had moved the capitol building to Columbus. But the governors and the major legislative leaders still lived in Chillicothe. The Chillicothe cabal made up the rules at home, then they rode up to Columbus to legalize in the capital what had already been decided at dinner tables in Chillicothe. It was perhaps justified since the population still hugged the Ohio River. But now the presence of the United States Bank in Chillicothe made a farce of Columbus as capital. And the governing that was done from the chair of director of the Bank of the United States turned the Western state-governors into lance corporals.

Unknown to the lawyer the fortress of Chillicothe was preparing for his arrival with flattering concern. In the Cross Keys Tavern, Justin Bolding sat down opposite Gideon Schaacht.

"Things are working according to schedule, Gideon. Major Armstrong has arrived. He brought four men with him."

But the young man's sitting motion was arrested. Through unmoving lips Schaacht rasped, "Don't sit down here." Bolding was surprised, he stood with his knees frozen at the half-bent position. "You forgetting you're auditor of this state?" Schaacht said. "Charged with collecting a hundred thousand dollars from my bank? How do you think you look at my table?"

"Everybody knows I worked for you."

"They will now. Sit down. It's done now."

"Just wanted to tell you the arrangements and tell you that I'm going to tell Armstrong who the collector is, so he can be watching for him."

"Don't tell him."

"Don't tell him?"

"That's right. He'll be more alert if he doesn't know. He'll watch everybody."

"You act like they might actually try to collect. How can they if I don't issue the warrant?"

"Blair may make you."

"Why do you worry about Blair so much?"

"Why don't you worry about him more?"

"Why should I, Gideon? Judge Byrd, everybody . . . says they can't collect that tax. Even their own governor. Blair's just bull-headed blind dumb."

Schaacht surged to within ten inches of Bolding's nose. He spaced his

hushed words in a bludgeoning monotone, "Have you got past wean-
ing and not learned yet that all the monuments in this world are built
in honor of men who are bull-headed . . . blind . . . dumb!"

With less assurance Bolding now clutched at the obvious, "But
we've got the Marshall decision against him and me in the auditor's
office, what can he do?"

"Don't know. But get back up to Columbus where the auditor is
supposed to be."

"How about the injunction from Judge Byrd prohibiting me from
collecting the tax?"

"The judge has it ready. Stop and see him. Take it with you."

Jonathan Blair walked into the office of the auditor of state in the
Borough of Columbus on the thirteenth of September.

"Bolding, I'm on my way down to Chillicothe just to see everything
goes all right. You issued the auditor's warrant to your collector yet?"

"There's not to be any collection, Jonathan," Bolding said smugly.

"No collection?"

"No."

"Who says?"

Bolding was obviously prepared. He had the two papers laid out
in front of him on the blotter of his desk. He merely revolved the
blotter, shoved it toward Blair, and said, "Injunction. Signed by Judge
Byrd, United States Circuit Court sitting in Chillicothe. Prohibits
me from proceeding to collect the tax."

Bolding leaned back and folded his arms. But he then immediately
unfolded them and leaned forward for he saw no alarm on the face of
Jonathan Blair.

Blair read slowly. He read this time as a dull man reads, tracing each
word with his short finger.

"Good Lord, Blair, you can see what it is! Just look at the signature!"

Blair continued to read slowly.

"It's a simple injunction, Blair!"

Blair held his place with his finger. "You're to be envied, Bolding,
that you find eighteen hundred and nineteen years of law . . . simple.
The development of a piece of paper which will stop party number
one from injuring party number two is a miraculous substitute for
bloodshed. Any piece of paper which achieves this . . . is *not* simple!"

After a quarter-hour of study Blair walked toward the door without a word, forcing Bolding to demand, "Well, what did you find?"

"That you should have studied with me another six months."

Bolding showed a moment of panic.

"You don't have an injunction there. You have the bank bill in chancery to the court and a subpoena to answer. That doesn't add up to injunction."

"How could a simple mistake like that be made?"

"I repeat it is not simple to stop a state from collecting a tax which has been passed into law."

"Then if it's not simple," Bolding suggested, "how come you know all about it?"

"Because this was a logical step for you to take and I therefore set out to find out precisely what kind of an instrument you would need to stop the tax."

"Where are you going?"

"To ask Judge Pease a question," Blair said.

"What question?"

"How to force you to issue the warrant to collect the tax."

The name of Judge Pease further unsettled the young auditor. And the calm purposefulness of Blair elevated the lawyer suddenly to a kind of equality in his mind with Schaacht, a view he had never before taken of the woods lawyer from Mesopotamia. It had been quite comforting a few moments ago to be on the side of Gideon Schaacht and John Marshall. But suddenly here was a man in a buckskin coat and in a big hurry, who said, "Bolding, you can be Schaacht's man or you can be auditor of this state. But you better not try to be both."

Blair moved for the door. Bolding said, "Wait!"

The young auditor sat down and wrote the warrant ordering collection of the tax from the United States Bank. He handed it to Blair. "You can take it down to Chillicothe with you. On the fifteenth of September give it to the man who hands you a half-dime embedded in a chunk of lead. He will look for you in the Cross Keys Tavern."

"How will he know I have the warrant?"

"I told him you would probably stop to check on me, and that if anything went wrong with the injunction I would send the warrant by you."

"And you will now rush to tell Schaacht that the tax will be collected?"

"No. I will rush to get a new injunction."

Blair took the warrant and left. He mounted directly and rode south toward Chillicothe. Bolding did the same.

At the Salt Creek crossing Blair pulled up short at a small fire which smoldered there. What startled him was the presence of three Indians. The center one was Silver Pigeon. Beside him was Squindatee and another one whom Blair did not know.

"What brings you down here, Pigeon?"

"To find a medicine doctor, of course."

"Did you find one?"

"Yes. In the circle town we find one."

"He will come?" Blair was surprised.

"Yes."

"How soon?"

"As soon as we show him money."

"Pigeon, I'm glad."

"I know. You are not a bad man, lawyer. We will let the doctor come to your town when your people get the sickness. You help pay."

Blair had no sufficient thanks for this unearned generosity.

"Do not thank us, lawyer. We know."

The Indian studied him a minute, then he said, "Your horse breathes fast. What chases you?"

"The young apprentice lawyer. The one that was with me. Remember?"

"The handsome one? The Bolding?"

"Yes. I need to get to Chillicothe ahead of him. He will stop the . . . you wouldn't understand, perhaps."

"He will stop the law you make? The tax?"

Blair was forever amazed at Silver Pigeon. He said, "Yes."

Pigeon sprang to his feet. "How long do you need to be ahead of him?"

The other two sprang up, compelled by Pigeon's act.

"How long do you need?" Pigeon repeated.

"A day and a night and a day."

"*Ina un du se seesta!*" commanded the Pigeon. Squindatee kicked the fire apart.

"Meshewa!"

The other Indian grabbed the horses, and the three Indians were suddenly mounted. The Pigeon said, "Lawyer, we will slow him down. You will have a day and a night and a day. Go!"

As Blair sat in the Cross Keys Tavern in Chillicothe a gnawing suspicion came upon him. Watching the customers in the tavern he saw none who would make a logical collector for a hundred-thousand-dollar tax. Stuttgart was there, probably handling a case before Judge Byrd's United States Circuit Court which was sitting. There were the usual well-dressed out-of-town men who came into the Cross Keys to fortify themselves for their interview at the United States Bank. If one watched closely, he would see these men leave the Cross Keys, and then he would see them come back an hour later, mad, disappointed or frightened.

Blair heard fragments of conversation in the tavern: "Why they call the damn thing a bank anyway" . . . "Say they haven't made a loan in six months" . . . "Own most of Cincinnati now. What they gonna do with it? Answer me that! So they own it, but what good will it do 'em?" . . . "Tomorrow's the day they're supposed to collect that tax. Hope they do" . . . "Aye, like to see 'em run the bastards plumb to hell."

In the midst of one overheard conversation, Blair had a strange experience. He heard his own name mentioned in connection with the tax, mentioned by a man Blair didn't know, and by a man who didn't know him. The man used the word "Blair" as though it meant a man who knew many things, a man to be counted on, a skillful man. The speaker who used the word "Blair" was better dressed than Blair. It was a strange experience for the lawyer.

But as he looked around the Cross Keys for a man whom Bolding might have appointed collector he saw no likely person. He held the sealed warrant in his hand, and he began to suspect that Bolding had played him a trick.

It would have been very clever of Bolding to appoint Blair himself, and to let Blair sit through the fifteenth of September with the warrant in his own pocket, never realizing that he was the one empowered to collect the tax. This would cover Bolding perfectly. He would have complied with the Crowbar Law. It would be Blair's own fault if the tax were not collected. It would be impossible for Blair to explain to the legislature or to the public why the tax was not collected.

Blair broke open the seal. The opening sentence leaped out at him: "The bearer is hereby commanded to proceed to the United States Branch Bank at Chillicothe on September 15th ult. to demand the tax of $100,000 from the cashier. Should the cashier fail to comply the bearer is commanded to *proceed by violence if necessary* to the vaults of——"

Blair's face burned. There was no individual named. Only "the bearer." Surely that must be Bolding's maneuver. Blair was completely unprepared for this. How do you collect one hundred thousand dollars out from under the nose of a career major who is hungry for a pair of silver eagles? Blair needed help. That's why he was so glad to see the big pair of shoulders that waded along above the heads of the crowd in the Cross Keys.

"Christofferson!"

Brute turned and came eagerly over to Blair's table. The big man sat down.

"Brute, I've got a problem." The lawyer slid the warrant over in front of the sheep man. Christofferson read it and grinned. His answer surprised Blair.

"I thought you'd never get here," he folded the warrant in his big hands.

"*You* thought *I'd* never get here?"

"Yes." Christofferson reached into his pocket. On the table he laid a blob of lead which enfolded a silver half-dime.

"You?"

"Me."

"But you were . . . with Armstrong up on the target range."

Chistofferson grinned. He pocketed the warrant. Blair asked, "Does Armstrong know you're the one?"

"Don't think so. Might."

"But I told Hope you'd not be in this."

"Blair, there's not much time. We need your help."

"But you were in with Ault on that railing that was made as a gift for the bank. I figured you're on the side of the bank."

"Blair, it's your time to listen. We've got things arranged so that . . ."

"Is Ault in on it?"

"No. He's gone home. You listen now. We are going to try to get the money out of the bank. But there's only two of us, Gavagan and me. We want you to do two things: first, you be with Schaacht at five o'clock tomorrow. Wherever he is, you be with him. And second, join us as soon as you can on the Scioto Road, north. If we are followed we will drop the money with you and let them chase us north in an empty wagon. The best place to hide the money for a while will be right here in Chillicothe. You bring it back here somewhere."

Blair nodded, speechless.

"We will come back for you, or we'll send somebody."

"Christofferson, one question. What are you doing this for?"

"For two thousand dollars."

"Then I guess you'll do a good job."

Chapter 16: "PROCEED BY VIOLENCE"

AT five o'clock on the fifteenth day of September, year of 18 and 19, J. Blair, lawyer, leaned against the long draught board in the tavern known as Cross Keys, town of Chillicothe, Territory North and West of The Ohio River.

He drew on his cigar with the extra deep pull that is only enjoyed by a throat numbed by drink. His face had the grin of cordiality that flushes out of a mug of sour-mash whisky. And he talked to his companion at the rail spontaneously, just as though his unguarded geniality were perfectly reciprocated by the tall sober army officer.

For the fifth time in as many minutes he offered a cigar to the major who refused again. The two had their backs to the bar. The major also declined drink. He studied the lawyer carefully.

A tall man wearing a white cravat and a white gold-threaded waistcoat rose from one of the tables and came over to confront the two. The tall one grinned and said, "Mr. Blair, you're giving a poor imitation of a man overindulging his cup." The tall one turned to the major, "Major, I don't know whether it's for your benefit or mine. But I know Mr. Blair didn't come all the way down to Chillicothe to drink whisky. I suggest when Mr. Blair drinks he drinks for a purpose, and I suggest you get on over to the bank and see if there's anything going on."

The major left.

The tall man took the major's place at the bar. The lawyer pulled out a cigar, "Have a cigar, Mr. Schaacht."

Schaacht declined. But Blair had the aggressive hospitality of the draught room. Schaacht accepted the weed with dawning amusement and studied the lawyer as he bit the end off between large even teeth.

"Maybe you *are* in your cups at that, Blair. I heard you used to drink a lot."

"You know a lot about me, eh, Mr. Schaacht?"

The man behind the bar handed forward a burning stick which Schaacht applied to his cigar, all the while studying Blair. Smoke came out of his mouth as he said, "I know enough to suspect you're sober as Judge Byrd right this minute."

Blair laughed genially and as he did so whisky from his tankard sloshed up and arched over onto the gold-threaded white waistcoat. Schaacht's face contracted and his hand flashed to his pocket kerchief which he used to brush off his waistcoat. His mouth clamped his cigar.

Blair whipped out his own handkerchief, "I'm sorry, sir. Let me fix it."

Schaacht brushed him aside. But Blair insisted. "I'll get that vest washed. I'll get you a drink."

Schaacht straightened up and watched the lawyer. The vexation on his face turned to amused assurance as he reappraised the lawyer. "You *have* had a few at that, Blair. It's all right. Leave it. Bernard! Another whisky for the lawyer . . . and myself."

The tankards were refilled and Schaacht clapped the lawyer on the back cordially.

"You and your boys have come down for the hundred thousand dollars, no doubt, Mr. Blair?" Schaacht threw his head back and laughed. "Let's have another round right away, Bernard, to toast Mr. Blair's coming for the hundred thousand!"

The big man's laugh was taken up in a ripple that washed along the length of the crowded bar.

Blair slapped his mug down on the bar and laughed with them. "I'll drink to that!" he grinned. "Where the hell is my hundred thousand dollars?"

The laugh surged off the end of the bar and around the room. Men looked up from tables and grinned. A few scowled at Blair in disappointment.

"How will you have it, sir?" Schaacht roared. "In twenties or tens or solid bullion?"

Blair grasped his chin in thought. "Well, if it's all the same to you, sir, I'll take it in quarters. I brought a wagon along to haul it in."

Schaacht laughed. Blair laughed. The long line of loungers laughed at the most fantastic proposal ever.

Brutus Christofferson stood at the new walnut rail in the bank. Riddle took the twenty dollar United States Bank note from him and counted into his palm a handful of silver and copper and gold. "We don't usually redeem such small notes in specie," he said irritably.

"I know," Christofferson said. "But I thought I better redeem this bill in coin before those critters collect that tax from you folks. They told me you might not be able to redeem after that."

Riddle sighed in strained tolerance at this quip which was already stale to his ears, "There'll be no tax collected from *this* bank."

"Well, just in case," Christofferson said.

"All right. There's your money."

"I'm not familiar with all these different kinds of coins. So I'll just go over to the bench there and count them careful."

"It's all there," Riddle turned to other business, marvelling at the stupidity of the woodsmen in this country.

Christofferson sat at the bench counting and recounting the coins as though he had never seen coins before.

Major Armstrong walked in. "Anything happen, Riddle?"

"No. Been quiet."

"Well, don't forget, Mulvane is right outside the door. You holler if anything looks foul."

Armstrong turned to Christofferson. "Cash in a note, Christofferson?"

"Yeah, thought I'd best cash it before they collect that tax."

Armstrong grinned at Riddle and shrugged. Then he said, "Brute, when you go back up to Mespo will you take a message back to my men?"

"Sure."

"When you leaving?"

"Tonight. Better write it out now."

Armstrong stood at the extreme left edge of the new walnut railing, writing a note.

Christofferson rose and walked to the extreme right edge of the railing. He rubbed his hand over the smooth walnut as if admiring Slasher's work, which in fact he was. Neither the major nor the cashier paid any attention as his big hands felt along the near edge of the railing. Nor did they notice when his fingernail found a joint in the apparently solid walnut railing. Christofferson's fingernail ran along a three-foot length of the walnut, and quietly lifted off a curved section, revealing a trough in the rail.

Armstrong finished the note, folded it and turned toward Christofferson. But the note fell from his hands. The major was looking at two black holes in the muzzles of two Stikes-built hand guns.

The major's hands were starting to rise in slow amazement.

"No, Major. Don't lift the hands. Put them in the pants pockets."

"You! You're the one?"

"Put yours in your pockets, too, Mr. Riddle," Christofferson said.

Christofferson held the pistols low, beneath the window level. Armstrong said, "Christofferson, I'll teach you to hang."

"You might, Major. But don't forget you also taught me to shoot."

Armstrong exhaled through his teeth, "Damnit yes. I even taught you to shoot."

"Major, move over to that railing and unhook the four chains that hold that big walnut disk with the bank crest on it."

Armstrong looked confused. But then he walked over and unhooked the four chains which extended out from the round medallion to the four corners of the first section of railing, which was the gift to the bank from Mesopotamia. It left him holding a large round medallion twenty inches in diameter from which extended four substantial chains with hooks on the ends. When it had been a part of the railing it had looked purely decorative. But now that he held it in his hands Armstrong noticed that it lost all decorative appearance and seemed like a tool of some kind.

Christofferson eyed both Riddle and Armstrong like a sheep dog as he laid one gun down on the railing long enough to extract the warrant from his pocket. He snapped it open with one hand and let it glide through the air to land at Riddle's feet.

"Don't move your feet, Riddle. Just bend over far enough to read that paper. You'll see it says to give me one hundred thousand dollars, and you'll see it's signed by your old friend Bolding.''

Riddle read it.

"This is preposterous. We have had an injunction issued forbidding this collection.''

"I don't know anything about that part. How are we going to do this? You going to hand it over? Or do we do like it says in the third paragraph?''

Riddle read the third paragraph:

> ". . . after demand and refusal of payment of aforesaid tax, if he cannot find in the banking room sufficient monies, the collector is hereby commanded to enter and search every closet, vault, chest, box, strong box, and to seize forcibly sufficient monies to satisfy the terms of this . . .''

"It's unbelievable!'' Riddle straightened up. "If you get it you'll have to seize it.''

Riddle moved three steps sideways toward the bell pull-rope in the hall that led to the back.

"Stand still! Where were you going, Mister?''

"To pull the bell rope,'' Riddle said.

"No! Stand still!''

"I always ring the bell at five and a quarter o'clock,'' Riddle said.

"But it should only ring once. You would ring an alarm.''

"All I want to do is . . .''

Armstrong barked, "At ease, Riddle! You're not dealing with a fool! He's a cute one. I know him. Stand still.''

Riddle said petulantly, "Then he should want the bell to ring on time as usual.''

Christofferson said, "The bell will ring.''

"It will ring?'' Riddle laughed. *"How* will it ring?''

Armstrong looked at the railing, studying if he could grab Christofferson when he tried to get over the railing to the bell pull-rope.

"No, Major,'' Brute said. "I will not try to ring it. But it will ring.''

Riddle laughed.

"By your clock,'' Brute said, "it needs two and a half minutes yet till ringing time. We will stand still for two and a half minutes and then the bell will ring.''

Christofferson knew it was a dangerous two and a half minutes. In two and a half minutes someone could come to the door of the bank. In two and a half minutes Armstrong could do a lot of thinking, and Christofferson knew it would be good thinking. So he said, "Major, I didn't plan you'd be here like this. And I don't want you to think for two and a half minutes because you might think of something I didn't think of. So I'll talk."

"It's all right, Christofferson. Keep quiet. We'll just wait it out."

"No. I'd rather tell you how I figure. I figure you're thinking I won't shoot because a shot would alarm your men. Then I'd not be able to get the money. And you're right about that part."

"Just keep quiet, Christofferson."

"But if I was just interested in the idea of Mr. Blair's tax I could shoot because this warrant says I can. But I got to confess I'm not too much carried off by Blair's tax on principle; I want the two thousand dollars that goes to the collector. It's not the principle, it's the money. So I'd likely not fire off a gun to alert your men. That would stop me gettin' my hands on the two thousand. I know you'll figure that far. But what you might not figure . . ."

"At ease, Christofferson! We're waiting, like you said! What more you want?"

"I know, but you might not figure this way . . . that if I get the two thousand I can get Hope some more sheep. But if I don't get it, and if I can get rid of you, I can bring her own sheep back down out of the woods."

"You aren't the kind, Christofferson, to shoot a man down for a few miserable sheep."

"I know it, Major. I don't feel like that kind of man either. I'm not sure myself if I would fire or if I wouldn't. But all I know is there's not much I wouldn't do to keep from facin' Hope to tell her you caught up with the sheep, and me havin' none to take their place for her. And truth is, you been gettin' kind of close to our hidin' place a couple times this summer."

"What's all this talk add up to?"

"Just wanted you to know, if you was to break away right now and make a grab for me or holler for one of your men, I don't know if I'd have the gump to squeeze off these triggers or not. Probably not. But I'm that far into this thing now, I wouldn't bet much on myself not to."

"Don't worry, I'll not chance it."

"Well, I know this fat one over here won't. But I figured you might . . . knowin' me as well as you do after all these months of chasin' me. I think if I was in your place I might chance it, knowing me like I do."

"Sounds too much like an invitation," Armstrong said dryly. "Besides, you still haven't got the money out of this building yet, nor out of the town."

"That's true. I think we got that figured, though."

"Doubt it. You probably know where my men are stationed. They can see the back and the front."

"That's true. You did an almighty good job of placin' them. We might not make it. But I hope we do."

"We?"

"Well, I don't want to go into that."

Armstrong looked at the clock.

"Minute to go yet," Brute said. "I hope you'll keep standin' there like that."

"Shut up, will you! I'm waiting!"

"Some day," Christofferson said after a while, "if this miserable money trouble clears up, you and I ought to have a drink like men, Major, instead of . . . like we are."

"Shut up, and do whatever you're going to do."

"Only half a minute more, Major."

Over in the Cross Keys Tavern Gideon Schaacht pulled his large ornate watch from a small pocket over his flat stomach. He opened the cover and said, "Well, Mr. Blair, I guess you won't be collecting the hundred thousand today. We close up in about half a minute."

Blair snapped limp fingers in sodden anguish. "Here I went and waishted the whole af'ernoon! Well, what time you open up 'morrow morning, Mr. Schaacht?"

The crowd laughed. But Schaacht didn't laugh. "Blair, you aren't the joking kind. I think I just better explain a few things to you. We've got an injunction against this ridiculous tax of yours."

"I know that. And you've got your boy in the auditor's office."

"That's right, Blair. Then why aren't you more worried?"

"I a-a-m worried, Schaacht. Wouldn' you worry if you jus' lost hunderd thousan' dollars?"

The crowd laughed.

"And we've ordered a new bell for the bank that can be heard all over town."

"I heard about that," Blair said.

"And I know what Christofferson is down here for."

"I suppose you do."

"And I also know you wouldn't be happy to have anything happen to him. Wouldn't make you exactly a hero up in your town. They like him. Especially his wife."

"That's right."

"So I'd just like to take you out and show you where Armstrong's men are posted. I want to show you what would happen to a man that tried to take a trunkful of money out of that bank."

"Just le's have one more, Misser Schaacht, 'fore we inspect the breas'-works. Bernard! Whisky for Misser Schaacht."

Schaacht scratched his chin.

In the United States Branch Bank in Chillicothe the clock on the wall suddenly cleared its throat like an old hen and three men snapped their heads to watch. The long ornate minute-hand backed up a quarter-inch and kicked a few times to scratch itself, then it jumped forward a half-inch to register a quarter beyond five o'clock.

Riddle said, "Hah! There it goes, see! Fifteen after five and your bell isn't going to . . ."

But the banker's jowl quivered and his scalp moved.

O-n-g-g-g-g-g!

The faint crack of a distant rifle drifted into the room seconds after the bell rang. Perhaps only the three men in this room plus one other knew how the bell was rung that day in Chillicothe. Christofferson did not have time to enjoy their amazement.

"Major, step over to the door and shove home that bolt!"

Armstrong tarried over the job, but he complied.

"Riddle, lead the way back into the vault! Hands stay in your pocket! Walk wide of that bell rope! Major, follow Riddle!"

In the vault room Christofferson said, "Open it, Riddle."

Riddle hesitated.

Armstrong said, "Riddle, I taught him to shoot. Open it. He can't get it out of the building anyhow."

Riddle unlocked the vault with a key. He swung back an iron door.

"Start counting, Mr. Riddle. I want the larger bills, so there won't be so much to tote. But I want it in United States Bank notes."

"We don't have a hundred thousand in only United States Bank notes."

"Then give me what you've got. Then go to the other kind. Mr. Blair said John Piatt notes are pretty good. And any eastern notes will be all right. And we'll take all the gold eagles you have. Commence."

Riddle counted money into a cloth bag.

Outside the bank building a wagon pulled up, driven by Matthew Gavagan. Gavagan dismounted. Mulvane said, "When are you men going back up to Mespo?"

"Be leavin' tonight, I guess."

"When you go back up, the sergeant wants you to take some mail and a message back up to the rest of the platoon."

"All right."

"What's on the wagon, Gavagan?"

"The smith had me to bring this new bell over for the bank. Guess they're gonna put it up tonight. He'll be along soon."

"Oh."

Inside the vault of the United States Branch Bank Brutus Christofferson said, "How much you got now, Mr. Riddle?"

"Depends on how you compute it."

"What do you mean?"

"Well, if you count the John Piatt notes as a discount of only 20 per cent, we've already got . . . let me see . . ."

"Let me heft the bag," Christofferson shouldered Riddle aside impatiently.

"It hefts like a hundred thousand. Pick it up now."

"I'll want a receipt, Christofferson."

"You'll get your receipt from the treasurer of the State of Ohio. Now carry it up those stairs to the second floor."

Riddle looked surprised. So did Armstrong.

"Riddle, you go first. Major, you're next."

As they climbed the stairs Brute said, "Don't get near that bell rope. I'm that far in this now that I'm a mite flustered. Any loud ringin' noise would like to set my fingers jumpin'."

At the top of the stairs the shepherd said, "Riddle, open the little door there to the bell. Reach outdoors and slide the bell in this way on the railing. Pull it inside the building."

Riddle moved slowly, exploring every opportunity he might have to set off an alarm. But Christofferson stood close to him.

"Good, Riddle. Now tip the bell easy on its side, and mind the clapper."

Riddle rotated the bell and Christofferson shoved a table under it with his foot.

"Now cram that bag of bullion and notes inside the bell. That's what I said! Inside the bell!"

Riddle complied and stood back smugly, because the arrangement was far from satisfactory. The money slid out of the smooth inner surface of the bell. But Hussong said, "Now Major, if Slasher's work is as good as usual, that walnut disk should just fit inside the lip of that bell. Fit it in there."

Armstrong looked at the walnut medallion and then at the cashier. Both of them looked at the disk as though seeing it for the first time.

"Go ahead, Major."

Tranced, Armstrong moved to the bell. He fitted the disk into the lip of the bell, and many things now fit together. The very bevel on the edge of the walnut medallion, which had appeared to be strictly decorative, fit the skew of the bell so that as Armstrong pressed it into place, air flushed out around it.

"Now if you'll just take those four chains, Riddle, and loop them up so they meet at the top of the bell, they should just hook together nice."

In amazement Riddle looped the chains up over the top of the bell and struggled to connect the hooks.

"It'll be a tight fit, Riddle. You'll have to force it."

Riddle complied and stepped back from the bell. Christofferson did not step closer, but he squinted sharply at the connection.

"Now, Mr. Riddle, that isn't a good fit you made there. That one hook doesn't look all the way in."

"That's as far as it'll go."

"You think it'll hold?"

"Looks like it would."

"Well, would you be satisfied to be suspended from it, hooked that way?"

Riddle shuddered and moved quickly to the bell. With the heel of his fleshy hand he pounded the hook. It snapped suddenly into place, giving the whole container a nice adjustment. The eagle was outer-

most on the walnut medallion, and the words "United States Bank
. . . Chillicothe" were carved in a circle around it.

Christofferson carefully laid one gun down within snatching distance. He drew a knife and sawed it through the bell pull rope
which he held fast under his foot. He sheathed the knife and pulled
the bell rope up through the hole in the floor, handing one end to
Armstrong.

"A cavalry knot please, Major, tied to the chain at the top of the
bell."

Armstrong complied and then Christofferson motioned him back.
The big man again carefully laid one pistol down no more than ten
inches from his hand. He grabbed the rope, wound it several times
around his sledge-sized forearm, placed his foot on the bell and pulled,
testing the knot. Satisfied, he snaked the rope out through the bell
door so that the end of it fell over the top of the bell support-bracket
and then down to the ground outside.

He watched the rope until he saw the slack suddenly go out of it.
Then he turned to the cashier, "Mr. Riddle, I want you to call out
two words, not real loud, just a turkey gobble above normal. Call out
'lower away.' But do it quietly just once to kind of practice. And
if you call out anything else, I reckon you know I'm scairt enough
now that the shakin' of my miserable arm is near squeezin' off this
hand gun without you excite me none."

"Lower away," the cashier said with an excess of caution.

"Pretty fair," Christofferson said. "But your fiddle strings are screwed
too tight. Make it deeper and relaxed like you talk to a man that's
trying to borrow money. Once more, quiet like."

Riddle promptly pulled his chin in against his jowls to deepen his
voice and to show obedience. "Lower away!"

"That's just nice, Mr. Riddle. Now put more wind in it."

"Lower away!" the cashier boomed.

Christofferson pressed his boot against the bell so it just cleared
the shelf. Instantly he resumed his guard stance, one hand gun-bear-
ing directly on the major's middle, the other on the cashier's. The
three watched the rope slide slowly over the bracket.

Outside the bank and below the bell, Matthew Gavagan payed the
rope out slowly through his hands, lowering the bell gently. The
slowness and apparent ease with which he handled the rope indicated
a light load. But ex-Corporal Mulvane, beside him, noticed the rope

left red marks on the heel of Gavagan's hand and on his forearm. He was about to remark, but Gavagan said, "Mulvane, just take this rope and pay it out easy while I back the wagon under it. Want to set the old bell right on the tail of the wagon so's it won't be too tough to unload. Thank ye."

Mulvane leaned his rifle against the wall of the bank and fed the rope out, though by misjudging the weight he let it slip a bit too much at first.

The sergeant came roaring across the road. "Mulvane!" He stormed up to the corporal boiling over at his cracked sun-baked lips in a steady stream. "Mulvane! How many times do I tell you that when you're on guard duty for me you keep that rifle in your hands. I don't care if they cut your head off, you keep that rifle in your hands until I relieve you. Understand?"

Gavagan took back the rope.

Mulvane said, "Hell, he only asked me to give him a . . ."

"Never mind what he only asked. If Jesus Christ or the major himself asks you . . . when I say 'guard under arms,' I mean 'guard under arms.' That means a gun, not a rope. You need somethin' done you call me. Understand?"

Mulvane grabbed up his rifle. The sergeant took the rope from Gavagan. "I'll do anything needs doin'. Just you keep that rifle in your hands like it was growed there."

The sergeant lowered the bell absently as he eyed his errant guard. Gavagan leaped up on the wagon and pulled out his knife. The bell jarred the wagon.

"Heavy damn bell," the sergeant observed.

"Yeah, them bells are heavier'n they look," Gavagan said.

Gavagan sliced the rope. He handed the cut end to the sergeant and said, "Now would ya just be tyin' that rope to the new bell there, Sergeant? I thank ye."

Gavagan jumped down from the wagon, slammed up the tailgate and drove home the bolts.

"Hurry up, Christofferson!" he yelled. "We're ready!" The sergeant looked a query. "With the new bell," Gavagan explained.

Keeping his eyes aloft Gavagan walked over behind ex-Corporal Mulvane. "Can I take a drink out of your canteen, Corporal? No, you hold your gun, like the sergeant says. I'll get it."

Still watching aloft, Gavagan untied the leather pouch on the back of Mulvane's shot belt. He took out the wooden bottle, drank, and let a little run off the lip of the bottle and under the frizzen and over the flash pan of Mulvane's rifle lock which was near the soldier's hip. He returned the bottle to the pouch, wiped his mouth and exhaled in loud appreciation. "Ah, nothing like water to dampen your stomach." Then louder, "Hurry up, Christofferson!"

Aloft on the second floor of the United States Branch Bank Christofferson said to the cashier, "Now once more, Mr. Riddle, call out, 'Hoist 'er up!' "

Christofferson looked down at his shaking hands which drew Riddle's attention to the same, and the cashier anxiously boomed out, "Hoist 'er up!"

The three watched the rope travel over the brace in the opposite direction now.

Christofferson waggled his two-hand guns herding the major and the cashier over to the far side of the room. "Lie down on your stomachs, your feet toward me."

They looked at the nervous face of Brute Christofferson and they complied quickly.

"I don't mind tellin' you both I'm a little conflustered at this point. Like you said, Major, this is the worst part right here. So I'm just sayin' the longer you lay there the better. I know you'll do what you have to do soon as you figure I'm gone. That's all right. But it'll be up to you to decide when I'm gone. Wouldn't hurry it none."

Christofferson belted one pistol and removed his boots with his free hand. Armstrong's head moved.

"No, I'm not gone yet!"

Armstrong's head elaborately hit the floor.

Christofferson walked out on the bell shelf just as the new bell clanked up against the bracket. He tossed his boots and his other pistol into Gavagan's wagon below. He stooped to get a good grip on the bell rope and he swung his body off the bell shelf. As the big man's hands burned down the rope his heavy body slammed against the side of the bank and twirled. The baffled sergeant below held onto the rope and was jerked forward, but recovered to watch the big man slide down toward him. But before he could make sense of it a large pair of wool feet smothered his face and shoved him to the ground.

Christofferson hit the ground. Gavagan leaped to the box of the wagon. Brute grabbed the tailgate and vaulted over. Gavagan cracked the silk over the horses . . . who plunged the rig west in a clatter of fright.

From his back on the ground the sergeant yelled, "Fire! For God's sake, fire!"

Mulvane squeezed off his trigger which delivered a sickening *phsst* to his ear and a wet glob of black powder to his eye.

Gavagan leaped back off the box to kneel low in the wagon bed where Christofferson was already on his belly.

At the corner of First and Water Roads a long black barrel stabbed out the second-floor window to flash in the setting sun. The horses surged in fright as a point blank explosion filled the street.

Gavagan caught the glint off another barrel which swung in a tracking arc from the first floor windows at First and Church. Gavagan hawed sharp to the right giving the rifle the narrowness of the tailgate. He heard the ripping of wood beside him and he raised up to explode the silk over the heads of the frenzied team before they could reload.

Then there was nothing but the plunging pandemonium of the wagon hammering north over the hard clay ruts and fossilized hoof marks of Church Street toward the Cross Keys Tavern.

Gideon Schaacht's mouth was still ajar listening for more rifle shots when he looked down to see an extremely sober Jonathan Blair opening a brass padlock in haste. He was about to speak, but the lawyer was gone. Schaacht moved swiftly to follow through the crowd which was already surging for the door, some already out.

Jonathan Blair forced his way out the door and then turned to slam the door shut against the crowd. By a steady push he was unable to close it against the human bodies which thrust out through it. So he suddenly opened it wide throwing them off balance and then he slammed it home and threw his shoulder against it long enough to slip the lock through the hasp and snap it shut.

The wagon did not stop, but it slowed up, the wild-eyed horses not knowing what to expect. Blair grabbed the gunnel between the front and rear wheels and sprang up onto the side. Christofferson rose up and hauled him in. Gavagan cracked the silk over the terrified team.

Chapter 17: TO SATISFY THIS WARRANT

THE WAGON rammed north through the woods. The right rear wheel flung a spoke far ahead of the team. Yet the team moved so fast that the off-mare's chest ran into it before it hit the ground.

Gavagan gave the mare no time to worry. He exploded the cracker over her ears and they hammered north; the wagon timber creaked, crosstree bolts screeched; they surged and lurched up the Columbus Road. Blair was thankful Stikes had built special axles for Gavagan's wagon.

Christofferson lay on his belly where Blair could see the dark red spot on his right trouser leg spread at the calf.

"Brute, you got to get those pants off and look at it! You're hit!"

"Not yet." Christofferson hammered the chain coupling loose at the top of the bell.

From his kneeling position at the lines Gavagan turned his head long enough to yell, "Christofferson, you're hit. Open up them pants and see to it!"

Blair crawled forward and grabbed Christofferson's short boots. But the knife edge of the big man's hand cracked down on Blair's wrist bashing it on the bed of the wagon.

"Not yet!" he yelled, and he counted out one hundred gold eagles from the tax money. Over the rushing wind he yelled, "Blair, I'm takin' a thousand of mine in gold coins. The other thousand in United States Bank notes. And I'm takin' it now. You want to count to see I'm only takin' two thousand?"

"The hell with that!" Blair yelled. "Open up those pants and look at that leg!"

"In a minute," Brute said. He placed half the hundred-dollar United States Bank notes in the bottom of one boot and half in the other. Then he pulled on the boots.

"Brute, you damn fool! We got to tend to that leg!" Blair rose up on his knees and grabbed hold of Brute's right boot.

"Not yet, I tell ya, Blair! I got somethin' to do yet!"

Blair nevertheless tugged at the boot. But the flat of Brute's big hand came down on the back of Blair's head and the lawyer's face picked up splinters on the wagon bed. Christofferson's left boot planted itself gently but firmly on Blair's back ribs, pinning the lawyer to the sideboards and the wagon bed. The jolting of the floorboards pounded his face as he turned it to watch Christofferson.

He saw the big shepherd take out his knife and slit the stitching between the inner and outer layer of leather in his short boots. He poured half the gold eagles between the two layers of leather in his right boot, dispersing them. The shepherd's face was grim, as a man who works against time. Every motion accomplished work. A few gold eagles spilled on the wagon bed. But time was worth more than ten dollars a second to Brute. He left the spilled coins. His face contorted in pain as he straightened his right leg and pulled his left leg in to where he could slit that boot top also. Without interrupting his work he yelled, "Blair, watch to the rear!" He slid the rifle over to Blair and he poured the rest of the gold coins between the layers of leather in his left boot-top, flattening them out. He rolled the top of each boot into a cuff, sealing them. He cut two leather whang strips off the sling of one of Gavagan's rifles and he wrapped one around the top of his left boot, pulled it very tight and tied it. He winced as he pulled his right leg in to do the same. Christofferson's fortune was safe in his boots.

He now braced himself in a sitting position with his hands flat on the wagon bed behind him. He closed his eyes and his lips drew back in pain. He sighed and said, "Now!"

Blair picked up the knife and slit Christofferson's pant leg. The un-coagulated redness that met his eyes was a sickening sight he hadn't seen since the Battle of the Thames in Canada with Harrison. The cloth stuck to the red mass. Blair clamped his jaw and went to work.

"Gavagan! Your shirt!"

With one hand on the lines Gavagan started to take off his shirt.

"No! Rip it!"

Gavagan stole a glance at the leg and he ripped the right side of his shirt off. Blair took Gavagan's canteen of whisky, he squeezed open Christofferson's jaws by pressure at the hinges, and he poured in enough whisky to drunken a bull. Blair folded half of Gavagan's shirt into a bunch and jammed it into the red cavity in Brute's leg. He jerked the other whang strip off Gavagan's rifle and bound the shirt in place so tight Christofferson winced.

The big man now opened his eyes for the first time and gaped at his own leg. His face drained white, his arms melted and the huge torso sagged to the wagon deck.

Gavagan tried to steer around the largest tree roots.

"The Brute can't stand blood," he yelled. "That's why he wanted to finish first."

Blair took off Brute's belt and strapped it around the enormous thigh, high up.

"Gavagan, there's a doctor at Circleville!"

"Yeah! I'll get him there, don't worry! But if I do that, I can't worry about the money, too. Take the money and get over the side, Blair. I'll come back for you. Get in the woods and hide!"

Blair looked around the bed of the wagon.

"Take it in the bag!" Gavagan yelled.

But a man walking around in the woods with a cloth bag full of money would be marked. Blair crawled up to the front of the wagon and pawed through the miscellany the wagoner kept there. He pulled out two old army blankets Gavagan had brought home from the war.

"Got a harness needle and twine?"

Gavagan opened the seat box and pulled out a roll of twine with a huge needle stuck in it. Blair jammed the twine in his pocket. He grabbed the blankets, Brute's powder-and-ball pouch and one of the hand guns, and the bag of money. He crawled to the side of the wagon. But Gavagan poked him with the butt of the whip and jerked his head to the rear. Blair looked and saw riders behind them.

Gavagan yelled, "Wait for the bend at Deer Creek! When I cross the creek, I'll have to slow up going up the far bank. Go over the tailgate! Good luck!"

At Deer Creek, Blair blessed Gavagan's skill. The wagoner splashed across the creek, and just as the wagon tilted to climb the other bank Gavagan sidled her through a stand of cattails. Jonathan Blair went out over the tailgate into the cattails and waded back downstream toward Chillicothe.

He was a good forty rods back downstream by the time the riders came plunging across the ford.

It was getting dark fast. Blair spread one of the blankets on the ground, and opened the bag. He was glad Brute had chosen bills of large denomination. Quickly he spread the hundred dollar and five hundred dollar bank notes out on the blanket. He laid the other blanket over the bank notes and curled in the edges of the blankets. With the harness twine he sewed up the edges in great loose stitches. Then he ran the harness needle through each pile of bills and through both layers of cloth, quilting Ohio's tax between a pair of U.S. Army blankets.

He sliced the cloth bag in half, rolled the coin and small bullion in the two halves and twisted the cloth. These two rolls of metal he sewed into opposite edges of the quilt. He curled the edges of the blankets under and sewed a hem in great six-inch stitches. He rolled the blanket into the smallest possible bundle and stood up to see how far he was from the road. It was too dark to see.

It was easy to tell, though, because from the road now came the sound of slow southbound horsehooves and a voice calling, "Halloo from the road!"

Blair was somewhat surprised then to hear a responding voice considerably closer to him, "Halloo from the field!"

Blair turned back deeper into the tree line and sought the creek again. He had just splashed back into the creek when his scalp crawled. Behind him in the creek came still a louder answer, "Halloo from the creek! You're gettin too far ahead of me, Mulvane! Patrol slower. Zigzag back and forth. Not so fast. Whatever bent them cattails can't be far from here."

Blair stood rooted like a water heron, with one foot lifted and his breath arrested.

From farther to the east now came a fourth call, "Halloo from the woods! Nothin' over here so far."

And much louder now from directly behind him, "Halloo the creek. Slow it down and guide on center. I heard some splashin'. Touch your flank man on both ends of your zigzag. If you fire, fire only to the south."

Slowly Blair lowered his right foot behind him onto the shoreline debris. When he touched shoreline driftwood he pressed down slowly, compacting the material underfoot, testing to see if it would crackle. It did not. He pressed his boot down to solid footing. He shifted his weight back onto his right foot and slowly raised his left boot out of the water. As it broke the surface it made a slight sound, "doip." He froze.

"Slow it down and guide on center!" The voice was close behind him.

Blair got his left foot on solid ground. He took a few steps away from the creek, compacting the swamp brush slowly under each foot before he shifted his weight forward.

"Halloo the creek! We got somethin' here. Take it slow, in toward the center."

Blair tried another step toward the road, but his boots sucked mud. Instantly the call, "Slower still!"

Blair sank slowly to the marshy ground, huddled. He knew now why Harrison had once boasted, "My Major Armstrong is the only officer who's developed a patrol tactic that can flush a Shawanee out of the Black Swamp." Armstrong had a reputation in early 1814 for his patrols. He had trained his men to patrol in a thin line through woods and marsh. Each man zigged to his right then zagged to his left, and on each leg of the zigzag he made contact with a man on his right and his left, each of whom was doing the same, so the line always remained straight, and Armstrong could control it from center. He trained his men to maintain contact in the dark and to fire only in one direction to prevent accidental casualties. He had successfully conducted such patrols even on a half-mile front.

The major had written paragraph thirty-two of Chapter Ten in the new Light Infantry tactical hand book. And he practiced what he preached this night. It was a thorough, searching, merciless comb. The teeth were riflemen. And suddenly Blair knew how it felt to be a rabbit or a fox or a Shawanee.

In the dark it would come. He wondered if the hunted target ever saw the muzzle-flash, or did the bullet travel faster than the flash? He had heard wounded men say you were hit before you heard the discharge, but it didn't start to hurt until you heard the shot. Then you knew who it was, and you got madder than you've ever been; but then you got madder still because you couldn't do anything about it. You felt that you were the only man in the world who had ever been shot.

Blair was mad already, and the shot wasn't even fired. He was mad at the calm, atrocious intention of the hunt; what they dared to take from some woman's son out here in the swamp . . . the ultimate larceny, robbing a man of the future, robbing him of even tomorrow. And this they did self-righteously.

"Slow it down! And remember, no talk, no parley. Just shoot. They're full of tricks. You saw!"

The voice was on the off-tack. But Blair heard the boots tramp back into the creek, then across it, then out on Blair's side. He supposed in daylight tomorrow the faces of strangers would look down at him. Perhaps some of them would be women. They'd think of sons they lost in the war. The men would be calm about it. Might go right over to the Cross Keys Tavern for a drink. Some one would lean on the bar at the exact same place where a live lawyer had leaned yesterday. "He stood right there . . . right exactly there," someone would say. "In the chest they got him."

The boots approached, pulling at the mud. Blair breathed in short breaths over stiffened jaws, not enough so his chest moved. He looked down so the whites of his eyes wouldn't show. He wanted to cover his white shirt-front more, but didn't dare move. Perhaps his bowed head would hide the white of his shirt. His spine was arched and it ached to be straightened, but he held.

The boots squelched toward him.

In the chest would be best. Not the stomach. Butchel had had it in the stomach at the battle of Thames, and it was the worst. But the chest could be bad, too, like Captain Smythe. But not as bad as the neck and lower face. If it could be the leg. There was extra flesh there. But the lawyer remembered Christofferson. The chest was best. The chest or the leg.

The boots stopped and the only sound was the drumming of Blair's pulse. He told himself it only *seemed* loud. It was not possible for others to hear a man's heart beat, surely.

A filmy, maddening soft insect walked up Blair's neck, walked out on the underside of his chin with disgusting softness. Blair thickened his jowls to deaden the repulsive tickle, but he did not move. The thing walked up over his lips. He longed to blow out air to blast it away. But he only closed his mouth, careful not to touch his teeth. From the effort of holding still he felt that his body was quivering. But he could not control this.

The air from his nostrils apparently angered the soft thing that crawled on him. It held on and climbed up beside his nose. He did not move.

From the opposite direction another pair of boots slushed through the marsh toward where the major stood stock-still.

"That you, Major?"

"Yes, Mulvane. Anything?"

"Nothing."

"All right. Continue."

Both pairs of boots turned outward from Blair and receded in op-posite directions.

Ever so slowly the patrol passed by Blair to the south. Blair held still. He gauged their distance by their calls, "Halloo from the creek." And fainter, "Halloo from the field!" "Halloo from the road!"

Not again in a hundred times would Armstrong's combination of zigs and zags leave a gap just big enough to miss a man in its fine-tooth comb.

When the voices became faint enough Blair rose slowly. He moved quickly out of the trees into the brush, out of the brush into the field, from the field to the road, then across the road into another field, and then south.

Jonathan Blair decided that there was only one safe place for him-self and for one hundred thousand dollars of bank money this night.

When the lawyer arrived at the stable in back of the Cross Keys Tavern in Chillicothe, he picked up one of the curry brushes. He had it poised over his trouser leg when the stable boy said, "I'll do that, sir. Which hoss?"

"The bay with the black boots."

He took the brush from Blair and went to work on the bay. Blair reached for another brush, and when the boy worked the off-flank, Blair surreptitiously applied the brush to his own trousers which were full of burrs and seeds and sticks. He swabbed off his own boots and saddle-soaped them.

"Which saddle, sir?"

"That Kentucky cavalry one. But wait till I blanket him."

"Blanket him, sir?"

"Yeah, chills."

"Chills? Oh, no, sir. He's in fine shape. I noticed when I fed them."

"This is an odd one," Blair said.

"All right. Then let me get you a better blanket."

"No!" Blair calmed his voice. "Sorry. But, has to be just so. I'll handle it."

Blair threw the heavy quilted blankets over the bay. The coins weighted it down nicely over the flanks. He hooked the blanket over the bay's chest with a huge horse blanket pin. "All right. The saddle now."

Blair led his horse right up Church Street to Water Street to Paint Street. There were lanterns walking around in the streets and a lot of men. The talk was excited. Blair guided away from groups and lanterns. He headed down Paint Street. He thought he knew the safest place in the West for the bank's money and for himself right now. But he knew that if he had guessed wrong, he would be mortally wrong. There'd be no half way.

He listened closely to the snatches of talk, learning as much as he could.

"Went right down . . . I mean *right* down the center of this street, they did. Right in front of . . . I mean *right* in front of everybody . . . broad daylight . . . I mean broad."

"You never see anything like it. Just as calm they was . . . like . . ."

"Didn't get much start, though."

"No, but they had that rig rollin' like Harrison's cavalry."

"Notice the team he had? Big. That was no dray team."

"Personally, myself, I hope they're to Circleville already."

And when the lawyer was five houses down Paint Street he had the strange sensation again of hearing his own name come out of the dark, as though it were public property. "Don't know if he was with 'em or not, but you can hand it to that Blair. Nobody thought it would come off."

When he came to the tall narrow brick house, Blair tied his lines to the hitching rail in front. Double knot. He walked up the short walk to the tall forbidding doors of the Schaacht residence. He pulled the big ring knocker. Instantly, as though the house were waiting for news, one of the big doors swung inward.

She stood there with her hand on the latch, her mouth ajar in surprise. The silence elongated into awkwardness until she laughed.

"Well, the last person I expected to . . . you have more nerve than sense, Mr. Blair. Come in."

Blair took off his broad brim felt and was over the threshold.

"Take Mr. Blair's mount to the barn, Kentuck," she said to the white-stockinged Negro.

"No," Blair said. "Thanks, no. He'll be fine right there."

Blair held the door open with his foot. "There is one thing, though.

Could . . . ah . . . I notice you have a post lamp near the hitch rail. Could you light it?"

Her head cocked in query.

"Your horse is afraid of the dark?"

Blair twirled his wide-brimmed hat and grinned, "Well . . . ah . . . that way I could see my horse from the house. Little worried about him."

Kentuck started out the door. "Ah'll take 'n put him in the barn. I see y'all got him blanketed. Ah'll jest . . ."

Kentuck looked up in surprise. The fingers which now gripped his upper arm seemed too strong for the polite smile on the lawyer's face. "Thank you, Kentuck. But I'd rather just have him where he is."

Blair followed her toward the dining room. Perfume whispered back to him. And he marveled that he was so recently in a rotting swamp inhaling its stinking exhalations and his own fear-soaked sweat. He observed the flexuous folds of her swirling skirt and breathed deep.

"Where've you been," she said over her shoulder, "during the excitement?"

"I guess I missed it."

She gestured to the long table sparkling with twelve place settings. "You can see you disrupted things at this house. They're all out helping the search."

"Don't blame me. It's the *auditor's* job to see to the collection of taxes."

She measured him a moment and motioned him to a place at the end of the table. She walked to the other end and sat in Schaacht's place. Between them stretched a long table, ten empty chairs, and a hundred thousand dollars.

Conversation was cryptic. Blair was glad that he had a stomach, a throat and a face to eat with; but Miss Schaacht said, "You seem to have a light appetite, Mr. Blair."

"Yeah," Blair said. "Well, you don't get much exercise in my line of work."

Kentuck came in bringing food and news which he received from people who came periodically to the front door. "Miss Virginia, a man jes came say they got one of the two of them holed up in the Scioto marshes north of town."

"One of *two,* Kentuck? I thought there were *three.*"

She looked at Blair.

And again much later Kentuck returned to announce, "Major Armstrong called in his men from all around these counties. He's gon 'ave fifty sojers by mornin' combin' the whole place an' on up to C'lumbus."

At that Blair stood up. "Could we finish the wine in the music room, Miss Schaacht?"

"Why?"

"Uh . . . like to hear you play. Don't see many pianofortes in this country you know."

She smiled.

"*You* can listen to music *tonight?*"

"Why not?"

Blair immediately chose the couch from which he could see out the front window, his reason for wanting to be in the music room.

His bay stood patiently by the post lamp. While Virginia Schaacht settled to the piano, Blair reclined a little so that he could look between her arms and her lap out through the window to the hitch rail. To change his glance from the keyboard to his horse was only a matter of focus.

Virginia Schaacht played in a fortissimo which set the room to throbbing. There was an oceanic sweep to her music which caused a man to think of his accomplishments. With her music for background, suddenly they seemed good. It firmed a man in his purpose. If there was music like this when men faced their great trials, a man would give a better account of himself. But there never was, unless you carried your own inside.

She looked over her shoulder at him. She was very perceptive, and she saw what the music was doing for him. So she changed.

The light, tinkly thing she played next put the laugh to everything, and she knew it. But he had caught a moment.

"Kentuck reported there was some activity up at the bank," she said. "Would you take me up there?"

Blair considered this a moment. "Don't think it would be safe for you," he said.

"For me?" she asked with crinkled dimples. "Or for you?"

He said. "We will go."

Blair untied his bay.

"It's close enough I'd planned to walk," she said.

"I'll just lead him along with us."

"You won't need him. And I thought maybe you'd walk me back afterwards."

"I will. But I'll just walk him along with us to warm him up a bit. Worried about him some."

There were many lanterns at the bank. Men swarmed around the outside of it, and inside it, and up onto the bell shelf on the second story. A sparse ring of Armstrong's men stood at port arms around the bank, keeping out unauthorized people.

Blair listened to the remarks in the crowd of watchers. "They think maybe the money never went out of the bank. Think the gee might have hid it inside and made as if he took it. Come back for it later."

". . . think they can find something one of them dropped or something. They say a hundred thousand would close down the bank."

". . . waste of time. Riddle says he knows the money was in the bell."

"But he don't know if the bell ever hit the wagon."

"The sergeant already said it did."

"But Schaacht don't believe it."

A possessive bystander, self-appointed guide to the historic scene, came up to Blair. "That's the new bell there. Here's where the old bell hit the ground."

"I see," Blair said.

"Then they went up Paint and down Water and up Church. They say they picked up that lawyer, Blair, at the Cross Keys."

"Oh," Blair strove for brevity.

Virginia Schaacht started to speak. Blair gripped her arm.

"They're lookin' here at the bank. The money maybe never left here. They say that Blair's a canny one. Might have stirred up a ruckus, figurin' to come back later when everything's good and cater-wampussed."

"Uh-huh."

Virginia Schaacht said, "Maybe you could save them a lot of looking, Jonathan."

"Me?"

Disappointed in the lack of reaction, the excitement-monger left to inform others.

Through the crowd now strode two men, one Blair recognized. The short, heavy one wore a colonel's uniform. The taller one wore a weathered major's leaf and chagrin. The short one was saying, "I didn't expect to give my personal attention to a one-platoon assignment, Major. Have you got it guarded against a second surprise?"

"Yes, sir."

"What strength do you have in pursuit now?"

"About fifty men, sir."

"What report from the patrol in the swamp on the one that got away?"

"None, sir. But we've got him bottled in. As soon as daylight breaks, sir, we'll ——"

"Daylight, hell, Major! Get up there and flush him out tonight!"

"Yes, sir." Armstrong saluted and reached for his horse with the callous grip of a man trying to hold together a career. The major's horse-holder stepped out of the way as the major wheeled in the crowd. But the humiliation was not over.

"Armstrong!"

"Yes, sir."

"Not you personally, you fool! *Send* somebody. You stay here at the center of things and command this unit . . . if you know what command means."

"Yes, sir." The major dismounted heavily. The difference between the rank of major and lieutenant colonel was usually just a six-bit chip of silver, but for Armstrong now it would be a hundred thousand dollars worth. For the benefit of the colonel he barked officiously, "Sergeant! Mount a patrol for the swamp!"

"And report hourly!" added the colonel.

This last indignity perhaps would not have seared the major's soul so raw if he had observed that it was in turn for the benefit of Gideon Schaacht who now loomed out of the dark at the colonel's elbow.

"Got it yet, Colonel?"

"Gideon, we've dispatched a patrol of . . ."

"Spare me your dispatching and your patrolling, Colonel. My report will simply say you got the money or you did not get the money!"

In the dark Virginia Schaacht looked up at the lawyer. "Your law will break a lot of men, Mr. Blair."

"My law will *make* a lot of men, Miss Schaacht."

Schaacht saw Blair. He parted the crowd and approached. "Blair!"

But abruptly he turned and yelled, "Colonel! Don't waste any more time looking around here. It won't be near here if Blair's here."

A few in the crowd looked at Blair when they heard his name and then their heads went together and they stared at him. Schaacht said, "Blair, you've got nerve standing here. Your boys are in trouble."

"You forget, Schaacht, they have a warrant. They're legal. You're not."

Virginia Schaacht said, "Where's Justin, Father?"

"He's over at Judge Byrd's getting a new injunction. And late he is about it." Schaacht turned to Blair. "You want it legal. All right, Mister, you better warn your boys just how legal we can get."

"How legal is that?"

"Shootin' legal. Over the signature of Judge Byrd."

"I'll worry about that," Blair said. "Meanwhile you might want to warn *yours*. Namely . . . the auditor better decide which side he's on because if he leaves me a shilling's worth of excuse I'll sue him for dereliction of duty to the state. That won't be hard if he's not in Columbus to receive the tax money. Amount of the damages will be one hundred thousand dollars." Blair turned to Virginia Schaacht. "He'll be an old man when he gets out."

Her sophistication slipped enough for Blair to see her swallow.

The helpful chatterer turned up again at Blair's elbow.

"Pardon me, sir. I found this gold eagle right here on the ground 'side your horse. It your'n?"

Blair looked at the coin in the dirty palm. He sidled close to his bay in the dark and ran one hand along the bottom edge of the blanket.

"I say, I found this coin there in the . . ."

"No." Blair said. "Not mine. Keep it."

"But it must be your'n."

"No."

Virginia Schaacht took a close interest in this.

"Well, I'll keep it then," the man said. "But right by your horse I found it."

Gideon Schaacht's attention was drawn to the business.

Virginia Schaacht leaned up against the bay. Blair put his foot in the stirrup. The chatterer bent to the ground. "Here's another. *Must* be your'n, Mister."

"No."

"Look in your pocket and see."

"All right. They probably *are* mine," Blair said, reaching for the coins.

Schaacht stepped closer. "Now wait a minute, Blair! Just what do you mean '*probably*' yours?" He turned to the chatterer, "Where'd you find those?"

"Right here on the ground," the man said, anxious to have something made of it.

Schaacht snatched the coins from Blair, examined them. "Hah! Colonel! Come here!"

The colonel broke through the crowd.

"Look at these! Tell your men there may be a trail of gold coins leadin' us right to 'em."

The colonel acted on this suggestion with flattering alacrity. He looked at Blair. "Sir, let me borrow your mount! I want to round up a few of my men and follow this up."

"Sorry, Colonel. I need it."

"You can contact my Major Armstrong," the colonel said. "Tell him I said to loan you one of our horses. Can't you see I'm losing time?"

The colonel grabbed the bay's bridle. Instantly Blair's knuckles hammered the corded inside of the officer's wrist, springing open the grip. The colonel held his wrist, shocked.

Virginia Schaacht stepped forward. Her hand was in the pocket of her habit which she held out away from her body so that all could see her finger sticking out through the bottom of the patch pocket. "Gentlemen, I'm afraid this is wasted motion. I seem to be the one with a hole in the pocket. I had a few eagles in it when I left the house. They seem to be gone." She turned to the finder. "Please keep one as a reward."

Blair studied the woman closely. It was impossible for him to tell if Virginia Schaacht had had two gold coins with her or not. It was impossible for him to tell anything about Virginia Schaacht except that the high curve of her cheek promised a kind of nobility, and the agile corners of her mouth denied it.

Blair backed his bay out of the crowd. "I trust, Miss Schaacht, you'll find sufficient escort home."

Blair rode to the stable at the Cross Keys. The stable boy reached for the lines. "No thanks," Blair said. "He's in bad shape. I'll sleep here with him tonight. You got any tonic?"

Chapter 18: THE CARRIER

FROM THE talk in the stable of the Cross Keys Blair heard how the search spread out from Chillicothe. Each patrol was armed with thirteen rounds of ammunition per man and a copy of the new injunction. This second injunction, issued after the collection of the tax, prohibited the collectors from delivering the money into the treasury of the state of Ohio, and commanded them to return it to the custody of the United States Bank.

Patrols combed east and west and south from Chillicothe, but Armstrong himself led the one up the road north to Columbus and its attendant trails and traces along the Scioto River.

Blair learned that in Columbus troops surrounded the state office building to prevent transfer of the funds from the warranted collector to the treasurer of state, or to the auditor, though the auditor was not expected to coopcrate in receiving the funds.

Excitement in Chillicothe itself dwindled some. Troops were no longer wasted guarding the bank. There were few people in the street on the nineteenth of September, year of 18 and 19. But even those few saw nothing alarming in the lonesome sight of the now familiar buckskin-clad lawyer, leading his blanketed horse north out of Chillicothe. The ferryman said, "Horse is no better, sir?"

"None."

"You tried leeching?"

"Yeah."

"You try sulfur fumes?"

"Yeah."

"Try feedin' 'im a pound of ground Peruvian bark?"

"No. Is that good?"

"Fixed up the land clerk's York State Pacer."

"I better try it."

"You want me to put you back ashore then?"

"No. Cross over. I'll try to get some at Circleville. Peruvian bark you say?"

As Blair rode along the trail north, slowly, he did not examine the

281

blanket, nor feel it. In fact he conducted himself exactly as though he were being watched, which is exactly the feeling he had. Occasionally he slapped the back of his neck, as though at a fly, using the pretext to look behind him suddenly. But he saw nothing.

As he rode, Blair pondered how to transfer the funds from himself to the treasurer. He believed that he would be able to ride through Columbus right out in the open, with no question. He had had time to improve the quilting job on the blanket. But he knew that any man carrying anything at all, even a blanket, into or toward the treasurer's office would be stopped and searched, and the new injunction would be served upon him.

He knew, too, with Armstrong hungering and thirsting for a lieutenant colonel's leaf, any man resisting the injunction would be summarily shot.

Armstrong was at that ticklish point in an army career where a brilliant war record was beginning to fade and the momentum from a number of swift promotions had run down. A little shove would still push him over the next rank. But a little more delay would mire him in permanent inertia. So Armstrong rode his men hard.

And therein lay more of his trouble. His sheer competence with line troops intimidated and discomfitted the regimental commander. Thus Armstrong was uncomfortable to have around the headquarters mess room, but invaluable to have in charge of troops in the field. So while the two new majors lounged at the colonel's elbow in Cincinnati as adjutant and quartermaster, Armstrong was dispatched to the field on a sheep hunt and a bank-guard detail.

Not the least of Armstrong's abilities as an officer was precision enforcement of his own orders. He was careful how he phrased them; then he enforced to the letter. And Blair could imagine what kind of orders had been issued this week.

Blair also knew that the one hundred thousand dollars could not be squeezed into small space. Nor could it be deposited in another bank and a bank check issued to the treasurer of state, because no alert banker would accept this money.

No man would be permitted to walk into that treasurer's office carrying any more than a pair of gloves.

As Blair churned this over in his mind, he came to a conclusion. There was only one possible carrier for the hundred thousand dollars . . . Armstrong himself, or one of his men.

And as he rode along, in thought Blair sought some way to get Armstrong himself to carry the money into the treasurer.

"Hey, lawyer!"

Blair yanked his hand gun out of his belt and hied the bay around. But the soldier behind him sat his horse quietly, his rifle slung harmlessly across his back, a grin on his face.

"Put it down, lawyer." The soldier spurred gently and his horse eased onto the road, approaching Blair. "We aren't going to grab you. Just follow you. The major figures you know where it is."

Blair did not know the soldier well, but he recognized him as the one called O'Fallon; he'd been up on the sheep-hunt detail at Mesopotamia, an eager young soldier with a career to make.

O'Fallon's hand signal was executed with the unnatural perfection of the manual-trained recruit. But it brought two more riders out of the woods promptly to fall in beside Blair.

"Just be prepared, you got company with you for the next however-long-it-takes. You'll never be lonesome."

They rode north toward Circleville.

"I can't go very fast, O'Fallon. Sick horse."

"Still? Well, no hurry. Just go where you're going."

They rode in silence for the most part. Blair was wondering if it were possible somehow to use these soldiers to get the money into the treasurer's office. Periodically he wondered if perhaps they already knew where the money was.

When they rode into Scippo Creek, Chief Cornstalk's old Shawanee Village, Blair saw ahead a strangely familiar figure sitting quietly on a dappled draft horse. As they closed the distance Blair knew it was Joe Hussong.

Hussong heeled his heavy-shouldered horse in alongside Blair, displacing one of the soldiers.

"'Lo, Jonathan. I was down tradin' for some packin' salt. I'll ride back with ya."

This was strange. Hussong would ordinarilly have hollered out some inquiry about the tax collection. Unless he had heard. And Fitchburg was boiling salt this year right in Hosmer Village. Hussong looked at each of the soldiers, then reined his horse closer to Blair. "Jonathan . . . uh . . . you got any gear or anything to be picked up anywheres? I got Daisy here. Good broad rump in case you got legal books or any duffle from the legislature session needs carryin' home."

Blair looked at the three soldiers and then he reached his right hand down to pat the blanket.

"Thanks, Joe. But nothing except what's with me right now."

As they crossed a neck of the Pickaway Plains, O'Fallon became alert because another rider now fell in alongside, the same way Hussong had. Startling to Blair, too, it was William Tyng. Tyng said, " 'Lo, Joe. 'Lo, Jonathan. I was down seein' if the new wool mill would pay in eastern money for rolled wool fleeces. No luck. They're buyin', but not payin' in eastern money. I'll ride back with ya."

The six men attracted some attention riding through Circleville. People came out of the cabins and pointed to the civilians in the group. One bold youngster yelled to O'Fallon, "They the ones that took it? They the robbers?"

The word "robbers" jerked Blair's head around to look at the boy. But he was not a malicious kid. He was obviously repeating a word he had heard. Could they be referring to a legitimate tax levy this way?

But he was in for another surprise. Just a little north of the last house in Circleville, Denaro fell in with the column.

"Hallo, men! I was down talking to the vino man. But already he got too much grape. No business. We ride back together, eh?"

Blair looked back at Denaro. The Italian face was naive simplicity. The forehead wrinkled in constant worry, the eyebrows arched high in a perpetual question mark at the hardships and terrors of life. But denying this artless face, Blair distinctly saw one olive-colored eyelid lower unmistakably. And suddenly Blair realized a wonderful new dimension in Antonio Denaro.

Blair looked to see if O'Fallon had also seen it. He hadn't. But he had seen enough to recognize that all these men were from Mesopotamia, and all armed. It was common enough for a farmer from the north counties to go casually armed, even to his own fields. But these firearms were all charged and the flash pans covered, ready.

O'Fallon dropped back from the now sizable group of riders, signalling his two soldiers with him. They put their heads together briefly, and then suddenly two of the soldiers stretched their horses out into long, flat, ground-covering gates toward Columbus.

The Mesopotamians looked at each other. And in the same incredible manner, as the party proceeded north, they picked up at various trail crossings Amos Exeter, Asa Buttrick, Aaron Fitchburg.

Their explanations of their business here brought a grin to Blair's face. Their presence brought a great warmth in his chest. He said to Tyng, "Great that you happened to be down this way. Good to have your company."

"Good for us to have yours, Jonathan. You done a thing or two for us all right . . . for the whole country."

When O'Fallon was blocked from view by several riders, Hussong came alongside close. He reached out and felt of the blankets on Blair's horse. He grabbed a fistful of blanket and felt the stiff crinkle inside. He pursed his lips in understanding. "It should be warm enough for him."

Blair said, "How are the sheep up home?"

"Good."

"And the shepherds?"

"Bad. One of 'em at least."

"Oh?

"Yeah. Couldn't find the doctor at Circleville. They came straight on through."

"And Matt?"

"Arrested. But he got the word to us about you."

Hussong dropped back.

They were at the halfway tavern between Circleville and Columbus. No reinforcement had arrived for O'Fallon. Blair decided to stop for the night, for he still had no solution for transferring the funds from himself to the treasurer. And the entrance of this crowd into Columbus would draw attention.

They fed themselves and the animals at the tavern, but they did not spend the night in it. Blair did not want to be caught inside any kind of enclosure.

They moved well off to the east of the road and camped in the woods. Hussong built a long narrow fire.

"Three of us will sleep on one side of it, well back from it. Three of us on the other," he said to Blair as they spancelled the horses. "Anybody passing near or through us will be silhouetted against the fire from both sides. O'Fallon can sleep where he wants."

"Hussong," Blair said, "did you see anybody behind us on the way here?"

"Nobody but O'Fallon. Why?"

"Ever feel like you're being watched, and don't know who?"

"Yeah. You feel that way now?"

"Yeah. All day."

"Well, sure. The soldiers."

"I suppose so. All the same, Hussong, you better take the blanket on your side of the fire. You and Tyng lie on it."

"We will, don't worry. And we'll stake it into the ground."

The Mesopotamians set up a guard. However, this proved unnecessary. O'Fallon left a mark out on the road which guided in the reinforcements which Armstrong sent down to him. His original two men, plus two more. The troops set up a one-man rotating guard. So the civilians abandoned their system.

The ground was cold. But in addition to this Blair felt watched, even as he lay between Buttrick and Fitchburg. Buttrick's large, soft body found the ground hard. But when he did finally get to sleep, he slept loudly. Fitchburg was an older man. His tawny old muscles were cold, and he moved around a lot. Between them Blair also lay awake long after even Fitchburg slept.

The sounds of the woods seemed more numerous and louder than they should. But then Blair reasoned that he was considerably south of Mesopotamia. The insects and animals might have a longer summer.

The lawyer dozed off, but he was more frequently wakened by two owls, calling and answering. They seemed to grow louder or closer together. But sounds are more piercing at night. Blair dozed.

Suddenly, though, he was awake. Not just conscious, but bolt upright. And not from any noise, but from the lack of it, as when the rain stops abruptly.

Then suddenly from behind him there was a thumping, unguarded running, as something plunged through the dry interlaced underbrush. Blair whirled around to his rear. The other two were up, suddenly facing away from the fire.

Throughout the camp now Blair heard men grabbing for rifles. A few locks clicked back to full cock.

"Halt!"

The civilians and the soldiers were staring into the dark to the west.

"Halt!"

There was more than one running person or animal.

"Halt!"

But it was a foolish command. What would you fire at?

But two did.

"Hold that fire! You can't see anything!" It was Mulvane's voice.

Suddenly, though, from the east, Hussong's voice. "It's this side! Hey!"

Then you could just see a flitter of a silhouette dash through the center. It flayed through the fire, dragging a stick. The fire flared up, lighting the center and effectively dropping a curtain of black around the outside of the bivouac.

"Hey! The blanket!"

Blair's stomach turned over. He ran across the fire toward Hussong. But Hussong was gone, crashing east through the woods. So was the blanket.

Two of the men fired east.

"Hold them damned guns! You can't see nothin'."

The blanket was gone. Tyng held up the palms of both hands to Blair in an anguish of helpless apology.

"I don't know. I don't *know*, Blair! We sat up to see what was the ruckus to the west. There was a tug. It was gone to the east."

In a frenzy of atonement Tyng grabbed his gun. "We'll get it, Blair! We'll get the blanket!" He plunged east into the black. Buttrick went huffing to the east also.

Blair looked at O'Fallon, who said, "Blair! Is that blanket gone!"

Open-mouthed and in blank amazement, Blair asked, "And just what does that blanket mean to you, O'Fallon?"

"A hundred thousand dollars and promotion to sergeant!" O'Fallon said.

"You mean you were going to let me ride it right into the hands of . . ."

"Seemed like the safest way with a man like you, Blair."

"But it looks like Hussong outfoxed us both, O'Fallon."

Denaro said, "No, Blair! Not Hussong."

"Who then?"

Denaro shrugged.

The lawyer walked to his horse. Quickly he untied the spancel rope. O'Fallon had followed him. Blair said, "One thing, O'Fallon. If you knew, how come Armstrong sent only you two men?"

"When I sent for reserves I didn't know for sure about the blanket."

"Oh, what convinced you?"

O'Fallon pointed to Blair's bay. "I noticed your horse wasn't bad enough off to need the blanket at night."

Fitchburg had come up beside Blair. "Shall we chase off after 'em with Hussong?"

"No. No point in it."

O'Fallon said, "What do you mean, no point, Blair?"

But the lawyer was mounted and pushing west through the brush toward the road.

"Halt!"

But O'Fallon's bewilderment gave Blair plenty of start. On the main road, he headed north.

Daybreak brought him to Columbus. But he skirted Columbus wide and rode north toward Mesopotamia.

It was the midmorning of the twenty-second of September that J. Blair walked into the cabin of Hope Christofferson. She noticed two things strange about him. The horse he tied outside was not his own. And by looking at him she could judge that his own was spent out somewhere south of here.

Second, he had a red-splotched rag around his right arm, just above the muscle, and the sleeve of his buckskin coat was ripped. And this did not go with the Jonathan Blair she knew.

Hope Christofferson had seen a share of blood in her day. She had been the one to bandage Joe Hussong's father's eye during the Rontondee raid in '11. She was there when Hosmer's daughter miscarried. They brought Jim Hawkins to her place after he axed his foot. Hope's own cabin was right now hung with washed white rags stained with various shades of pink. And the one in her hands at the moment was stained dark brown with spots of bright vermilion. But the redness on Blair's arm stopped her for a moment. However, she looked at the closed door to her other room, then at Blair.

"I'll get to yours next," she said. "A husband comes first."

He grinned. Hope had a clear-cut, comfortable code that did her choosing for her. Blair knew some judges who could learn from her.

She was gone into the other room. And then she was back, surprised that he was still standing.

"I didn't come for that," he said. "Want to talk to Brute."

"Not now," she said, and then seeing that he was not hurting, she charged, "And you said he'd not be mixed in this!"

"Hope, I didn't know."

"You knew."

"Hope, some day he'll tell you. Right now I've got to ask him a question about the money. It's gone."

"He's weak from losing blood. Can't you be satisfied yet?"

"Hope, it's a hundred thousand dollars."

"That's more money than makes sense. But it's not worth riskin' Brute's strength for . . . he's got that little."

"But Hope, Brute could tell me whether . . . I mean, it could be that Hussong and the others saw a way to get the money for themselves. It would pay a lot of mortgages." But he could see talk would make no difference. He brushed by Hope and grabbed the leather door-pull to the bedroom. But the splinter in her voice held him.

"Jonathan, I never laid old man Hosmer to your door. But Brute . . . I would."

Blair let go the door.

He rode over to the Hussong place. He didn't go in the cabin but rode up into the wooded section. He found what he was afraid he would find, a fresh dug hole in the ground, with dirt piled up.

He rode back down to the shed. Tim Flannerty was feeding Hussong's hogs. Blair said, "Tim, is Joe Hussong around?"

"No, Mister Blair, that's why I'm tendin' hogs for him."

"What's the hole up back for?"

"The hole?"

Blair watched the lad's face closely. "The hole in the ground."

"Oh, that? That's fer buryin'. Mister Joe says a natural dyin' hog's got to be buried direct he dies to keep it from spreadin'. He lost three last week. Keeps a hole dug, ready."

Blair had no choice but to believe the lad. He heeled his borrowed stallion north by west, up the old Harrison War Road toward Upper Sandusky and the Indian towns.

Chapter 19: RECEIVED THIS DATE

THOSE WHO knew where to point could point to the skeletons of careers and of men in the Northwest who had underestimated the Silver Pigeon.

J. Blair had made many mistakes in the Northwest, but this one he never made.

Four men sat at the table of the Reverend Seth Gershom. Blair ate hungrily, Gershom nervously. Rontondee ate with his hands. Silver Pigeon did likewise, and Blair paid attention to this. He knew that The Pigeon liked to eat with a knife and fork. The fact that The Pigeon tonight ate with his hands might be only for the benefit of Rontondee, leader of the unreconciled Wyandots in Upper Sandusky. Rontondee would love to go among the disgruntled faction and mimic Silver Pigeon eating with a fork.

But Blair thought the fact that Pigeon ate tonight with his hands was more for his own benefit. Pigeon kept two distinct faces, the civilized and the savage. With one face he fought the eighteen United States with its own civilized tools, the bad dollar, the treaty, the contract. If these failed he was apt to fight with the Indian tools, and when he soberly put his mind to the Indian ways he had forgotten more savagery than Rontondee could even imagine when sweating drunk.

Pigeon's eating by hand served notice on Blair that he was dealing with the *Indian* Chief on *Indian* terms tonight.

The Pigeon said, kindly enough, "What brings you, lawyer?"

"As sub-agent I'm to make a report on conditions."

"This means . . . how many of us? What health? How do we behave our people?"

"Yes."

"I can help you quick. How many? Nine hundred eighty-three. How do we behave? Very fine. Health? Gratitude to our own efforts, the health will soon be good."

"The pox is mending?"

"Yes. We have the doctor. He puts the sick ones in four cabins. Keeps the well ones away. This doctor is good. He takes money. But he is still good."

"Much money?" Blair asked.

"Much." Pigeon looked across at Blair. "But nothing is too much for a good medicine man."

Blair dropped the money question.

"And *your* money, lawyer? Did you get it from the bank? We held your man for you."

"I guess everything went all right."

"Good. I am glad you got whatever you wanted." Pigeon gnawed a wing clean. "Sometime you will show The Pigeon how to count some of the bills, please? Tell how much is the different colors and pictures on the money. Which is good? Which is bad?"

"Why do you want to know?" But Blair wished he hadn't asked. Fawn, standing behind The Pigeon, nodded her head, negative.

Pigeon threw his bones on the trencher. "You come to make the report, lawyer. But where is the feather for writing?"

Blair gulped a drink of water. Then he pointed to the preacher. "Figured I could borrow some from Reverend Gershom."

The meal proceeded with only the cracking of bones and the scraping of fork tines on trenchers until The Pigeon pushed back his bench.

"Get your paper and writing feather, lawyer, and I will take you around to the huts tonight to see our people."

Blair studied the dark eyes a moment, then lifted his gaze two fingers above Pigeon's head. Behind the chief a gentle chin moved slowly from side to side. Blair searched her eyes. Pigeon whirled to look behind him. But Fawn was quick. She swiped at a sluggish September fly as if it were the cause of her nodding.

"Well, lawyer, are you ready?"

Blair thought Rontondee rose from the table with too much eagerness.

Blair studied Gershom. Gershom buried his beak, and perhaps his conscience, in his mug of coffee. At least Blair thought he saw relief slacken the minister's lank frame when he answered, "I guess I won't go with you tonight, Pigeon. I'm tired."

Rontondee stiffened and looked at The Pigeon disappointed. But The Pigeon was gracious. "Yah, I should have think. I will send

Squindatee take care your pony. You have many friends here, Blair. Squindatee and Mudeater are arguing still which feeds the lawyer's pony. I chose Squindatee. So maybe you will go by the Mudeater's hut tomorrow to make him feel proud, too."

Pigeon started to leave, but . . . "Here he is now."

Mudeater, a short skinny Indian, burst into the hut, walked to Blair holding out his cupped hands which contained a belt of wampum, and chattering in Wyandot. Blair only understood that it was a gift from sixteen remaining Wyandots of the Turtle clan, Mudeater's group. Pigeon strolled over and took the belt from Blair's hands. He pointed to the figures on the wampum belt. "In your language, lawyer, this belt would say, 'gratitude to white man who brings land, blankets, hoes, axes and——' " The Pigeon's dark face turned darker with hurt and anger. But he recovered and smiled casually. "And they also think you brought the new medicine man. Well, it is all right for them to think you did it."

For two days Blair walked around the Indian town which was crowded with gangs of dogs, squaws who looked as old and brown as the leaves, shrunken old braves who looked as old as the trees from which the leaves fell, and naked black-haired, broad-footed children who seemed as numerous as the leaves.

Blair slept in the loft of Gershom's cabin. He made a convincing display of writing a report. But at the end of the second day The Pigeon came up beside him and said, "To make the letter to your great white war chief you will perhaps go over the many acres of the reserve to see some improvements we make away from the town. Tomorrow Rontondee and I take you to see the dam we make."

"You seem to get along better with Rontondee lately, Pigeon. At least, these two days."

"For some things Rontondee is good. He has not been turned womanlike by the Gershom. Do you want to go tomorrow?"

"I guess not tomorrow, Pigeon."

On the second night, when Gershom got up from the table to close the shed door, Fawn was cleaning off the table. She kept her eyes on the trenchers and equipment, but her husky voice said, "The lawyer should stay in large groups of Indians, not alone. Or go home."

"What do you mean?"

"My brother can not only read wampum belts and some white man's writing, lawyer. He can read better still the face."

"What does he read on my face, Fawn?"

But Gershom returned and Fawn carried the trenchers to a clay pot of steaming water.

On the third day he talked to the young doctor from Circleville. They had given him the best hut, next to Gershom's and Pigeon's. Blair was pleasantly surprised at the candor. "No, I'm not certificated. But I've reached *legal practitioner*. My preceptor was Drake, Cincinnati. But I'm as good as all *licensed physicians,* and better than a few of the *society members*."

"Why did you come up here?"

"I want money to get to Transylvania to attend the lectures."

"What kind of money they pay you in?"

"Is that some business of yours, sir?"

"I'm Indian sub-agent. Supposed to see to things."

"Oh. Well, the pay is to be in U.S. Bank notes, which is more than I can say for Circleville."

"They pay you a lot, I suppose?"

But The Pigeon came up then. Conversation ended.

In Gershom's cabin that night Blair said, "I notice The Pigeon was at one of your services, Gershom. You convert him?"

"No."

"Then why does he come?"

"When The Pigeon makes a contract, he keeps it. His attendance is part of a bargain. His presence brings some of the roughnecks in."

"And what is your part of the bargain?"

Gershom leaned forward as if to begin a long explanation. Then he said, "Have some more whisky, Jonathan." And he left.

Late in the same evening, Blair went to sleep in the loft. He was only beginning to realize what had been drained out of him in the last week. He lay on the loft trying to figure where The Pigeon might hide a blanket full of money in this town. He wondered if it were coincidence that Pigeon had been down near Chillicothe just before the tax collection.

Vaguely he heard Rontondee enter below and tell Reverend Gershom in English that he was wanted to pray for the sick Jonathan Pointer. Later still he heard Mudeater come in and talk to Fawn in Wyandot. She was wanted for something. Blair knew Fawn helped in the bringing of babies, and she was the only one who could get the old Mingo woman to stop bringing her cow and its attendant flies into the hut where there were two new and sick babies. Fawn also was the only one who could push old Red Jacket's spine so the bones snapped back in place. She was the only one that could keep the young Chippewa woman from trying to exchange her baby for that of the lighter skinned, nearly identical baby of the quarterblood woman Seshawan McCullough.

Blair thought nothing of it while the two talked in rapid whonking Wyandot. But when the door closed after Fawn, Blair found himself more awake. Until this moment he had not realized the comfort he had been taking from her soft brown presence.

Blair was a man accustomed to aloneness. So he recognized this as not the absence of a friend, but the presence of danger. There was no noise in the cabin beyond the draft in the smoldering hearth. Yet the room throbbed with another human presence.

Blair made sleeping sounds and thrashed around as a man does in half-sleep, and under cover of this noise he crawled close enough to the edge of the loft to look down.

The Indian on the floor below had selected a relaxed, leaning-back position which he could hold without moving a muscle. His hands were clasped around his knees. His head leaned back against the wall, commanding a view of the loft.

The hearth occasionally sputtered and snapped, fanning up a glow which lighted the immobile cheek of Rontondee. The glow showed his nearest eye to be open.

Blair lay still.

On the following night the Reverend Gershom was again summoned out of his cabin to break an argument between two Christian Wyandots and three non-Christian Mingoes who had straggled into the reserve. Fawn was called to help find the Chippewa woman who had removed Seshawan McCullough's nearly white baby from the McCullough hut and made off.

And again, when Fawn left, an Indian silhouette slid to the floor to wait. It was The Pigeon himself.

It brought Blair a flashing revelation. If the Pigeon had a large amount of money to hide from white men, who would he best make custodian of it? Obviously a white man. What white men did he have available? Several quarterblooded whites lived among the Wyandots. But nowhere in the Northwest could he find a safer vault than the cabin of Seth Gershom.

And in that cabin, in case The Pigeon were not always able to trust Gershom, was another pair of perceptive Indian eyes, Pigeon's sister, the Fawn.

The facts fell together like one of Judge Pease's decisions.

Those who brushed lightly against Jonathan Blair in the world which straddled the old Greenville Treaty Line were apt to mark his gentle manner and note it down to unsureness. Oddly enough his fault lay exactly the opposite way. The quiet voice of Jonathan Blair stemmed from a monstrous overconfidence which hated to bludgeon people unless a crisis warranted it.

This became manifest now in the preposterous action of the lawyer which jolted him noisily to his feet and brought him to the edge of the loft, standing.

Pigeon rose slowly at the commotion, startled by the sight of the lawyer standing above him on the edge of the loft. His amazement at the leap left him open-mouthed even as the lawyer's weight crashed into him.

But the impact which flattened the Indian against the puncheon floor flooded protective rage through his hard body, and alerted every one of his long slippery muscles into writhing action. His torso wrenched out from under the lawyer as the heel of his right hand came down on the back of the lawyer's head, driving the white face into the splintery puncheons.

The lawyer was still an instant, but before the Indian could pull his legs under him to rise, the lawyer's knee was in his stomach, pinching the flesh of his belly against his lower ribs. Pigeon doubled in pain and Blair was on his chest, pinioning his wrists to the floor.

"Where is it, Pigeon?"

The Pigeon writhed to the left and right, but the lawyer was solid on his chest.

"Where is it, Pigeon?"

The Pigeon said, "Over there."

Blair turned his head to look, and as he did a sharp knee jabbed him in the back, straightening him up. The Pigeon was suddenly on his feet, and stooping to draw something shiny from the thong around his leg. In the gloom of the room, Blair felt around the floor. The leg of the reverend's Bible stand came to his hand. He brought it up in front of his face in time to absorb Pigeon's knife. Pigeon jerked back the blade, but the Bible stand came attached to it. He banged the stand on the floor snapping the point off his knife. Before he could jab again, Blair had hold of both his wrists.

Pigeon jerked his arms to free them, thus pulling Blair from side to side and forward and backward. But the lawyer held on and backed the Indian slowly against the loft ladder.

They struggled in winded grunts. Blair was awkward, but a great calm came over him and his strength amazed the Indian.

The Pigeon let his arms go slack. Blair was letting go when he felt the surge of power return as Pigeon drove the broken knife toward his chest. The lawyer fell back, grabbed the Indian's wrist and yanked him down.

But Pigeon's wrists were slippery with sweat and they revolved within Blair's grip. As they rolled and struggled wordlessly Blair hammered Pigeon's wrists against the puncheons, to pound the knife loose. But the Indian was leather. Besides, he had learned now to twist his wrist so that the blade scraped and pricked Blair's forearm. Blood ran down Blair's arm, but he learned to jam his thumbnail between the bones of Pigeon's wrist in a way that brought relief from the blade.

The necessity to hold Pigeon's wrists gave the Indian full play against Blair's body and enabled the Indian to lift Blair up from the floor occasionally and then shove him down against the puncheons so his teeth jarred.

But Blair noticed that the Indian also gasped for breath now. He supposed the air burned in Pigeon's chest as it did in his own. The knife blade slid between two puncheons and Blair hammered the Indian's wrist, snapping four inches off the blade. What remained was a jagged iron.

The Pigeon was strong, but his strength this night was multiplied in blessed hot release against a single white man instead of a hundred elusive tentacles of white government. Blair paid for the militia Indian massacre of '13 by having his spine jammed against the stone hearth so his brain jostled in his skull. He paid for the Duncan McArthur Treaty by being yanked upright so his arms sucked in their sockets. He paid for The Pigeon's smoldering years with a backful of splinters as he was dragged across the floor and then jerked upright and spun around. Blair still held the Indian's wrists, but his arms were crossed now, as were the Indian's. Sweat blurred Blair's vision or perhaps he would have seen the knee which rammed his groin to spring his grip and melt his will.

He floated to the floor.

A warm streak across his cheek and down across his chest muscles brought stinging strength back in time to dodge the second pass of the knife which had just slashed him with red.

Blair's hand found the hearth shovel which he flung in one motion at The Pigeon's head. The Indian ducked. Blair was on his feet and had hold of the wrists again.

Blair was not as elaborately muscled as the Indian, but his legs were thick and his hands were strong. The staunch legs now pushed the Indian back against the loft ladder again. Blair yielded his left arm a little allowing Pigeon a stroke of the knife. Then he jammed the brown elbow against the loft ladder so that The Pigeon filled the cabin with an agonizing roar. His hand sprang open, fingers outstretched and strumming like cords. Blair kicked the knife into the hearth.

Against the loft ladder Pigeon's shiny chest heaved in exhaustion and pain. Blair held him there with the hearth shovel which he anchored behind a loft pole, and he panted, "You stole it!"

"Yah! If I did, I stole it from the stealers!"

"That's different!" Blair gasped. "It was owed to us. Didn't take it for m'self. For my people!"

"Different?" The Pigeon was broken-winded, but he managed a laugh. "How different? What did I take it for? Myself? Look at me. What did I buy for myself? I bought a medicine man! Different, did you say, Blair? How do I steal different than you steal?"

The question was unanswerable.

Pigeon's own arguments recharged his own body and he pushed against the shovel. But Blair had it anchored securely.

The door swung open. The Fawn stood on the threshold. "Stop!" she said. "The sergeant comes with soldiers."

The Pigeon relaxed. "Good," he said. "Bring them. Tell them Blair is here."

"*Neethetha kitchokema,*" she said, which sobered Pigeon's face. But then a faint flicker of a grin reappeared. "Even so, tell them the lawyer is here."

Blair released his grip on the shovel.

"They can search a lot better than I can, Pigeon, if there's many of them."

The Pigeon sobered again, and he walked toward the door. His sister

threw her doeskin coat over him. He stared at her hard and meaning-
fully, Blair thought, with instructions.

Blair sagged to the bench at the eating table. The blood from the
gash in his chest flowed fast in the sweat down over his chest and then
sideways in the folds of his torso and down his flanks. Blair grabbed
a red cloth and started to wrap it around his waist to stop the satura-
tion of his doeskin trousers. But he noticed it was Fawn's red shawl
from the French traders, and put it down. However, she came over
to him and herself wrapped the shawl around his waist.

"Sit still," she said.

She went into her room in the back and returned with a pitch pine
knot as big as a man's fist. She lighted this at the hearth.

"In there," she said.

She took him by the arm and led him into her part of the cabin
where he sagged to the bunk.

"Is The Pigeon all right?" she asked.

"I think so."

"Down." She pressed him down flat. But he was upright again instantly because of the splinters in his back.

"All right, sit then."

She poured him a mug from the reverend's crock, which he drank
sparingly at first. But the liquor would not bring the usual pleasant
sting to his hot throat, so he upended the mug and emptied it.

She swabbed down his chest with a wet soft doeskin. She grasped
his shoulders and bowed them forward, closing the gash on his chest.
She then soaked a long strip of doeskin and plastered it over the gash,
rough side to his skin. The strip began to turn red, but she ran
the back of her finger down over the strip. As the water squeezed out,
it stuck to his chest. She wound two dry strips around the barrel of
his chest.

"Over," she said, and Blair lay chest down on the fur-covered bunk.

His head was turned to the side. He could not see his own back,
but he noticed that after she looked, she poured him another mug of
whisky. It cut into his throat better. She poured another, but when
he reached for it, she poured half of it over his back. The coldness of
it arched him back against the grain of his spine. But splinters arched
him forward again.

He winced each time she pulled one out.

"Stay still! Pulls open chest."

She gave him the rest of the whisky which spread a comfort through his warm body. Her cool hands moving lightly over his shoulders became pleasant except for the periodic nicks as she pulled out splinters.

As she worked lower on his back, the nicks became hotter, but her hands became cooler and more tender. The groove down his spine was deep, flanked by strong ridges of muscle which reservoired the whisky. She used this to rub over the places from which she drew splinters. Her fingers were a light breeze.

Her hands slowed up as her attention drifted from him to something else. He rolled to look at her.

"I found the cheahha."

"What?"

"The little one. Fawn finds it. The Chippewa woman took it. Hide him in empty hut."

"Did you give it back to . . ."

"Yes," she said reluctantly. "To Seshawan McCullough."

He rose on one elbow to study her. "Not black hair on the cheahha," she said. "Brown, like this." She grabbed a handful of the beaver blanket. Then she dropped it and took hold of the bear skin. "Like this," she said. But she dropped the bear skin then and her hand enmeshed in the short hair at the back of Blair's head. She clawed her hand gently through it, over the top of his head toward his forehead.

"Like this," she said. "Like this it is brown."

She leaned forward and blew into Blair's hair like Squindatee examining a beaver pelt, and just as critically. Her lips parted as she examined him with even more intensity than Squindatee at a fur trade. Her tremulant weight was soon against him, tenderly.

Her loveliness in the eyes of Jonathan Blair this night was classic. She was mercifully cool hands, and a warmth of urgent breath against his face. His elbow slid out from under him beneath her precious weight. His arm went around her to speak a gentle, unhurried language, neither Wyandot nor English.

Blair thought briefly of the sergeant and the troops who had just ridden into town. Then he thought of the hundred thousand dollars which both he and the sergeant sought. Then his head lost perspective; or perhaps gained it in the crook of a copper-colored elbow where a pulse alternated with the throb in his temples.

Well south of the Indian lands, in the caucus room of the tavern called The Red Lion in the Borough of Columbus sat a group which had come to be known as the Chillicothe cabal. They were waiting for someone.

Each of the persons in this room, if he were to appear on the roads of the Borough of Columbus, or of Chillicothe, or on the log sidewalks of Cincinnati, would be a figure of influence in his own right.

The heavy-set, heavy-lidded Riddle, who sat placid like a sleepy eagle, had been dispensing loans for the United States Bank long enough to have built a solid base of patronage in Cincinnati, Louisville, Steubenville, Columbus, Dayton, and as far northwest as Detroit. His leaden stare made a borrower crawl and contort, and his traplike mind for figures, it was said, could calculate a man's ability to repay down to the last dollar. But borrowers who were desperate enough to crawl low enough, and borrowers who did not make the mistake of going over Riddle's head to Schaacht, could at times get loans from Riddle.

Word passed among small bankers and large farmers and merchants as to just how to approach Riddle. By the similarity of approach lately, he was beginning to suspect that there had been some comparing of notes. But this, too, was a kind of fame not unpleasant to Riddle.

Every loan application to the bank was ultimately approved by Schaacht in person. But as the borrowers had studied Riddle, so Riddle had studied Schaacht. Often as not he would present the applications of his pets unfavorably to Schaacht, saying the man's security was only double or triple the amount of the loan, or some other overcautious demurrer. To which Schaacht would often as not say, "Good God, Riddle, do you want, blood?" He would scrawl his approval on the loan.

And if some of the pets of Riddle were slow to pay, Riddle would often recommend to Schaacht such fierce collection measures that even Schaacht would yell, "Riddle, you must be the bastard that sold Jesus for thirty pieces of silver. Extend the loan sixty days!"

So Riddle was an influence in the West.

Duncan McArthur, speaker of the assembly, piled his muddy boots on the round table and whacked off flakes with a rifle ramrod. When the West had needed soldiers his Indian-baiting truculence had boosted him. His boasts had been comforting to the nervous settle-

ments along the river; and since he made good on them he had served
the West. The West had thanked him with a generalship and speaker-
ship of the house. If he did not know a great deal about treaty making
or legislation, that was not as important as keeping Tecumseh off
men's backs. And he might be needed again. From his knowledge of
militia officers, his influence in the assembly and his seat on the board
of the U.S. Bank, he also could call favors from two or three important men in every major Western settlement, and would be recognized
in every Western tavern and army post.

On McArthur's right was the slim-fingered, brocade-vested Tremaine
with morocco shoes. Most of the group wondered what a Cincinnati
man was doing here. But no one asked. If he was here today, he was
important.

On McArthur's left was that fortunate kind of man, a self-possessed
youngster who had learned to pull up a chair as though he belonged,
and by the very presumption proving that he did. For Justin Bolding
knew that though the numbers discussed at this table were bigger
and the cigars came from farther south, the principles and motives
were the very same as those being discussed by his young contempo-
raries out in the common room of The Red Lion. He knew, too, that
he would be put to the test as soon as his elders at this table could
manage it . . . which would be soon; and he knew also that he would
be competent.

Major Armstrong was here and there were others in the room of
equal stature. And viewed thus individually they were impressive, but
grouped here in this room, they would soon be as a group of children.

Bolding knew that Gideon Schaacht was arriving when McArthur
swung his boots casually but quickly down off the table. Tremaine
stopped fingering his watch chain. Even Riddle's upper lids raised
a little.

Gideon Schaacht yanked out a chair for his daughter and said,
"Well, what have you all accomplished?"

The veterans of such meetings made no stammering attempts to
answer. But Tremaine, not realizing how much information normally
came to Schaacht from all quarters, began a recapitulation of news
which was interrupted fiercely by Schaacht. "We know all that! Good
God. What have you done about the money?"

Armstrong gave an account of the military side since O'Fallon's in-
cident, concluding, "So, since the big Christofferson is in his cabin in

Mespo, and the wagoner, Gavagan, is arrested, we believe that Blair knows where the money is, and is gone after it his damn self. He was last seen goin' north out of Mespo, so I've got a sergeant taking a patrol up into that Indian town with instructions to let Blair find the money, then bring in Blair."

Justing Bolding waited until the meeting came to its lowest ebb, when everyone was embarrassed at not having an idea and would welcome one from anywhere without jealousy. Yet he did not wait so long as to give Schaacht time to propose an idea of his own. He cleared his throat and every eye was on him. "I suggest, Major Armstrong, you don't capture Blair if he *does* have the money."

Bolding enjoyed their surprise a little too long. Schaacht said, "Come on! Come on!"

"Just keep a ring of troops around Columbus to prevent him from delivering the money to me or the treasurer. If he delivers that money into my office or the treasurer's office, I've got to accept it. And once he delivers that money to me or the treasurer his wild scheme has a sort of official blessing on it. After all, it *is* a state law; constitutional or not, it's a law. But if he does *not* deliver it into the treasury . . . and since he's not the official collector anyhow . . . then in the eyes of the nation and the Congress and Mr. Monroe . . . well, the whole thing is reduced to"— he shrugged—"grand larceny. And how long can one man keep a hundred thousand dollars safe in these woods?"

Riddle's wattles reddened. "And we lose a hundred thousand dollars to a gang of woods robbers!"

Bolding didn't even bother to defend his idea. Schaacht did. "Yes, Riddle! We lose a hundred thousand dollars, but we win the principle of the thing; and we lose it only *once*. Not once *every* year. You can stand it once. The Baltimore branch lost three times that to its own embezzling cashier."

McArthur grinned. "We change Blair from a crusader to a crook." While the others savored the idea with relish, Schaacht had already dispatched Riddle to tell the editor of the *Freeman's Chronicle* that it looked as though the money had fallen into the hands of thieves, and it was no longer expected at the treasury.

Riddle glanced at Bolding suggesting that he should run such errands, but Bolding sat still.

Schaacht said, "Bolding, you've got a head on you! Just let Blair try to preserve a hundred thousand dollars in those woods. Why some of his own Mesopotamia grannymothers would skin him for a tenth that much. Every rifle in the woods will be looking for him. Armstrong, your job now is to make it impossible for Blair to deliver that money to the auditor or the treasurer. Don't catch him, but make it look like you intend to."

"I'll get out messengers." Armstrong scrambled to his feet, but he was arrested, as were the others, by a quiet contralto voice, much like Schaacht's, except it was sweet and mellifluous.

"Just a minute," she said. "Justin, when you proposed this scheme, were you aware a man could get shot trying to husband a hundred thousand dollars out there, with the way blocked for him to bring it on in?"

Bolding smiled, taking silent credit for the knowledge, whether he had it or not. Armstrong said, "Ma'am, he could get shot, stabbed, drowned, beat to death or all four combined. There was a drover stabbed dead in the stable of The Swan last night over one miserable Spanish doubloon. Half the men in the West have gone back to packin' what money they got in their boots, and honest farmers are drove to waylayin' strangers on the trails."

Virginia Schaacht kept staring straight at Bolding. "Did you see Riddle's sick mare, Justin, when they shot her? How the lead went in through the forehead bone and came tearing out behind, rolling the side of her neck off?"

Bolding swallowed and turned red.

The only sound was the whispering of levantine silk falling into vertical folds as she rose and left the room in disgust.

Blair had no idea how much time had passed when he woke. The pine knot still flickered in the drafty cabin beside the bunk. But he did know what woke him, the faintest stiffness in the blanket under his cheek. The fur rugs had parted so that his whiskered face lay on a rough army blanket. He did not move his face, but he reached his right hand up slowly and clutched a handful of the blanket, only long enough to hear the brittle crinkle inside it.

It made sense. Where better could Pigeon hide the money than under the person of his sister, in the house of the Reverend Gershom? Gershom's silence now made sense, too. Gershom's bargains were hard, and he honored his side to the letter, expecting the same in return.

Blair had contracted to deliver a doctor to Upper Sandusky. He had defaulted. Pigeon had therefore made his own arrangements about a doctor, which involved money. Gershom would never interfere under such conditions. Other things fell into place. Pigeon's occasional tongue-in-cheek attendance at the Reverend Gershom's services could be part of a bargain for Gershom's custodianship of the money.

Blair lifted his head just enough to clear the blankets, and he rolled around to look at Fawn. She slept with a smile, hugging herself. He raised his torso ever so slowly from the bunk. The slowness of the rise required muscular strain which broke open his chest gash; but he continued until he was sitting upright. He lifted one leg clear of the bunk and found the floor. Then he transferred his weight slowly to his feet.

He rolled back the fur rug on his edge of the bunk, revealing the quilted blankets containing the money. Keeping his eyes on Fawn he tugged at the quilt lightly. The far edge of it was pinned under her.

She drew her knees up in languorous slumber. She turned her head toward where Blair had lain and her smile sweetened. Blair wondered, how in the midst of male-made turmoil did some women still smile so trusting lovely. Didn't they know about the world? Or did they know and still smile that way? Were they all-knowing, or all-blind? Anyway, it was wonderful.

He snapped back to danger, because, though she did not open her eyes, she rolled, unfolding one somnolent arm, extending it to where he had been. Blair moved like a panther so that he was under the arm when it settled. It seemed to satisfy her dream. He lifted her gently, kissed her slowly, and jerked the blanket from under.

In the front room he found his coat and gun and then he paused long enough for one of those gestures which had often defeated him. Gershom's quill was there and foolscap. While measuring time in heartbeats, he scrawled:

Sorry, Pigeon.

Blair

In Gershom's shed Blair did not risk the noise and fumbling of saddling up, especially after his borrowed stallion woke with such a loud start.

A half-mile into the woods, the trail narrowed. Blair saddled.

Blair lost all track of time because of the way he slept. He rode south through Mesopotamia in darkness without stopping. But he thought it was probably the third night when under his thighs he felt the tired stallion begin to yearn forward with new speed. Looking ahead he saw why. The bright patch of moonlit clearing ahead was Boxford's where the horse belonged. He dismounted before she came out into the opening. He had trouble holding the barn-bound stallion still while he inspected. But something didn't look right. He studied the Boxford cabin and sheds.

The trouble was the bearskin which hung over the doorway of the last shed which was usually open and unoccupied. There was an extra horse at Boxford's. It would be normal for Armstrong to station a man here.

But Blair wanted to trade off Boxford's stallion for his own bay. He wrapped the stallion's lines around a tall butt and circled toward the sheds.

He was halfway there when the stallion split the night with a scolding whinny. Blair froze like a stump. The whinny brought Boxford's hulk into the lighted cabin doorway. It also brought a woman's silhouette out past him. It was a silhouette that could fit twice inside Mrs. Boxford's shadow and it marched out into the moonlight and down past all the sheds to the last one.

The stallion issued another shrill complaint. With the woman standing by the shed where his bay was and with Boxford unsaddling the stallion, Blair decided to wait it out. But the woman's voice said, quietly, "Blair?"

And Boxford answered, "Yeah, this is the one he relayed off."

Her voice had the snap of her father, "Blair!"

He stood rooted.

Boxford said, "It's all right, Blair. The young lady has a message for you. I wouldn't call you out if I didn't think she was on your side of this thing."

Boxford couldn't know how often the sides had changed lately. Blair kept quiet. But the two closed towards Blair until she saw him.

"Come inside, Blair," she said. "I came up this far with one of Armstrong's men. Something to tell you."

"I guess you'd best tell me here, Miss Schaacht. I'm not going in any buildings tonight."

"All right. Do you have the money?"

"Nor am I answering any questions."

"The point is the game is changed. The trick is no longer to get the money back. Just keep you from delivering it."

Blair whistled slowly as he grasped their idea.

"This is Virginia Schaacht telling me this?" Blair alerted. "Daughter of Gideon Schaacht?"

"Yes."

"So I can be led right into Columbus, nice and easy?"

"No. I came to help you get the money in."

"And I should believe this?"

"I think I could prove it in the cabin."

"Any troops in there, Boxford?"

"No, Blair. Just her. She's been real domestic here waitin' for you. Matter of fact, she's just been sittin', sewin' on a dress."

"Her? Sewing?" Blair backed up.

"Sewing."

"You both go first."

Blair carried in his blankets, staying well behind the other two.

Mrs. Boxford looked at Blair and got him hot acorn coffee and fingered his eyes. "Boy, your eyes are ringed down to your face bones. You'll be sleepin' here tonight."

"Afraid not, Mrs. Boxford. Miss Schaacht, you mentioned proof?"

Mrs. Boxford reached to relieve him of the blankets. He tightened his grip. "I'll just keep 'em handy, Mrs. Boxford, thanks."

Virginia Schaacht left the room and returned carrying a grey wool dress, wool so fine it hung and fell into every indentation. She displayed it to him. Boxford said, "Yeah, that's the dress she's been sewin' on, Blair."

Blair said, "Uh-huh. But the proof you spoke of?"

Virginia Schaacht smiled and said, "And notice this special petticoat, Jonathan."

Blair colored as she flipped back the hem of the dress, revealing a multiruffled affair underneath, the color of which alone made a man feel he'd got into the wrong room. It was nice, though. But Blair felt he was being laughed at. She left the delicate thing exposed, and said, "I took a lesson from you sewing horse blankets, Jonathan. The story's around now, how you sew a pretty fine horse blanket."

Boxford looked puzzled. Mrs. Boxford's hand went to her startled eyebrows, "Horse blankets?"

But Blair was watching Virginia Schaacht's fingers. Deftly they were working through the ruffles, and Blair saw her fingers duck in and out of what seemed to be a hundred little pockets in the thing. You didn't notice the openings among all those feminine ruffles and frills. Blair suddenly made bold to finger the garment. He looked into her eyes now and said, "You?"

"Together we'll walk in to the auditor," she said.

"Why should I trust you?"

"Perhaps you shouldn't."

Mr. and Mrs. Boxford looked at each other and left the kitchen in case there was to be a proposal or something; but not before they heard the lawyer say, "Miss Schaacht, that's the most beautiful gown I've ever seen."

Blair and the girl went to work immediately. In the young Republic of America, no woman had ever worn as valuable a dress as Virginia Schaacht pulled over her fine shoulders that night.

On the twenty-sixth day of September, 18 and 19, a light, four-wheel chaise drove toward the clapboard building which was already being called the state office building in the Borough of Columbus. It was remarked not only because it was one of only two such chaises seen north of Chillicothe, but because Virginia Schaacht sat in the right hand seat, composed. The beauty of her face began with the bones, which is why the men stopped to look at her. Then, there was a certain at-homeness about the way this woman swayed beside this man, which was odd considering what antagonisms should be between them at this moment; which is why the women stopped to watch.

As for the lawyer, the natives of this town had not seen him much, but they had nevertheless seen a remarkable change in him. Having observed it, they had a feeling of ownership of this man. When he had first come here his face had been a little vague of contour. Today, though, his cheekbones were pronounced, because the skin was tighter over the face. The mouth, less full, but more of a mouth at that, straight across. The nose had flattened out some, and a small, faint blue "x"-shaped scar on the bridge added to the folklore of this town. Today some noticed a diagonal slash on his left cheek, rather recent.

His hair was dark and curly, lying close to the head except at the neck where it bulged a little over the collar of his buckskin shortcoat. The face displayed some wear and some growth . . . and power.

On this day the bystanders watched the lawyer, J. Blair, rein the chaise to a stop in front of the clapboard state office building. The lawyer made no effort to get out of the chaise immediately, but sat, allowing the corporal to go all over the entire vehicle, unfolding a pair of horse blankets in the back boot and inspecting them carefully. The soldier's motions were apologetic, but the lawyer made it easy for him. A major of infantry stood off from the carriage watching. The corporal finished his inspection and then called something to the major. The major made a gesture, and the corporal shrugged and asked the lawyer to step out of the carriage. The lawyer displayed some papers from his pockets. The soldier walked around in back of him and looked. The lawyer opened his coat, but there was a call from the major and the lawyer took off the coat. The soldier inspected it and stepped back.

The attorney took the woman's elbow, helping her dismount. They started toward the doorway of the clapboard building. Again the major yelled.

Bolder bystanders moved closer.

"Who you going in to see?" the major asked.

"Treasurer of state or the auditor," the lawyer answered.

"What for?"

Blair laughed. "Why, to deliver the money, of course. Better inspect my wallet."

No humor lightened the major's on-duty face. He gestured for Blair to open his coat, which was done. With apologies the officer looked at the woman who wore a grey dress and carried a bundle of dark green levantine silk. "I'm sorry, Ma'am, but I don't know who's who anymore, with your friend Bolding being first on one side, then the other. It's in your father's interest."

"Oh," she said. "You mean this? Why, certainly."

She handed him the silk. He held it up and let it unroll down. The bystanders smiled. The major colored and handed her back the dress. "I'm taking it later to Mrs. Deshler for some alterations," she explained.

"Yes, Ma'am."

The major looked at Blair. "I'll accompany you to the treasurer's door."

They went into the clapboard building.

The treasurer's office was empty. They went to the auditor's office on the second floor. Bolding stood up like a shot. He looked beyond Blair and Miss Schaacht to Armstrong, who stood in the doorway. But Armstrong only gave him back a shrug. "The lawyer was searched before he came in, Bolding."

Relief flooded Bolding's face. Then he studied Blair, and smiled easily. "I see you bring no bells with you, Blair. What can I do for you?"

"I want to discuss some business of the State of Ohio," he glanced at Armstrong. "In the absence of any representatives of the Federal Government . . . that is *official* representatives."

Armstrong stepped barely outside. Bolding closed the door. "You're in strange company, Virginia, considering whose daughter you are."

She looked down at her gloves. "Yes, Justin, I guess I am." Then she lifted her chin above his barb. Bolding was uncomfortable as he noticed that Blair and Virginia Schaacht, though they stood far apart, gave a strange illusion of standing together, relaxed and easy. He said, "Well?"

Blair said, "I want you to write out a receipt for $100,000 minus $2,000 for the fee of the collector, minus $3,000 more."

"What?"

"You heard."

"But why? Time enough when the money arrives, *if* it does."

"When the money is delivered, it may be necessary to deliver it in a hurry. It will be in the interests of Ohio to effect the transfer as quickly as possible, in view of the Federal troops on duty here."

"But there's a Federal injunction."

"That does not concern you. The injunction forbids the collector from delivering. It does not prohibit you from accepting."

Bolding walked to the window and looked as far up and down the road as he could. "You expect the delivery to be made soon?"

"Very soon."

Bolding went to the door, opened it. There was a soldier there. Bolding only looked at him. But the soldier went quickly down the stairs. Blair walked to the window and looked down. He saw Armstrong pointing out sentry stations, and he saw soldiers moving to them quickly, forming a large, rough circle around the building.

Bolding shoved home the bolt on his door quickly. But Blair noticed it, and was pleased.

"All right, Blair," the auditor said, "if it will ease your mind I will write out the receipt. I won't sign it, of course, until the money is on this table."

"Fair enough. And I would like to have the treasurer sent for."

This was done. The door was bolted again.

Bolding put down his quill and passed the paper over to Blair with a patronizing smile:

> *Received from bearer on behalf of the State of Ohio on the* ——*th*
> *ult., year of* ————, *$95,000, representing tax levy by State of*
> *Ohio on The Bank of the United States.*
> SIGNED: ———— *Auditor of State*
> SIGNED:———— *Treasurer of State*

"When and if the money should ever turn up we will deliver this receipt to the bearer of the funds," Bolding said confidently. "Will that be satisfactory?"

Blair studied it.

"We'll want the state seal on it." He handed it back.

Bolding chuckled, "Yes, *sir!*"

The auditor handed it to Mr. Curry, the treasurer. "Would you go to your office and get the seal, Mr. Curry?"

Pink flushed into Curry's white paper-textured face and he reached into his waistcoat pocket, producing the seal on the end of a short shaft.

Bolding was startled. "You knew it would be needed, Mr. Curry?"

"No," mumbled Curry. "That is . . . uh . . . what I mean, I usually carry it with me. Uh . . . that is . . . lately."

"Why? Did you expect it would be needed?"

"Well, I . . . uh . . ." Curry straightened some. "I *hoped* it would be needed, Mr. Bolding. Didn't you, sir?"

Bolding's composure melted some. Curry worked silently, but with ill-concealed expectancy.

Blair inspected the seal, blew on the cooling wax and casually handed the paper to Bolding. "You can fill in the date now."

"What?" Bolding's rising pitch betrayed him. But he settled back. "What date?"

"Today's date."

Bolding laughed. "All right, sir. Done. Now what?"

"Now you can both sign it."

Bolding folded his arms and laughed. "You taught me better than that, Blair. When the money comes, I'll sign."

"Very well. Fair enough."

Blair walked to the door, checked the bolt. He walked to the window and looked out at Armstrong's alert sentries. He closed the inside shutters on the window.

"What the devil are you doing, Blair!"

The lawyer said quietly, "Gentlemen, would you face the other way?"

"Not on your life, Blair! And I warn you if you put a strong hand on us, we'll have the sentry in here."

"I don't intend to touch you, Bolding. Just turn around as a matter of courtesy to Miss Schaacht."

Curry's crinkled paper face showed the beginning of a grin and then the beginning of a blush. He turned his back. Bolding said, "Curry, are you crazy?" Bolding grabbed the hearth poker to defend himself.

Blair took the green silk dress from the girl and stepped in front of her, facing Bolding. "All right, Miss Schaacht. At these stakes I guess we'll not stand on modesty."

Blair, facing Bolding, saw the auditor's jaw drop at the sight of a flurry of pristine, red-piped ruffles which foamed out beyond Blair's screening body. The fact is the lawyer himself was immensely aware of the rustling behind him.

The absence of voices and the surprise on the face of the auditor caused the treasurer to turn back toward Blair. But the snowstorm of lace which frothed out from behind Blair jogged his Adam's apple and pivoted him back away. Red flushed into the veins of his parchment-thin ears, like red maple leaves in October.

Blair sensed the moment when the dress slipped up over her head. He kept his feet planted wide, but he twisted to hand her the green dress and to take the wool dress from her. A brief vision of round arms and shoulders above a white something-or-other jarred his head. The base of her throat was flushed with some embarrassment but her mouth and chin denied this in matter-of-fact determination, completely admirable. She stooped to step into the green dress, but her head raised, pointedly reminding him that he was looking . . . overlong.

Blair stood silently until she finally stepped out from behind him, face flushed above a green dress.

Blair walked to Bolding's desk and placed the grey wool dress on it. He furled back the hem. Bolding had lost himself to candid amazement.

Blair grabbed two handfuls of the ruffled petticoat which was attached to the inside of the dress. He pulled in opposite directions and the petticoat ripped. It covered the desk with money.

In the same instant, that petticoat bulged the eyes of the auditor, brought a grin to the face of the treasurer, and laughed at the last decision of the Chief Justice of the young Republic of America.

No thought was given to the ripped petticoat, for the four people in this room well understood that what ripped beyond repair here today was the sovereignty of the Federal Government over its states, the safety of the United States Bank in the West, or the possibility of peace between Jonathan Blair and Gideon Schaacht . . . however you chose to look at it.

To Jonathan Blair, it meant the sheep of Hope Emerson could come down out of the woods.

Chapter 20: THE TRESPASSERS

THE U. S. Bank versus Messrs. Christofferson, Gavagan, Curry, Bolding for trespass, contempt and recovery."

Extremes were well understood in the settlement of Hosmer Village, lately more often known as Mesopotamia. Twenty years of survival thirty miles north of where the double-rutted trail dwindled to single-axle width had depended upon extremists.

A man needed not to be a good shot, but a superior shot. Sam Hosmer had not worked hard, he had worked like an ox to haul the first crops out of the forest. In the raising of hogs, Joe Hussong could not be merely clever, he needed sheer cunning. And those who had not been extremists had gone back east or had gone down beneath the twenty-two stone markers in the burial yard. That's why the survival of Jonathan Blair had been little understood here. But in November they understood.

The townsmen of Hosmer Village accurately measured the new

stature of Jonathan Blair in the West by the immensity of the charges now hurled against him. These were extremes, and they were understood.

Culpepper looked out the new glass window of Hosmer's Store, which was proprietored now by Asa Buttrick, and he said, "God'l mighty, would ya look at that lawyer out there feedin' his bay so quiet and gentle? How'd a man ever guess he was such a hell-eatin' demon as they got him writ down here for!"

The newspapers which they all labored over, were the ones which Asa Buttrick had just brought up from downstate.

"They're suin' Blair's people just like they was bandits," Culpepper said. "Blair called it a simple tax collection. But it appears by *The Western Spy* here the central gover'mint calls it grand larceny."

Other papers called it other names:

> "The Governor of Ohio does not support his own people and has declared, 'I view the confiscation in the most odious light, and from my very soul I detest it. I am ashamed it has happened in Ohio.' However your editor hastens to add that he would have been proud to have had it happen in Indiana."
>
> *Vincennes Western Star*

> "We reprint the Pittsburgh paper which reprints the Philadelphia paper which quotes the president of the U. S. Bank as saying, 'This outrage cannot be paralleled under a government of law, and if the defendants are sustained by the courts, they have struck at the vitals of the Constitution, and union among the states will dissolve.'"
>
> *Miami Intelligencer*

> "It has often been stated that the United States will one day divide at the Alleghenies into two countries. Easterners are now saying the first blow has been struck, and this paper says if they wish to consider this the second Boston Tea Party, let them. We are ready."
>
> *Western Herald and Steubenville Gazette*

"And to think that's him that stirred up the whole caterwampus . . . right out there feedin' his bay like nothing happened." Culpepper shook his head.

"That's him," Buttrick said. "He said he was gonna drive that Schaacht outa here, and it looks like by Jehovah he did."

"That don't follow," Exeter said. "They got Bolding in jail. They got Gavagan in jail. They got Curry in jail, and they're gonna put Christofferson in jail as soon as his leg cures. Does that look like Blair won?"

Buttrick said, "If Blair's got friends enough in the legislature to get the tax law passed, he's got friends enough to get them all out of jail."

"That don't follow either," Exeter said. "Looks by these papers like Blair's friends got kind of scarce all of a sudden since Judge Byrd announced he's holdin' Christofferson and them on $250,000 bail."

"Christ!" Culpepper said, "is there that much money?"

"The Bank can't sue those individuals," Buttrick explained from the world-wide knowledge of a man who got to Cincinnati once a month. "They have to sue the State of Ohio. That's who took the money."

But Exeter, from his more accurate newspaper said, "Maybe so, but that's not who they got in jail. Who they got in jail is Gavagan, and Bolding and Curry. And if I read right, that's who they're suin'."

Which happened to be the fact of the matter.

"And I don't mind 'cedin' Blair started a big thing. But looks like *we'll* have to finish it, like everything he starts. 'Less we intend Christofferson and Gavagan to stay in jail. I don't mind about that Bolding the least part. But the others." Exeter shrugged with good effect.

In the jail at Columbus, Justin Bolding was not in the main building. The debtors had swollen the population of the prison beyond capacity. Seventeen long, shedlike cabins had been built around the jail. Captain Vance's Franklin County Dragoons patrolled the grounds and were glad of the militia money.

Bolding was in one of the cabins. The resident dwellers were not referred to as prisoners, because some of the best of Western society were there. They walked around outdoors, restricted only within the sentry paths.

It was an awkward situation, in which Captain Vance commanding the Dragoons was seen each morning upon his arrival to salute several of the inmates who had been in his regiment in the late English war, much his senior. Also, Sergeant Blakely was on duty as a guard on Monday. On Tuesday he was an inmate.

But Bolding was not a debtor prisoner. Two Franklin Dragoons were therefore stationed outside his cabin. Visitors were not deterred from bringing food. They were encouraged by the officials who could not supply adequate rations.

Justin Bolding was first surprised that he was allowed visitors; but more than this he was surprised that any visitors came. Worse, though, was the unsettling nature of the visits.

On the third week of his imprisonment, they still came. Not so many as before. But a few.

He stood still under the palsied inspection of a white-maned specter of the great rebellion. The old man ran his eyes up one side of Bolding and down the other with the audacity of age. Then he presented an unsteady tangle of bony fingers to be shaken by Bolding. Bolding gripped it gently, then he winced as the old man squashed his hand like a bird's wing.

"Good work, boy," the old man rasped. Bolding did not reply, for he suspected sarcasm. But after his hand was released, the old man grabbed it again. "Strong stomach it took to issue that order. Good work, boy. We're behind ya!"

Bolding sat down on his bunk.

Outside the cabin occasionally a stranger would come up to one of the sentries and apparently ask a question. The sentry would then point to Bolding's cabin, and the stranger would stare in. A square block of a man entered the cabin. "You Bolding? The one that issued the warrant for the tax?"

"Yes."

"Huh. Expected an older man." The block shoved out a square hand. "Name's Adonijah Heth. I can do anything, you let me know. I got the forge down the road aways. We know what you did."

"You do?" Bolding was careful. If these brazen black eyes knew as much as they seemed, then this offer of friendship was surely facetious. "What do you mean you know what I did?"

"We know ya stuck by your guns and sent them collectors after the money from the Bank when you was ordered not to."

The mitered hand shook Bolding's and left him liking very much the blunt admiration of a blunt man. Bolding was tasting for the first time the strongest of liquors—reward for fundamental service to men. But it curdled as he swallowed.

Even before the time for the distribution of evening rations to the prisoners, the unconfined prisoners lined up to receive the corn bread, salt, coffee and salt pork with which they would prepare their own meal. The confined prisoners had their meals brought to them. From his doorway, Bolding stood watching the slow moving line. In it he saw a woman in a sheepskin coat. She had a small pale girl with her who carried one of the vessels. The child kept leaning out of the line, counting the number of people ahead of her. Then she would argue with the woman in the sheepskin coat. The woman, girl really, would pat the child's head.

Corporal Johanson brought Bolding's ration which included a crumbling square of corn bread. Bolding pointed to the small pale girl. The corporal delivered it to her. The woman's eyes followed back over the route of the corn bread to Bolding.

She turned to the man behind her and then left the line, coming over to the doorway of Bolding's cabin.

"You're Bolding, the auditor. My husband says you got spine, what you did."

Bolding forked in a mouthful of slumgullion.

"He says the men will not stand for it that you stay in prison because of it. He says it is in the papers from Dayton."

Bolding was just going to nod to her, but he was caught in this lie of omission, because over her shoulder he saw the unreadable face of Virginia Schaacht.

He said to the woman in sheepskin. "Lady, does your husband know what part I had in the legislation behind that tax law?"

"How would he know? But I'm sure it was grand. Did you make the tax?"

Bolding now noticed that a Franklin Dragoon had arrived with Virginia Schaacht. The Dragoon stepped over to talk quietly with Corporal Johanson. Bolding also saw an unmistakably mischievous interest on Virignia Schaacht's face as to how he would answer the lady in sheepskin. He swallowed another forkful of slumgullion. "Well, I guess to keep the record straight, madam, you'd better tell your husband that I am the same Justin Bolding who, on the floor of the assembly represented the side of . . ." Bolding seemed to choke on the slumgullion. "You'd better tell him once and for all that I represented the interests of . . . I tried to maneuver for . . ."

"Oh, he already knows you're a smart one," the woman interrupted. "They're all sayin' it. Though I wouldn't know about the details."

He saw Virginia Schaacht's faint dimples wink in amusement.

"Now wait a minute, Ma'am, I'm trying to tell you something. Listen close now. I'm telling you that . . ."

But Corporal Johanson interrupted. "Bolding, this man just brought a note from up yonder." The corporal leaned his rifle up against the cabin wall and abandoned his cautious and watchful demeanor. "You're bailed."

Bolding's eyebrows queried the corporal. The corporal's thumb motion evicted the auditor. "We need the room."

"Bailed by whom, Corporal?"

Johanson emancipated a stream of eating-tobacco nectar. "Does it matter?"

"It might. Who bails me?"

The corporal spit. "Schaacht, of course."

The sheepskin-coated woman exclaimed, "But that's . . . the one!" Her hand went to her mouth.

Bolding sat down.

"We'll be needing the space," the corporal said.

"Find it elsewhere, Corporal. I'm staying."

"You're what!"

"You can't bail a man that doesn't want to be bailed."

The sheepskin-coated woman nodded and smiled as though she had said this. The corporal shrugged.

The dents in Virginia Schaacht's cheeks disappeared.

Blair planned his arrival at Columbus to catch the circuit court when it came through again. He was in search of a good lawyer. After opposing each other all afternoon in the courtroom, the lawyers came across the ruts of High Street to The Red Lion, laughing and talking together. The judge walked across separately, but he permitted the lawyers to join him at the dinner board each night.

Blair approached the table after they were all seated so that he could sit in a certain place. He wished to talk across the whole length of the table so that Ewing and Stanhope would have to answer his questions loud and plain and for record.

He hoped there would not be a lot of fuss upon his arrival. But Stuttgart was there, and he exclaimed, "Blair! How long y'all been heah? Ev'body's lookin' for ya! Includin' the federal lawyers I heah! You sure did it big, Mistah Blair! Big! They say that old man Schaacht is stompin' up the . . ."

Other exclamations broke out. But Judge Pease glared them silent. He waggled his hand.

"Mr. Blair has had enough of explaining and gasping. Let's give him peace at least amongst the bar."

Pease leaned close to Ewing and said something. Ewing studied Blair and nodded at what he heard.

Pease said, "Mr. Blair, this is Mr. Ewing."

"How do you do, sir."

"Hello, Blair. Naturally I know about you. Everybody's heard. Glad to meet you."

While he had his attention Blair waded right in. He said, "Judge Pease, I tried Jacob Burnet as you suggested."

"Would he take the case?"

"No."

"You try the others?"

"Yes, sir. I asked Curtain of Dayton, and Colonel Johnson."

These names commanded Ewing's attention. Judge Pease said, "And?"

"They won't take it."

"What's the matter with Bela Hult? He's man enough and he's a good lawyer and some standing at the bar."

"He'll take it if I insist. But we both agreed a man of more reputation is needed. Either reputation or ability. Besides it's costing Hult's people dear he says, for what he had to do with it."

Pease resumed eating his soup, but his head snapped up as Blair's next remark went like a bullet to Ewing. "The truth is, Mr. Ewing, I came here tonight to ask you to take the defense."

The heads at the table snapped from Blair to Ewing.

Ewing lowered his chicken bone slowly. His eyes challenged Blair for forcing this public decision.

The other lawyers, ineligible for the assignment, were free to enjoy the tension. Ewing borrowed time, "Are you referring to the defense of the collectors of the tax against the suit of the U. S. Bank in Federal Circuit Court in Chillicothe?"

Blair ignored the question in favor of his food. The length of the silence was emphasized by the chuckling of Judge Pease's soup sluicing through his poor teeth.

"It needs a big man," Blair said. "A man of great ability and knowledge. It needs you, sir."

The judge's soup fairly gurgled.

"There'll just be the treasurer, Mr. Curry, and a man named Gavagan and one named Christofferson to defend, sir."

"What about the auditor?" asked Ewing. "Young Bolding."

A snicker started around the table, but Pease glared the young lawyers down.

"He's being bailed I hear," Blair said. "And I expect charges to be dropped in his case. Will you do it, Mr. Ewing?"

Ewing straightened up with excessive forthrightness. "Mr. Blair, whoever takes that case must be available to thoroughly research it. I expect to go to Washington in the winter. I must decline." He looked around the table, preventing any facial comments. Judge Pease sucked his soup.

Blair's comment was eloquent. He only ate.

For long seconds there was nothing but Judge Pease's soup, as Blair punished the great man with silence.

"Salt, please," Ewing said. But he had to reach for it himself.

There was more soup through the judge's teeth.

"All right!" Ewing said. "All right. I'll take the defense."

Blair looked up.

"If," continued Ewing, "you'll get me Jacob Burnet for associate counsel."

They exchanged glares.

"Perhaps you didn't hear me say I can't get him," Blair said. Pease studied Blair as if he had never seen him before.

Blair turned abruptly to Henry Stanhope. "Mr. Stanhope, I heard your preceptor was Tuttle of Philadelphia; and that you won a case in bona confiscata before the upper bench in Pennsylvania against Bouvier."

Stanhope kept his eyes on the table. He wiped his mouth slowly with the hand linen. But every lawyer saw his mind was racing.

"Ours is really only a routine collection of tax by confiscation," Blair continued. "Same as a state would proceed against any debtor."

Stanhope was not one to be bowled off his feet. He waited for the proposition to be fully stated.

"Chance for an exceptional young lawyer to skip five years of will writing, dower settling, petty crime and woods circuits."

"Or nail himself to it forever, Mr. Blair. The federal isn't calling it taxation. They're calling it trespass and larceny and a few more."

"But our side is clear cut. The action complied with a state law and a warrant from the auditor."

"Then why don't you defend them, sir?"

Blair slapped the table with a flat hand. "Because I've chucked a life into petit juries on this woods circuit. And in fifteen years I don't know fifteen cents worth of law, nor the feel of a federal court, nor the whims of Judge Byrd, that's why!"

Stanhope looked about to answer, but Blair cut him off. "Never mind. The job's not for such a cautious young man."

Stanhope reddened and stood up. "I'm not cautious because of the law involved! But if you'd stop and think a minute, if the plaintiff plans to rely on the Marshall decision, they'll choose some arch Federalist for counsel. The Federal circuit judge will be the same. They'll have fought the rebellion together, fought Jefferson together and then along comes me for the defense in the face of a Marshall decision. Does it look like a win?"

Blair ate.

"But I'll do this," Stanhope said. "You get your Colonel Hult to face the bench, and I'll be his second counsel. It would be a politic combination. I saw him at The Swan. I'll get him."

Stanhope stepped outside The Red Lion and sent a stable hand for Colonel Bela Hult over at The Swan.

Hult came in and shook hands with Blair in silence. He nodded to the others and sat down.

"Will Mr. Ewing do it, Jonathan?"

"No, Bela. We're asking you."

"Burnet and the others? No?"

"No. Will you take it, Bela?"

Blair looked into the saddest pair of hound eyes he'd ever seen on a man. He was looking at a man who wanted to say, "yes." But a man who was thinking about Coshocton, and what they had lost there already. "Jonathan, I . . ." Hult took out his pocket linen and swabbed the undersides of his chin. "Jonathan, you think I'm the best we got for it, huh?"

Blair looked at his friend and he surprised even himself. "No, Bela. I don't think so. We'll look some more."

The following evening Blair went to the prison to talk to Gavagan. Gavagan was all right. He said, "Tell Flannerty's boy to cut the black's feed in half when he's not workin'. And don't use the hair collar on him."

"I'll tell him, Matt."

Blair went to see Mr. Curry. Curry was frail and he was cold. But he seemed proud to be in prison.

"Don't you worry any, Blair. We'll beat them."

"You might be in here awhile."

"Don't you worry about that." Blair was leaving the prison.

"Did you find one?" The voice in the dark was a woman. He stopped and Virginia Schaacht caught up to him.

"Find what?"

"It's pretty well over the territory that you're looking for a lawyer with stomach to stand for the defendants against the Republic."

"People know I'm looking?"

"And the more time goes by," she said, "the more nobody wants the job."

"I'll get somebody. And somebody good! Plenty are against the Bank."

"Trouble with you, Jonathan, you mistake Mesopotamia for the whole territory. You mistake talk for action. Your friends talk strong in the taverns. But they won't stand to the bar and talk against Gideon Schaacht."

"All right. All right. Don't tell me what I already know. Help me find the man I need!"

"There *is* one that's man enough to stand in court against father."

"With a brain in his head?"

"He's smart enough."

"Anybody ever heard of him?"

"Lately he's achieving something of a name for himself."

"Wouldn't be one your father wants to put in my camp . . . like he did the auditor?"

"No."

"You think this man would do it?"

"Yes."

Blair stopped, "Who is he? Take me to him."

"No. I wouldn't put you in touch with this man until you've really found out how many others of your so-called supporters will back out."

"I need him now!"

"No."

"What's the matter with him?"

"Nothing. But you won't accept him until you're desperate."

"I'm already des . . . hah! No doubt. If he was worth a damn he would have come forward by now."

Blair walked faster.

"Like your others have?" She kept up to him.

"Besides," Blair said, "I don't know any good reason you should be on my side. What are you after?"

The exertion of keeping up with Blair colored her face. "I should think I'd done enough that I don't have to go into that," she said.

"Tell me this man's name. I'll see him myself."

"No point in it," she smiled. "Even if you knew the name, you wouldn't believe he could help you . . . until you're desperate."

Blair was puzzled. This woman had reasons not to help him. And she was not helping. Yet there was a teasing quality in her as though she would take him to this great man, if he would crawl low enough.

He tipped his broad-brimmed, low-crowned beaver. "I won't get that desperate."

On his third evening in Columbus, Blair's attention was grasped by a horse tied in front of The Red Lion. Only Culpepper brushed the coat so ostentatiously that it had a changing evanescent grain like mahogany. Culpepper's presence in Columbus was confirmed because next to the chestnut was Mike Stikes' big white mare. They must have come down together. But Stikes had not been to Columbus since . . . in fact he'd never been.

Blair hurried into The Swan. He didn't see them in the ordinary room. He hurried into the tap room. But he slowed up then because of the way Stikes and Culpepper leaned so intently toward Judge Pease. The men's backs were mostly toward Blair. But as he approached he heard Stikes say, "So we figured, Judge, that you could tell us the names of some of those good hundred-dollar lawyers down in these parts."

"You wasted your time comin' down here, men," Pease said. "Y'oughta know Blair is gettin' the best lawyer he can."

"We heard he's not havin' any luck."

"No. But he's tryin' the best. Been turned down by Burnet, Stanhope, Ewing and a fine lot of others. Huh. A fine lot. You think you can do better than Blair can?"

"Tisn't that, Judge," Stikes said. "But we figured when Blair asks them, it's all full of complications. Somethin' about the way Blair goes at a thing that gets it all tangled up in right against wrong and all that. But if we asked the lawyer to take the job, we'd just say 'get Gavagan and Christofferson out of the law.' "

"Oh? And what reasons would you suggest this lawyer give the court for setting them free?"

"Because it's blamed important."

"Why?"

"Why, because Gavagan does our haulin' for us. He's got the only six-wheel hundred-hundred rig up our way. The rest of us can't go runnin' off all the time and haul stuff down to the water courses and bring back iron and seed and salt etsetra."

Culpepper added, "And Christofferson's leg is bad and Miss Hope does nothing but tend him and stand by him, and won't leave him."

"Is that bad?" asked the Judge.

"Yeah, y'see while she's tendin' him nobody's watchin' out for them Merino sheep, and they got a touch with Merinos like nobody but Adam Rotch hisself. And 'rinos might save us. Only thing bringing bankable money these days."

Blair stood rooted, listening.

Pease said, "I see. But that's not law. And the Bank has bought the best law brains in the country to prosecute."

"Prosecute?"

"Yes, for the bank. Schaacht has got J. Harrison Inge in here from Pittsburgh."

The name obviously didn't mean anything to Stikes or Culpepper. But it stood up the short hairs on Blair's neck. J. Harrison Inge. The Western waters navigation case . . . decision favorable to the federal. The national road case . . . decision favorable to the federal. The Revolutionary Officers' Pension case . . . decision favorable to the federal.

Stikes said, "Well, we don't know anything about him, but we got a man looks pretty good to us."

"Who?"

"Stuttgart."

Judge Pease never got into personalities. A long pause covered his thoughts, and then he said, "Don't you realize he was working for a client who was fighting the tax bill?"

"We don't know about that," Culpepper said, "but he gives a nice speech and knows a lot of words. That carries it off, don't it?"

Blair saw Judge Pease shake his finger in Culpepper's face. He couldn't hear the words.

Betsy Deshler answered Blair's knock. She read him before he spoke, and said, "She's over at Sullivant's."

Blair crossed the Scioto in the dark. His admission at Sullivant's was cool. But from within came the music of Virginia Schaacht at the pianoforte. Blair accepted the proffered chair immune to the coolness of the offer. The music filled the small room and made it a throbbing cathedral. Blair knew it was probably because he hadn't heard much music in the woods. Yet, he could not discount it. The chords invaded him through the very wood of the floor; and in the middle of it was the straight back of Virginia Schaacht. Seen thus, with her hands moving to new sets of notes while the previous notes were still rising through the air, she was fine.

She saw him there once, but she played right on until the end. The resonance seemed to be still in the air, flickering the candles even after she moved away from the instrument.

She made it easy for him. "Are you ready at last, Jonathan?"

"Yes."

The others looked startled as Blair and Miss Schaacht abruptly left the house.

Once outside she said, "I thought you'd never come."

"Just tell me who he is and in what city," Blair said. "I'll go get him."

"I think I would have to be the one to ask him."

"Well, you could give me a note. I could ride faster alone to wherever he is."

"He isn't that far away. In fact, he's right here in Columbus."

"In Columbus!"

"You'll meet him soon enough."

She indicated the direction and Blair walked as fast as she could follow in the dark. He led the way.

"What's the man's name?" he asked.

"It isn't that his name is so much," she explained. "But lately he's displayed a strong potential."

"What cases has he won?"

"Point is he has every motive for defeating the Bank and defending the robbers."

Blair stopped.

"I mean the *collectors*."

They resumed.

"What motives?"

"Ever hear the legend about the drunken beggar who was found in the gutter outside the good Duke's palace?"

"No. Can you walk faster?"

"He was mistaken for the Duke by the Duke's servants. They washed him, put him in the Duke's bed. Next morning they shaved him and dressed him in the Duke's clothes."

"Are we going the right direction?" Blair asked.

"Then they sat him in the Duke's chair and ushered in the supplicants waiting to see him. And the drunken beggar became in fact the Duke, and a good one."

"Let's hurry."

"Well, it's the same with the man we're going to see," she said.

"He's a drunk?"

"No. But he's been on the federalist side of things. Oddly enough, though, the people have credited him with the collection of the bank tax."

"They what!"

"And he seems to like the Duke's clothes. Quite becoming to him."

"I don't know who could be credited . . . unless perhaps O'Shaughnessy who changed his vote and persuaded six others to . . . hey, we're going into the prison bounds!"

"So? You said some of the best people are in prison these days."

"Not the best *lawyers*."

"Well, he's not a debtor prisoner."

"Why are you so eager to take me to this man?"

"Gratitude."

"Huh? Why?"

"Because you made a man out of him."

Blair increased the pace. A suspicion squirmed into his head, making him impatient.

Virginia Schaacht reached for the latch thong of one of the cabins. She pulled open the door.

Blair stepped into the dark cabin. A silhouette against the hearth rose and extended a hand to Blair.

Blair reached for it, but then suddenly he withdrew his own hand. "Bolding!"

Blair bulled for the door. Virginia Schaacht snapped the latch and stood athwart.

"Wait a minute, Jonathan! Until you've thought it out. Who pleads better than a man in his own defense?"

"Huh! Which Bolding would he plea for? The auditor of the State of Ohio? Or, the chore boy of the Federal Bank?"

Blair moved close enough so his words were damp against Bolding's face, "In fact, just who the hell *are* you Bolding? You decided yet?"

And to Virginia Schaacht, Blair said, "And even if *you* know which side he's on, you know I don't need an auditor or a bank clerk! I need a *lawyer!*"

"He *is* a lawyer, but for a little matter of a signature on a piece of certificate paper."

"Oh *is* he! Just what entitles him to be called a lawyer!"

There was an impish moment of relish for Miss Schaacht. "Why, his training, of course," she smiled. "Or wasn't that so good?"

Chapter 21: THE DOCTOR

MESOPOTAMIA had a nod, a nod of the head that was a kind of jury. You can't live up in the woods, two hundred miles north of the river and pass a man without speaking. Same time, there's a limit. So the nod was for the newcomer, the nod was for the defaulter, for the man who reported sick the day of a barn-raising or a road-mending.

Lately the nod was for Blair.

Jonathan Blair had long since learned to live without the slapping of hands on his leather back in Exeter's tavern. But at least he had always been a comfortable man to drink with. Always quick to buy his round. Didn't have much about himself that was worth telling, but always listened to the others with admiration.

Seemed to absorb what Stikes had to say about the proper way to break in a new rifle; and if Blair was at the table, Slasher always expanded more about the merits of cherry timber for inside wood over ash, Hussong spread himself more than usual about how he'd improved the Mesopotamia spotted hog over what Woodbridge had done with it. If Blair was there just quietly listening, every man seemed more of a hero. Because Blair mostly just sat there studying them in a way that made a man feel important.

Now it was different, though. *They* studied Blair. This say-nothing fellow who bent no iron, dug no dirt, carved no wood, boiled no salt, it turned out now he was not just a by-sitter. Suddenly he was the middle of the town . . . in fact, the whole county. And every man's troubles . . . if you followed them back . . . somehow suddenly started with Blair.

Like Hope's sheep hiding up in the woods somewhere . . . that went back to Blair. Like Stikes' bounty land warrant not going through yet.

Then there was the debt hanging over all of them. Wasn't Blair's fault Mesopotamia Hog & Trust notes went bad. But it had been Blair got them mixed up with the U. S. Bank. Take Christofferson lying up in the hut with a shot-up leg. Wasn't Blair's fault, maybe that the pain was moving toward the knee. But take it back a step. It was Blair bulled through that Crowbar Bank Tax. Looked like a good idea for a time, but now Gavagan was in jail. And most every man's troubles went back to money, therefore to Blair. That would be all right except these were vague, mysterious troubles a man couldn't get his axe into, or his gun sights on, or his ox hitched to, or his hands on.

So Blair was accustomed lately to just nodding, and getting just a nod back, which he did now with the men at the next table as he clanked his empty mug down on Exeter's counter and walked out. He nodded again to Stikes as he passed the forge and again to Buttrick and those on the porch of the store.

He was used to it. Didn't bother him much. But he could read the nod these days. And the nod this day said, "Christofferson's leg."

But at the Christofferson place, Blair nodded to the Federal sentries outside the place.

Inside he nodded to Hope who nodded back. He knew he should have been thinking about Christofferson. That's why he came here.

But as his eye went around the room he was instead soaking up the signs of how this woman was taking care of her man. The whole room was Christofferson's leg. Yards and yards of washed bandages. A wrapper of store tea. Bottles of medicine. The sheep tools hadn't been used lately. To be the husband of Hope apparently was to be everything.

He asked, "Any better?"

"Some. The doctor is in there now."

"Hope, I came to tell you I haven't got the right lawyer yet for Brute and Gavagan. But I will. They'll have the best. We'll get him free before he ever has to leave this house."

She dismissed that subject with a wave and a deep breath.

"You may hear that I've failed. But I'm still at it."

"Jonathan, you overjudge your law business. I don't need a good lawyer. I need a doctor that knows what a chunk of lead does to the flesh."

The doctor came out of Brute's room and closed the door. He was a cheerful, brisk man of fifty with Philadelphia breeches, shiny from the saddle. The doctor had chin hair, but none grew on the back of his neck. It didn't seem right to Blair for a doctor to come out of a sick room so cheerfully, and with such unseemly interest in arranging the items in his bag just so.

Blair knew nothing of medicine, but he compared the doctor's display of his lancets, leeches and cups to the way Stuttgart flaunted his new copy of *McClean's Pleadings* in the courtroom. He noticed, though, that Hope was apparently taking comfort from the strong medical smell and the view of the object which looked like a pair of glass doorknobs, one end filled with green liquid, the other with red. The doctor wrapped it in velvet cloth.

"Pulsometer," he explained to Hope. "The bubbles show your husband's pulse to be a little rapid. But, not unduly. I've given more laudanum to ease him."

Hope reached for a leather bag. She counted out gold coin. There were some instructions and the doctor left in an aroma of sassafras, juniper, and geranium.

"He doing any good?" Blair asked.

"I don't think he's the right kind of a doctor for Brute. This doctor knows about fevers and agues and downstate ailments, but not bullets."

"Hope . . ." But Blair didn't know either.

She was tired and she raised neither her eyes nor her voice to him. She just said, "Jonathan, you want to do something for me, don't get me a lawyer. Get me a doctor."

"I'll go south tonight."

"Not south. I hear that Doctor Saul Brooks has got the pox near cured up there in the Indian town. Gershom said he seems to know a thing or two beyond leeching and pills. I want him."

"Him! But Hope, The Pigeon would no more let me get . . . that is, I took the money away from Pigeon. If I step back in there, they'll . . ."

Hope was nodding silently and impatiently. "All right. But that's what I need."

"Listen, Hope. Not only me. If *any* man from Mesopotamia sets foot in that Indian town and attempts to take that doctor . . ."

But she nodded her head some more, and started to move toward the bedroom. "I see, Jonathan."

Suddenly he had her by the shoulders. "All right, Hope. All right. Doctor Saul Brooks."

She turned back to him, and he let go of her, relieved.

"But it will take money," he said. "Brooks made it plain he wants to go to Transylvania Medical College in Lexington. We'll have to have money."

"There isn't any. Not that kind."

"Brute's two thousand dollars, I mean."

"He won't spend it for anything. Says it's for Merino rams only."

"Take it from him." Blair was impatient.

"Can't. He keeps it in his boots. And he keeps his boots on."

"When he sleeps take them off."

"He doesn't sleep."

"Then take them anyhow!"

"Did you ever try . . . from Brute?"

Blair kneaded his forehead with his knuckles. "Then you see what chance we have."

But she was nodding again and she turned to Brute's door. Hope seldom asked anything. And when she did, she only asked once.

Blair forced her to face him. "All right. All right. Don't go. Saul Brooks."

Of the many obstacles Blair foresaw, the chief one was Saul Brooks, himself. For, from his brief contact with the young doctor, Blair already suspected the presence there of a slightly unhandy streak of character.

Blair found Asa Buttrick in the store. "Asa, you've been ordering quinine out of Cincinnati for that Brooks up in the Indian town, haven't you?"

"Got some waiting for him here now."

"I'll take it up to him. I'm going up."

"Oh, you will, eh, Blair. Fine. You got ninety dollars?"

"Ninety!"

"Ninety."

"What is it, a barrel full or something?"

"Tha-ree ounces, mister." Buttrick leaned over the counter and unfolded three fat fingers in Blair's face. "Three."

Buttrick put the tiny package on the counter.

"What color currency does he pay in?"

"U. S. Bank notes."

"How does he pick it up? In person?"

"Nope. The Pigeon sends that old Captain Michael down here for it on horseback. And there's five big bucks come in with him, armed. They don't say one word. Just walk in that door there. The old man grunts and plunks down the cash. The old man holds the medicine like eggs, and the others are watchin' over him like he was Tecumseh's sacred ghost. They go up that trail . . . and gone."

"How long has this package been waiting here for him?"

"He's overdue a week now," Buttrick said with concern.

"Hmmm."

"Hmmm what?"

"I may be able to do business with the doctor at that."

"What for?"

"For Brute."

"I wouldn't have any truck with a money-hungry, Indian-lovin' son of a bitch that turns down white trade for Indian money."

"Except to sell him the medicine, huh, Asa?"

Buttrick's wattles jostled as though he'd been plucked.

Up in the Indian town, Blair had to use the smallest signs to read the minds of Brooks and Pigeon. And the chief sign he had that the Pigeon had perhaps not told Brooks about the U. S. Bank funds, was the fact that Silver Pigeon allowed the lawyer to sit here at Gershom's

table with them. The Pigeon made no reference to the bank, nor to
money, nor to Blair's last visit here.

Gershom ate in silence. The Pigeon talked. Brooks ate fast and his
mind was back in the Indian huts. His hair was blond and tied behind
his head queued into a tube of unpolished snakeskin. His oblivion to
the other conversation was plain by the abrupt, irrelevant remarks
he inserted.

"Just because that number-four hut is cured up now doesn't mean it
doesn't get the whitewash tomorrow like the rest, Pigeon."

Pigeon's face went blank, then it grinned. "Yes, Doctor, like the rest.
What you call number four is Squindatee's hut."

"Number four is easier."

"That is all right, Doctor. You call it number four. We whitewash."

Pigeon asked Blair how the pox and marsh fever and ague were
down the Scioto Valley.

Brooks interjected, "And remember, Pigeon, I want those cow flaps
shoveled away from the cabins tomorrow."

"Yes, Doctor."

And later Brooks said, "Also, that Mudeater fellow, he's well. He
just likes the medicine. Keep him out of the line tomorrow."

"Yes, Doctor."

"And go now and check on Squindatee that he's in his hut."

"Yes, Doctor Brooks. Right after eating."

"Now."

The Pigeon grinned and went out.

Blair decided to strike quickly. He said, "Doctor, I came up here to
ask you to come down to Hosmer Village to fix a man's leg."

Gershom's great hawk eyes bored into Blair. Fawn came from the
back room. Brooks looked at Blair and then as though the lawyer's
request were not worthy of answer, he scraped the last of the bacon
onto his trencher, and ate.

"I said we'd be grateful if you'd come down to Hosmer Village,
Doctor Brooks, and tend a man's leg."

"There's doctors enough around to set legs for white men," Brooks
said. "I came up here to wring the pox out of these Indians, and I've
done it nearly. Then I go to Transylvania to hear the lectures. I came
up here to get money for that. And that's what I'm going to do."

"That needs a lot of money, doesn't it?"

"Yup." Brooks finished his coffee. "And they're payin' me a lot."

"You sure they've got the money, Brooks?"

"They've had everything else they said they had. And they've co-operated, too. Did you see how those huts are cleaned up?"

"How do you know they have the money?"

"They showed it to me when I first came up here." Brooks got up and put on his coat. "And they been payin' for the medicine I called for right along."

"Could you just come down to Hosmer Village for thirty days, say, to take care of this man's leg?"

"Thirty days to set a leg?"

"It's not broken, Doctor."

"What then?"

"It's shot."

Brooks shoved out his lower lip. But he said, "There's doctors in Columbus."

"That's what we got, Doctor. But the leg is swollen up. Red in places. Dark blue in others."

"Where is the red?"

"Around the mashed part."

"And the blue area?"

"It's not an area. It's streaks."

"Streaks! Why didn't you say streaks? What's the doctor doing for it?"

"He put a lot of ground up hickory bark around it."

"Bark!"

Fawn watched the doctor become absorbed and she glared at Blair.

"This doctor . . . is he a Homeopath or a Botanic?"

"How would we know?"

"Well did he say if he studied under Thompson or under . . . what is your doctor's name? Did he use large amounts of Calomel?"

"We don't know these things, Doctor."

"Look, it's important. If he is a Homeopath, maybe that bark thing is legitimate. They believe in inducing mild symptoms of the thing they're trying to cure. But if he's not a Homeopath-type doctor, his bark thing may be just plain no-count pract . . . what's his name?"

"Brooks, you got to come look at our man!"

Brooks suddenly woke up. He put on his hat. "No, sir. That's how I'm five years late getting to the lectures at Transylvania. Always it was 'just look at this one more patient please.' And always I stayed a year." Brooks's blue eyes accused the whole room. "That's why I

stand here today . . . ignorant! I don't know if bark induces an immunity or not. I'm neither a bona fide Homeopath nor a Botanic, nor
even a horse doctor! I always put off the lectures. I've seen it happen
to others. So I fix your man's leg. And while I'm doing it I don't learn
how to fix a thousand other men's legs! Good day!"

Brooks went out of the cabin. Gershom rose up from the table.
When he had reached his full six foot four he yelled, "Blair, can't you
leave us anything up here! You think it's right to come up here and
take our doctor when you couldn't even help us get one? What are you
thinking of!"

"I'm thinking of a man with a shot leg. I didn't say it was right.
I just said I'm up here to get a doctor for Christofferson."

"Huh! You thinking of the man with the leg?" Gershom sneered.
"Or his wife!"

The cabin door opened and bit off the talk. Brooks leaned in, "Blair,
how long has this wound been open?"

"Since before I was up here last."

"Since before you were . . . good God! What part of the leg?"

"The calf."

"A clean hole or . . ."

"No, all mashed."

Brooks was drawn into the room as if by magnet.

"Does the man eat?"

"A little."

"Sleep?"

"Very little."

Fawn walked in front of Brooks and looked into his face, "It is
time now," she said, "for Mudeater's cheah-ha to be born perhaps."
Brooks alerted. "Yes. Besides, I said I'm going to Transylvania."

He turned to go. But Blair grabbed him by the only handle he could
find.

"Transylvania! All right!" Blair rose. "If the Indians have paid you
enough to go to Transylvania, they did it with money that was got for
them by Brute Christofferson. He got shot in the leg getting it. You'll
owe your education to Christofferson, Doctor."

Gershom grabbed Blair's arm. But Blair rose and shrugged loose
from the preacher's claw. "And if they *don't* pay you enough for
Transylvania, Hosmer Village will."

Brooks scowled, "I'll take mine from the Indians."

"Will you? They don't have it to give, Brooks."

Brooks laughed.

"All right, laugh. But have you asked for money yet?"

"No. But I will."

The door opened and The Pigeon stepped in. His quick face took in the room. "What is this loud talk?"

"There he is," Blair said to Brooks. "Ask him now."

But Brooks just stood there looking at Blair. "That's a low way to get a doctor, Blair."

"Is it? Then think this one over Brooks. Why do they let your last shipment of quinine sit so long in the store down at Hosmer Village? Ask them if they have the money to pay for it?"

Brooks turned to the Indian. "Have you the money for the quinine, Pigeon?"

"Uh . . . yes, Doctor."

"Then why haven't you sent for it?"

"I did not know it comes so soon. Apparently Mr. Blair looks out for our interests. He maybe sits all day to see if the Indian quinine comes."

Blair said, "Pigeon, we only want the doctor for thirty days. It's for Christofferson."

Pigeon mimicked bitterly in a whining singsong. "We only want the doctor for thirty days." He dropped the mimic. "But when I asked *you* for a doctor, what did you give me? Talk only. Now, get out, Blair!"

"Pigeon, damn it, you don't need the doctor any more. He's got your town fixed up. We need him!"

The powerful Indian moved on Blair, but these two had measured each other before and apparently it was not necessary again. The Silver Pigeon's voice came out hoarse, "Try and get him, Blair. Try it!"

"I didn't want it on that basis, Pigeon," Blair said. "I only wanted to borrow him. But if that's the way it is . . ." Blair turned to the doctor, "Brooks, I suggest you ask The Pigeon for your money now."

Brooks said, "I suggest you get out."

Pigeon smiled. Blair walked out.

But apparently the doctor did ask for his money. Because two days later as Blair waited impatiently on the trail south of Upper Sandusky, he saw a small Indian pony approaching. The pony carried a man, and two bulges astride the saddle. Behind was a pack pony with two bulges. It was the silhouette of a doctor in the Northwest Territory.

Blair dropped down the trail quietly, two miles south, to a defile where the trail went between two granite faces, nearly perpendicular. In nervous times or war times, smart men never rode through the defile which was known as Navarre's Pinch because of the time that Slover Navarre's squatters trapped Armstrong's scouts there. You could still see traces of the little side trail which circumvented the Pinch like a toll dodge. But it was a laborious climb and seldom used, mostly at night, and when there was trouble.

Blair checked his rope which was fastened to the top of a birch which was pulled down across the path so that its top was down behind the south face of the granite bluff. He thought he had done everything exactly as he had heard Navarre describe his trick in Exeter's Tavern. For all he knew he might even have the very same birch tree. Navarre had said you should have an axe to activate the pinch. But Blair felt the edge of his heavy knife and hoped. The convolutions of the ground afforded him cover and yet allowed him to watch the cut. He saw the doctor's pony approach. Brooks's mind was apparently already at Transylvania, and the pony picked his own way down the trail.

Blair waited until the pony had picked his way to the place where both forehooves had stepped over the trunk of the bent-over birch.

The lawyer laid his knife over the rope and hit the back of the blade with a rock.

The doctor heard the click. But it was too late. The birch swished up noisily, its top branches fighting with other branches.

The trunk came up under the pony's belly, slammed him against the face of granite and then spun him around sideways. The pack-horse guide rein halted the spin with a jerk.

The birch whished on by to the upright position.

Brooks was on the ground scrambling for his rifle which was rolling down the rocky incline. Blair jumped on his back, pulling the doctor's arms up behind him until the latter's face was in the rocky path. The lawyer took no chance, for the young doctor looked strong. He roped the two wrists together and then wrapped the end of the rope around the windings between the wrists.

Brooks had seen so much unspeakable conduct up here already this past few days that he was neither outraged nor excited. Only taciturn. With Blair's help he remounted his pony and rode ahead of Blair.

Thus did the doctor and the lawyer enter Mesopotamia in the winter of the year of Christofferson's leg.

Exeter and Hawkins, Fitchburg and Stikes, Culpepper and Faith Hawkins and some others crowded into Christofferson's room behind Blair and the doctor.

Christofferson lay there, white. Hope had washed him and combed his hair. His usually whiskerless face had grown a beard long enough so that you could see here and there speckles of gray in it. His eyes were smoldering black in an expressionless face. Hope had drawn a sheet over him.

Exeter said, "Just tell me which bag you want brought in, Doctor."

Brooks stood there, eyeing Christofferson. "I don't want any of them brought in. I told you I'm on my way to Transylvania. I just want to be untied."

"I'll bring in all the bags then, Doctor," Exeter said. And the bags he brought in were not new like the other doctor's.

Brooks said, "I told you I'm not a certificated M.D. anyhow. I'm only a legal practitioner. And I can see even by this man's face that he needs the best."

Hope Christofferson said, "You're the best as far as we're concerned, Doctor. We heard what you did up at the Indian town."

Blair said, "Look, Brooks. All we ask is you take care of Christofferson and then stay here thirty days so we're sure you did it right."

Brooks glared contempt at Blair. "You want a guarantee, huh?"

"Sure, but we're willing to pay for it."

"Do you guarantee court victories, lawyer?"

Christofferson's voice was weak. "Blair, get that man out of here. I didn't ask for him. The doctor we got is doin' good enough. And he's willing."

Blair ignored the big, helpless Christofferson.

"Brooks, I told you we'll pay your way to Transylvania."

"I've been told that before you know."

"I guarantee it. Every man in this town will pledge a part of it."

There were sharp intakes of breath around the room. Brooks saw it. "That their idea, Blair? Or just yours?"

Exeter said, "It's just his, Doc. We got along all right without a doc so far."

Blair pointed to the tavernkeeper. "And we got a full buryin' yard to show for it, Exeter. Your share is twenty dollars. Mike, yours is thirty-five. Buttrick, we'll count on you for forty dollars."

"Now wait a minute, Blair!"

But Blair walked over to Buttrick, "How was Elizabeth's cough when you left the house this morning, Asa?"

Buttrick's jowls backed up, "Well, all right, I admit it'd be a good thing to have a doctor here. But forty dollars!"

Hussong next began to protest, but Hope cut him off, "You'll be the first to want him, Joe, if the hog cholera comes back. You been buryin' about two a month."

She had hit Hussong where it hurt. "All right, Hope. But twenty-five is all I'll go." Hussong whirled to examine the doctor critically. "And how do I know he knows anything about hogs?"

Brooks turned red to the roots of his blond hair. "You can take your hogs to the devil, mister. I wouldn't so much as . . ."

"All right. All right," Hussong said. "You're ornery enough you probably know your business."

"My business isn't hogs!"

"Yeah, but I can tell you got the stuff to catch on fast. I'll go for twenty-five dollars worth of the doctor."

Brooks was speechless. But Hope brought in her leather bag and counted out sixteen dollars in gold and silver. Blair took a pencil and scraps of paper out of one of the doctor's bags and got signed notes from the others for pledges toward the doctor's tuition to Transylvania.

He stuffed them in the doctor's chest pocket. "There's part of it. And here's Hope's share in cash. And I'll get the rest . . . in writing."

Exeter had an afterthought. "But don't forget, Brooks, that means you got to stay here thirty days and *then,* after you get this schoolin', you got to come back here and settle."

Blair glared at Exeter. Brooks laughed. "Oh, is that so? No thank you, gentlemen. If this is a sample of your town, I've already had too much. I'll be goin' now."

Brooks moved to the door. The crowd moved out of his way with unflattering alacrity. Exeter even flung open the door with a flourish. Blair sagged. Then suddenly he called, "Doctor!"

Brooks turned around, quietly defiant. But he was not prepared for Blair. The lawyer suddenly threw back the sheet over Christofferson's leg.

The room went silent. Brooks stared.

The puncheon floor creaked as Brooks, with a trancelike expression, moved slowly to the bedside.

When his hands were freed, Brooks took hold of Christofferson's knee gently. Christofferson winced in pain. Brooks let go. He took hold of Christofferson's leg up higher where it did not hurt. Then he moved his hand lower in succeeding grips until Christofferson stiffened in pain.

"All right, sorry."

Brooks's face was contorted with concentration as he examined Christofferson. His mouth was open and his lips pulled back as though he were squinting into a hot fire. Without taking his eyes off the leg, he opened his bag. He soaked some wisps of fleece in some clear liquid that smelled like Amos Exeter's tavern, and he swabbed over the wound, after he had propped Brute's leg up where he could see the underside. Mesopotamia craned its neck.

Brooks stood up, "I want whisky."

"What?" Hope asked.

"Whisky. The strongest you've got." He measured Christofferson. "About a quart and a half."

Exeter said, "I got just the thing." Exeter scrambled out with importance.

Brooks untied Christofferson's boot and took hold of it gently to pull.

"Leave the boots alone, Doctor!" Christofferson said.

Brooks ignored the patient. Christofferson kicked, "Leave 'em alone, Doc."

Brooks looked up, surprised. Hope said quietly to Mr. Brooks, "If you could leave him his boots it would ease his mind."

Brooks glared.

"I know it's hard for you to work," Hope said. "But if you just could leave his boots on I'd be obliged to you."

Brooks' face softened. "All right. He can leave them on . . . unfortunately."

When the whisky came, Brooks directed Hope to feed it to her husband. She gave him a cupful. "More," Brooks said.

She gave him more and Brooks looked up from his bag, out of which he had gotten some leather straps, "Give it all to him."

As Brooks worked he frequently looked at Christofferson's face and felt his pulse at the wrist, and laid out instruments. At one point he said in a quiet tone which Blair found too matter-of-fact, "Everyone out of here. The wife can stay."

Brooks studied the faces of the men in the room and then he pointed to Stikes and to Blair. "You and you, wait in the other room. I'll need you later."

Mesopotamia went out, but not far out. They stood near the cabin speculating and comparing opinions of the doctor. Strangely most agreed with Hussong, "I favor a little cussedness in a doctor. Means he's got to know his trade."

But talk was cut short by a shattering roar like the dehorning of a bull. They surged back into the cabin.

Brooks was against the cabin wall. Around his throat was the massive hand of Brutus Christofferson and across his chest was Brute's great forearm. Christofferson kept his weight on his right leg, his left pantleg was slit revealing the inflamed calf muscle, big around as the gaskin of a draught horse. In Brooks' hand was a small shiny, silver saw.

Christofferson let go. Brooks sagged to the floor. The patient seized the doctor's leather bags one at a time and pitched them through the thin doeskin window.

Brooks rose from the floor unruffled, "Get off that leg, you crazy ox!"

"All right! But I'll keep it! I thought it was a doctor Blair brought! When I want a leg butchered off, I'll get Hussong! Now get out!"

The reactions in the room varied.

This much, though, was apparent to all, including Brooks. If he wanted to leave now, he would not be stopped.

But he did not leave.

In the days that followed Mesopotamia became accustomed to the blunt, unsmiling face of Saul Brooks. It was an odd thing about him . . . a man didn't like to go up and ask him to look at an ailment because of the way he looked straight at a man as though he'd heard all this before. It made you think you shouldn't be troubling him with this. You should be glad you were alive and keep quiet. Without saying anything at all, he had the town pretty quick so that Charlotta McGuire didn't much enjoy telling him about that mysterious ache in her head. Yet Camelia Flannerty somehow understood that she was quite welcome to call him over to look at her brother, Tim, when he was down, even though Hank Flannerty hadn't signed one of the pledges to buy a piece of the doctor.

But even though Elizabeth Buttrick's cough improved and Tim Flannerty got cured quick and Aaron Fitchburgh was made spry, it was a disquieting thing to watch Brooks ride his Indian pony out to the Christofferson place every other morning, knowing what he was trying to persuade Hope to do. And you had the feeling that after he'd done the awful thing he would just wash his hands and pack up his bags and go eat his supper. Mesopotamia had a pain in its leg just thinking about poor Brute. Each man had his own horrible vision of the awful procedure. And a simple thing like Saul Brooks passing could make every leg in the store hurt and take the laughs out of Exeter's stories.

When you'd pass a man like that you'd just nod, and that's all except some of the older women shuddered a little. As for the younger women, well it was more like a shiver, unpleasant a little, but exciting. In fact Elizabeth Buttrick confessed to Camelia Flannerty she'd like to take a comb and run through that blond hair and straighten it out a little. Also take that snakeskin thing off his queue and tie it with some black ribbon. But when they passed him in front of the store, Camelia Flannerty said to Elizabeth out of the side of her mouth, "But when you see him, can you picture yourself doing that for him?"

And they nodded as they passed him.

Every morning he carried a crock of special whisky out to the Christofferson place. But he always brought it back, unused. And one day he rode back to the common with a great blue-black spot under his eye, about the size of Christofferson's knuckles.

When thirty days of Saul Brooks were up, Blair had a tough assignment. It was in the store that it happened. Hussong said, "All right. So the thirty days is up. So let him leave, I'll not stop him if he's that kind of turncoat."

"No turncoat," Blair said. "That was the bargain. But we've got to pay him the money we pledged. Today's the day."

Hussong's laugh recruited support behind him, "Ho-ho. Blair, count me out. I didn't get twenty-five dollars worth. The two times I asked him to come out to check my sows he refused. Me pay?" Hussong waved a big hand.

Exeter followed up, "I ain't had a sick day since he come. I should pay twenty dollars for not bein' sick?"

"Well, you may get your money's worth yet, Exeter," Blair said, "because it's probably going to make you sick to know you *got* to pay, like we agreed. It's not Brooks' fault you didn't get sick."

Charlotta McGuire was there. She said, "Jonathan, we called Saul Brooks about my head noises. He said to call him when they got as loud as a horse stompin' into the barn. But they never got that loud. Why should we pay?"

Blair grinned. "Charlotta, if you don't get a view of the gates of hell, will you take back the money you paid to the Reverend Gershom?"

But Exeter, riding the popular side, said, "No joke, Blair. We don't pay."

It was along in there that the blunt face of Saul Brooks appeared in the doorway. He said, "Blair, I overheard the trouble."

"Don't worry, Brooks, they'll pay. But up here we pay hard just by nature. Insures we get full measure. But you'll get your money."

"I know I will," Brooks said.

Hussong asked, "And just what makes you so all-fired sure of that, Mr. Brooks?"

Brooks reached in his pocket and pulled out some slips of paper which he handed to Blair. "Because Mr. Blair here will see to it."

Even Blair cooled to the offensive assurance of Brooks, "Me?"

"Yes, Blair. You commandeered my services. I guess I have the same privilege. You're a lawyer. The circuit court gets up this way now I understand. Here are the contracts. Yours to collect."

"Contracts!" said Exeter.

"Yes. I believe those notes you signed constitute contracts, wouldn't you say, Mr. Blair?"

It was too much. Hussong hung his thumbs in his chest pockets and leaned his elbows back on the counter behind him. "All right Mr. Lawyer. Collect."

The argument was little further along when Hope came into the store. She commanded attention because of the red under her eyes and because of the urgent way she marched directly over to Brooks.

"Now, Mr. Brooks!"

"You've persuaded him?"

"No. But I know now what you said is true. It's got to be done. And it's got to be now."

"I doubt if I can even get the straps on him. I've never seen his strength anywhere."

Hope looked around the store. None volunteered. Her eyes lingered on Stikes, who stood it for a minute and then said, "Hope, I will if you say, but . . ."

She looked at Buttrick. Buttrick's face quivered. "Hope, I couldn't."

Hope looked at Hussong. The hog farmer studied the floor, but when he looked up she was still looking at him. "All right, Hope. I'll come." Then he looked around in anger, "And you'll come, too, Buttrick. Least you can do! And you, Mike, and Exeter. Let's go, Brooks, and get it done."

But Brooks did not move. Hope tugged at his sleeve. Brooks shoved out his jaw. "You can think what you want, Mrs. Christofferson. But I'm not going until a certain matter is settled here."

Hussong looked at the slips of paper in Blair's hands. Blair's own mouth fell open. Hussong said, "My God. Even at a time like this!"

Hope looked baffled. Hussong explained, "The bastard wants to be sure he gets his money. Why I'd sooner . . ."

Hope looked around the room and last at Hussong. "Please, Joe."

Hussong glared at Brooks in loathing. But he slid his fist into the pocket of his breeches and addressed the room. "All right, men, for Hope."

And the hard knuckles of Mesopotamia went slowly into its pockets and came out with cash.

Hope said, "Please hurry!"

At the Christofferson cabin Brooks silently laid back the cover and spread apart the slit pant leg of Brutus Christofferson.

He grasped Christofferson's knee very lightly, but it must have been like a needle in the eye to Brute. He pressed his finger into the out-side of the thigh and Brute still winced. He ripped the trouser leg up higher and touched the hip bone. He pressed harder than before, but Brute still stiffened.

Quickly now Brooks pulled Christofferson's shirt out of his belt and examined his flank. He touched it with his hand and Brute rolled away from him.

Brooks exhaled, and pulled the cover back over Brute's leg. He picked up his bag and walked out of the cabin. They followed him out.

Hope's face was misery and her eyes were wet. Brooks said, "At the knee I could have saved it. Even at the thigh I begged you. At the hip there was a chance. But now? No point to put him through the pain."

Men are sparse enough in the great Northwest that you don't pass even a miserable buck Mingo in silence. But there's a limit to everything. So when Saul Brooks rode his lead pony south across the common toward the ford and Transylvania College somewhere south of the Ohio River in the Kentuck Country, his only farewell was a nod from the porch of the store in Mesopotamia.

Chapter 22: HUNDRED-DOLLAR LAWYER

HOPE CHRISTOFFERSON could see now why Blair had been so anxious to find what Stikes called a hundred-dollar lawyer.

Jonathan Blair had always seemed like a downtown sort of man to her. She had always been able to imagine him walking into the finest house in the world and handing his hat to the house man. But as she looked at him in his buckskin jacket here in the old legislature hall, among these downstaters in Chillicothe where the Federal circuit court was in session, she could see that he was up-county people like herself and like Matt Gavagan, next to her, and like Mike Stikes who sat behind the rail which they called the bar.

Hope Christofferson was here to see that they got it all straight about Brute and his part in it. When they came up to Hosmer Village to move the sick man down to the Chillicothe courtroom, she had had Doc Brooks tell them to get out and leave him alone, which they had done upon her agreeing to be present.

But today, she could see by how many people had come crowding into the courtroom how important the thing was that Jonathan Blair had got them all mixed up in. There were women in this courtroom who had obviously never worn linsey next to their skin, and there were men here with morocco leather shoes and wrist cuffs like women.

The room was full and many of them were studying Jonathan Blair. You might see some buckskin behind the bar in an Ohio circuit court, but you didn't expect to see it in front of a federal bench any more.

Hope was a little proud of Blair in that he seemed to know what this was all about and understood everything.

Once in a while he'd look over at her and Gavagan and that Mr. Curry and he'd smile as if to say they shouldn't worry.

But still she noticed that he looked anxiously over at the two finely dressed men who sat at the opposite end of the table from him. These men had a bigger pile of papers than Blair, and a bigger pile of books. And their books, like their clothes, were new. She noticed too, that Blair's ruffle-fronted shirt which looked so white and fine up in Hosmer Village, looked bedraggled and yellowish here when it was seen directly opposite the chest full of Philadelphia ruffles.

Everybody knows that clothes don't make the man. But they told a story here today. The auditors who sat closest to the bar in good black cloth coats were there to see Schaacht win. Hope wondered why Bolding didn't get bailed out and go over and sit with his friends. But instead Bolding sat here with herself and Gavagan and Curry, being defended by Blair.

But the clothes of the largest part of the auditors here showed them to be on Blair's side of the discussion. After three years of money grief the cloth on the settlers' backs had worn so thin you could see bare character showing through. You could tell by the way they studied Blair that they liked their representative. But you could also tell they wished he had another lawyer to assist him the way the opposition did.

And whenever he got up to speak, they strained forward with him. On the faces of some you could see the wish that he'd bear down on the judges a little harder, and that he'd stomp around more like the opposition did.

J. Harrison Inge walked around a courtroom as if it were his. The opposing counsel, the auditors and the judges on the bench became his guests. And they were to sit quietly and not disturb his thoughts as he walked around. In fact, the auditors absorbed the uneasy feeling that they were not even guests, but eavesdroppers. Inge was alone in the room with the judges, it seemed, in private conversation; not so much a conversation either, but a seminar in which Inge appeared to instruct the judges.

Inge was a very red man, aggressively red. His hair was red, with grey threads. It disappeared into a long, thin, black silk queue. His face was thin and his skin was thin, and the light came through his veinous ears, red. The thin membrane between his nostrils was prominent and very red when the light shone through it. He was that pale-eyelashed kind of redhead who looks cold as ice and smart as a trap.

He inspired no affection. But he inspired great quiet from the bench, the gallery, the jury. You could say what you wanted about him, but you didn't say it very loud. Among the bar itself, he had perhaps no friends. But he had many admirers. The gallery today was packed with seasoned Western lawyers who had ridden long distances for a chance to hear J. Harrison Inge at the bar. They wished he had better opposition.

But you could not watch J. Harrison Inge without learning the trade of the advocate. When Blair objected to a question, Inge instantly withdrew even before the judge ruled, and moved on to another question, as if the first was unimportant anyhow, giving the distinct impression to the entire court that the defense counsel was concerning himself with trivia. But Blair learned to watch for the same question to recur a few seconds later in disguise.

Occasionally when Blair would object, Inge would close his eyes briefly as though his good nature could barely stand much more such nonsense. On one occasion, after three such consecutive objections from Blair, Inge started a question, paused in the middle of it and turned to Blair as if expecting an objection. By reflex Blair rose, but finding he had nothing to object to yet, he sat down.

"See? The defense objects to me just on general principle!"

Inge smiled. The gallery chuckled. Blair burned.

The more alert ones not only admired Inge, but they admired his client also. For they now observed Gideon Schaacht rise from the gallery, walk up to the bailiff and hand in a note. The bailiff walked over to the advocate's table and handed the note to Inge. Inge turned the note over and looked at the back of it. Then he placed it face down on the table. And while Jonathan Blair made a serious point on the inadequacy of this court to decide the question, Inge let the curiosity in the room build up to the point that even Mike Stikes wished Blair would sit down so they could hear what was in the note.

When the best of Blair's argument was over, Inge stood up slowly and said, "Your honors, I beg leave to interrupt because of an offer just brought to me by my client."

"Go ahead," said Byrd.

"Well, since my client is not interested in discomfiting any of the defendants, since his only desire is the return of the stolen——"

"Object!" said Blair. "The word 'stolen.' Unwarranted assumption to prejudice the court. That's what we're here to try, whether it's stolen or not."

"Sustained."

Inge closed his lips at the interference and amended. "Since his only desire is the return of the money to the bank, he would like the defendants to have comfortable quarters during trial. He has therefore arranged to raise the two hundred fifty thousand dollars bail for the defendants."

"Object!" said Blair.

"What grounds?"

"Attempt to influence the jury, favor of the plaintiff. These details can be arranged in chambers."

Inge said, "I ask only that defense counsel do me the courtesy to ask his clients if they would like to accept this bail, so that we can make the necessary arrangements. Your clients would no doubt prefer to sleep at the inn."

Inge looked at the well-dressed Bolding. Bolding said nothing. But Gavagan blurted, "Naturally we'd rather sleep in the——" Hope's elbow silenced him and she said, "We'll stay in the jail. A few more days won't matter."

Bolding nodded.

Judge Byrd said, "Bench sustains the defendant. These details can be handled privately."

Blair watched Bolding. Bolding could certainly play a part to perfection. To look at him one would think he despised the bank's offer.

But the bail offer from the plaintiff indicated that Schaacht was afraid of having any martyrs on his hands.

It came Blair's turn. He walked slowly from the advocate's table to the bench in the hush that usually precedes the defense's first major speech. As he walked he studied Judge Byrd. It was a good face, a reasonable face, a face of considerable courage. But it was a professionally blank face. It offered neither encouragement nor discouragement. Blair was disappointed at this. Not because he expected favor at this point. But this remarkably complete blankness was a trait of young judges leaning over backwards to be judges. Now Judge Byrd was an old hand on the bench. Old enough and respected enough that he could afford to smile at the advocates, ask after their health, he was even known to josh an approaching attorney at times with, "Now, Ned, let's have it straight this time."

But today Judge Byrd had on his young judge's mask. Which meant that he was aware that he had a landmark case on his hands this time. Blair watched Byrd fold his hands and compose himself as he wished posterity to view him.

This was bad. Blair knew that a judge can be so preoccupied with phrasing his decision for the printed page that he makes his decision the way he thinks history should be made to read.

Blair did not blame the judge particularly. He asked himself, "If I sat there, would I be deciding whether states can tax the Federal Government? Or would I be deciding whether Christofferson and Gavagan should go to jail?"

In any case Blair could see the judge had braced himself to make history, so Blair knew he would be disappointed at what he was about to hear. And it was in fact very true that as Blair talked the judge's face betrayed resentment. Blair was saying, ". . . and so I maintain that we have here no suit, and that if we did have a suit, this court is not entitled to exercise jurisdiction. The bill of the plaintiff should be made out against the State of Ohio . . . not against the individuals, Gavagan, Christofferson, and Curry."

Byrd leaned forward and put on a pair of glasses. "Do you omit Bolding's name on purpose?"

Blair still did not think of Bolding as one of the defendants. He corrected himself and continued. "The acts complained of by the plaintiff," continued Blair, "are the acts of the legislature; the party charged with aggression and trespass is the state legislature; the relief prayed is against the acts of the legislature. Therefore, this court must dismiss the case or stay proceedings until proper parties are made."

Judge Byrd wiped his glasses as if to see if he heard right. He obviously was not pleased.

"Are you presuming to say, sir, that there is then only one court in the world which can try this case, and that is the United States Supreme Court?"

The laughter came from the auditors, not from the judge. But even that faded when Blair's answer cut through the room. "I am saying exactly that, sir."

The auditors looked at each other uncertain whether to laugh or what. But neither J. Harrison Inge, nor the judge, nor Gideon Schaacht laughed. They only looked at Blair, surprised.

Byrd recessed five minutes to consider the point. He returned to announce that, where the proceeding is *in rem,* the court could and would definitely act upon the subject matter of the controversy. "So proceed."

Jonathan Blair, up-county lawyer from Mesopotamia, then proceeded to the great pleasure of the audience to draw an extremely persuasive and understandable counterattack against the Bank of the United States, a condemnation of the Bank's disastrous policies to the population of the state. In this section, he was frequently interrupted by objections from J. Harrison Inge, most of them sustained.

He then proved that the collection of the tax, loosely referred to by the plaintiff as "the robbery" was by confiscation, an accepted method of collection of any state debt.

But he was at his best near the end of the third day of the trial when he brazenly attacked the very foundations of the bank case. On the day preceding, J. Harrison Inge had traded heavily on Marshall's late decision. It had given him a close which rang with authority. Judge Byrd was comforted at the thorough documentation which relieved him of going against Chief Justice John Marshall.

But on the morning of the third day, Blair shattered all that.

"The great mistake of Mr. Inge was way back in the beginning," Blair said, "when he framed the Bank's charges against my clients. His charges assume that the Bank of U. S. is not subject to the taxing power of the State of Ohio, because he believes, like most of us, that the U. S. Bank is an agency of the federal government.

"Allow me to show you that this is not so."

The entire courtroom leaned forward.

"The Bank of the U. S. is no more an agency of the U. S. Government, than the Cross Keys Tavern across the road."

There were laughs in the gallery. But they died from lack of reaction from Blair.

"In fact the Cross Keys Tavern may be more of a federal agency than the U. S. Bank. As I remember when General Harrison mobilized the third regiment here, the troops spent three to four hours a day in the Cross Keys Tavern. The proprietor then might have well named it the U. S. Tavern because it served the U. S. Troops.

"Now, the U. S. Bank is the same thing. It is nothing more than a private business establishment which is in the business of making loans for profit."

Blair now went into a detailed story of the origin of the bank in Philadelphia by private individuals. He called to the stand several witnesses who were stockholders in the bank. He forced them to explain how they had not had to lay out much cash for the stock, drawing out the fact that they had paid for their stock from subsequent dividends.

"Now then, if it is just a private business establishment, how did it come by the sacred title of U. S. Bank? Well, one of the customers of this bank is the United States Government. The U. S. borrows money from the bank for which I might add it pays a good interest. In addition, the United States needs to have its money stored in various places in this country so that it can pay its bills. The U. S. genially agrees that in exchange for the dubious privilege of storing its money in these banks . . . which are called Federal Depositories . . . it will not draw this money out suddenly. But I would like to point out how handy this is for Mr. Schaacht. While this money is on deposit, Mr. Schaacht is permitted to loan it out, on interest. Now since the bank is going to handle so much of federal funds, your government thinks it wise to hold a few seats on the board of directors. They therefore purchase a few shares of stock in the bank, the same as you and I are privileged to do, and just as you and I might buy shares in the Cross Keys Tavern, if Mr. Higgins were selling."

The laymen in the gallery were leaning forward with their mouths open. The U. S. Bank dwindled before them to a tavern; and in fact, as they looked at Mr. Riddle sitting there, he did indeed begin to look like a bartender.

"Now, just as Mr. Higgins might have named his tavern the U. S. Tavern because of selling whisky to the U. S. troops, so the bank in question named itself the U. S. Bank because the U. S. was one of its customers. Now, I believe this court would not say it would be unconstitutional for the legislature of the State of Ohio to pass any tax they desired on the tavern of Mr. Higgins. Why then can that same legislature not tax in the same way this bank of Mr. Schaacht's?"

Blair sat down.

He had scored, and he knew it, not only by the buzz of vehement approval which swept the gallery, but by the slackened jaw and unguarded expression on the face of Gideon Schaacht. For just a moment, Blair saw naked attention on Schaacht's face. Schaacht jolted alert angrily when Blair caught him in this moment of impressed repose.

Attention of the gallery now shifted with a smile to J. Harrison Inge, opposite Blair.

Inge walked to the bench with his arms behind his back. He stifled a yawn, as though the case were exceedingly routine. And it must be admitted in his favor that it had the effect of calming down the court and deprecating Blair's last speech.

"Plaintiff begs leave to remove a juror, the third one from the left."

Blair studied the third face from the left. "On what grounds, pray?"

"The decision lies with the judge, Mr. Blair. But the juryman had applied for a loan to the bank and was refused. Naturally he would be prejudiced against my client."

Blair came forward. "Perhaps so, but no more than the other eleven. It is impossible for you to empanel an unprejudiced jury in this state."

"Sir?"

"And as to its being the judge's discretion, I believe you err, sir. I I believe it is at my discretion."

"Yours?"

"Yes. We were put to considerable delay on your account. I find now that you may only withdraw a juror on account of misconduct of the juror, or with my consent."

Byrd said he would recess to consider.

During the recess the attorneys for both sides retired to the Cross Keys Tavern. Poorly clad men crowded around Blair and wished him well. It gave him a good feeling.

But when the bell summoned them back to the courtroom, he saw something which rasped the raw ends of his nerves. Walking down the street to the courthouse came Justin Bolding, accompanied by the federal guard assigned to hold him. But he came from the direction of Schaacht's house. And beside him, looking up at him, walked Virginia Schaacht. Blair stopped in the middle of the road to watch. Others stared with him. Seconds later Gideon Schaacht, surrounded by five men, came walking toward the courthouse, smiling.

Blair did not like the taste of it.

Inside the old legislature hall, Blair moved through the crowd toward the bar. Stuttgart, who was present as an auditor, caught his sleeve and congratulated him on his handling thus far.

"And I'm especially pleased to heah ya'll gettin' an assistant," Stuttgart said. "Makes us all feel kind of sheepish, the way nobody had spine enough to stand up with you. But I hear you got a good assistant now, Blair. Ya'll deserve it."

"An assistant?"

"Yeah, we figured you picked him. That's the talk."

Blair walked inside the bar, bewildered. Maybe Bela Hult had decided to come in with him.

But it wasn't Hult.

Judge Byrd announced that a new counsel for defense had been admitted. And would be allowed to speak on the point under discussion. Blair watched in amazement. The bailiff walked over to the defendant's box and opened the gate, admitting to the inner rectangle of the bar. . . . Justin Bolding.

Bolding smiled at Blair and walked toward the center of the bar. But Blair was on his feet. "Sir, what do you mean you're admitting this man to speak for the defense?"

Byrd said, "Well, naturally I assumed the request originated with you, Blair. You are directing the defense I presume."

"Yes, I am, and I neither requested, nor will I permit this man to speak."

"I'm afraid you have nothing to say about it."

"Not only am I persuaded that he does not have the loyalty to my side of the argument, but he is not even an attorney."

"Are you forgetting that a defendant can speak for himself in any court? Apparently Mr. Bolding has elected to do that."

Blair stared in unbelief. So tightly was Bolding bound to Schaacht and the bank, that Blair had forgotten the ironic twist which made Bolding one of the defendants. A man as smart as Gideon Schaacht would not forget this, though. Blair sank slowly to his chair.

Justin Bolding addressed the bench with impressive poise.

"Your honor, may I proceed with Mr. Blair's point that it is impossible to select an impartial jury for plaintiff."

"You may."

Bolding addressed the jury. "Gentlemen, do you have any money in your pockets? Will you get it out, please?"

The jurymen looked puzzled, but they pulled out their money. Bolding selected the fifth man from the bailiff's box. He was big and whiskered and his hair was doubled into a thick club queue in the back. His neck was thick, and his chin whiskers were a half-inch long. Bolding picked up a twenty-dollar bill from the juryman's hand.

"What is a dollar?" Bolding asked.

"Huh?" The juryman's forehead wrinkled.

"What is this I have taken from you?"

"Why, it's a twenty-dollar bill. Bank of Muskingum currency."

"But what is it?"

"Why just what I said."

"I mean how did you get it? Do you remember?"

"Sure. That's for twenty hundred-pound spotted hogs, paid to me by Muskingum Packing Company."

"But what did you do to the hogs?"

"Why, I raised 'em, fed 'em, notched their ears. I gelded 'em, fattened 'em, slaughtered 'em and hauled 'em to town and unloaded 'em. Didn't you ever raise hogs?"

The court laughed, except J. Harrison Inge, and Gideon Schaacht.

Bolding grinned, genially. He had good courtroom presence. He said, "How much time would you say you spent on those hogs?"

"Why, takes about a year to get these skinny critters up to a hundred pounds. You know that."

"But I mean how much time, say in hours, would you say you spent on just these twenty hogs?"

"Oh, I see. Why, maybe if you filled it in solid . . . thirty days."

"Thirty days. All right. And for that thirty days labor you got this twenty-dollar bill."

"Right. And damned lucky to get it the way hogs are gluttin' the Muskingum."

"So, it would be safe to say that this twenty-dollar bill is really thirty days of your time?"

"Uh . . . ayeah."

"All right." Bolding reached into his pocket and pulled out a five-dollar bill, a U. S. Bank note. "Now, would you swap me this twenty-dollar Muskingum Bank note for this five-dollar bill? It's a U. S. Bank note."

"You're dang right I will." The juryman reached for the bill. Bolding gave it to him.

"Now don't you want to know how I got this five-dollar bill?" Bolding asked.

"Dang right I do."

"Well, I got it by going to the Cincinnati money market. I sold a thin packet of ordinary local bank notes to get this U. S. Bank note. The transaction took me about an hour. So you might say this five-dollar bill represents four hours of my time. You have just swapped me thirty days of your labor, for four hours of my labor. Do you like that?"

The juryman turned red in the neck and forehead. But under the constraint of his strange surroundings he sat down, injured to the soul.

Bolding turned to the bench. "A dollar is a unit of work. This juryman who produces solid worth in the form of hog flesh has just traded me thirty days of his work for four hours of mine. That's what the Bank of the U. S. did to him. I could repeat the same transaction with most every member of this jury. Do you tell me that every man on this jury, or any jury, won't be prejudiced against the bank, Mr. Inge? Shall I continue?"

Byrd scowled at Bolding. "Bolding, you confuse me. Are you arguing for the defense or are you supporting Mr. Inge's request to withdraw a juror?"

"I am proving Mr. Blair's point that it will be impossible for the plaintiff to find a jury, and therefore we should not be delayed while they try."

Byrd pulled his chin. "Mr. Bolding, you have made a point which deserves the most serious consideration. Recessed until tomorrow."

Bolding smiled at Blair. Blair did not smile back.

The following morning Judge Byrd announced his decision to discharge the jury with the consent of the defense. J. Harrison Inge smiled.

The trial began over again before Judge Byrd.

Charles Willing Byrd then found the defendants guilty of trespass against the close of the United States Bank, and liable for returning $100,000 to the United States Bank, plus court costs, plus interest on that portion of the money which was in gold bullion or specie. The prisoners were to remain in custody or be freed on $250,000 bail.

And Jonathan Blair traced his defeat directly to the day Judge

Byrd decided to dismiss the jury, which was the day Justin Bolding interfered to make his courtroom essay on the subject, "What is a dollar?"

At the bar in the Cross Keys Tavern Jonathan Blair observed how quickly the fruits of victory came to Gideon Schaacht. When it had looked as if Schaacht could lose the case, men talked more boldly to Schaacht, including debtors. But now he was back in power more firmly than ever, and the men of the West rushed around him to listen to his words of wisdom.

But Gideon Schaacht moved away from them and walked to the bar where he ordered a Monongahela for Jonathan Blair.

"No, thanks," said Blair.

"Have it your own way, Blair. But two like us should work together. I could keep a lawyer of your ability busy and wealthy."

"How?"

"Well, naturally I will proceed with collections and foreclosures now that the court has established our right to be here. That's lawyer work, Blair. And I could use you."

Blair's tankard came off the bar and knocked the glass out of Schaacht's hand. "Schaacht, I said I'd drive you out, and I will. You'll foreclose nothing!"

Schaacht looked at his broken glass on the floor and then he laughed. "How will you stop me, Mr. Blair?"

"I will take State of Ohio legal protection away from you. I will see that sheriffs won't foreclose your mortgages, courts won't try your debt instruments, constables and sheriffs won't protect your money. I'll leave you all by your damned self."

Schaacht laughed. "I've been that way before, Blair."

"Well, don't dismiss your lawyer, you'll need him."

Schaacht's laugh followed Blair out into the road and to his dinner and to his bed, and all along the trail up to Columbus.

Chapter 23: THE FULCRUM

THE jailkeep at Chillicothe had never had such a fancy customer as this J. Bolding, one that insisted on wash water twice a day and was now handing his coat and waistcoat out to him through the bars to be taken to the tailor for pressing. "And mind, tell him to stick it on a hanger when he's done, Constable." The swelling constable was on the point of making a counter suggestion for the lodging of the coat, but he withheld it because of the intimidating stature of the visitors who now approached to see Bolding.

That girl who was so striking pretty that you couldn't look her steady in the face, now came in with her father, Gideon Schaacht.

Schaacht waited until the jailer was out of rumor range and then he said, "Bolding, I see you did learn something from Blair after all."

"What do you mean, sir?"

"Getting rid of that jury was the smartest stroke I've seen in a courtroom for a long time. A Federalist appointee on the bench, confronted by a case in violation of Marshall's own decision!" Schaacht threw back his big head and laughed. "Beautiful!"

Justin Bolding smiled. Virginia Schaacht studied this smile. He smiled at her, too. But that was not good enough for Miss Schaacht.

She said, "Well? What do you have to say to these congratulations?"

Bolding grinned. "I say I wish you two would get out of here. Your presence embarrasses me. You forgetting I'm the hero of the debtors, Gideon?"

Schaacht froze off the new first-name familiarity. But Bolding's grin held like dried plaster.

Schaacht said, "But you've got to get out of here now, Bolding, and get up to Mesopotamia. I want to know what Blair's up to."

"What makes you think he's up to something?"

"Because of the way he left here. I'll have horses ready for you in the morning."

"Don't arrange bail on my account, Mr. Schaacht."

Schaacht squinted into Bolding's grin, "What did you mean by that?"

"I mean I don't think I want any more favors from you, Mr. Schaacht."

Virginia was interested. Schaacht was puzzled.

"I mean I think Blair can help me more than you can."

"Blair!"

"Sure, show me another law student as young as I who will get a chance to recite in the Supreme Court of the United States."

"Supreme Court!" Schaacht thought he saw the joke and he laughed. But Bolding didn't. He said, "Certainly. Blair will appeal. It's presumptuous, but you forget what you've made of Blair. He doesn't even seem to know it himself. But this state and three others are watching that man now. If he only had the sense to know it, Illinois Territory would give him a lot of help. Indiana, too, and Kentucky. They all have crowbar laws drawn up, patterned after his. If he succeeds, they're all going to pass those laws. They'll pressure Blair to carry on. He'll appeal because he worries about people. You said yourself he's tougher than a man that work for fees."

"The Supreme Court!" Schaacht breathed, without laughing. But the laugh broke out again. "But . . . *Blair!* Blair in the Supreme Court!"

"I didn't say Blair would go to the Supreme Court; I said he'll appeal. He won't have so much trouble getting a good man to take the case for him now. Ewing, Corwin, or Hurley over in Indiana, they'd all love a chance at it. And *I* go with the case, whether he likes it or not. I'm the *defendant,* remember?" Bolding let it sink in. Then, "You're better off to keep me in jail, aren't you?"

Schaacht admired brains, wherever he found them. "Hmm." He reached through the bars and whacked Bolding's shoulder. "Y-e-a-h."

Riddle came puffing into the jail with some papers in his hand. "Gideon, if you'll sign these requests to the county sheriffs, we can start debtor and collection and foreclosure proceedings in a week, beginning in Cincinnati."

Schaacht chewed the inside of his cheek and studied the floor. "That's not soon enough, Riddle. And we'll have to start first in Mesopotamia. Get all our people in my office right now. And the complete debtor list! Now! Hear me?"

The swiftness and the mightiness of Gideon Schaacht in the West were well known to Jonathan Blair. But it now suddenly struck Hope

Christofferson with an impact Blair had never been able to convey to her. Hope measured all men against her heroes. And to her the great man of the West was Adam Rotch. He was the man who had brought to the West a salable product, a stuff which would hold its value until you could get it to market. When nothing else would sell, you could usually get metal money for a Merino fleece.

Yet this great man was now humbled by Schaacht. That Schaacht could sit in Chillicothe and yet somehow reach way up to Big Sippo Creek a mile east of the Tuscarawas, somewhere in the new Stark County, to lay strong hands on Adam Rotch was to Hope the height of power. Yet it had been done.

As Blair and Hope traveled north toward Mesopotamia through the Borough of Columbus, she saw a circle of beautiful dirty Merinos nuzzled into a circle for warmth. And in the center of the circle stood the great Quaker.

Around the Merinos stood a group of men, haggling over price. Rotch had brought part of his flock here to Columbus to sell off enough to clear a United States Bank mortgage. But the bids were low. Men were beginning to understand that Merinos were like gold. But they had no gold to exchange for them.

Rotch was delighted to see Hope Christofferson because of her knowledge and understanding of Merinos.

"My husband has got hold of two thousand dollars, Mr. Rotch. He wants me to get three good breeder rams with it, and if possible, ewes to match."

Rotch was firm, but kindly. "Mrs. Christofferson, for the kind of flock you're building, don't buy the kind of ram that comes three for two thousand dollars with ewes thrown in. I have two here you should consider."

To Blair's amazement Rotch remembered the names of each of Hope's rams and inquired after the health of Galahad. Rotch said, "All right, with those rams you need a longer combing wool type. And you should, if you can afford it, purchase one or two of these ewes who have a good record for bearing twins and triplets. These two rams I'm advising you to own are producing sheep which yield about eighty to a hundred hanks to the fleece. Since your flock is small, you need that."

But Hope could only afford one at the price Rotch had on them, and she insisted on looking at three cheaper quarter bloods. But

Rotch was adamant. "My sister, you are wrong. You must learn. Buy everything else as paltry as you can. But for the ram, look for the costliest you can find."

But between the two rams Rotch recommended she could not decide. She asked him which he would choose.

Rotch shrugged and sighed. "If I should pick the one for you, and if he should come down sick, you would think the other might have stayed well."

Hope studied the two rams for a half hour. She felt them all over, measured the hanks of fleece, scraped the hooves and studied the ear tags. Finally she said, "How long since they've been fed?"

"Four hours."

"Give me some fodder, and I will choose my ram."

The men who had been trying to buy the sheep were piqued at being ignored by Rotch in favor of a woman. And now while she made up her woman's mind, one of the buyers said, "Hey, Rotch, if the lady wants to go through some hocus-pocus while she decides, you could at least tell the rest of us the prices of these."

Rotch froze the speaker. "Sir, I suggest you would do well to watch this lady who is one of the best breeders of Merinos west of Pittsburgh, and she is working under the most difficult pasturage conditions imaginable. You probably know about her."

One of the men said, "You mean that's that woman that's got her flock hid up under the Greenville Line, and half the United States Army is up huntin' 'em?"

Rotch nodded his head and the men now eagerly grouped around to watch this woman who said she needed fodder to select between two rams.

Rotch placed the two prize rams on the other side of his wagons. Then he scooped a handful of fodder out of his small wagon and started toward the two select rams. Hope said, "No, Mr. Rotch. Let them see it, then take it over there about six paces."

The two rams eyed Rotch and turned around to keep him under surveillance as he circled them and then walked away from them.

Rotch placed the fodder on the ground, and looked back at Hope, puzzled. Hope watched the rams.

The smaller, but darker, of the two pricked up his ears and stuck his head up in the air. His orange-spotted black nose flickered a moment, and suddenly he marched briskly to the fodder. The other followed.

"That's him in front," Hope said.

Rotch raised his eyebrows and smiled. The crowd of men looked at each other and grinned. Hope removed her boot and paid for the ram.

It was painfully evident, almost as soon as Blair and Hope reached Mesopotamia, that the long hand of Gideon Schaacht had preceded them here. It had turned Mesopotamia in against itself in a way that wrenched Blair.

The long hand of Schaacht was manifest here in a new secrecy in contacting Blair which was foreign to the days when Sam Hosmer fought the town's battles. Time was, if there was trouble here Sam Hosmer would yell the whole length of Exeter's bar, "Hey, Blair. Buttrick is tryin' to collect from me for a shipment of rope that got sunk on a keelboat out of Pittsburgh. Do I have to pay him, or don't I?"

That's how it used to be. But now they came to Blair privately. Amos Exeter, the elected constable, was the first. He rapped on Blair's door after every light on the common was out.

"Blair, I need to talk to ya."

When they sat down in Blair's cabin, Exeter's face fought with itself. His chin was out with self-righteous determination. His forehead was wrinkled with shame.

"Jonathan, we heard what happened at the trial. Everybody says you did right good. We was surprised . . . I mean they said it was somethin' to see the way you stood up to them down there, just as good as a regular lawyer . . . I mean just as good as . . . I mean, they said you would of won it if that Bolding didn't trick you, the way he did."

A new directness had crept into Blair's speech in the last half-year, the same that comes to mechanics and craftsmen when they change from dreamers to doers. He said, "Thanks. But you didn't come for that."

"Nope. Didn't. Y'see, fact is, you lost the case."

"Yes."

"So that means Schaacht can move in now."

"Yes."

"I'm constable. And Ault says I got to serve the foreclose notice on the debtors. Says I got to start with Hussong."

"That's your job. If he pays you the twenty-five cents per writ, you've got to serve it."

"But I can't serve the writ on Hussong. He's . . . well, he's in my tavern every day. And he's my . . . he's . . . well, he's like to flare off, too."

"That's right. But there's a way out."

Exeter leaned forward gratefully. "How?"

"Nothin' says you can't resign, does it?"

Exeter sank an inch and revolved his hat over his finger. "Yeah, somethin' does."

"What?"

"Well, I . . . well, after all I *am* constable. It's my *duty*."

"Duty never sat that heavy on you before, Amos. What other reason?"

"Well, fact is, Ault thinks he can get me an extension if I'll help him execute the foreclosures."

Blair saw more than he wanted to see. Schaacht was organized. He stood up. "Your problem, Amos."

Exeter flared off. "Yeah, now it's *my* problem. *You* lost the case, and it's *my* problem! Huh!"

The next one to come was Adams. He too came late at night.

"Amos wants to deputize me to help him serve notice on Hussong."

"Did you accept?"

"He says I can't refuse deputation."

"He's right."

"But I can't serve no writ on Joe. He's . . . he's my next neighbor."

Blair grinned, "And besides he's tough, huh, Adams? Shoots quick."

"Yeah. So what do I do? If I can't refuse the deputation?"

"I never saw you to worry about a point of law that fine, Adams."

"It ain't the law side of it."

"What then?"

"Well that Exeter's built a fence around me that's pig tight, horse high and bull strong."

"How's that?"

"He says if I do it, Ault will get me an extension on my debt."

Blair poured them both a gourd of whisky and sat down.

The next to come was Mike Stikes and then Jim Hawkins and

then a few more. But the day that opened Blair's eyes the widest was perhaps the day that Emanuel Ault walked in. Blair wished Ault had come like the others, after dark. Instead he came in broad daylight. When Blair opened the door he saw a few men on the porch of Hosmer's Store, watching. Ault said, "Yeah, I know, Blair. You don't much like to be mixed with me. But I guess we can't help it. We're in trouble."

"How am I tangled with any trouble of yours, Ault?"

"You got to help me get Hope's mortgage back from that preacher, Gershom."

"Sorry. Not interested."

"I know. But you will be."

"How so?"

"Well, you know Schaacht wants me to collect from Hope, bein' as I'm head of the Mesopotamia Hog and Trust. Says the case is too well known around the state. She's got to be brought in line or he'll have trouble all over the state."

"That's his problem, not yours."

"He made it mine, Blair. He says he'll have me locked up for criminal neglect if I don't close her out. You think he could get a lawyer to make that stick?"

"Might."

"Well, suppose you were his lawyer against me. You think you could make a case against me?"

Blair thought a moment. "Yeah, guess I could. But Schaacht wouldn't put you in jail."

"Why wouldn't he?"

"Because you're no good to him in jail."

"He says I'll be an example then to the new man that he'll put in as head of the Mesopotamia Bank which owes the United States Bank. He says that way the new man will see to the foreclosures."

"An outsider couldn't run our bank," Blair said. "Not and foreclose against these people."

"Schaacht don't mean an outsider."

"Who then?"

"You!"

Blair leaned back and laughed. "The man is crazy. I wouldn't take the job."

"He says you'll have to."

Blair laughed again. "How so?"

"He's not sayin'. He just says wait and see."

Blair slapped the table with the flat of his hand and roared. But then the laugh faded fast as Blair faced squarely the record of Gideon Schaacht for keeping his promises.

Ault said, "I notice you're not laughin' all of a sudden. I'll expect you'll deliver that mortgage paper from Gershom right soon now."

Thus the town closed upon itself so fast that Ault was not five minutes out of Blair's cabin before Mike Stikes appeared. With him was Hussong, Hawkins, Hope Christofferson and five others. When they walked in Stikes and Hope and Hawkins sat down, the others stood up. Stikes only said, "We saw Ault comin' out of here, Jonathan."

He expected some kind of an answer to this, obviously. But he was in no hurry. He sat there crimping the edges of a sheet of copper with a pair of pliers.

But Blair had no answer and so made none. Without looking up Stikes said, "We got quite a surprise when you went down there to the big court and gave it back good to those professional lawyers. I mean those expensive ones. They said that one you was fightin' against gets maybe two three hundred dollars. And we heard some say you licked him if it had been called fair. But seein' Ault walk out of your place, well we just wondered what we're supposed to think about that."

"You, too, Hope?" Blair asked. "You wondered, too?"

"I wasn't wondering about anything, Jonathan, until just now when Ault told me you'd be plannin' a trip up to see Gershom pretty soon. Naturally it set me a bit nervous."

Blair looked at Hussong. "You, too, Joe? You want to know where I stand?"

"I thought I knew pretty close, Jonathan. Seemed to me you was heart and soul with us, all you went through and everything. All I know is I'm over in Hosmer's Store just now . . . these men were there with me. I'm buying some seed from Buttrick for next spring. Wanted to try some of that Kentucky gourdseed corn to thicken the hogs. Just as I got it all picked out and Buttrick's agreed I should get credit for it, up comes Ault and says something to him, quiet. Next thing Buttrick don't want to mark me any more credit on

his big book. He ain't sure I'm gonna be here to harvest it. I ask him
how come, and he points to Ault. And Ault says, 'Ask Blair.' So
here I am . . . askin'.''

It was a reasonable enough statement. But Blair flared, "Why
doesn't somebody in this town try trusting somebody? You avoid
each other on the common. You sneak over to my cabin one at a
time. Time was when old Sam was here we'd bring our troubles up
right out in the open over at the tavern. A man would help another
man, and we didn't try to kill each other off.''

Hussong said, "I'll admit it was better when old Sam was here,
but whose fault is it that he ain't?''

Blair turned dark. "I'll take my share of the blame, Hussong, but
you were the one went bustin' into the bank to save your own skin,
and to the devil with everybody else. Now instead of each of ya
lookin' out for your own skin, why don't ya look for a way we can
all come out of it!''

Hussong moved on Blair, but Stikes waved him back. He continued
bending the edges of the sheet of copper. "You told us a mouthful
there all right, Jonathan. But this money thing is beyond most of us.
We got to look to you to lead us out. And lately, looks as though
you might know the road. But before you get riled at us you got to
admit your Crowbar Law didn't come off so good. Started off fine,
but it backdrafted on us, and looks like it'll burn us all out. You didn't
do it right.''

Blair stood up. "Do you know how it should have been done?''

"Think maybe I do.''

Old man Stikes' quiet presumption left Blair speechless. "Y'see,
Blair, I think you're doin' more lately to fill old Hosmer's shoes
around here than anybody. But they're still a little too big for ya.
They got to callin' your law a 'crowbar' law. Now I'm no lawyer. But
it wasn't really any crowbar at all. To have a crowbar you got to
have a fulcrum.''

Stikes held up the pliers casually and worked them back and forth
as though studying their action himself. He squeezed a coiled strip
of copper flat.

"Now take if it was Hosmer made that law, Hosmer would have put
a fulcrum in it. Hosmer, y'might say, had a lot of crowbar laws
around here, remember? And we always did what he said, remember?
Because he knew more about crowbar laws than you do, Jonathan.

He always had a fulcrum to work his lever against. Remember? If you didn't stand a turn at guard watch, you didn't get to come in the blockhouse when Rontondee come down here raidin'. And so forth. See what I mean, Jonathan?"

There was silence in the cabin, as they watched the idea sink into Jonathan Blair. Blair grinned. "Mike, you're a damned fine lawyer."

" 'Course I don't know how you do this." The old man was pleased. "But you see what I mean, boy?"

"Yeah, Mike. I do."

Jonathan Blair saddled up in the dark. He pulled his stirrups up two and a half inches shorter than usual. The bay got the point, and raced south for the Borough of Columbus.

The way the action appeared on the first page of John C. Gardiner's *Freeman's Chronicle* was not entirely fair to Jonathan Blair, due to two facts: first, the editor could not afford to offend the men who opposed Blair so bitterly; and second, Blair's speech was so long that the editor ran out of lower case "e's" toward the end. Since the United States Bank had begun refusing Franklinton Bank notes, the *Freeman's Chronicle* had not been able to buy a single stick of new type. And it was necessary to use what "e's" were available on the paying advertisements. Yet by the careful language of the editor it was obvious that he knew this was a story which would be copied by every editor with whom he exchanged papers. His article said:

Fulcrum Law

The General Assembly of this state was amazed on Thursday last to hear a long and impassioned speech by Jonathan Blair of Mesopotamia. Blair is the author of the so-called Crowbar Law which recently attempted to evict the Bank of the United States from the West.

Blair began his speech by announcing that the legislature should not be depressed over the recent adverse decision of Charles Willing Byrd in the United States court at Chillicothe. He said that the court at Chillicothe had no authority to pass judgment upon a law made by this legislature. He said that at the conclusion of his argument here today he would ask the legislature to pass still another law which would become the fulcrum for the Crowbar Law.

Here Mr. Blair walked up and down the aisle and talked so rapidly that your editor was not able to write down all his remarks. But he said, "I therefore recommend that this Legislature should declare the Bank of the United States to be an outcast beyond the pale of Ohio law. Every jailer in this state should be forbidden to receive into his custody any person committed at the suit of the bank, or for any injury done to it. Justices of the peace, judges and grand juries should no longer take cognizance of any wrong committed on the property of the bank, though it were burglary, robbery, or arson . . . since our tax for these services has been disallowed."

The silence in the lower house was deafening as Mr. Blair went on with his staggering proposal. The members looked stricken. Mr. Blair noticed this and he said, "Yes, I can see some of you making faces of distaste for the benefit of the gallery." With his hands in his pants pockets Mr. Blair turned to look up at the improvised gallery where sat Miss Virginia Schaacht, Mr. Gideon Schaacht, Mr. Riddle and Mr. Rouff. "But let me tell you that if you miss the opportunity to vote for the bill which I am about to present, you have passed the last chance to prevent the most utter economic devastation which shall ever have descended on a region. You will return to your homes from this session to see your neighbors' lands and chattels knocked down under auction hammers for pennies on the dollar."

When Mr. Blair sat down to listen to the reading of his so-called Fulcrum Bill, the house remained in such a silent state of shock that the clerk forgot to rise to read the bill. In this paus , R pr s ntativ Tr main took th floor and ask d for adjournm nt. Th motion was b ing nt rtain d by th sp ak r. But R pr s ntativ B la Hult from Coshocton County ros and call d a point of ord r.

Th bill was imm diat ly giv n its first r ading on Monday, 12th ult., D c mb r. W go to pr ss b for th vot . But full t xt of th bill is r produc d on pag four.

Public Notice

The highest price will be paid for genuine bank notes on Boston, New York, or Philadelphia banks. Also for other good eastern bank paper. Apply at auction office or contact me at The Red Lion. Elias Phillips.

Public Notice

The subscriber intends opening a school on the 21st inst. in the house lately foreclosed on Uriah Johnson on High Street. Courses of instruction will be arithmetic, surveying, dialing, reading. Tuition must be paid in U.S. Bank notes or in some good eastern bankable money.

S. Jamison

N.B. None need apply but such as allow of moderate correction when necessary.

THE SUBSCRIBER

. . . will sacrifice a good Pennsylvania stallion, roane in exchange for $4.00 in metal money which is desperately needed to pay a certain debt. There is also a fair condition coach to go with him for $5.00 in bankable money.

Jules Standish

Notice

The following produce will be accepted in payment for subscriptions to the Chronicle at the following rates:

Whisky ....14¢ gal.
Dressed Deerskins ....75¢

But the subscribers would accommodate the editor by paying in bankable currency, as some of this is needed for the purchase of new type from Pittsburgh, particularly "e's," both capital and small case.

Notice

Choice lands are now available at low rates because of the necessity to foreclose many parcels in this area. Apply to J. Riddle. In person or by mail at the Chillicothe office of the U. S. Bank.

*　　*　　*

Blair returned to Mesopotamia late in the night. The town was dark and he unsaddled, fed the bay and went to his bunk.

Next morning Tim Flannerty saw Blair's bay in the shed and therefore came into the cabin to wake up the lawyer. "Thought you'd want to know about it, Mr. Blair. Reverend Gershom's come down. Miss Hope got him to come down to hold a special church this morning to ask that Mr. Christofferson's leg gets better."

Blair sat up. "Is it worse, Tim?"

"Yeah. Swelled up big. My old man says Mr. Christofferson is hurtin' real bad. He saw the rams Miss Hope bought, and liked 'em fine. Then he got worse."

Blair pulled on his pants. Tim brought his boots over.

The lawyer entered the blockhouse just as the Reverend Gershom was finishing up. Hope sat there in the front as the others streamed out of the church. A few of the old-timers, including the lawyer, went up and gathered around Hope. She saw Blair and he could tell she was glad he was there.

Gershom said, "Hope, before we go out to see Brute, I brought something down with me for you. You might as well keep this piece of paper. I keep worrying about if I should lose it." Gershom reached in his inside coat pocket. Then he reached in his waistcoat pocket.

Blair noticed the first frightened look he'd ever seen on the minister's face. Gershom began slapping all his pockets.

"I can't find it!" he roared.

Hussong was watching with alarm also. He said, "Reverend, was that Hope's mortgage paper? The one you brought Ault to his knees with?"

"Yes. Yes, but I've lost it."

"Lost it, hell! Did you stay the night in Exeter's Tavern last night?"

"Yes. Yes."

"Did you lock your door?"

"Never do."

"Come on over to Exeter's Tavern," Hussong said. "That miserable Emanuel Ault and that miserable Exeter are closer'n thin hogs on a cold night lately. They're fixin' to make Hope the first one foreclosed because that Schaacht's got a mean streak about her. And I'm s'posed to be next, because if they can close me down they figure the others'll give up easy. But I'm tellin' you I'll hang that Ault up on a slaughter hook first. I notice neither of them skunks was in church this mornin'. Come on."

But they didn't have to go beyond the outside of the blockhouse. Exeter stood there sheepishly. Ault stood there smugly.

Ault said, "Serve the papers on both of 'em, Exeter."

Exeter reached in his pocket nervously. "Hope, we had to do it this way. You got to be first and Hussong second. We couldn't chance it any other way. The church is the only place where there's no firearms these days. If we went to Hussong's place, we know he's got a rifle propped through a hole by the cabin door. And Brute's that mad in the head lately he'd shoot before he thought it out good. So we had to do it like this."

"Do what, Amos?" Hope said.

"We got to serve the writs for the debt. You always wanted to be treated like the rest of the men, Hope. We're all pretty tough up here. I know you'd serve it on me if you could save your place."

Hussong said, "Did you let Ault into that tavern last night, Exeter?"

"He would have got it whether I let him in or not, Hussong. He was gonna waylay the preacher and swipe it anyhow."

Exeter's face jarred under the glare of the big hog farmer. But he bulled his way through. He pulled out the paper and handed it toward Hope. "Might as well get it over with, Hope. You got to sign that I gave you this paper . . ."

But before he had finished the sentence he was up in the air, stretched out lengthwise and he came down on the frozen ground with a thud like a dropped rock that made all the watchers wince. Hussong did not let go of Exeter's arm. He flung it so that Exeter's own hand hit him in the stomach. Hussong snatched the papers out of Exeter's limp hand and began to tear them. As he did so, Ault yelled, "You got the writ in your hand, Hussong! You been served!"

Hussong dropped the papers in a rage. "I'll serve you!" He grabbed two handfuls of Ault's coat front and swung him against the blockhouse so the wind came out of him in a grunt. But Ault was tough physically and morally. He swung a rocklike fist at Hussong's jaw. He missed the jaw, but struck the neck, turning the hog farmer's face purple and his brain red. Hussong stormed at Ault. Blair grabbed Hussong from the rear. Stikes grabbed Ault. Hussong surged from side to side, breaking Blair's grip. But Gershom then grabbed him. Hussong roared like a stuck boar, "You damned lawyer, Blair! If you can't help, for God's sake get out of our way at least!"

Blair reached into his pocket and pulled out a copy of the *Freeman's Chronicle*. He poked a stick through it and jammed it into a hole in the blockhouse wall.

"Read it," he said.

They crowded around the paper.

ACT TO WITHDRAW FROM THE BANK OF U.S. THE
PROTECTION AND AID OF THE LAWS OF THIS STATE

Sec. 1   It shall not be lawful for any sheriff or keeper of a jail to commit any person arrested upon a mesne process or taken or charged in execution of the suit of the President or Directors or the Bank of U.S.

Sec. 2   It shall not be lawful for any judge, j.p., or other officer to receive or deliver any proof or writ or deed to which the Bank of U.S. may be a party.

Sec. 3   Fines for sheriffs, constables, judges, notaries public or j.p.'s who violate this act will be $500 and summary removal from office.

Jos. Richardson
HOUSE
Allen Trimble
SENATE

Mike Stikes broke out in a grin which was a pleasure for Blair to see. "Now ya got some real leverage, boy!"

Hussong read it aloud for Hope, who turned to Blair. "Jonathan, that means they can't touch us, doesn't it?"

"Not unless we lose our appeal on the Crowbar Law, Hope. And it gives us some time to think."

Hope exhaled, and her face was lighted with a relaxed beauty which made a man want to grab hold of her and tell her she deserved it.

There was even an exhausted sort of sweet smile there which didn't change until Tim Flannerty came running up.

"Miss Hope! He wanted ya, at the cabin!"

Hope ran stumbling toward her mount.

"No use to hurry, Miss Hope. Not now."

Chapter 24: THE MESOPOTAMIAN

MESOPOTAMIA had no way to measure the thing which happened to it now. It could not be said that Mesopotamia was a place of affection. The earnestness of survival here brought a reserve to the town, for though you shared your whisky with your neighbor today, you might need to refuse to share your oats with him tomorrow, or your salt or gunpowder. But in one respect this town was a family, for though they had lashed Hank Flannerty on the bare back thirty-nine times for larceny, they would permit no outsider to touch Hank Flannerty, and they had once forcibly delivered Flannerty out of the county jail.

Likewise, when one of their number was elevated by the outside world, each Mesopotamian took unto himself a handful of the honor. And they had had many honors. Indeed nature's own refining process insured that any who survived this far north and west should be greater men than elsewhere.

Mesopotamia had produced Sam Hosmer. They had produced Thomas Woodbridge, who had developed the Mesopotamia Hog, heaviest breed in the West to date. They had produced Mike Stikes, whose Stikes Rifles were already known as far as The Illinois Country. They had produced Hope Christofferson who was known across at least three counties as the woman whose sheep were making Major Armstrong the laughing stock of the army.

So Mesopotamia was accustomed to honor. But what happened now to Jonathan Blair shook even Mesopotamia's complacency.

In the tavern Culpepper said, "My God!"

Buttrick said, "Not only that, the legislature *insisted* he be the one."

Stikes said, "Darnation, there'll be no more five-dollar law cases handled around here, 'less we get in another lawyer."

Hope Christofferson cut five inches out of the sleeves of the late Brutus Christofferson's white shirt. She washed it and dried it in the sun. Mike Stikes polished a piece of iron so smooth you could hardly feel the pits, and he took it out to Hope's place. She heated it at the hearth and she ironed the shirt. She handed it to Jonathan and said, "When you take it off at night, hang it over a chair. Those inn hangers will let Brute's shoulders hang off the ends too far."

"Thank you, Hope, but what about the sleeves?"

"I shortened them."

"Enough?"

"Yes."

"How do you know?"

She colored. "There was a time or two I had occasion to know the length of your arm, Jonathan."

Even the new settler, Isaac Steese, the tanner, was in the spirit of it. He came over with a fine pair of saddle bags, one side of which had compartments for Blair's three law books.

The word even got up to the Indian town at Upper Sandusky. Fawn stepped silently into Blair's cabin. She handed him a light tan rough-buck trouser belt. It was sparsely decorated with polished animal teeth.

"From the Silver Pigeon?" Blair asked.

"No. From Mudeater. He waits for me outside the town."

Blair smiled, "Tell the Mudeater I like it. Almost as much as if it was from you." Blair grinned.

"From me, this. The white man's goodbye." She rose to the toes of her moccasins and kissed him on the mouth. She giggled and left the cabin.

From Buttrick, Blair got advice. From Joe Hussong, Blair received great tribute. "Jonathan, it's a big thing. You're like . . . why it's like finding a full-blooded Bedford boar hid in a passle of woods pigs."

Blair rode south across the ford wearing the colors of Mesopotamia in leather and brass and a clean white shirt, cut to fit.

Jonathan Blair had never felt so incompetent. Standing once in Hope Christofferson's shed when Guinevere and Evangeline were both dropping twin lambs in the same hour, the other men had been sweating-busy and Blair had stood by stupidly, not knowing where to turn his hand.

Today he felt that same cowlike ineptness as he stood up in the cellar of the Capitol in the city of Washington, Republic of America. The others stood up absently, continuing to study their papers and

confer. Even the opposing attorneys stood up automatically and continued talking in whispers, not even glancing toward the great white
bench which rose at the far end of the room. The gay and chattering
guests in the gallery only subdued their small talk as much as Hope's
sheep at feeding time. There was more discipline and respect in a
Western circuit court held in a tavern. But Blair naively paid attention
to the marshal of the court.

"Yea! Yea! Yea! Yea! The Supreme Court of the United States is
now in session. All persons having business before the court will be
heard! God save the United States and this honorable court!"

There was more. But Blair's eye wandered around the cellar. He
was partly disappointed that the highest justice bench in the land
was tucked in a remote corner of the cellar under the Capitol. But on
the other hand he was glad there was no overwhelming grandeur.

The small room was pie-shaped, the bench at the apex. It was
about the proper size for a county courtroom in, say, Columbus.

The place was so crowded that the judges now entered from a side
door and were helped into their robes by the clerk right in front of
everybody.

Blair immediately spotted the great man, not because of his bearing
or dress, but because of his height. John Marshall apparently stepped
on the hem of his robe and couldn't get it up over his shoulders. The
chief justice laughed among the judges as though there were no
attorneys or spectators present. The laugh encouraged Blair; it was
too hearty for an intriguer, and too spontaneous for a bigot. It was
a fair man, Blair felt.

John Marshall's iron-grey hair was tied in a blunt club behind his
head. On his way to the center seat at the bench he reached a long
arm up to rub the moisture off the cellar-type window and he apparently commented on the weather to Judge Story. Good God, didn't
he know the whole Western economy was about to be put into his
hand! He wiped a window with it.

Since no one paid any attention to the judges during this settling-
down process, Blair looked around behind him. A bas-relief hung on
the wall above the heads of the gallery. Justice leaned on her sword
and held the scale in her other hand. Blair looked over where the
opposing attorneys sat. They had caught him gawking about, and
they were smiling. They were very well-dressed young men, and very
self-assured. Blair looked down at his buckskin trousers. He colored

and glared back. But they were still looking at him, in fact with even more interest. Suddenly he knew why, because Bolding was tugging at his coat sleeve. Everyone else had sat down.

Since there was talking in the air even after the judges were seated, Blair walked over to the two confident young men.

"Pardon me, could you tell me when we begin?"

The one with edging on his lapels smiled tolerantly and said, "Any minute now."

Blair said, "I notice the marshal handed each judge some little envelopes, and they are each writing now. Was I supposed to submit an envelope of some kind?"

The edged lapels looked at the one with the sleepy eyelids and grinned, then back to Blair. "You mean you don't know about the envelopes?"

"No."

"Well, don't worry about them," the lapels patronized him. "The judges are answering their invitations. The court season is quite a social affair."

Blair got through the openings for both sides. The attorney general, William Wirt, who sat to the left of the six justices stated the case for the Bank. Blair was studying the gallery with awe, for this was a completely unique gallery of auditors. On Judge Pease's circuit in the West, Blair was accustomed to a gallery in which each auditor had already made up his mind and was violently in favor of one side and opposed to the other. This gallery was different. It showed no concern how the play would come out, so long as it was a good performance.

The attorney general droned on ". . . appealed from circuit court in Chillicothe . . . the appellants pray for a reversal of the lower court's decree, contending it is erroneous for the following seven reasons . . ."

Jonathan Blair wondered how his seven reasons sounded to the people in this court. Studying the two young lawyers at the far end of the table, he could not tell. They didn't even seem to be listening.

But Blair noticed that the chief justice interrupted and said, "Repeat the appellants' sixth reason please, Mr. Wirt."

Blair was encouraged. This was his most important argument, and John Marshall had singled it out in a flash. There would be justice in this court, and Jonathan Blair was well prepared, through long and laborious study.

Blair was relieved to find that he could stand up and talk. He was extremely self-conscious, but he had prepared so well that he got through his opening all right. Also, the sharp attention and the unpretentious smile of the chief justice encouraged him.

He sat down when he had outlined his case, and the floor went to the confident young man with the ribbed-silk edging on his lapels. His opening gun seemed to blast the floor out from under Blair's case:

> "We decline arguing the right of the State of Ohio to tax the bank, considering that question as formally determined by the former decision of this court in McCullough vs. Maryland, which was supported by irresistible arguments by Mr. Henry Clay and Mr. Daniel Webster, to which we could add no further illustration.

> "But this is not like the law of Maryland, a case of taxation. Ohio's law was enacted for the purpose of expelling the bank from the State of Ohio, by inflicting penalties amounting to prohibition. It inflicted penalties on the bank greater than the bank's entire annual income. It was a confiscation . . . not a tax!

> "It is obvious that if one state could in this manner expel one of the branches of the bank from its territory, then every state may do the same. And thus this great institution of the national government would be destroyed by the local governments. Can you imagine what kind of a Federal Government we would have if it were forced to trust its states not to destroy it?"

Blair bounced to his feet, "You're already trusting the states not to destroy you! Take the land tax itself. The Federal Government derives income from selling off the public domain in the Western states. Now, we states have an agreement with the general government not to tax the land until after it's sold. But we have only to make the tax law prohibitive, and the United States will not sell another acre in the West. But we seem to have exercised that privilege with restraint and justice. We could name a dozen other examples where the states have only to pass a new law, and there is no Federal Government. But we have not done this.

> "Now you said the tax was designed to drive the bank out of the state. You are quite right. But since when has the tax not been a

legitimate form of protest or coercion under this democratic form
of government? I should think the Federal Government would
examine its bank and see what makes it so obnoxious to the states."

Blair sat down. He had roused the interest of the spectators. John
Marshall smiled faintly at Blair. He said, "Mr. Blair, every attorney
has his first time before this court. But would you please remember
not to address your opponents, but the bench; and hereafter wait
until the plaintiff has concluded."

The edged lapels grinned. John Marshall added, "However, do
not under any circumstances allow the rules of the court to interfere
with your enthusiasm for your side. We're here to listen to the best
that can be said, both ways."

By God, that's a good judge, Blair thought, on Monday.

On Tuesday, Blair was certain he observed a definite change in his
two young opponents. They spoke with more alacrity. This seemed to
be in direct response to a big change in the make-up of the gallery
on Tuesday.

Bolding called it to Blair's attention. "I think you must have been
making your points yesterday. The women kind of got crowded out
today. These vultures are all business. See that one next to the post
there, with the side whiskers? That's Langdon Cheves . . . president
of the whole U.S. Bank. And you see that coat in the empty seat next
to him? I guess you know who owns that, don't you?"

"Yeah," Blair squinted at the great fur-collared coat. "That's
Schaacht's."

"That's right."

The presence of Schaacht and Cheves in the courtroom sharpened
Blair's arguments. He even felt Judges Marshall and Story leaning
forward to hear better when he said:

"The question whether the bank of U.S. is exempt from the
taxing power of the states depends upon the nature and character of the bank. If it stands on the same foundation with the
mint and the post office, we admit that Ohio cannot tax it.

"But banking is a private trade. The convenience and profit of
private men is the object of any bank. It's the object of your
private banks here in Washington, same as it was the object of

my neighbors, Mike Stikes, and Tom Woodbridge, and Sam Hosmer, and Jim Hawkins when we formed the Mesopotamia Hog & Trust up in my town."

Laughter burst from the gallery. But there was no laughter from the bench. They all leaned forward, eyes on Blair.

"Now Mr. Cheves' bank here," Blair pointed to Cheves, "his U.S. Bank, is not one whit different from the Mesopotamia Hog & Trust."

There was more laughter. Even the great hawkish face of Gideon Schaacht flickered as Langdon Cheves reddened.

"Except," Blair said, "that when Sam Hosmer's signature was signed to a dollar bill, everybody knew what it stood for. But Mr. Cheves keeps us all guessing what he's going to do next. One day he was happy to loan us money. The next day he wanted it all back."

Langdon Cheves glared at Gideon Schaacht. Marshall now frowned a little at Blair, holding him down. So Blair said, "Let's build a bank, right here in this courtroom, the way Mr. Cheves' bank was built, and then decide if the states can tax it.

"Suppose that the individuals who are to build this bank live not in one city, like Mesopotamia. Suppose they live in all parts of the country and they join together for the purpose of establishing a bank with a capital of $28,000,000. They collect this capital together in the city of Philadelphia and begin trading as bankers. Fine.

"Now, not finding sufficient borrowers for their capital in Philadelphia they establish a branch in New York, one in Boston, one in Baltimore, where they do a profitable business. It is perfectly clear that the business thus transacted must be subject to the laws of the various states.

"Now, on a given date the Federal Government decides that it would be good to become a customer of this bank, that is, borrow money. Therefore our government makes a contract with this bank, which becomes a charter and makes the bank a corporation.

"Now, the mere creation of a corporation does not confer political power or character. So this very same court decided in Dartmouth College vs. Woodward. This is not my thinking, but your own." Blair paused. "However I agree with you heartily."

Marshall smiled.

Blair was interrupted by the hasty and noisy exit from the gallery of Gideon Schaacht. Schaacht was not a man who could move without being noticed. And as he left now suddenly, heads swayed together to identify him. Nor was Schaacht a man to make motion without accomplishing something.

Blair did not know what Schaacht accomplished, but on the following morning he did notice a tremendous increase in the number of attorneys in the gallery. They carried brief covers, and they were a well-dressed crowd. Blair felt shabby. His shirt was now soiled, though he had preserved it every night.

Blair came to a breaking-off place in his argument on Wednesday, and John Marshall recognized the attorneys for the bank. Neither of the young men rose, though. In fact, they sat there looking down at the table, as though they were waiting for something.

During this strange pause Gideon Schaacht arrived and sat down beside Cheves, nodding in a way that even Blair could read from his distance to mean, "It's all arranged."

Schaacht, absorbed in the court action, left his daughter to find her own seat.

John Marshall again asked the attorneys for the bank to proceed. The young men looked over at Langdon Cheves and then the heavily eyelidded one rose. He faced the bench as if he were about to speak but he held his tongue and looked behind him. A set of loud ringing footsteps echoed down the cellar corridors, which was what the young attorney was apparently waiting for. As the bootfalls grew louder the young attorney slowly sat down. The gallery leaned out to watch the doorway.

A tall man, obviously much at home in these corridors, strode into the courtroom. His hair was worn in a short queue with a black ribbon. His shoulders were broad. His neck was thick and his manner was preoccupied in the way of men who habitually step from one policy-level meeting into another. He walked to the plaintiff's end of the table. The two young attorneys rose. The large man asked four or five brusque questions; his eyes demanded quick answers. Then his glance swept across the bench and the gallery. He cut off the talk with an impatient nod, and walked toward the apex of the courtroom.

Blair was dumfounded.

Henry Clay addressed the bench, for the United States Bank.

Henry Clay's arrival to bolster the bank's attack caused the court to take a new look at this buckskin-clad lawyer, that he should deserve such an opponent.

Bolding grinned and said quietly, "You've got them worried, Blair. Plenty worried."

Blair looked over at the gallery. With his face contorted into a question mark he sought out the serene face of Virginia Schaacht. She smiled at him. And she brought her hand to her forehead in a kind of salute.

Bolding observed this. "But don't get the idea you won't have to stay on your toes," he said testily.

Blair's head snapped back to the bench.

Henry Clay worked in bold strokes. It seemed to Blair he had risen above technicalities. He apparently had practiced before the Supreme Court enough so that he wasn't expected to concern himself with laws and cases. He swept grandly into philosophy, history, patriotism.

"Mr. Blair is helping us to find it unjust that the U.S. Bank be exempt from taxation by referring us to the homey example of his local bank in Meso . . . Mesopotomy . . ."

Chief Justice Marshall grinned and corrected, "Mesopotamia, it is, Mr. Clay. The Mesopotamia Hog & Trust Company."

The first tier of lawyers in the gallery smiled and nodded back at the judge, confirming the pronunciation.

"Anyway," Clay continued, "we who have created governments, either federal or state, know that the power to create a U.S. Bank must infer a power effectually to protect, preserve and sustain. A grant of the end is necessarily a grant of the means. The bank is as much a servant of the government as the Treasury

Department, and I presume Mr. Blair would not have Ohio tax the U.S. Treasury.

"Mr. Blair claims that the lower Federal court at Chillicothe had no right to hear the case. But if that privilege be taken away, the bank is stripped of its power . . . and so is the nation. In fact, we have no nation. The next step is the drawing of guns . . . in fact, that step is already here. Because the men whom Mr. Blair asks us to protect have already drawn weapons against an agency of the Federal Government, and I say we should perhaps not be talking of a simple trespass and larceny, we should perhaps be trying a case of treason!"

Blair studied in his room at the inn. Many lawyers had come up to him after the day in court. Several of them brought him books with pages marked. Blair's progress was slow because Clay had talked so fast that he had not been able to take complete notes.

Justin Bolding entered Blair's room, accompanied and guarded by a U.S. marshal. He said, "Jonathan, did you see page sixteen of my notes?" Then noticing his pile of notes, still folded on Blair's bed, "No. I see you haven't. But I got down most everything Clay said and some good suggestions in there for rebuttal. Aren't you going to look at them?"

Blair rolled Bolding's notes into a club with which he tapped the back of his fist while he looked at the younger man. "Bolding, I don't feel confident using them."

"You don't think I have any brains?"

"I'm afraid you have too many for me, Bolding. Nothing tells me you're not Schaacht's man still. I think your speech licked me in the Chillicothe court. I can't keep up with you."

Bolding shrugged and pulled the marshal toward the door.

The bell on the church was ringing out eleven o'clock when Blair answered his door next. It was a wide-eyed porter who dropped a naval officer's sea bag, "I was told to bring this to the buckskin lawyer."

"Who told you to bring them?"

Blair opened the bag and pulled out a white shirt, a white waist-coat, a good tweed tail coat and light grey wool trousers.

Blair threw them in the corner, and went back to work. An hour later he went over and picked up the clothes and hung them in the closet.

He worked late that night. When he went to bed his head was so full of the possible attacks Mr. Clay might make that he had trouble sleeping, and he woke with a great hunger.

He shaved hastily and went down to the common room for breakfast. It was there that he overheard the conversation from the next room. The two men talked like lawyers.

"The blighter makes a damned good case. But he makes it so deuced hard for the judges to take his part. Every lawyer in the city is watching, and that fool dresses himself like a pole pusher on a keelboat."

"Why not, if that's the way they dress out in his country? Don't forget he's even north of Columbus."

"Well, sure, if it wasn't an act, he could borrow a coat. But he flaunts a wild-eyed Jeffersonian costume in front of the judges . . . on top of that he admits his bank robbery was a deliberate attempt to break down Federal authority. Marshall spent a lifetime *establishing* Federal authority. Now Marshall's a fair man . . . but you hold up what looks like the ghost of Tom Jefferson in front of him, and talk about tearin' apart the Federal, while wearing wild-eyed backwoods buckskins . . . What's the judge going to think?"

"Judges don't make decisions on clothes."

"How long have you been practicing?" asked the other attorney.

Jonathan Blair went back up to his room and took off his leather coat. He walked into the courtroom in a tweed coat with a velvet collar. It looked good. Blair's chest and his square shoulders filled the coat well. But he didn't feel easy. Especially he felt uneasy when John Marshall looked down on him in surprise, and something that Blair took to be disappointment.

The courtroom was filled on the sixth day so that men were standing around the outside edges of the room, and in the corridor leading in. Mr. Clay talked almost unbrokenly all day. Blair made a short rebuttal that didn't seem to injure Clay's vast, sprawling, diffuse argument.

Blair felt that the rich cloth clothes on his own back were better than the law which came out of him. The sleeves of the coat fitted perfectly according to custom, but the cuffs covered so much of his hand that Blair felt like a short man on a tall horse. He felt ineffective, in fact he was.

On the seventh day Jonathan Blair entered a few minutes late, wearing his leather. Blair busied himself immediately with his notes, and in whispered conversation with Bolding.

But those who interested themselves in the nuances of courtroom action noticed that the chief justice looked over to observe Blair. The justice smiled very faintly, and it seemed with some pleasurable relief. The chief justice's smile was reflected in a ripple along the first row of lawyers in the gallery who now felt they owned a little part of Blair, having watched him grow up a half a notch in a single day to the place where he knew enough to wear his own mantle.

Mr. Clay seemed aware that he was involved in no casual case. He put on his tragical tone, "Consider then that Bolding employed Christofferson and Gavagan to do an illegal act. That he is therefore jointly responsible for it is as well settled as any principle of law. Mr. Blair, in attempting to narrow the field says that Bolding was only executing his legal duty under the laws of Ohio. Who then are we to hold accountable, Mr. Blair?"

Justice Marshall coughed and smiled. "Will you address the bench, please, Mr. Clay?"

"In fact," Clay warmed to his work, "to treat this as a simple trespass and larceny is only a wrist slap. This was an attempt at the total destruction of the Bank in Ohio . . . which means an attempt to expel the Federal Government and wreck the union."

Blair rebutted vigorously. "Sirs, the question of the wreckage of the union is not under appeal.

"But to return to the bank's ability to jail the state auditor in the performance of his duty. Does this mean that the State of Ohio might sue the government mail contractor for delivering letters and jail him? I insist you must give us one or the other.

"The carriages and horses of the mail contractor is a stronger case than that of the bank for exemption from taxes. Public service is his first great object. Yet we may tax him. But in the case of the bank the private trade of the company is the great object of pursuit, and the public business is incidental and subordinate. Yet we cannot tax the bank.

"The mail contractor takes the risk of a hazardous contract in the public service, and pays taxes. But the bank, on the contrary, receives a special pecuniary advantage resulting in profit to its stockholders in transacting private business, and cannot be taxed. In Mesopotamia we don't do things this way."

The attorneys in attendance observed now that as Mr. Clay approached the bench he was taking snuff with both hands, and was generally distraught. He walked to the bench and talked privately to Justice Marshall. Marshall in turn addressed Blair across the whole court. "Mr. Clay requests a recess."

Blair hesitated. Bolding whispered, "I'd grant it. Strengthen your side."

Blair said, "Agreed."

During the recess two attorneys arrived at Blair's table, one from Carolina and one from Kentucky. "Our state legislatures have sent us to assist you, Mr. Blair," the Kentuckian said. "We don't want to get in the way. But put us to work. There's other states coming too, I hear."

Jonathan Blair took great hope from this.

But after the recess his hopes fell. When counsel for the bank filed back in, there were the two young attorneys and Henry Clay. And now a newcomer joined the plaintiff's side. His appearance spread a hush through the room, and then a buzz of talk. The newcomer was serious, intense, dark haired and vigorous.

When the session reopened the side of the bank was represented by Daniel Webster.

Chapter 25: REPUGNANT TO THE REPUBLIC

WHEN THE case of the United States Bank vs. Justin Bolding, Matthew Gavagan, Brutus Christofferson et al. closed, almost everyone in Washington was on the side of the lawyer from Mesopotamia. He had made strong argument and good rebuttal. He had even taught some law to lawyers; two young sleek ones in particular had learned to beware the opponent who comes before the bench for a small fee and big convictions.

Chief Justice John Marshall had publicly remarked on the force of the Western lawyer's logic, and Henry Clay had personally congratulated him, had even walked with him three blocks toward his inn.

Langdon Cheves and Gideon Schaacht had paid him the ultimate tribute, by engaging Henry Clay and Daniel Webster, the most formidable team then practicing in the capital.

But in the crowded courtroom Blair only heard snatches of the decision over the pounding of the blood in his head.

"The court therefore feels that the United States Bank is a necessary and proper measure for carrying on the fiscal operations of the government . . . full pressure of the appellants' argument is felt, but . . . nation would stand stripped, naked of defensive armor, unable to execute its laws . . . bank is not considered a private corporation . . . power to tax is the power to destroy . . . hence the tax law of the State of Ohio is much more objectionable than that of Maryland . . . therefore *repugnant to the law* of the Republic . . . sum of $100,000 taken unlawfully from the bank . . . court directs restitution thereof and . . . dissenting opinion will be read by Justice Johnson."

The justice got no further than that when Blair saw Gideon Schaacht go into action. Schaacht leaned over to talk to a young grey-suited man next to him, who was apparently present for this express purpose. The young grey suit hurried out of the gallery, like a man well fortified with previous instructions.

Blair addressed the bench. "Do you know what begins now? Do you know what starts to happen now? Do you?"

The gavel fell. Bolding and two Kentucky attorneys tugged Blair down.

"It's started already! Now it begins!"

The marshal rapped. The chief justice said the dissent would be read tomorrow.

As Blair struggled out of the courtroom his eye fell on the bas-relief in the rear of the room. Though many men, strangers to Blair, crowded around him and talked loudly, he was able to notice that the figure of Justice in the relief was not blindfolded, and instead of holding the scale delicately, the sculptor had her grab it with such a firm fist that it seemed to Blair the balance could not swing either way of its own accord.

In the tavern which was below the inn, strange hands beat on Blair's back and jaws full of teeth entered his vision just above the rim of his tankard. The tankard was pulled from his hand many times and refilled by the bar man who could tell by the crowd around him that this lawyer was a man to be well served.

He never heard the name Blair around here before; but any fool could tell by the way they were asking him to stay on here and take marine cases with this firm and land-grant cases for that firm, and British war-damage claim cases for this one . . . anyone could tell this was a lawyer you'd hear about around this town from now on.

Also, you could tell by the way he paid no attention to them and just stared straight ahead thinking his own thoughts . . . you could tell by that . . . he was a strong man. Didn't even bother looking pleased for all the handsome things they were saying about him and all the fine offers they were making him.

But probably none at this table knew what was going through the head of the lawyer. The lawyer was wondering how soon the news would get back to a place called Hosmer Village, or Mesopotamia.

How soon would Elizabeth Hosmer know that Blair had lost old Sam's fight? How soon would Hope Christofferson know that Brute's last great two-thousand-dollar gesture was canceled out like an Owl Creek Bank note? How soon would Gavagan know he was not a collector, but an outlaw?

Blair lifted his saddle bag of law books up onto the tavern table. He felt of the leather that Isaac Steese had oak-tanned and stitched and tooled. How soon would Isaac Steese know that his saddle bag was better than the lawyer?

One thing about Gideon Schaacht, he was a man. He sat now in the side room of the Irving House facing the president and one third of the board of directors of the United States Bank, including the Federal representatives. But they found he was a hard man to put on the carpet. He would not squirm and yell.

He sat erect, but not erect enough to give them much satisfaction. His hands lay still on the arms of the chair. They did not twist or rub the wood.

Not only that, he had seated himself at the foot of the table opposite Langdon Cheves. And in truth if you could not hear who was speaking, the foot of the table would look more like the head of it. Even when being interrogated, Gideon Schaacht looked natural at the end of the table. You could not imagine him in one of the seats along the side, where men with more seniority and experience were sitting in obscurity.

Langdon Cheves said, "Schaacht, you were lucky today."

"I think you mean we were all lucky today, Mr. Cheves. If they had driven my branch out, the rest of you wouldn't last a month either."

"Nevertheless," Cheves said, "you were lucky. But your problem has just started. You have mortgages on half the State of Ohio. But can you close them? You've loaned out more of our good capital on less convertible security, than any other two branches put together. You've got the people mad enough that they're near ready to secede. And the board and myself are anxious to hear your exact plans for foreclosure. How can you get them off the land, and if you do, how can you convert the land to cash if you drive the people out?"

"Well, the first thing I will do is ask you to procure some Federal manpower to help me. The second thing I will do is remind you gentlemen that it isn't exclusively my problem. It's yours, too."

"But you created it," Cheves said. "You loaned too much, too fast. Then you tightened up credit faster than I intended you to. Now you have made a national martyr out of a place called Mesopotamia. Half the city of Washington has adopted that town to its heart, and that back-woods lawyer with it. It's become a catch word around here for pluck. Just this morning I congratulated the hackney on his team getting us to the courthouse on time through the rain. He said, 'Yes, sir. Them's Mesopotamia-style nags.' Point is, if that lawyer and that town take a notion to resist, you won't be able to close out any other town either. They'll all say, 'We're doing like Mesopotamia.' And Clay says it's not at all preposterous that you have opened a battle for Western independence. Lewis and Clark and then Burr almost broke the West loose. You may have done it better."

"By the same token, Mr. Cheves, if I can collect in Mesopotamia, I can collect throughout the rest of the territory with no trouble. I intend closing out those Mesopotamia mortgages first."

"How can you do it with half the country watching Mesopotamia now?"

"It will be done quietly and with dispatch."

"How?"

"By the selection of a certain collector, who will know just how to handle it."

"Who?"

Schaacht seemed on the point of answering the question. But then he said, "If I told you his name I would have to amplify endlessly. He's here in this city, and if I'm to get him, I should get him immediately. So if you'll excuse me, gentlemen."

Schaacht rose. But Cheves said, "Look here, Gideon, we're answerable to the stockholders, and we deserve some explanation."

Schaacht knew both the risk and the power of playing a weak hand boldly. He said, "I require a certain amount of autonomy. If you don't care for that method of operation, perhaps one of these men would like to replace me at the head of the Western branch of the bank."

There being no reply he put on his hat. He left no affection behind him. But on the other hand he left no room for meddlers.

At the tavern where Blair drank steadily now, the group of men around his table had thinned, but it had simmered down to men of some substance, who had specific proposals they wished to talk over with Blair. But Blair just drank.

One thing about Schaacht, when it was time to be tough, he never shrank from the moment. And this was the moment.

Blair first became aware of someone's approach when the chairs began scraping back from the table. He saw a skirt opposite him, and all the men standing and bending slightly at the waist. Then beside the skirt was a pair of fine tight wool breeches. Blair's eyes followed up to a brocaded waistcoat and on up to the hawk face of Gideon Schaacht.

The introductions were over. Still Blair did not rise. Schaacht extended a long arm and a hand across the table to Blair. "It was a good fight, Jonathan."

Blair ignored the hand, shoving out his lower lip and drinking from his mug. The eyes held.

"I don't blame you. You had a lot of heart in it, Jonathan, and you lost. There's a lot say you should have won, including two dissenting judges."

Most of the men standing around the table knew Schaacht and his daughter. The banker genially invited them to be seated, and he sat himself. He said, "Gentlemen, I couldn't help overhearing your proposals to Mr. Blair. That's why I came when I did. Mr. Blair won't be accepting any of them, I'm sure. In respect to a tough and worthy opponent, I myself intend to make him the best offer of all. So he will not be staying here in Washington. He will be going back to his well-loved town of Mesopotamia," Schaacht grinned, "which he has made the pet of Washington."

Blair hoisted a cynical, intoxicated eyebrow. But Schaacht said, "Yes, it'll be tough to face them, Jonathan, but you'll go back. You're not the kind who could run away from them."

"You don't think so, huh?" Blair drank. "Catch me dead back there. String me to Stikes' forge, feet up."

"It'll be tough. But you'll go back."

"Think so, huh, Schaacht?"

"I know so."

"Just how you know this?"

Schaacht reached in his breeches pocket and pulled out three small pieces of black slate which had been chiselled into the shape of grave markers.

"Because Mesopotamia has too much in this thing. You cost them too much to run out now."

"Like what?"

Schaacht threw one of the miniature gravestones on the table in front of Blair. "Like Sam Hosmer."

Blair stared at the gravestone, but gave no answer.

Schaacht threw another one down, "Like Brute Christofferson."

Blair stared at the small slate gravestones, and reached out for one. But he pulled his hand back quickly as another one hit the table and danced like a half-dollar.

"Or like Hope Christofferson's Merinos that are going to pot somewhere up in the woods."

A fourth one hit the table top.

"Or like the doctor you took away from the Silver Pigeon. How many did he lose after you took his doctor away, Jonathan?"

Blair fingered a gravestone and looked up at Schaacht, "Winowa lotta troubleda make ya poin', dinya, Mister Schaacht. Lotta trouble."

"Yeah. I did, Blair. Wanted to be sure you got it."

"Well, I gotta poin' fer you, Mister Schaa. You're the one killed old Sam, an' Brute, an' sent 'rinos up in the woods, *and* took the doctor outa Upper Sandusky. You hadna broke our money, be there yet."

"I know the bank made some mistakes, Jonathan."

"*Some* mistakes! Jees Christ, listena him! *Some* mistakes! Ya saved the goddamned bank and ya ruined the West. Thas trouble with damned U. S. Bank, anyhow. Everybody raises 'em up on pedestal like doctors or preachers or somethin'. Like they had the interests of community at heart or somethin'. Fact is, you're just plain ordinary damn businessmen, walkin' aroun' holier 'n hell. Nobody understands that. Fact is, you don' even unnestand where money comes from. You think it comes from some bigger bank'n yours. You're crazier'n hell. That isn't money. Y'know where money comes from? Money comes from when Mike Stikes takes a goddamned bar of iron and changes it into that pair of hinges you got on your oversize front door down Chillicothe. Thas what money is. Stikes makes it, you don't. And Hussong, when he takes a li'l skinny woods pig and cross breeds it and cross breeds it up to a big fat pig 'at can har'ly stan' up it's so fat. Thas what money is. Wha' you know 'bout money?"

Schaacht's face held steady under the insult. In fact he said, "We're beginning to learn about that, Jonathan. I understand more than you think about that. But I also know the bank's job is to give Joe Hussong time to make those three generations of pigs. We feed them until he gets to the fat pig. I know that now."

"Yah, you know; the hell you know."

"Well, at least I know enough to know that *you* know it. That's why I want to hire you."

"You! Hire me!" Blair put his head back and laughed.

"I'll pay you well."

"You got a million dollars a day to pay me, Schaacht? Thas my startin' pay, work for you, hah!"

The others around the table watched for Schaacht's reaction. It seemed he would take anything from this lawyer tonight.

"You'll see that you're one of the few who could handle this job for me, Blair. I don't expect you'll take it for love of me. But you'll take it because . . ."

"Because of your beau'ful daughter? Take even more'n that, Schaacht."

Virginia Schaacht hardly moved an eyelid.

"You'll take it," Schaacht said, "because you have always understood that you have to have people on the land to make it worth anything. I also understand it now."

"Whas 'at got to do with it? Wha' you think I'm gon do for you, Schaacht?"

"You're going back up to Mesopotamia."

"For what?"

"As my collector."

"W-h-a-t?"

"You'll be the collector for the U.S. Bank. You're the man for the job."

Blair sobered like a shot. He rose slowly, gripping the edge of the table. Schaacht sat with his fingers in opposite pockets of his waistcoat.

"Why you crazy misbeguided damned fool, Schaacht!"

Blair lifted up the near edge of the table and shoved the whole over onto Schaacht. Virgina saw it coming and deftly rose and side-stepped. Schaacht was too well composed, and he thought he knew the lawyer too well. He went down under the table and the sliding mugs and the spillage.

Blair walked out into the cold night air.

Gideon Schaacht separated himself from the lumber and the broken crockery. He brushed himself off, not much damaged.

BOOK III

Chapter 26: THE COLLECTOR

ALL I know is, we're fair game now!" Joe Hussong announced to Hosmer's Store in general and Asa Buttrick in particular.

Buttrick read aloud a few more paragraphs from the *Freeman's Chronicle*. It was the fifth account of the trial that Buttrick had read to Mesopotamia. And they still listened hungrily where it said about Jonathan Blair, the frontier lawyer, and how he brought Mesopotamia into the trial.

Two people in particular grew an inch or two taller when they heard the fine accounts of Blair. One was young Tim Flannerty, who had always called the lawyer "Mr. Blair." Tim Flannerty had had Blair's cabin cleaned up for him for a week now, against the lawyer's return. Importantly, he had borrowed a few items around town which he needed "to get Mr. Blair's place ready."

The widow, Hope Christofferson, also listened intently whenever an account of the trial was read.

Hussong, however, always came back to the main point. "What good is it? The fact is he *lost*. And Ault says there's a U.S. Bank collector on his way up here now to start the dirty work. What do we do about *him?*"

Buttrick said, "Our Blair has probably learned a lot since he's away. I say he'll show us what to do."

"And I say your Blair won't be back, Buttrick. If he did so fine, he'll have himself a job of law there in Washington or down in Chillicothe or Cincinnati. I say we've seen the last of him."

Buttrick challenged this.

"All right," Hussong put on his hat. "You can all sit around and wait on your lawyer to come back. But I've got two hundred and sixty-two hogs that have got to be made plans for, before this collector comes to make the plans *for* me."

Young Tim said, "Mr. Blair will be back."

"How do you know, son?" the hog farmer wanted to know.

"Because . . . uh . . . should I tell them, Miss Hope?"

Hope was puzzled. "Why, yes, if you know for sure, Tim."

The lad polished his boot toes on the backs of his trouser legs, "Because Miss Hope got a letter."

Hope colored as the eyes converged on her, especially Faith Hawkins' and Camelia Flannerty's and Elizabeth Buttrick's. Elizabeth asked, "Did you, Hope?"

"Yes."

"Well, what in thunder did he say?" Hussong roared.

"He'll be back. He's got a plan."

"You might have told us that, Hope."

Elizabeth Buttrick's rosebud mouth distorted as she bit her lower lip in thought. "Hope, could it be you haven't *read* that letter? I mean . . . anyone of us will be glad to read it to you, Hope."

Hope's chin raised a fraction, "He wouldn't write if he weren't comin' home . . . that is, back. And he wouldn't come back unless he had a plan. Besides the way the letters slant on the page, it's strong-handed and confident. He'll be back. And he'll know what to do."

Mesopotamia looked at the floor and held its tongue. Asa Buttrick motioned his daughter silent, but Camelia Flannerty barged right into it, "Why don't you get it out and let *us* read it, Hope?"

Young Tim scolded, "A girl your age should know, Camelia. Suppose there was some . . . some man-woman talk in there or somethin'."

Hussong said, "It's your business about that part, Hope. But I got two hundred sixty-two hogs that can't wait around on bashfulness . . . not if there's a collector half way to here already."

Halfway up from Columbus Jonathan Blair felt the excitement in the horseflesh under him as the bay surged toward familiar ground.

But the lawyer reined down, dreading the familiar. He would not have believed any man could put him in this position. But Schaacht had been blunt when he returned to Blair's inn the next morning. "Either you handle the foreclosures with certain leniencies which I will grant, or I handle them in my own way, which will be . . ." And before Schaacht even finished Blair had visualized a train of wagons pulling out of Mesopotamia dispossessed.

Then Schaacht showed him the advertisements the bank had already ordered placed in eastern papers advertising bargains in already improved Western farms, foreclosure prices.

Blair had driven a bargain with Schaacht, a good one. But it wouldn't sound so good in the tap room of Exeter's Tavern. Blair couldn't even imagine himself telling them the terms. He hoped they would throw him out of town when they did hear.

Midday brought him to Boxford's Cabin, which meant he'd come into Mespo at dusk or after dark, which was good.

But he hadn't figured on Tim Flannerty. Even grown-ups admitted that Young Tim was second sighted; like an animal he knew about things he'd never seen, and when things were going to happen. These past three days he'd taken to keeping a vigil late afternoons south of the ford where sundown silhouetted a wagon or a rider for a moment on the ridge. Young Tim had taken just one look at the outline of the bay with the saddlebag bulges and the rider with the low-crowned, broad-brimmed hat, and he was clattering bareback toward town, yelling, "He's back."

They met the lawyer at the ford. Everyone was there. They took him right to Exeter's Tavern, stood him to the bar, and crowded around. The *Freeman's Chronicle* was pegged up over the mug rack, the Supreme Court case well outlined in thumb prints.

For half an hour they asked him questions and told him what they'd heard about the case. They told him about the two new settlers who had moved up, and then came the lull in the talk when most questions seemed to be answered. Tim Flannerty stood there watching as though he had made Blair with his own two hands. Hope studied him quietly.

That's when Joe Hussong said, "Jonathan, it's good you're back in time to help. Ault says there's a U.S. Bank collector assigned to come up and collect or close us down. We figure you'll know what we can do about it and who he is. Do you know him?"

The lawyer swallowed. He looked around at the circle of faces. "I thought you knew," he said.

"Knew what?"

Blair asked, "Hope, didn't you tell them . . . in my letter?"

"I told them what I figured was in it, Jonathan."

Buttrick said, "Well, Hope figured it might be private, Jonathan." He laughed, "And a good right she'd have to think that, the way you been moonin' after her for years."

The laughter in the room quenched quickly because it was not re-flected on the lawyer's face.

"I'm the collector," he said.

They had never met this man before, this man who drank by himself in the tavern every day. This was an empty man, that could look right through you, listen to your story, and then just sit there, not answer-ing. This was a man that didn't care what you called him or what you thought of him, apparently.

This was a stranger. This was a man that was nodding when you were only half through talking to him. He'd heard it before. But also this was a tough man, who never smiled, tough in the way a man can be who has no friends to lose.

He could look Antonio Denaro right in the eye and say, "The part you're to mark off to give back to the government you can choose yourself. But the part you are to mark off to give to the bank is just where I tell you. Right where I drew those lines."

"But Mr. Blair! Right in the middle you took. Take over here. Take over there. But right in the middle! All the grapes! That is my whole . . ."

"Right where I marked it, Denaro. Not here. Not there. Right here."

"Why? Why the best part?"

"Because that's the way it's got to be."

"Tam you, Blair!" Ten years of backaches from bending over the tender grape-shoots welled up inside Antonio Denaro and spilled over. He wiped the paper onto the floor and spit on it. He plunged across the table and grabbed Blair's throat, "You tam lawyer you!"

But the lawyer had been through this many times this month and he pelted Denaro in the exposed ribs with a fist that had learned its power lately. Denaro's grip melted. Blair grabbed his slack arm, spun him away from him and shoved him stumbling over the bench into the floor.

Denaro rose slowly, drawing a splinter out of his palm. Blair picked the paper off the floor. "Sign this, Denaro. Or worry about your own settlement."

"Blair, I only . . . I only want . . ."

"You want to pay your debts and keep your grapes, too. Sign it."

Denaro signed.

Even Tim Flannerty no longer liked to come to the Blair cabin. But his father, Hank, made him come because the lawyer paid in metal coin.

Tim Flannerty picked up the bench and swept the place, while the lawyer sat there studying a plat of Mesopotamia. "Mr. Blair, why did you . . . I mean old Tony Denaro, he . . ."

"He doesn't understand that he'll come out of it with something at least." The lawyer did not snap at Tim as the boy expected. "Denaro doesn't understand that we are trying to get a new land law passed, whereby the government will let Tony keep as much of his land as his first three payments will cover, instead of taking it all."

"Who is going to get the law passed, Mr. Blair?"

"Gideon Schaacht."

"You mean he's on *our* side? Is he your friend?"

"No."

"Then why will he do it?"

"Because I've got hold of his ear, and he's got hold of mine. We're both twisting. Understand? And the devil catches the one that loses his grip. Understand?"

"Maybe. The grip you got is a kind of secret grip maybe, Mr. Blair? You can't let it out?"

The lawyer threw down the plat of Mesopotamia and leaped to grab the boy's hand. "God bless you, boy! God bless you! That's exactly it!" Then he poured himself a drink of whisky and he was back studying the map of the town again.

"But how you going to make the rough ones hold still for it, Mr. Blair? Joe Hussong and Adams and those?"

"I wish to God I knew, boy."

Day after day the lawyer sat with his whisky and his plat of Mesopotamia. And when anybody came into the cabin, which they only did when they were called . . . summoned, then the lawyer covered up the map.

But Tim came early one morning when the lawyer was drunk asleep, slumped over the plat. Hadn't been to bed at all. And he saw that the lawyer had drawn the craziest zigzag lines over the farms on the map. He noticed a long skinny strip to be taken out of the Emerson farm. Hard to see how you'd farm it. Then there was a circular area marked out of the Hawkins farm. Seemed to be about where that rocky hill was on the Hawkins place. He was studying the way the lines took the heart out of the Fitchburg place when the lawyer jolted awake, "What are you looking at, boy!" He covered the map, "Get out of here!"

At Exeter's Tavern lately the talk was so much of Jonathan Blair, that it was no longer necessary to name him. If a man simply said, "he," it meant Blair. You could walk through the place and hear it any evening. It didn't matter much who the speaker was.

"He's crazier'n hell. Overdrank hisself."

"You mean the hell he's crazy. He's gettin' his, and plenty. He didn't sell us out cheap, you can bet on that."

"Way he's cuttin' up the farms makes no sense atall. None atall."

"I'll bet if you could see his master plat it'ud make a lot of sense. Make so much sense in fact that he won't let anybody have a look at it."

"That must be why he has a different one of us help him with each survey. So's nobody gets the whole picture."

"He sure learned surveyin' in a hurry."

"Yeah, and the son of a bitch learned it good. I tried to swoggle him out of three acres on the bias on your place when I was helpin' him. Caught me flat out. Made me run the line over."

"He's gettin' a good cut for hisself you can be sure. That's why he took Denaro's grapes. He always did like grapes."

There was laughter in one corner of the tavern. "So there's Blair standin' ankle deep in Hussong's hog wallow sightin' a survey line over to a quarter section marker. Know what Hussong did? He drove them hogs for the wallow on the dead run. Blair's feet was ten feet in the air. His face was ——" The speaker was too convulsed to continue.

"Yeah, very funny," said Culpepper. "But you notice all the good it did? Blair scooped the mud off and set right to work again. Y'noticed that, too, didn't ya?"

This convulsed the group again. "And then Hussong let that saved-up boar out of the pen and loosed him into all that mess of sows. Blair went . . ." The shrieking laughter was the consolation prize to beaten men.

But the laughter ended suddenly because Hussong was not beaten. "Stop laughin'! You stand here like it was a joke. Instead of standing around laughing, why don't you back me up! Am I the last one left that's man enough to stand up to a damned supple-souled lawyer!"

"What are we supposed to do, Joe?" Culpepper asked. "He's got all the right and all the law on his side."

"What are we supposed to do?" Hussong mimicked Culpepper. "What you're supposed to do is pay no attention to that survey of his. Use that land just like you always have. It's yours. One man. *One* man does all this to you. A little law talk and you whimper like the culls from a ten-pig litter."

Hussong's insults were food for these men. Here was a strong voice. Younger than most of them, Hussong was, but his neck was an arch of muscle. His black eyes could face down a cornered boar. His chest was heroic shaped. He rose up out of a heap of men looking like the statue of a general that was on the front of the Scioto *Gazette;* and his courage charged through a group like Exeter's special harvest-day whisky.

"Myself, I'm goin' right ahead and plant that patch he took away from me just like I never knew Blair. What can he do about it? Will he pick the land up and carry it away from me? Crimus! We're not fit to own land if we squeal so quick."

"Good talk, Hussong. But we'll see what you do when plantin' time comes."

"Damn you, I'll plant early. Fact you can *watch* me. I'll go to Buttrick's store in the mornin' and pick seed. I'm buyin' that fancy big-eared yellow he brought up from Virginia."

The word entered every cabin, except the lawyer's, by sunup.

Tim Flannerty entered Blair's cabin early.

"What do you want, boy?"

"Brought two hen eggs for your breakfast, Mr. Blair."

"I've still got the ones you brought yesterday."

"I forgot."

"Forgot?" Blair studied the boy. "What's on your mind, Tim?"

"Well, I just wondered if maybe you'd ought to go over to the store and git a new . . ." Tim looked around the room. He hadn't figured to the end of the sentence.

"A new what, boy? Why do you want me to go to the store?"

Tim breathed deep and shoved his jaw out, come what may. "Well you said you had a grip on his ear."

"Whose?"

"Schaacht's."

"Yes. Go on, boy."

"Well, you said it would be devil take the one that loses the grip first."

"Come on. What?"

"And your grip has something to do with . . . with . . ." Tim pointed to the plat of Mesopotamia which he knew to be under Blair's bunk.

"You never mind what my grip has to do with! Or the map, either!"

"Yes, Mr. Blair."

"And don't come in this cabin when I'm not in it!"

"Yes, sir!"

But the morning was one of those at the break point of winter when the snow-drained ground had dried just enough in spots to draw a man out on his land for the first pokings at the ground. A man would stay on his place if things were normal. So the crowd at the store was remarked by Blair.

He saw how men stepped onto the porch of the store, looked over at his cabin for a moment, and then stepped inside briskly. Tim had been trying to tell him something. The lawyer thought for a while.

Blair entered the store just as Hussong shouldered the keg of seed. He turned to the crowd. "Well, I guess you all saw, didn't you? Step up there like men and do the same. We . . . hello, Mr. Blair! You're just in time. Seed for this spring." He tapped the keg. "Special. Just right Buttrick tells me for that low place around the hog wallow."

"That land doesn't belong to you any more, Joe."

"Hah! That's the point I'm makin', Jonathan. I'm gamblin' premium seed prices that it does."

He walked deliberately to the door.

The lawyer said, "Asa, I guess you got paid in cash, didn't you?"

Buttrick didn't answer. But he looked worried.

"You better, Asa, if that seed's goin' in the ground anywhere near that hog wallow."

Buttrick looked around at the crowd. He tried to hold his ground, but even through the jowls you could see him swallow.

"Time that gets ankle high, it won't belong to Joe. That corn will be harvested by the new owner. Bank will be moving in new owners, bringing up their eastern buyers to do their choosing 'bout the time that seed breaks crust."

"Not on my place they won't," Joe said. But he saw the sick look

on Buttrick's face. "All right, Asa, if you're so squeeze-fisted worried
about your money, I'll pay cash."

He walked back and flung down the black and white currency
of the Bank of Steubenville. Buttrick fingered them gingerly and put
them down as though they offended his nose.

"What's the matter with them, Asa?"

Buttrick handed them back to the hog farmer. "If you're payin' me
with these, Joe, I'd need a bushel of them. Maybe you don't need so
much seed, Joe."

Hussong dropped the keg. He reached into his pocket. "I hoped
you'd not drive me to it, Buttrick. But I got a point to make at any
price. I'll cut your price to a third and pay in metal." He rang an
eagle and a half-eagle on the counter, so everybody could hear. "I
guess everybody understands that when Hussong pays for seed in
metal, he'll be there to harvest it all right."

Blair stopped him at the door again, and handed him the paper on
which was recorded the boundaries of the land Hussong was to
hand back to the bank. "You're on your own, then, Joe, to deal with
the bank."

"All right, Mr. Blair. All right!" And he turned to the crowd. "Come
on. You were with me last night. Step up and buy your seed."

As the pause in the store lengthened out, it looked as though Joe
Hussong were losing.

But Hope moved toward the counter. With no facial expression and
in a monotone she said, "Joe's called us. If we meant what was said,
now's the time to back him. I'll take the same as Joe bought, Asa."

Mesopotamia watched her with hope and admiration. "I used to
think Jonathan had the way out for us. But it looks like Joe's got
more our way of doin' things. I favor we risk it with him."

"But what do *you* risk, Hope?" Blair asked.

"Why the same as Joe."

"No you don't." Blair forced himself. "Your mortgage paper is in
the safe hands of Reverend Gershom, isn't it?"

The men and women in the store in Mesopotamia found reasons why
they had to leave.

Chapter 27: BLAIR'S BULLION

ON Monday Mesopotamia looked to Jonathan Blair like the same old town Sam Hosmer had carved out of the revolutionary bounty lands. But on Tuesday it looked to Blair rundown and gone to weeds.

The difference was the presence of the well-dressed downstater who rode beside him. It brought the faults of the place into sharp focus for the first time.

Blair had no knowledge of the soil. So he was surprised to find that today he was offended that Jim Hawkins had failed to add his usual four new furrows to his field this year. He hadn't even plowed up a quarter of the old field.

Old man Fitchburg had always lengthened his furrows by three or four horse lengths each spring. This year he stopped plowing way short of both headlands. Adams added a little fence each year to his pasture. This year he didn't even fix the old. This was the way men worked the land when the ownership was in doubt.

Today Blair also noticed how quickly the men matched their fields. Culpepper's field was growing back up to shoots and sprouts and weeds. And Culpepper hadn't trimmed his beard for a month. He had lost the snakeskin queue for his hair and never replaced it. It hung to his shoulders, unkempt. Susan Culpepper, too, was losing the starched look that she'd brought to Mesopotamia.

There wasn't enough planting going on to matter. Who would put seed in the ground when he didn't know who would harvest it?

Bolding said, "Even Hope's place doesn't look so good."

"Shut up," Blair said. "That's not what you're here to inspect anyhow."

"Fence is falling apart."

"You forgetting she's without a man?"

"Thought you were her man."

"Christofferson was her man. Remember? Got shot because of your damned bank."

"She looks kind of heavy, too."

"You ignorant bastard! She should look heavy in places now. Looks damn nice to me."

"You mean . . . ?"

"Yes! Even with a shot leg Christofferson was man enough for that. Which is a damn sight more than you can say."

"I didn't know."

"You wouldn't. You don't even know what you're doing. Here you are back working for Schaacht."

"There's a lot to be learned from Schaacht."

"Yeah. And a lot to be gained. Your woman, Virginia, was telling me how you were going to go into law for yourself."

"I was going to. But you wouldn't sign my certificate, remember?"

"Well, I've shown you the town. Now what else did your guardian angel want you to check?"

"Schaacht wants me to see if you've gotten the tracts measured off that go back to the bank. I'm to see them with my own eyes."

Blair rode over the town and showed the young man every one of the farms. He pointed out a few of the markers and then showed him the relinquishing papers by which each man gave part of the land back to the bank, listing the boundaries of the relinquished portions. Without riding to every single stake it was impossible for Bolding to see the exact shape of the tracts, but he could satisfy himself that the acreage was correct, and he could see that the surveys had been made conscientiously.

At the Denaro place Bolding said, "Now do you have a map of the area, showing these tracts?"

"No."

"No?"

"You heard me."

"Well, how can you run a thing like this without a map? I've got to have a map."

"Then go make one. You've got the boundaries all described."

"How can I make a map from these?"

"You're a lawyer. A lawyer has to be able to do that out here, Bolding. You had a chance to learn when you were up here with me. But you spent the time over with Camelia Flannerty."

Denaro sat on the steps of his hut watching them. Blair yelled, "Tony, how come you haven't broken any ground for this year?"

Denaro just sat and stared back.

Bolding said, "You see, Blair? You going to waste another ten years on this kind?"

Back at the cabin, Blair said, "All right. You've seen the land. I've done *my* part. Now what about Schaacht's? The new land law?"

"Yes, you've done your part. I'll tell him how well you've done it. And I'll give him these relinquishing papers you've had signed." Bolding reached for the papers.

Blair pulled them back. His tone was dead weight. "I guess you didn't understand me. Has Schaacht got the land law through, and what proof did you bring?"

"Well, Jonathan, there's been a little . . ."

"Jonathan, nothing!" Blair rose. "He has or he hasn't. Which?"

"He hasn't. He's run into trouble. The eastern members of the house aren't partial . . ."

"The devil with who's partial and who isn't! His bargain is to get the land law through!"

"He's having trouble."

"Then get out of here! What do you mean inspecting my half of the bargain, when you come to tell me he hasn't got his half . . ."

"I'm to bring back those papers."

"You'll bring back hell!" Blair buttoned the papers inside his shirt.

Bolding stayed at Exeter's inn. Blair drank. He kept the relinquishment papers under his shirt, day and night.

Blair goaded and scolded the Mesopotamians to plant, but they would not plant. Bolding grinned.

Blair went to Hope. Hope was good to look at lately, filled out nicely, had a soft look to her. And in his state of near intoxication, Blair stared longer than even a brash man should—sober.

"Hope, for everybody's sake, help. Get Flannerty to plow your field and plant for you."

"Easy for you to say, Jonathan. But I've used up seed for feed. Asa won't sell seed without cash. Can't blame him."

"Mean you're not gonna do *anything?*"

"I'm going to the blockhouse tomorrow night when Reverend Gershom comes to pray. That's how bad things are. You better go, too."

Blair went to Buttrick. "For the love of something, Asa, let that seed out. What good'll it do dry rotting in your store?"

"Makes nice talk, Jonathan. But you keep to legalizin'. I'll keep store."

Ault, the banker, was there and he snickered. Blair said, "Yes, laugh! But if you knew how to run a bank you'd find some way for the people to do business!"

Ault laughed again. "I'm just waitin' for you lawyers to show me how to do that . . . like you showed the U.S. Bank, huh, Bolding?"

Bolding smiled.

"I may do just that!" Blair yelled. "You think they got no money, huh? You don' even know wh' a damned dollar is! I'll show ya. I'll show whole damn bunch a ya. Always said I'd show yuh wha' dollar is, Bolding. Now's time."

Blair lurched for the door, but there was drunken purposefulness in his lunge that choked off laughter. "Come on over the blockhouse ri' now. Ri' now, I said. All of yuh! An' go on over the tavern. Get 'm out."

The Reverend Seth Gershom scolded his children with an extended asparagus stalk of a finger to save them from the more vindictive wrath of The Maker whom he held back with the flat of his other hand. But his patience was now tried by the lawyer who feared neither as he lumbered unsteadily down the middle aisle, fortified against embarrassment and damnation by whisky and anger.

The lawyer sat down in the front row with his eyes levelled impatiently at Gershom.

Gershom closed his service quickly; and before he finished his last words Blair was walking up onto the platform. Gershom abandoned the rostrum. Blair gripped it. He looked down over his townsmen with a whiskied disgust that compelled their attention.

"The women can go home," he said. "But the head of every house will stay. 'Case you're not minded to do as I say, let me tell you the news. Schaacht didn't get our land law through. We did our part of the bargain. He didn't do his. That means I can give a few orders around here. Do as I say tonight, I'll hang onto your signed relinquishment papers. Any man contrary-minded, I'll turn his paper over to Bolding tonight. Wash my hands of him. Women and kids leave now."

There was no laughter. The women left.

Hope Christofferson and the widow Shane stayed.

Blair's tone was softened, "Hope, if you're not up to it, you can go home."

"I'll stay."

The lawyer froze up again and he was sobering fast. He said, "Mike Stikes, how big is this blockhouse?"

Stikes looked surprised. "Forty by forty, inside size."

"How many square feet is that?"

"Sixteen hundred, naturally."

"All right. Twelve hundred square feet. You can count on gettin' no sleep tonight, any of you. Soon's I get through talkin' every man'll go bring his axe and any iron nails he's got. Mike Stikes'll supervise. Each man'll build himself a cubicle in this blockhouse, thirty-two square feet, outside size. Leave an aisle down the middle. If there isn't room inside, you'll have to add on. Each man'll carve his name on his own stall. But start movin' fast because no man's going to put his head to pillow till we're done!"

Stikes rose. "Blair, you got hold of us where we can't fight back. So we'll do it. But old Sam, when he had us like that, he always let us know what we were doing and what for. Stand up there and play Christ if you want. But you'll get a sight more done if you let us know what in blazes we're doin'."

"Don't think you'd understand if you were told. Nobody's plantin'. Nobody's plowin'. Nobody's adding on to their huts for the young. Don't you know whether you lose your land or not, you got to eat; you got to have clothes, you got to have shoes for the horses?"

"Just how are these stalls going to fix that, Mr. Lawyer?"

"It's going to give us some damned money, that's what. So Buttrick'll stop sittin' on good seed corn. So you'll fix the busted plows. So Hope will let her rams stand to stud."

"Don't see how this'll do it."

"No, and you won't see it any better if I explain it. But by this time next week you're each going to see that those cubicles are filled. Stikes, you're going to fill yours with horseshoes. Exeter, you're going to fill yours with whisky. Understand?"

Blair noticed a certain wave of light pass over the crowd. He also noticed a certain new alacrity in the movements.

Even those who did not understand seemed glad of the activity. And there had not been such a clamor in the air in Mesopotamia since the building of the blockhouse.

Stikes ordered men around as in the old days. Trees went down on the common. Fires were lit for warmth, women came back with rations in the middle of the night. The air carried the smell of new oak chips, even some laughter, and a lot of loud talk. It did not get finished that night, but ran on into the evening of the next day.

But as the fires were relit that night at dusk the clearing at Mesopotamia was wider by the absence of many trees. The blockhouse was unfamiliar from the inside and the outside.

And even before further instructions Stikes was clanking horseshoes into his cubicle. He ran out of horseshoes and he began throwing in door latches and hinges.

Hope Christofferson was filling hers with fleeces. Isaac Steese, the tanner, did not have to comply because he was one of the first few debt-free men in Hosmer Village. But he saw the sense of it, and he piled hides three feet high in his stall. Steese leaned over backwards to co-operate with Mesopotamia, in an effort to get Mrs. Steese accepted at this place.

Three things were against Mrs. Steese here. First, her skin had an olive darkness which you didn't much see yet west of the Hudson except for Denaro. Second, she was beautiful in a way that straightened the lips of the women in town; third, she had a bright orange dress with a thousand ruffles that kind of winked when she walked. And she wore it every evening as soon as the meal was done. Deliberately, women said, she thought up reasons to go to Hosmer's store as soon as she had the flagrant dress on. However, the men reminded their wives that every woman who saw her in the store must also have been in the store, and a little color around town was a good thing.

As the cubicles filled up, there were arguments, too. Culpepper was damned if he'd haul his corn in where every man could see how much he had. Blair said, "You'll do as I say."

"You're ordering me to put it in?"

"That's right."

"By what right?"

"By this right." Blair pointed to Bolding. "I'll hand him your relinquishing paper before I'll argue another five minutes, Culpepper. And glad to be rid of it."

Culpepper went for his wagon.

Hank Flannerty asked, "What am I supposed to put in mine, Blair? I got nothing."

"You've got your labor."

"So what's that? What do I put in the blockhouse?"

"Get that calendar off Buttrick's wall. You got two hundred ninety-five days' worth of labor left this year. Rip off the first seventy days, and put the rest of the calendar in the bank."

"In the what?"

"In your cubicle."

"You mean you had me build that big cubicle just to hang a damn calendar in?"

"Yes, and what's more, as each day goes by see to it you come in here and mark off one day that's not available any more."

Flannerty shrugged off the stupidity of lawyers.

By the fourth day, the stalls were nearly full. Hussong said, "What about you, Blair? What in hell are you going to put in your stall that's worth a damn?"

"I'm not answering to you or anybody else, Hussong." But as he saw the physical goods of Mesopotamia pile up in the cubicles, he wished he had as clear-cut a contribution to this world as most everyone else. He wished he could count his, and feel it, and measure it and weigh it on Buttrick's scales.

But he addressed himself to Bolding. "See to it every man gets a slip for each item he puts in the bin. Stikes gets a hundred slips, each should say, 'redeemable for one horseshoe.'"

A few overheard this conversation. Hussong protested, "Yeah, but how do we know Stikes don't get more slips of one-horseshoe paper than he's got horseshoes? I been through this with old Sam Hosmer, remember? How do we know we don't get another barrel of nails?"

"Because you're damn well going to trust me. That's how."

"So we trust you. What stops somebody else writin' up some more slips that look just like the ones Bolding writes?"

The hog man's point was valid. Blair grabbed his chin.

Exeter said, "We got to have some kind of paper that there's no more like it anywhere in town. Ault, you got any more of those Mesopotamia Hog & Trust blank notes with the wavy lines on the edge?"

"No." Ault could see what was making, and it worried him, as it should have. "And any paper you put it on could be reproduced by most anyone."

Buttrick said, "Let's get Mike Stikes to stamp them out on straps of barrel-hoop iron."

Stikes said, "Iron's too dear. The value's to be in the blockhouse, not in the receipt. I see what Blair's doin'."

Justin Bolding was watching with a certain admiration.

There were other suggestions, but none was rascal-proof.

There was a small cackling laugh from Exeter. "If ya want somethin' that can't be imitated this side of the ocean," he said, "there it goes right now." He pointed off across the common.

Angelina Steese was walking toward Hosmer's Store. She carried a wooden bucket over her arm. Under her short coat the orange ruffles winked and sparkled in the moonlight.

There were bass-voiced chuckles. "I'll say she can't be doubled."

"I mean the dress," Exeter said. "There ain't one like that this side of Pittsburgh."

"I mean the woman," Culpepper said. "None like that either, worse luck."

Isaac Steese approached the blockhouse with another armload of hides. The talk faded so fast he noticed it. Looking across the common he guessed the reason and bristled, "Anybody here got something to say I should hear?"

There was no answer until Steese's glare came around to the lawyer.

"Yes, Isaac," the lawyer said. "We want Angelina's dress."

Steese slammed down the hides and stiffened up, "What's the meaning of that kind of talk?"

"Can you get us Angelina's dress?" Blair asked. "We want to cut it up. It's different from anything around."

"Since when is it your business if she wears a different dress? I'm about tired of the ——"

Blair held up his hand. "We need a kind of certificate that can't be counterfeited, Isaac."

The pounce went out of the tanner. "Oh." He smiled. "Yes, it is a very rare cloth. She got it from the . . ." his face clouded. "But cut it up?"

"It's important, Isaac."

The tanner rubbed his bark-stained hand across the back of his neck. "I s-e-e. Important." He cupped his hands to his mouth. "An-ge-lin—a!"

Thus it was that there were issued to the townsmen of Mesopotamia, small rectangles of orange silk on which were lettered faintly in ink, units of goods. In some cases it was handy to make large denominations.

The pieces of silk issued to Mike Stikes read: "Stikes . . . 4 iron shoes."

It happened that Stikes immediately swapped several of these pieces of silk to Culpepper for ones which read: "Culp. 5 bu. corn."

When Stikes collected the corn, Blair collected a piece of Angelina's orange dress and took it out of circulation.

And as the squares of silk began changing hands among the cabins, the hard-faced lawyer moved his blankets into the blockhouse and slept there. He ordered a two-man armed watch around the blockhouse at all times. And Stikes was in charge of seeing to it.

There was no geniality between the lawyer and his townsmen. For his speech grew even shorter, his tone more forbidding, and he watched over the exchange of silk slips for goods with the frigid fanaticism of . . . well, like Sam Hosmer.

But there came a day when Bolding said to the lawyer, "I see. I understand now."

And the lawyer could do without the smiles and small talk of his townsmen, for there was planting going on in Mesopotamia.

Bolding said, "I'm supposed to take those relinquishment papers to Schaacht so that he can line up his buyers, Blair."

"Then you better help him get his law through. Because you'll be empty-handed until it does."

"He said I was to tell you he needed help from you on this end."

"*I* should help him!"

"He said you'd know how, Blair. But I explained to him you didn't have any connections out here that were big enough to be of any help."

The young man's bland remark widened Blair's nostrils and narrowed his eyes. "Oh, you did, did you, Bolding?"

"Certainly. If you could get to Harrison, or Burnet or old Nicholas Longworth. Men like that. But after all, who could *you* contact up here that would have any weight in Washington on this ——"

"It just happens, young Mr. Bolding, that I have the best contact in the world. The best and the biggest, and the most powerful . . . and he lives right here."

Bolding grinned. "Blair, you're drinking too much."

"There he goes right now." Blair pointed out the door.

"Him? Why, that's only Adams."

"Yep. Only Adams. But he's about to become the most important man in the country. Adams!"

Elisha Adams sulked into Blair's cabin. The lawyer was giving too many orders lately. Blair said, "Elisha, do you know anybody out of town?"

"Don't think so."

"Think, damn it! Anybody down the Miami, the Licking, the Scioto?"

"Did once know a squatter up on Maumee. And one up on the Auglaize. One is Johnson, other is Navarre."

Blair wrote down the names. "Anybody else? Where did you buy that ox?"

"Man down below Boxford's Cabin, name of Maddern."

Before he was through Blair got ten names from Adams. People outside of Hosmer Village. Adams left and Bolding said, "Can't say I'm impressed with your influential man."

"No? You should be. Adams is about as much of a recluse as you'd find anywhere. Yet Adams knows ten men in the territory, reaches all the way down to Vincennes. Now if Adams knows ten men, everybody else in this town knows ten. And each of the ten men known to each man in Mesopotamia, knows ten other men. And each of *those* ten men, knows ten others. And it can go on, Bolding. On and on and on."

"I'm not overwhelmed, Mr. Blair," Bolding grinned.

"S'pose not, but maybe the United States Congress will be. Go over to the store. Tell Buttrick I want four hundred sheets of foolscap. Take what he has and tell him to get more. Then come back. You're going to help me . . . on behalf of Schaacht, of course."

Blair looked up in *Morehead's Pleading and Practice* on how to write out a memorial to Congress. He wrote down that since over half of the men in the West were debtors to the general government, any attempt at wholesale foreclosures would produce resistance which could result in violence, even civil war, at best it would create a vagrant, destitute Western population ripe for organization into a separate union. "Therefore, we request permission to relinquish as much of each man's claim as he cannot pay for, with the privilege of applying the money already paid against that part of the tract on which he has built his improvements."

Blair kept it short, and at the head of it he addressed a note to the recipient, instructing him to sign the memorial as a petition and return it to Jonathan Blair, Mesopotamia, after first making ten copies and mailing them to ten friends, who are instructed to keep the chain going in the same manner.

When Bolding returned the lawyer sat him to his table and said, "Copy that."

"How many?"

"Until you run out of paper."

As Bolding wore blisters on his fingers, Blair took the letters to Mesopotamians and explained to them, and superintended the addressing of them. Each man addressed one to ten others.

Isolated in the place called Mesopotamia, the lawyer, Jonathan Blair, had no visual proof that he had reached out a big open hand to the West. But if he could have visited any ten of the most considerable towns west of the Alleghenies he would have detected the hopeful excitement which now began to infiltrate the vast woods.

Men who had not received a letter in ten years were surprised at the stores and at the inns to be called to the desk and asked to pay eight cents postage for a letter. Further, when these men opened the letters now they found them signed by an old acquaintance. They scratched their heads and remembered. And the letters were hope.

Storekeepers in Zanesville, Defiance, Piqua, who wrote their own letters on ironed gun-powder packages were now asked, "How come you don't have any writin' paper in this 'ere store? Get some."

Four times in one week the innkeeper in Dayton was asked, "How much does it cost to get ten letters writ?"

The whole merit of the scheme seemed to be the low level at which it was aimed. These letters were not ripped open hurriedly by busy attorneys and merchants and legislators, cynical of results and familiar with petitions. These letters were peeled open slowly by blunt fingers which had been carefully washed first. They were opened reverently by men who had counted out the eight cents postage slowly. They were read by men who studied out the message letter by letter with the help of neighbors. They were labored over by some who were at that moment packing their gear onto wagons to move west for a free squat . . . men who had found out that five years' accumulation of family and animals and land-breaking tools no longer fits onto one wagon.

The letters seeped laboriously down the Scioto, branched across to the Miami, the Licking, the Muskingum. They filtered north to the Auglaize and south along Deer Creek, Darby, Paint. A few dribbled north to the headwaters of the Maumee and then into the new settlement of Toledo. They simmered down the Mohican, the Tuscarawas, a few flowed up the Cuyahoga to a little clearing at Cleveland.

They picked up volume and momentum on the Ohio River and eddied up around the big bend and then up into Indiana against the current of Silver Creek, Indian Creek, up the Little Pigeon, the Big Pigeon . . . up the Wabash to Vincennes.

Then up the Illinois to Peoria, Peru, and a settlement called Chicago . . . a few to Kankakee.

The letters swirled heavily into St. Louis and many flooded down into the Kentuck Country.

And the first one came back in March.

The second one came in April.

And in the month of May, postmasters from Fort Pitt to Fort Wayne to St. Louis were asking, "How do you route a letter to a place called Mesopotamia?"

As the summer burned through the trees, corn broke through the crust of Mesopotamia. There was no silver in town worth counting or stealing. And even there were fewer slips of Angelina's ruffles still circulating because they were being turned in for goods.

But as the little orange fragments of Angelina's dress became fewer and harder to come by, there was still some reassurance in Mesopotamia, because at least you could damn well always tell a man's credit rating in town by the height of his pile of goods in the stall at the blockhouse.

To the anger and chagrin of Emanuel Ault the blockhouse came to be called the Second Mesopotamia Hog & Trust Bank. And the scraps of Angelina's ruffles were laughingly called "Blair's Bullion." They laughed . . . yes. But the petticoat currency was the oddest kind of a joke. A stranger passing through joined in the laughter one day. He left two teeth on the floor of Exeter's tap room.

And it was a kind of lesson for Justin Bolding the day Blair walked into Buttrick's store. The lawyer said, "Asa, you said you have forty-four more letters that came in for me. So I'd owe you three and a half dollars postage. But I've run out of silver."

Buttrick reached up for the bundle of letters. "That's all right, Jonathan. I'll accept silk."

Nor did the men miss the twinkle of ruffles over the hips of Angelina Steese, for as Faith Hawkins unjustly observed, "She makes that linsey skirt swish just as bad. You'd think she wanted to turn that to money, too."

Chapter 28: THE ESTRAYS

THE return of Matthew Gavagan to Mesopotamia in the fall gave the place a semblance of old times. His laugh boomed across the tavern and the store and the common. He had bells now for the hames of his team, and two great red plumes which he had made in jail.

The place had an old-time look in another way, too. In addition to the two guards which paced around the old blockhouse to keep the white men honest, there were now two more to keep the red men out. There was hunger at the Indian town at Upper Sandusky, and straggler Wyandots filtered down to Mesopotamia to beg at first, and then to steal. A man had to watch his grain and his pasture.

But Gavagan had his harness leather greased up and he gleefully helped Blair load the fat packets of petitions in his wagon.

"These oughta show the bastards what's what! Blair, how long will it take them Congressmen to read all of these?"

"They'll just read a few and count the rest," Blair said.

"How'll they know you didn't fake 'em?"

"No man alive could assemble so many different kinds of paper and spelling."

The town watched the loading in silence. They were impressed by the vast bulk of the letters that had poured into Mesopotamia. But they had seen Gavagan's wagon haul disastrous wagonloads of Blair's schemes before.

But the lawyer ran this town with a hard hand these days, worse than old man Hosmer. Before they pulled out, he lined up Stikes and Hussong and Hawkins. "You see there's a guard on that block-house day and night, same as always. And whenever anything comes out of that blockhouse, you see that the right amount of silk goes out of circulation."

"What if you're gone through harvest?" Stikes said. "There may be some want to put more back in the stalls . . . more than we got silk for."

Blair unbuckled the saddlebag that Steese had made for him. He pulled out a length of orange silk. "We still haven't used any of Angelina's matching petticoat," he said. "You keep it locked up, Stikes."

Denaro said, "Where did you leave the relinquish papers, Blair?"

Blair stared at him. "That's my business, Denaro. You tend the grapes."

"Huh," Denaro grunted. "We know what you do."

Gavagan and Stikes stopped at Boxford's clearing to ration the horses. They were just a mile south of Boxford's when Gavagan pulled up the horses. They were looking into the bores of two Stikes rifles. One was held by the Wyandot called Squindatee. The other was held apologetically, but firmly, by Mudeater.

Mudeater just stood there looking pained. Squindatee did the talk-ing. "The Pigeon says lawyer comes back to get corn for Indian town."

Blair did not move from the seat. "Out of the way, Mudeater. I told The Pigeon to see that there was planting up there last spring."

"Yah. But Rontondee and The Pigeon, big fight. Not enough plant. Lawyer helps now. Pigeon says so."

Blair pointed to the back of the wagon. "In the back. Papers. Important papers. We take them to great white father."

"Pigeon knows this. He says, 'the wagon goes, but the lawyer comes back to help.' "

"But I've got to be with the wagon, Squindatee."

"One man on the wagon is enough." Mudeater walked up to Squindatee, keeping his rifle always trained on the head of the horses. Mudeater grunted at Squindatee a few times and then backed up again.

Squindatee's face lighted up. "Yes, and the doctor, too. Pigeon says the lawyer will bring back the doctor. Seven Indians are sick and eight cheatas are sick." Squindatee raised his rifle which had slipped down.

Gavagan yelled, "You're crazy! Where do we get a doctor from! Now get out of the way!"

He raised the reins to snap them, but Blair held his arm. "Matt, The Pigeon doesn't make a proposition unless he's got a vice to squeeze it with, remember?" Blair turned to Squindatee, "And what if we drive right· on through, Squindatee?"

The answer was apparently so bad it embarrassed Squindatee. He looked down at his moccasins.

"Bad, Mr. Lawyer. Bad, Mr. Lawyer. Just come back."

"Or else?" Blair riled.

"Or else the sheep, Mr. Lawyer." Squindatee kept his eyes to the ground. Mudeater looked up in the air. "The Pigeon found the sheep. The Indians get food, no trouble. No food, no doctor . . . we show the major to find the sheep."

"The Pigeon lies."

"No."

"He does."

"No."

Blair looked at the pile of petitions in the back of the wagon. He ran the flat of his hand down one side of his face.

"Squindatee, The Pigeon lies. And the Squindatee and the Mudeater are my friends. They will not stop the wagon. I will prove it to you."

Keeping his eye on Squindatee, Blair motioned Gavagan forward with the other hand. Gavagan shut off his breath and snapped the reins. The wagon eased forward. Gavagan looked straight ahead, glancing neither right nor left. He breathed over rigid jaws as the wagon crawled to the top of a slight grade.

At the top of the grade Gavagan lifted the whip and cracked the silk. The wagon thundered down the reverse slope, protected by the rise. At the bottom of the grade there was a curve into the forest robbing the Indians of a straight shot.

As they rolled south Blair rode easily and then uneasily. At Columbus he said, "I'm sure The Pigeon was bluffing. If he knew where the sheep were, he'd have used it before."

And as they clattered through Circleville, he said, "But then maybe he found those sheep months ago. Been savin' it for a time like this. He's a long-sighted rascal."

At Chillicothe Gavagan's wagon attracted some notice. Citizens recognized it. And while it was tied up in front of the Cross Keys Tavern an ancient chatterer, a kind of chronicler of his times, explained to the curious persons, "This is the same wagon. This is the same one. And look. Look there. The bullet hole where the rifle ball chipped the edge of the tailgate. The bullet that got that giant in the leg. He died y'know. Yeah."

The chatterer walked all around the wagon. When he got back to the tailgate, people were already beginning to finger the bullet hole. And lest he be robbed of his identification with the wagon and his ownership of the West, the chatterer continued. "I was standin' right there off the head of Paint Street. I heard a shot. This wagon come roarin' down the street throwin' up the dust. I knew they got him. And I said to . . ."

Blair came out of the Cross Keys and relieved Gavagan at guarding the bundles of petitions so the wagoner could go in and eat.

The chatterer said, "That's him! That's the lawyer that started it all. Hey, Mister! Are you Blair?"

Young boys stepped up and fingered the hole in the tailgate of Gavagan's wagon. And around Chillicothe that night there were games played in which twelve-year-old soldiers fired at passing wagons.

Thus a kind of immortality had come to Brutus Christofferson, for already the legend of Blair's Robbery was building in the West.

Blair and Gavagan bunked down for the night in the back of the wagon on top of the petitions. They alternated watch. Their rifles were loaded.

The stableboy brought the message just after the eleven o'clock bell. Blair woke Gavagan.

"Stay awake, Matt. She wants me to come to her house."

"She?"

"The Schaacht woman. I'll see what she wants."

"I know what would be good for her," Gavagan grinned.

She met Blair in the music room, and the slope of her shoulders and the motion which turned her clothes to sculpture were justification enough for her being alive, Blair thought.

"I didn't think I'd have to send for you," she said.

"You knew we were coming?"

"Of course."

"Why?"

"Part of the plan."

"Whose plan?"

"Who plans best?"

"Schaacht, huh?"

"Yes."

"What's the proposal?"

"No proposal. Just an order." She held out her hand. "The re-linquishment papers. Riddle will take them to Washington. That's where the buyers are. They'll have a chance to look them over and buy them there."

Blair studied her in ever-increasing amazement. But he made no move to take the papers from under his shirt. She continued to hold out her hand, but neither in malice nor enjoyment apparently.

"You actually thought I'd give them to you?"

"I presume you will."

He laughed. "Why?"

Her regret seemed genuine. "We've got the sheep."

He controlled himself.

"Pigeon led Ault to them. Ault led Armstrong. They're being held on the common in Mesopotamia now."

"Let's suppose for the moment they are." Blair hooked his thumbs over his breeches pockets. He grinned. "Ault doesn't have Hope's chattel mortgage."

She nodded slowly. "Yes. Does now."

Blair wilted some. "But under the new laws, foreclosures have to be executed in the presence of a judge."

"That, too," she admitted. "Court comes there on circuit in four days. Judge Pease."

"But Bolding will . . ."

"Will argue for the bank." She almost apologized.

"Your goddamned darling. Many happy returns of him!" His open hand cause a red spot to spread on the side of her face and neck. But she did not step back. "Tell me more about what a man he will be some day!"

"There is nothing to tell, I'm afraid."

As they faced each other he knew she was with him. But he lashed into her. "This time you misfigured. You'll have the sheep, but not the relinquish papers until your old man gets the new land law through."

"You talk fine," she said without spirit, "but you'll give them to us. You see, it's the woman. The sheep woman."

"She has a name," he said with pique.

"I *know* her name," she said with feeling. "Her child is due. She was screaming and slapping at the soldiers. They knocked her down."

"*Who* did?"

"It was an accident. They couldn't help it. She was crazy, they said, like a wildcat."

Virginia Schaacht had reason to back up from him. But she didn't. And she even finished her message. "So we'll have the papers, and then we'll call the army off the sheep."

"You'll have hell!"

"Just how?"

"I'll go back and give your boy some pointers in the law."

She smiled, barely. "She's lucky."

"She?"

"The sheep woman."

He took her by the shoulders. "Could I trust you just once . . . for a favor?"

She was a stranger for the moment, swaying close to him, her eyes closed. "Would you please," she whispered.

"See that Gavagan gets to the right place in Washington with these petitions. It's in your old man's interest, anyway."

"I'll see to it, so help me. I'll go with him. I'll follow him in the light surrey."

She was up on tiptoes, offering him a hungry face. And Blair was no log.

Blair reached toward the Cross Keys. But he went two blocks out of his way. There was a brick house on one corner. No lights were on. Blair's knuckles beating on the door brought no answer. But when he began pounding with a rock, a light flared quickly inside. There was glass in the windows. A colored man answered the door, saying, "The doctor is retired. He will see you in the morning, sir."

"He'll see me tonight!"

"Are you sick, sir?"

"Yeah! Sick and tired! Get him up!"

"No, sir, my orders are . . ."

But Blair was inside the house, starting up the stairs. He had found action is the best argument. The colored man said, "All right, sir. I'll get him. Wait."

Brooks stood in the nightshirt wiping sleep from his face. He registered very little surprise. Blair looked around the house in appraisal. "Doing pretty good, aren't you, Doctor? You're quite a doctor now."

"No better than before." He looked at a framed certificate. "But now there's a paper to prove it."

"And Chillicothe pays twice as much to have its hand held by a man that writes 'M. D.' after his name, huh, Doctor?"

Brooks also inspected his own house now with approval. "That's right."

"So you settle where the pains are small and the fees are high."

"I did my share of the other kind."

"Not quite. You've got one more job to do up north, for Mesopotamia and for the Indians."

"Oh, no."

"Oh, yes."

"What makes you think so, Blair?"

"Because we figure we bought you that M.D. sign, Doctor. And we figure we got shortchanged."

"I don't. Now if you'll let me sleep."

"I'll help you sleep well nights, Doctor. I'll ease your conscience for you." Blair reached for Brooks' arm. But the young doctor's muscles were hard and slippery. All Blair got was a handful of nightshirt. And as he yanked the doctor towards the door, Brooks belted him in the chest. The colored man yelled, "I got him, Doctor Brooks!"

And a pair of big knuckled, pink palmed sledge hammers thudded down onto Blair's wrists, springing his grip.

Blair was outnumbered. "All right, Brooks! I'll remember you to the folks who paid your tuition."

The lawyer hurried to the Cross Keys Tavern. He explained hurriedly to Gavagan. Within the hour Blair rode north on the best-winded pony he could rent. At sunrise a puzzled Matt Gavagan rolled his wagon east toward the capital of the Republic, escorted by a surrey which struggled along in his ruts. When the ruts became more severe the wagoner more often turned his head to see the lovely dress jostling along behind him. However his enjoyment of the sight was shortened by the increasing truculence of the good-sized house man who drove

the surrey. Without saying a word the houseman made it apparent
in his first fifty miles that he had a good opinion of Miss Schaacht and
a poor one of Gavagan; and he would back up either of these opinions
if necessary.

There was surprise around the entire store when Jonathan Blair
stepped into Hosmer's Store where Judge Pease was hearing the foreclosure proceedings against the chattels of the widow of Brute Christofferson.

It was not a court. That is, the court was momentarily functioning
under the statute as reviewing-board for the foreclosure. But it looked
like a court because of the remarkable man, Pease. He sat at the
moment in front of Buttrick's counter between the sugar barrel and
the rolled calico. But the way he sat, square, but relaxed, with both
boots on the floor, he appeared to be sitting between the flag and a
marble pillar. Most of all every man felt assured that that great slash
of a mouth would call the case as he saw it, and how he saw it would
be good enough.

The panel of citizens called for under this proceeding were ranged
along the north wall. The west and south walls supported Mesopotamia who leaned against them.

Hope Christofferson sat alone on a bench on the south. Emanuel
Ault squatted on his haunches on the north wall, fingers interlaced and
moving constantly.

Justin Bolding stood composed before Judge Pease.

He looked up from his brief in amazement upon Blair's entry. But
Pease said, "Proceed."

Bolding said, "This then is the chattel mortgage signed by Miss
Hope at the time of her loan from the Mesopotamia Hog & Trust,
which mortgage is now signed over to the United States Bank . . .
and presented for collection on this day. Would you inspect it, sir?"

Bolding followed procedure to the letter. He had obviously been
to some preparation for this.

Pease read it quickly. He lifted his glasses in Hope's direction. "Your
standard mark, Mrs. Christofferson?"

"Yes."

The paper was in two halves and burned on one edge. The judge
handed them back to Bolding. "Proceed."

"You have inspected the animals listed on the mortgage, which are
now under guard on the common, Judge Pease. Therefore Mr. Ault

and I would like to spare the widow any further disturbance by quickly executing the instrument. If you will sign it, sir?"

Pease reached for the two halves of the instrument again. He said, "Your claim seems to be in order, Mr. Bolding. However, I presume six of the wethers and four of the young ewes and all the lambs are progeny of the animals covered by the instrument and are not subject to it."

"That would be a most liberal interpretation of the instrument, Judge Pease, in favor of the debtor, especially since only three of the animals are named, and the rest are lumped under the words 'pure-bred Merinos owned by' . . . and so forth. Yet we will not oppose that view."

"Next point," the judge continued. "Is the debtor represented by counsel or does she speak for herself?"

Hope Christofferson rose and walked forward. But she stopped when a male voice said, "Debtor is represented by counsel!"

Blair stepped forward, studying the floor. He lately walked a court-room very much at ease. Without looking up he said, "Debtor denies the claim of the bank for the following reasons. "

He walked back and forth a minute, his arms behind his back. He accurately judged the extent of the judge's patience, and consumed every second of it for thinking-time. When he opened up, he opened explicitly, distinctly and with enough boredom to indicate that the right so obviously lay with his side that it was somewhat insulting to take his own and the judge's time.

"Our young opponent for the bank has made a serious error, sir. He has seized the wrong sheep."

There was a sharp intake of breath around the room.

Bolding was on his feet by reflex. Blair paused to let him speak. But the young man had risen before he knew what to say, and Blair let him be caught thus awkwardly for a moment. Then, "I leave it to you, sir, but I don't think we are so much required to prove they have seized the wrong ones, I believe they must prove they have seized the right ones."

Pease scratched his chin, and narrowed his eyes.

Bolding was on his feet. "This is ridiculous! Not one single person in this town has even once suggested that these are the wrong Merinos, least of all Miss Hope, who has been handling them, stroking them, even feeding them . . . like long-lost pets."

"The law permits the debtor to make his best case, Mr. Bolding," Pease said. "Because the debtor has not raised the point before, does not preclude raising it now. However, since the debtor does raise the point, it is appropriate for him to make proof. Proceed."

Blair walked to Hope and leaned over her. Bracing his hands on his knees he talked quietly to her. She rose and left the store.

Blair said, "We are bringing in our witnesses, sir."

"Witnesses?"

The crowd craned to look out the door, and there were smiles as Hope led in every ram in the flock.

Bolding addressed Pease. "Sir! Are we to have a circus in the court!"

Pease studied the animals, answering absently, "This is not a court, Mr. Bolding. And it seems to me reasonable that to identify a chattel, we must examine it."

When silence set in, the rams huddled in the center of the store. The round, heavy-wooled heads pivoted nervously and the black faces peered out as blankly anxious as first-time witnesses the world over.

However, Galahad sensed the attention converging on Blair. He lowered his neck and moved slightly to Blair, the others following. The ram stopped then and cocked his head to watch Blair's mouth work and his hands move.

The lawyer said, "Since Judge Pease has thrown us the burden of proof, I will ask counsel for the bank to identify the ram named in this instrument, Aaron."

Bolding protested, "Well, damn it, I never said I knew Aaron from . . ." Bolding looked at the mortgage, ". . . from Galahad. I'm just representing the bank."

"Emanuel Ault," Blair said, "kindly identify me the ram named Aaron."

Ault rose, rubbing the top of his head. "Well, I . . ." He stammered and looked at the judge. But the judge sat impassive watching the sheep.

The men in the store looked at each other and leaned forward, studying the rams. Some put their heads together and whispered.

With her finger on her lips, Elizabeth Buttrick studied the rams in rapt absorption. Absently the finger left her mouth and pointed. Young Tim Flannerty slapped the older girl's hand down so hard it startled a cry from her. Ault whirled, but too late. The finger was back on her lips, her eyes contrite.

Ault studied the crowd. But they were careful not to let their eyes even linger long on one sheep.

Ault circled the sheep in the silent store. As he circled, the rams fidgeted and turned to follow him with their eyes, clustering tighter. From the center a big bold yearling stuck his head high and bleated at the banker.

Ault walked over beside Hope and called, "Aaron!" But since all the rams looked back at him, he got no indication. No ram broke from the pack.

Ault walked to the opposite side of the room, and while walking away from the rams he called, "Aaron!" He turned quickly. The comedian yearling broke from the group and sallied toward Ault. He stopped part way and studied Ault. Ault pointed to him. "That's Aaron."

Judge Pease said, "Correct, Mrs. Christofferson?"

"No. Most everyone in this room could tell you Aaron is no yearling. He sired most of my flock."

Bolding looked stricken, Ault mad.

Blair looked at Pease, hoping he'd gone far enough. Pease wiped his glasses. "I'm satisfied that ram is not the sire named Aaron, Mr. Blair. But I cannot conclude that Aaron is not in there somewhere." Pease put on his glasses and faced the reviewing group of citizens. "You men are sworn to tell the truth. On oath; you there, is the ram called Aaron in this stand of rams?"

Hussong bawled out, "Hell no, Judge. The ram Aaron is dead!"

"How do you know, sir?"

"I heard from Gavagan that Blair wrapped the ram, Aaron, around the neck of Gideon Schaacht. Cold, dead, stiff. In fact, y'might say it was Aaron started all the trouble. Least the wrapping of him around Schaacht's neck."

The judge did not smile. But his glasses needed wiping again. He said, "Then, Mr. Ault, you were apparently not aware that Aaron was not even in the witness . . . in this group?"

Ault did not answer.

Bolding was on his feet. "One ram doesn't prove it, sir."

"I would say you were right." The judge addressed Blair. "This reviewing board requires further demonstration of your contention that these are not the Merinos named in the instrument."

Blair approached cautiously now. "Yes, sir. I ask Mr. Ault to identify the ram, Galahad."

There was a sucking of breath around the room. Hope did not look at the sheep.

Ault approached again. He was intimidated this time. He called the name Galahad, though not loudly. When he did the spirited comedian broke out of the huddle again. Ault raised his arm at the ram, who ducked back in the pack.

Blair attempted now to dismiss quickly. "So you see, sir, we claim these are not the sheep in the instrument. These are estrays which the bank has picked up."

Young Bolding was bright, though, and his brain had been whirling. He demanded now that Hope prove she had ever owned these animals. Hope said, "If you'll take that lively yearling and turn him over, you'll find him tooth-marked twice, inside front leg. He was a twin and hard to wean. The ewe toothed him twice."

It was done and it was so. But Bolding was only seeking time. He said to Blair, "Sir, would you loan me your copy of the estray statute?"

Blair hesitated. Pease said, "The law is common property, Blair."

Blair went out to his saddlebag and brought in his book. Bolding studied it while they took out the sheep, and his face lighted up like found money.

He advanced on the judge with such confidence as stopped the hearts of the townsmen. "We stand corrected, Judge Pease. What we have here are definitely estrays, and we concede to the debtor's counsel that we must proceed under the law for estrayed animals. Under Section three of the law we therefore put these estrays up for auction to the highest bidder. Under Section four, all bids must be in currency satisfactory to the taker-up. And in this case that will be United States Bank notes."

Bolding sat down. Ault winked his congratulations. Hope's face paled. Hussong and the others leaned forward. They burned at the calmness of Jonathan Blair at this moment. A mere boy had put it over him.

But Blair moved slowly as if in thought. Judge Pease had a dislike for the setting of traps in the courtroom. Blair wished to conceal the trap which he had just snapped shut.

But there was small chance of it. Judge Pease already had his forehead in his right hand. He didn't even need to listen to know what Blair would say.

"Does Mr. Bolding stand unretractable on considering these animals as estrays, and the bank as the taker-up?" Blair was slack-voiced and humble.

"Absolutely, sir!" Bolding made it good and strong.

"Then the debtor will abide by the creditor's own interpretation." Hussong slapped his leg in anguish at such defeat. But Blair continued. "And if Mr. Bolding will consult Sections 5 and 6 of the statute he has chosen on estrays, Mrs. Christofferson cites the part which says, I believe . . ." Blair pulled his ear struggling to remember the exact words of the statute which he had voted on himself. "But if the owner can prove property and pay feed charges, the taker-up is obliged to turn the estrays over to the owner, allowing the owner forty days in which to raise the feed fees, reward money and cost of estray notice. If during this forty-day interval the owner shall find that the taker-up has abused, changed the marks, failed to feed, water and shelter, or in any way reduced the value of the stock, the taker-up is liable to action."

Bolding's jaw went slack.

Blair now addressed Ault. "My client, Mrs. Christofferson, will require the full forty days to raise the feed fees, Ault. You and Major Armstrong will be held strictly accountable for the health and condition of the animals during that period. I suggest you see to their fodder immediately."

Judge Pease was seen to wipe his glasses still again.

Hope Christofferson was not seen removing the plugs of cloth from the ears of the vexed and impatient Galahad.

Hank Flannerty, with an extra-straight face, explained to Major Armstrong in immense detail how the sheep should be husbanded by the bank for the next forty days, including, "And don't forget, Major, the Duchess there is due to drop her lambs 'bout day after tomorrow. She likes to be inside a shed when she does it, isn't that right, Miss Hope?"

Hope's hand covered her smile. She nodded.

Major Armstrong's face raised to the heavens and his eyes closed in a devoutly profane supplication which imperiled the salvation of every lawyer, sheep and banker within regimental jurisdiction.

Hank added, "And Lady Elaine there is due. Twins likely. She's quite skittery. Maybe one of your men could . . . Major, are you listening?"

Chapter 29: THE ORPHAN

BOLDING, it must be said, was a man to press his advantage if he won, but he did not whimper when he lost. He made his appearance in the tavern to face out the smiles of the victors. The grin on his face was costing him out of his soul, but he kept it pasted on good and wide.

"Well, you put it over me, Blair!"

Blair looked up briefly from the table in the tavern and then resumed counting the orange silk slips. He turned to Stikes in pique. "There's slips out circulating for six barrels of pickled pork, but there's only five barrels in the blockhouse, Stikes! How come?"

"Hell, Jonathan. Hussong has got the sixth slip and he said he'll bring the sixth bar'l in tonight. Why should we run back and forth with the slips when he's bringin' the bar'l in a couple hours?"

Blair flared. "Stikes, I told you not for two hours or two minutes are there to be more slips out than there is goods in the bank! You forgetting that's what happened to the first bank?"

"Yeah, but Hussong wouldn't do anything with the slip until he brought in the . . ."

"No? You forgetting Hussong was willing to risk gun fire in Hosmer's store to get the lock off a barrel of silver?"

"As I remember, it wasn't Hussong that killed old man Hosmer."

Stikes rose to go after Hussong. Blair told Bolding to sit down.

The loungers in the bar studied the lawyer truculently. Immediately after the trial over Hope's sheep they had set up a free one for him at the mug rack. But he had said, "Don't have time. Want to see you, Mike, about the count on those silk slips."

Culpepper had said, "Aw, c'mon, Jonathan, sure you got time for one drink of whisky to kind of celebrate."

But Blair had said, "Nope. And by the way, Culpepper, I see you cut some fence posts off that piece that you're going to relinquish to the bank. They're not yours to cut."

The lawyer went out of his way, it seemed, to keep his distance. All right, if a man wanted distance in this town, he'd get a lavish of it.

It riled them to see any man talk that way to old Mike Stikes, too. But it made them swearing nervous to see a man sit down now to whisky at the same table with the lawyer he just recently opposed, Bolding.

And who in hell was he anyway that he should hold them by the ears with those relinquishment papers riding under his shirt next to his skin?

Culpepper shoved his empty mug and his voice the length of the bar, "Don't have much time for the common people any more, does he? Not when he can drink with one of his own kind."

Blair said, "Bolding, I need some help. Throw in with me. With the nasty job ahead of us, you'll learn a lot of law with me."

"I'm learning more *opposite* you, Blair," the young man grinned. "As for going in with you . . ." he waved his hand around the inn. "Why? What have you got out of it?"

Blair looked around, too. "Yeah." He looked at the back of his hands. "Well, what you going to do then?"

"Head back to Schaacht, tell him I got whipped, and ask for my next assignment."

"Which will be?"

"To bring those eastern buyers back here, to buy up the relinquished lands."

"Uh-huh." Blair looked his age.

Bolding stood up. He slapped Blair on the shoulder. "So we'll have another go-around then, Jonathan. I'll get an education out of you yet."

Bolding's worldly departure was splintered by his being butted in the belly accidentally by Tim Flannerty who plunged through the door into the tavern.

"He's coming! He's coming across the ford right now!"

"Who?" Exeter wanted to know.

"Young Doc! The stony-faced one. He's coming on a horse right now!"

"Brooks? Y'mean Brooks?"

Exeter busied himself pouring the doctor a charge from the small keg in the back.

Bolding looked over at Blair in wonder.

Doctor Saul Brooks stepped through the door and looked around. Exclamations greeted him, and Exeter held out the mug of whisky. The doctor smiled, but the smile was fleeting and preoccupied. He by-passed the proffered whisky and walked over to Blair. He wore the new medical certificate in his carriage, Blair noticed. He wore it, too, in the direct speech of a man who has discovered his own value to the world . . . in good eastern currency.

"You wanted me up here. I've come to give you three weeks of work."

"Doctor, I want to thank you for . . ."

"You said the Indians were bad off with hunger sickness. Let's get started up there."

Blair now matched the young man's abruptness. "No, Brooks. They've got trouble bad up there. But they kind of used up their chances, far as we're concerned. We want you to see to Hope Christofferson's babe."

"I'll get the Indians done first," Brooks said. "And come back in time for Mrs. Christofferson. Babies aren't as serious as hunger sickness anyhow."

But Exeter had heard it, and the loungers walked over to the doctor and the lawyer. Adams was spokesman, "No, Doctor, you don't go up to the Indian town. You got work to do right here. Start out at my place. Kid's got the thick neck."

And they led him out.

For the next three days they kept the doctor so busy he hardly ate.

The doctor stopped in at Hope's all three days. On the third day he came to Blair's cabin. "Blair, I think you'd best come help me with Mrs. Christofferson."

"Me?" Blair was alarmed.

"Don't flatter yourself. You wouldn't be any help that way. But I want her to move into Exeter's Inn for the next few days. It could be any time now. And there'd be no way for her to let me know . . . being way out there."

"You explain that to her?"

428 JONATHAN BLAIR: *Bounty Lands Lawyer*

"Of course. She says she's got the Merinos back safe now. And with those soldiers tending to them, she won't leave the place. Says she'll take no more chances."

"Uh-huh."

"But she's got to learn that being near the doctor is more important than sheep, and she's got to get in here."

Blair rose from his table. "Thing or two I'll have to be telling you, Doctor. You wouldn't understand about the sheep. But I'll just put it this way. If that's the way she wants it, it's a lot more fitting in this case the doctor goes to the patient . . . instead of the other way around."

Brooks flattened his lips against his teeth and sighed. "You've got twenty days coming to you. Guess you can have it the way you want it. But if I'm going to get up and ride out to her place every two hours, I'm going to use your horse."

"You don't quite get me, Doctor. You're going to *sleep* out there . . . until it's time."

Blair went out with him.

Hope said, "Jonathan, I like the doctor fine. But . . . uh . . . this is a new thing for me. And I'm mostly in the habit of coming at new things alone . . . sort of at my own pace."

"This is one time you're not going to be alone," Blair said. "The doctor will see to your baby."

"Well, Jonathan, I think the doctor knows his trade . . . especially with that new certificate . . . but . . . uh, he's a man, and . . . uh . . . I thought maybe I'd have Angelina Steese come out and see to me."

"Angelina's never had a child. Maybe never even been present. If it must be a woman, we've got some here that know enough they could instruct the doctor. Why don't you pick one of them?"

"Well . . . uh . . . I've not been in on the womanly things in this town so much . . . I . . . I guess if that was the choice I'd take the doctor. But I'd feel strange, having him in the house here."

"Then he won't be in the house. He'll be in the shed."

Brooks' eyebrows went up, but he didn't say anything.

"When the time comes," Blair said, "you light a candle in the window, the doctor will do the rest."

Blair took Brooks by the arm and started to leave, but he turned back. "Hope, you *do* know how to tell?"

"I've heard how it is."

Blair rigged a bunk for Brooks in the shed.

At dusk on the sixth day after Saul Brooks' arrival, Blair was in his usual seat in the tavern when he noticed Exeter reach up behind the cup rack for his barrel hoop sledge, while keeping his eye on the front entrance. Same time he was aware of Adams reaching up over the hearth for the rifle there.

Blair looked at the door which was opening. The height of the doorway was filled by the frame of Chief Silver Pigeon. With his hand still on the door he stepped inside experimentally, but with apology to no man.

The tall Indian kept his eye on the sledge which came now end over end through the air. Pigeon calmly closed the door just enough to prevent the sledge flying out into the night. The door killed it, so that it plopped lightly into Pigeon's waiting hand, by the handle at that.

The Pigeon refused Exeter the honor of anger. From the doorway he addressed Blair. "I come only to say, you are a good man, lawyer. I come to say the Indians are sorry we did not believe you would bring us the doctor, but you did."

Blair's jaw dropped.

"I come to say we are glad you talked good enough to keep the sheep for Miss Hope."

"What in hell are you talkin' about?" roared Culpepper. "You got no doctor! Brooks is out at Hope's house right now."

"No. Blair sends the medicine doctor for us. We got him. Pigeon tossed the sledge gently back to Exeter, who only recovered from amazement in time to prevent it mashing his face.

The Indian was gone.

Culpepper hammered his mug on the bar in glee and laughed, "Can you figure the gall of that dumb Indian thinking . . ." But he stopped abruptly, as the suspicion hit all corners of the room simultaneously.

They funneled out through the door; and the chase began.

The Mesopotamians had learned not to follow Indians unless they had numbers. For this foray they had so many in the party that it left the village short-handed. They had been gone a day and a night and a day looking for the doctor. Blair was awakened by Stikes to stand his second turn at guarding the blockhouse while the moon was about an hour before sinking.

He walked groggily to the blockhouse when he heard a chinking on stone over by the burying yard. He lowered his rifle out in front of him, clicked the hammer back and walked slowly toward the burying ground. He saw a white garment busy there. He studied it until it focused, "Angelina!"

She stood up.

"What are you doing out, Angelina?"

But he saw right away. Beside the big grave marker of Brutus Christofferson was a small slab of slate.

"It's what Hope wanted me to do," she said. "It's over."

"Get Isaac to stand my turn at guard, Angelina. I'll go out."

"No. Better not now.

"Does she hurt?"

"Not in the body. I go back now."

The Mesopotamians returned from the hunt by noon. They had had so many in the party that they'd not even had to warm a single rifle barrel. They had the doctor in tow. Above and beyond that, though, and perhaps as valuable, they brought back eight deerskins full of potatoes and squash which the Indians had stolen from Hawkins.

They brought back, too, a warning. The Indians from whom they had taken the doctor and the potatoes were the leanest, most unlaughing Wyandots they had ever seen, not even barring before the war.

The meeting to set up a new guard system against the infiltrating Wyandots was arranged for three nights hence to allow time to get down to Boxford's Cabin and to get settlers up from that settlement which was also losing stuff to the vagrant Indians. They could help.

When the meeting took place, Jonathan Blair's opinion was not much wanted in this matter. But lately you didn't dare not listen to Blair. Now that he was meaner than sin and carrying those relinquish papers in his shirt, you didn't cross him much, not unless you could get some backing-up.

So they had to let Blair speak. And what he said was, "Seems to me we're forgetting what old Sam would have said to do. Here you sit, making plans to patrol the area. Armstrong urges you to it because that's his training. But old Sam would have said that costs too much. He would have said, 'Give 'em a little corn, a few potatoes. It's a cheap way to buy back your scalps.' A patrol may protect you for a week, but what about next week, and next winter? Come spring we can go there and show them how to plant . . ."

He was interrupted by a voice from the door, "White lawyer already showed us how to plant."

The men in the store whirled to the rear and began to rise, but they were halted by the strange sight in the doorway. The Silver Pigeon stood like an apparition from Tecumseh. But in his arm was no rifle, no knife. A better weapon, perhaps.

His arm cradled a bundle of beaver fur, shaped into a sack. Across the top of it was a panel of bleached deerskin sewn heavily with colored beads of the kind found commonly in any Indian trader's supply kit. The deerskin flap moved convulsively from some pressure underneath it.

The Pigeon addressed Blair as he advanced slowly toward him. "We ask for corn. We get none. We ask for medicine doctor. We get none. Would you like to be Silver Pigeon, who cannot feed his own people? Cannot cure his own sick ones? Would you like that, lawyer?"

The Pigeon walked straight up to Blair, commanding every ear in the place. "Well, you are going to find out if you would like it, lawyer. Right now you will find out."

He held the beaver bundle out to Blair, "Now let us see you take care of your own!"

Blair stood puzzled.

"Yas . . . take it! The Fawn says the lawyer should take it. Take care of it!"

The Pigeon pulled back the flap four inches. Every neck in the store stretched to look, and the rest of the men rose to see. But it was not necessary. For above the rim of the beaver fur everyone in the store could see the tiny tight-clenched red fist as big as a walnut which now quivered in hungry rage.

Blair went white.

"The Fawn is very sick, very weak. No doctor. No food. So you show us now. Here, take him. The lawyer is maybe more smart than Indians. Take him. See how it feels to watch it happen!"

The Pigeon was gone. And Blair faced it, as he had never seen it before . . . hunger . . . primeval, demanding, urgent beyond belief. Hunger was not a thing to be planned against this night. Hunger was not a thing to arrange guards for and plant crops for.

Hunger was right now.

By midnight Jonathan Blair had a new respect for the men in the village, some of whom had faced this thing before. Jim Hawkins had four children, Fitchburg five. He realized he had lived half of a lifetime without knowing the meaning of the question, "How is the baby?"

Suddenly this cliché ceased to be small talk. "How is the baby?" The answer could be panic. The question belittled every human concern. You could not follow such a question with trivia like "How did John Marshall decide the bank case?"

Jonathan Blair put down the hollow straw through which he had tried to pour milk; suddenly he understood many things. Many things more he did not understand.

Tim Flannerty returned to Blair's cabin.

"Did you find him, boy?"

"No, sir. Nobody's seen Dr. Brooks."

"Look again. And hurry."

"No more places to look. Culpepper thinks the Indians grabbed him off again while we were in the meeting. And he's sore at you about it. Says it's part your fault . . . for letting them think the doctor was for them."

"Huh!"

"And Mr. Blair . . . uh . . ."

"What? What!"

"Uh . . . he also said, it wouldn't matter if you could find the doc. He said there's nothing to do."

"He's crazy."

"Mr. Culpepper's raised a deal of colts."

When dawn grayed in, the babe was limp from hungry crying. Yet occasionally over an hour's time it mustered strength to furiously demand life of this world in a red-faced spasm of imperialism. But the only part of the world that was listening was Jonathan Blair and Tim Flannerty.

"He's gone limp again, Mr. Blair. Let's try the soaked cloth again, sir."

Blair soaked the shred of linen in milk. But the babe would have none of it.

"He knows that's not right for him," Blair said. "Won't take it."

The milk-soaked cloth annoyed the child and it cried.

"Now! His mouth is open now!" Tim said. "Try the mug again."

Blair tipped the mug so a thin stream of milk poured out. The babe closed its mouth and sputtered.

"He knows that's wrong. Put more wood on the fire, Tim."

Blair broke off a crumb of bread as small as his fingers would nip. But the babe would not open its mouth.

"What did Adams say again about the goat's milk? I said never mind the fire! What did Adams say . . ."

"I told you five times, Mr. Blair, there is none."

"Damn him!"

"He can't make the goat . . ."

"Where is Camelia with the . . . Jesus, look!"

The babe's transparent face turned livid so it seemed the blood would burst through the paper-thin skin. Blair scooped him up and ran out of the cabin with no shirt on.

He burst into Stikes' house. Stikes said, "Jonathan, did you hear they got the doctor again?"

"Never mind that! Help me."

Polly Stikes said, "It never worried you before, Jonathan."

They had nothing to suggest which he hadn't already tried.

Two doors in Mesopotamia did not even open to Jonathan Blair.

Culpepper's door opened. But he took one look at the beaver sack, and pointed to the burying yard. "That won't even begin to make it even as far as this house is concerned. The sooner the better."

Throughout the day Blair was constantly referred to the burying yard and to the stolen doctor.

By nightfall the lawyer was beside himself. And the most intolerable, unbelievable part of it to Blair was to watch out his front door and observe that while his effort was failing by the minute, Mesopotamia was going right on with its meeting this night to arrange for a better guard system. They walked slowly across the common to Exeter's Tavern . . . casually!

The child had stopped crying hours ago. The crying had been a knife in the ribs, but this was worse. Blair walked over to look down into the beaver bag. The silent, tiny, dark eyes delivered a concussive jolt to Blair's neck flesh. His miniature wrath smoldered out against the outrage of starvation . . . and stupidity. But the little hornet carried such a man-sized anger that it drained his strength and closed his eyes.

"By God . . . you're a man! And we need men!"

Blair closed the beaded deerskin flap and snatched up the fur as gently as haste permitted. As he ran across the common to the tavern he held it arms length in front of him to lessen the shock of his running.

At the tavern he tucked the bag under his arm and stalked among the tables straight up to the front where a four-inch platform had been built for Gershom's sermons.

Boxford stood there this moment explaining why Boxford's Cabin men should not have to guard the road which came south from Mesopotamia.

The percussion entrance of the lawyer hung Boxford in the middle of a sentence. He stepped back in wonder as the lawyer reached the platform and whirled on the crowd.

"I hope you're satisfied! Look at him!"

He tipped the babe up and pulled back the flap. "Take a good look! Too weak to move!"

Blair's voice softened to sarcasm. "Seems funny. All the kids we've had in this town . . . none of you know what to do! Or so you say! But I don't think you're that ignorant. I tried everything. Look at him! Just look is all I ask. And *do* something."

A feminine voice from the back called out, "There's some of us don't know what's burnin' you, Jonathan." It was Hope. "What's ailing the child? A case of fever?"

"No! A case of starving!"

"Well, we're not that hard put we can't feed a . . ." Something stopped Hope. She colored. "Are you saying that the babe . . ." But she rose slowly from her bench and walked forward.

As she crossed the long distance to the platform her cheeks were burning, her face a struggle between diffidence and determination.

"It just came to me what you're saying."

She reached over and opened farther the beaded-doeskin flap on the fur hood. "I'm not practiced in the matter. But for that he shouldn't go without."

She studied the child and then Blair, who stood stupidly.

"There's not time to stand around, it looks, Mister."

Blair snapped back to usefulness. With one hand he grabbed a chair and yanked it beside her. Hope turned it about facing the window and away from her townsmen. "I'd as leave you'd be a shield, Jonathan."

Blair stepped behind her chair. She sat down, somewhat like a queen. Blair gave his back to Mesopotamia and placed one hand on her shoulder.

The base of her throat blushed as her fingers nimbly freed the laces. He handed the child over her shoulder.

Jonathan Blair stood silent, seeing for the moment the wondrous great scheme of things and the great beauty of Mrs. Hope Christofferson.

He was unaware of the shuffling of feet as Mesopotamia moved out of the inn.

Though the town had the grace to leave the inn, they obviously did not go far. Because when the youngest Wyandot in the Northwest broke the silence with a shockingly happy laugh that ended in a hiccup as old as man, it was echoed back from outside in sudden laughter and then a resumption of adult voices beyond the door of the inn.

The widow Christofferson handed the babe up proudly and gently, not to spoil her good work. And the lawyer held him in one hand and in turn raised the woman up by the arm with his other hand.

Her eyes were on the fur hood, and the lawyer's eyes were on her. She became mindful of tying her laces which was made awkward by his arm around her waist, inclining her towards him the slightest . . . which, if she were aware of it, she did not seem to resist. "What was meant for my Swede's son," she said, "seems to do finely for a Wyandot."

She concentrated on the babe, which was somewhat pointless as already its eyes closed and its breath rippled the fur of the hood in sleep.

And now that it was over, the shyness returned to Hope, which the lawyer cured not by releasing her, but by pressing her against him so close that she could not see his face.

There were now certain things in which many of the women of Mesopotamia believed the shepherdess could use instruction. Therefore she began now quite frequently to receive callers. They were friendly women and they were agreeably surprised at the extreme neatness of Mrs. Christofferson's cabin, even envious of the fine linen on her pillow cases.

However, this interest in pillowcases had no direct effect on developments in the Northwest, unless it could be that there was something about the contrast between the snowy lace of the pillow and the bristly charcoal black hair of the Indian with the uncompromising little black eyes that made even Faith Hawkins kneel down by Hope's lap and reach out a finger to be seized by the vicious little fists.

In the broader sense, there was something about the cantankerous old-mannish bags under the eyes of the babe that made even Elizabeth Buttrick take a suddenly odd view of a hundred years of warfare between settlers and the original red proprietors of the land.

In his small way it could even be said that this insignificant and truculent Wyandot accomplished a job of representation that was failed by Tecumseh, White Eyes, Tarhe and Blue Jacket. For the widow Christofferson's conversation gradually took on a pattern.

"I s'pose there's more lambs up there like this put to range before they're weaned."

Angelina Steese said, "Yes, Dr. Brooks said the women are in straights. Lucky to save one out of four. No proper food."

Faith Hawkins said, "They're not used to planting. What planting's done is by the women. But the ones expecting can't see to it very well."

"Seems against nature to lose so many," Hope said, "when they're such a trouble to the dam to get them this far."

"Wouldn't take a lot of food," Elizabeth Buttrick said, "to see them through till next harvest . . . say if it was divided up among all of us and the Boxford's Cabin crowd. Least enough for the women."

Which was how it happened that Culpepper's dump wagon began making the rounds among the cabins in the clearing of Mesopotamia.

Culpepper looked as though he had bit into a wormy walnut. But he turned where Hope Christofferson told him to turn and stopped where she told him to stop. He waited while she climbed down off the wagon and went into each cabin. And the wagon was seen to go out the west road past the Hawkins place and turn up the Harrison road toward Upper Sandusky, the Indian town . . . heavily laden.

Chapter 30: THE FORECLOSURE

THE WORD came in October. Schaacht was coming up to Mesopotamia. He was bringing with him his cashier, Riddle. And he was bringing a handful of eastern buyers who were anxious to buy immediately and settle. He was bringing also power of attorney to buy foreclosed land for many more eastern buyers in response to his eastern campaign.

The news came into the store by Asa Buttrick who had been to Columbus, and it swept through Mesopotamia on the lips of Faith Hawkins like hail before harvest.

And it reflected onto Jonathan Blair like excommunication. They had lulled into thinking it would never happen. But now the woods became busy.

Antonio Denaro dug up every other grape vine in the vineyard. Stanley-the-Slasher was busy marking every merchantable black walnut tree in his stand for immediate cutting and hauling. When he began cutting he needed a lot of help, snaking them out of the relinquished tract.

Blair moved back out of the way of Slasher's axe swing. "Slasher, you got no right cutting timber on the relinquished tract. Doesn't belong to you."

"Huh!" Slasher's axe bites jarred the ground under their feet.

Slasher bit through the core. "Stand back, Blair! Or you'll get your brain bashed in!" The walnut crashed down spewing dried leaves and flinging dead branches and forest debris. It bounced once and settled, letting another eighth acre of open sky break into the part of the forest which now belonged to the United States Bank.

Over on the Culpepper place, Culpepper was digging a trench just inside the boundary of the tract he was relinquishing. The trench led across into the part Culpepper expected to retain. Two dozen hollow logs lay beside the trench and a pile of small stones laboriously hauled up from the ford in the river where he had gathered them.

"Quit staring, Blair! I'll explain it to you."

"You don't need to, Culpepper. I can see you're covering up that salt spring and running it underground over to the part you're keeping."

"You're damned right, bright boy. Now either get out of here or grab hold of those logs and help."

"It's illegal, Culpepper.'

"Illegal my foot! Why should I give Schaacht the best salt spring in town!"

"Because that's part of the relinquished tract."

Culpepper straightened up and held his mud-covered arms akimbo. "All right then explain me this, Mr. Lawyer. How come you took my salt spring away from me and ya left the one on Hope's place in the area she's keepin'."

Blair didn't answer.

"Yah! I thought so! We like Hope all right. But it sure stinks the way you divided things up. Looks like now a man's got to be Mr. Blair's special friend . . . or he'll lose his shirt." Culpepper made as if to take off his shirt. "Here, you want it, Mr. Lawyer? Take it!" He pursued Blair, holding out the shirt. "Take it, Mr. Lawyer, you got everything else!"

Blair walked away, putting up an umbrella of silence against Culpepper's rain of insults.

"But I guess you wouldn't need *my* shirt, would you, Lawyer? I guess you're gettin' taken care of pretty good. We know how it is, Blair. Hell of a thing when a man that does nothin' but read law books, and talk pretty and writes pretty ends up ownin' a whole town that was built by men that didn't have time to sit and read!"

Over on the Fitchburg place Aaron Fitchburg had a big fire burning at night in the uncleared woods which he was turning back to the bank. He had borrowed two small horse carts and he and his sons were stripping the rich four-inch mulch of black soil off the forest floor, hauling it up onto his truck patch and squash field.

The town crawled with activity and Jonathan Blair couldn't stop it.

Saul Brooks had come down from the Indian town. He was kept busy tending sprained backs, cut hands and bad blisters.

"What are you doing to these people, Blair?"

"What the hell do you care!" Blair exploded. "You've given us our twenty days. Now get on back to your paying customers in Chillicothe."

"I will as soon as I get Fitchburg's dislocated hip set back in place."

"Huh, is that a week's work?"

"Just about."

In Asa Buttrick's store Joe Hussong was about to roar like a bull. Tony Denaro was about to bawl. Judge Pease was there according to the foreclosure statute. Gideon Schaacht announced that he had been unable to get the new land law through the government, the one for which Blair and all these men had written petitions. He had left Bolding in Washington to continue the effort. But meanwhile he intended to take what was coming to the bank. He was under severe criticism by the bank board for not doing it sooner.

And Jonathan Blair was apparently knuckling under.

Schaacht said, "The relinquishment papers, please, Blair. You got them?" Riddle reached for them for Schaacht.

Blair didn't move.

"Well, have you got them?"

"Yeah. You got the receipts?"

"All right, all right. Riddle will make out the receipts. Let's have the relinquishment papers."

"Sure. When I see the receipts."

Schaacht sighed. "All right." He motioned Riddle to comply.

The business of preparing the receipts took some time, Blair showing him what names they should be made to, and Riddle each time cautiously referring to the original mortgage.

Handing over the relinquishments was a ticklish business, too, the way Blair handled it. He demanded that the settler have his hand on the receipt before he would turn over the relinquishment paper to Schaacht. The settlers snatched the receipts from Riddle with hate.

When the exchange was complete, Schaacht and Riddle studied the papers carefully for several minutes. Then Schaacht smiled and his face softened. "Jonathan, you've done a fine, thorough job, just as Bolding reported. Good work." He turned to Ault. "This is what *you* should have been able to do, Ault."

To Blair, in the presence of his townsmen, this was the kiss of witches. He clamped his jaw and looked at the floor. But Schaacht wouldn't quit. "Good work deserves good pay. You earned yourself a bonus."

Blair flattened his lips and faced it out.

Schaacht motioned to Riddle who counted out a pile of bills and carried them over to Blair, grinning.

Hussong's voice boomed out over the store. "Now ain't that just dandy, folks? Wouldn't want Jonathan not to make out, would you?"

The settlers remained in the store to enjoy Blair's humiliation. They had paid for the privilege, plenty.

Schaacht said, "Everything is in good order. Now I'd like to select parcels to fill the orders of men who are buying these tracts. Have you got a plat of the town, Blair, that shows how these lands lie?"

Blair silently reached in his pocket and pulled out a key. He handed it to Tim Flannerty.

Tim Flannerty returned in a moment with a large four-by-four-foot plat of the town. The lines of the original farms were fading brown ink. And while the ink of the boundaries had faded, the old parchment itself had darkened so that the whole was indistinct. Yet over this background of vagueness, the relinquished tracts were marked with jet black charcoal so that they stood out in sharp relief.

"Hah!" An exclamation escaped Amos Exeter involuntarily.

The contrasting colors were so striking, that to a man familiar with Mesopotamia it struck almost like the ringing of a great gong . . . what Blair had done. His selection of lands for relinquishment, taken as a whole, made a strange pattern indeed.

Tim Flannerty was not unaware of the role he was playing. When he erected the map on the counter of the store he did it with a certain bounce, strut and splash. He leaned it against the pile of packaged gunpowder on the counter. Then grabbing two of Buttrick's scale weights to keep the plat from slipping, he planked one down on each side of the map with an éclat which was a blowing of trumpets.

He winked at Blair, to get credit for knowing what was going on; and he stepped out of the way.

Around the store faint grins appeared, timorously at first, as they studied the map. Exeter elbowed the stern-faced Jim Dolk and whispered something, and the Dutchman's granite face lighted.

Culpepper's jaw dropped as he moved closer to the map, examining it in unbelief.

Mike Stikes was standing near the map. Keeping his eyes on it he reached into his pocket and pulled out a pair of calipers which he applied to the scale at the bottom of the plat and then to a specific farm on the map.

Schaacht seemed unaware of the stir in the room. He looked at the plat with apparent pleasure, "Blair, they look nice and neat. I'm glad to see they're mostly all well shaped. I was afraid you might try to slice me out a lot of odd shaped triangles and crescents. That's why I wanted to study the relinquish papers carefully. But I see you've done a neat job of it. In fact, as soon as you can get ready, I want you to pack up and move down to Coshocton. Want you to do the same thing down there."

"No. I'm through, Schaacht."

"What!"

"I'm through."

"More money you want?"

"No. Just not interested."

Schaacht was not a dull-witted man. He read in Blair's attitude and in his stance the relief of a man who had had a job to do, and who had finished it well, and was glad to be out of it. He sensed in Blair a kind of victory, which alerted him to mind the attitudes of the others in the room.

As Schaacht studied the settlers he saw not so much hate as he saw a few minutes before. He saw whimsy trying to break out on their faces.

Alarm darkened his face like pulling a curtain.

He stood up, "What's gone wrong here!"

Schaacht raked the room with threatening eyes. "Riddle, something's fouled here. Find out what!"

Riddle was a man who based his decisions on facts, signatures, correct mathematical totals. He could not understand how Schaacht, who ignored all of this kind of evidence, could be president of the bank instead of himself. Yet he knew that Gideon Schaacht, who operated on hunches, whims, the change in a man's tone of voice, the smallest nuances of human behavior, was more often right than himself. Therefore Riddle began to look for trouble. But he didn't know where to look.

It was Gideon Schaacht who walked up to the plat of Mesopotamia and studied it with growing alarm.

"Blair!"

Blair stood still, but the settlers observed a certain tenseness in him.

"Blair!"

Blair didn't move. But Riddle went scuttling over to be of help.

"Riddle! Why didn't you notice this when you gave out those receipts!"

"Notice what?"

"Look at that pattern of lands he turned over to us. What do you see?"

Riddle looked desperately, but he was not a man to understand land.

"Don't look at individual tracts, Riddle. Back off and look at it all."

Riddle complied, but saw nothing.

"How would you get into this one, for example?"

Riddle looked at the long narrow relinquished section which ran square across the middle of the Hussong, Denaro and Adams farms . . . but stopped short of the roads on both ends. It was an island of land completely surrounded on both sides and both ends by the lands of now hostile farmers. No entrance, no egress.

"And these here along the river! Surrounded on three sides by the property of the relinquishing farmers!"

"They're open on the river side," Riddle said.

"Yes. Sure. On the river side. So who can we sell them to? House-boaters? Can you find a customer for farms that you get to by canoe?"

Schaacht studied the map.

"And here we've got several divided by the river. Can you find me customers for farms this size that are split by a river?"

Schaacht studied the pattern more. He found the patchwork quilt to be the most ingenious scheme imaginable for rendering good land undesirable.

"Blair, you won't get away with this!"

"I have, Gideon."

"You can't keep me out of those lands. You've got to give me a right-of-way in there."

"Let's put it this way," Blair said. "You can try to make us give you a right-of-way."

Schaacht whirled on Judge Pease, "Tell him he's got to give me a right-of-way in there, Pease!"

"It's about like he said," the judge answered. "You can try to make him if you want."

Schaacht strode to Blair. "Now look, talk plainer!"

"Sure," Blair said "Right-of-ways, like any other incorporeal hered-itaments, have so far been held not to pass without a specific grant in writing. I have so far found two cases where they were denied where the land was completely surrounded by the grantor's land because the conveyance showed that no grant of right-of-way was intended.

"You can also have a right-of-way by proving previous uninterrupted usage for twenty years. But that would be hard," Blair explained. "You can also have a right-of-way by specific grant from the owner of abutting property. You'd have to ask these men about that."

Schaacht looked around at the circle of faces. Hussong crossed his arms, leaned back and grinned at Schaacht. Culpepper did not let the lighting of a Conestoga prevent him from returning Schaacht's stare. Buttrick hooked his thumbs over his belt. Schaacht grabbed Blair by the shirt front. His three years in charge of Western finance were peeling off a little of his control.

"There's other ways, Blair! I'll get a right-of-way!"

"Yes, there are other ways. There's an easement of necessity. But burden of proof is on you. And I'd just like to handle the other side of the case. Particularly on your river properties where you can get in by boat."

Schaacht laid his high cranium in his bony hand which wiped down to his chin. But the face that came out from behind the hand was a more controlled, more powerful face than the one that went in. Schaacht had recovered from the shock, and he was dangerous as always. He even grinned. "All right, Blair. You're smart." He looked around the room, still grinning. They answered his grin with a degree of sportsmanship and fellowship. For Gideon Schaacht could be an appealing man. He would press an advantage when he had it. Everybody knew that. But he didn't whimper when he lost. That showed through, too. And Mesopotamia understood that kind of a man. Understood and respected.

"You're all pretty smart," Schaacht smiled. "You take care of each other. You're alert. You should be a good investment."

In testament to the power of Gideon Schaacht you could feel that store moving out to him, getting a chair ready for him, clearing a space for him at their bar. Blair worried.

"How about using some of that ability to help me out now? I've been fair with you I think," Schaacht said. "But what am I going to do about these properties? How can I sell them if I can't get to them? They're useless to me."

Blair said, "No, they're not, Schaacht."

"How not?"

"Well, since you can't get at them, we could probably be persuaded to work them for you . . . on shares for a while. Be a good thing for

the bank to be in the farming business so you'd understand a thing
or two about the West . . . if you're going to stay."

"But I'd be stuck with it forever. I could never get out of it. I could
never sell these lands."

"Yes you could."

"How?"

"If you understood anything about the country you'd see you have
the best group of prospects any man could ask for."

"Where?"

"Well, I imagine Tony Denaro would be happy to buy his grapes
back from you, if you take good care of them while they're yours."

Denaro lighted up.

"And Hussong would probably buy back his hog wallow from you
in a year or two or three . . . if your price is right. And Culpepper, he'll
probably buy back that land from you with the salt spring on it in a
year or so, if your deal is honest."

Blair waved his hand around the room. "These are your best
customers right here, Schaacht. Time you woke up to it. Here are men
that know enough about farming so they can borrow money from
your bank and make good enough use of it to pay you back your
interest just out of the crumbs left over. They can make more money
from a given hundred dollars than you can. That is, they could before
you ruined their currency for them."

Riddle, who was sensible of having made no contribution for
Schaacht all afternoon, tried now to recoup. Recognizing the new
giant in the room he went over close to Blair. With the air of a man
who is going to make everything all right, he said, "Now Mr. Blair,
let's all sit down around a table and work out a . . ."

But Tim Flannerty said, "Mr. Blair, it's time now. He was squallin'
like heck when I was over for the plat."

"If we could just sit down," Riddle continued with annoyance,
"and work out . . ."

Blair put his hand on Tim Flannerty's head and started for the
door. "*You* work it out, Mr. Riddle. I have an urgent appointment."

Blair and the boy walked slowly out of the store. Mrs. Hope
Christofferson blushed and left the store a few minutes later.

Jonathan Blair had no medals to show the world. He did not have
the largest hog ever seen north of Cincinnati, as Joe Hussong did. He

did not have the largest ear of corn grown north of Columbus, like the one Culpepper had nailed up over his hearth. He did not have a name that stood for something, like the word Stikes had come to mean "rifle."

But on this day he received a kind of medal, though he was not present to see it. Schaacht turned to Joe Hussong and he said, "Hussong, you seem to have quite a bit of 'say' in matters up here, let's step over to the map and talk this over."

"Won't do any good, Mr. Schaacht."

"Why not?"

"We could talk. But up here we don't make any moves until we talk to our lawyer. And he just left."

In the city of Washington a bright young man named Justin Bolding was being questioned by the congressional committee on public lands. The questions were put to him largely by Rufus King of New York State. And the young man answered boldly with answers which showed a natural knowledge of his subject and some study besides. He said, "Gentlemen, the fact is you have everything to gain by allowing the Western farmers to relinquish what they can't pay for and retain a piece of ground equivalent to the payments they've already paid in. You saw the petitions that our Mr. Blair forwarded. That only scratches the surface. Foreclose these men and you'll have a vagrant, wandering, squatting population of angry men. In fact, you might even have a new country on the other side of the Alleghenies.

"And they don't owe you anything either. You've already realized thirty-four million dollars in land sales in Ohio alone. And you took nine million acres of Ohio land to give away as Revolutionary Bounty Lands. So the West really paid for your army in the rebellion."

Bolding watched Rufus King carefully, so as not to overdo it. But he saw the great man nodding. King wanted him to go on. He did.

"Now I'm not suggesting that the Congress of the United States follow the lead of Gideon Schaacht, sir . . ."

"You may make that suggestion," King said, "God knows they need somebody's lead."

". . . but Mr. Schaacht is also creditor to the same people who owe you. Now he has decided to take back a small portion of the debtor's ground. Leave the farmer enough to get back on his feet. It's an enlightened policy which . . ."

King harrumphed. "However, don't unduly labor us with the merits of Mr. Schaacht. It just could be Mr. Schaacht is pulling himself out of a hole he never should have dug for himself. But go on."

"Point is," Bolding said, "if you should decide to foreclose, the government's Land Office would nullify a policy which already is in effect by the government's bank. The right hand cancels out the left . . ."

"Yes, yes," King said. "We see that. True, true. Point is, is Schaacht doing right? Be blunt, boy. Does Schaacht know what the hell he's doing out there? Answer me straight way, boy!"

Justin Bolding thought about his answer. Bolding had grown a lot in the last four years. He never was a babe in anybody's political woods. But now at a young age he was an old hand in the duel of departmental government, and he could find his way around political corridors as fast as they renovated the building. He was already long beyond and above the amateur intriguer who falls easily into a subtle invitation to murder a reputation.

He had advanced to the discovery that the eyebrow raiser who invites name slaughtering, for the moment is anxious to hear it; but tomorrow shuns the slanderer like any other murderer.

Bolding had taken the seminar so he knew that unqualified defamation and unqualified praise are both discounted 50 per cent.

He was even up to the place where he was about discovering that the trickiest answer, though the hardest to handle, was the petrified truth. He had run the course all the way back to that.

He said, "Put it this way, Mr. King, No eastern banker knew what he was doing at first. They were all learning. But Gideon Schaacht had the boldness to learn fast, and use what he learned, regardless of orders from Philadelphia and Washington. Now when he recalled those loans abruptly, he had not yet learned enough. He's trying to make up for it now. And he's man enough to do it. This Schaacht Land Bill is part of his attempt."

Rufus King clapped Bolding on the back so it stung. "Makes sense, boy. I want you to go down and tell the House what you just told us, when we make our report."

As they left the room King said, "Now, mind you say it without wavering, and good and loud." And when they were alone in the hall the older man said, "And . . . uh . . . I'll see to it somehow that the director of the bank knows you may have saved his job."

Taverns and cloak rooms around Washington buzzed with talk about the brilliant young man from the West, named Justin Bolding, who was trying to get a bill through the Congress. It was casually referred to as "that Bolding Bill."

Up on the east road out of Mesopotamia a recently familiar ritual was taking place on the Emerson farm, now referred to as the Christofferson place.

It interrupted a strange conference in the shed. Major John Armstrong of the Western regiment was accustomed to hold tight rein on his unit. But on this afternoon he was holding the foreshanks of a heavy-wooled ewe who was never called by name any more, but who was privately believed to be the ewe, Guinevere. The major held the sheep awkwardly as though he were proposing marriage under force and hoped to be rejected.

The widow Christofferson was saying, "So have your men shear closer to the skin like this, Major."

To the secret entertainment of a former Corporal Mulvane and a former Corporal O'Fallon, she cut off a hank of fleece and held it for the major to see.

He said, "But how in the . . . how do we get the animals to stand still for . . ."

But he was interrupted now by the important entrance of Tim Flannerty who said, "Time, Miss Hope! In fact, past time."

The major said, "Just one minute. Now . . ."

But the widow seemed to forget about sheep. With a certain embarrassment, which the ex-corporals found lovely to watch she left abruptly.

Guinevere landed, plop, on her knees. The major rose and dusted his own off in disgust.

Hope Christofferson received the beaver-fur bundle almost automatically and swept gracefully toward the cabin.

Blair and Tim Flannerty stopped at the door, and the widow Christofferson paused a moment to say, "Jonathan, it looks like you butted them clean head on this time. And won out."

"Too early to say, Hope. Gideon Schaacht is not to be played with.

And he hasn't left town yet. He's talking about pinning me with the part of the hundred thousand dollars that was missing. The part that Brute got and some that Pigeon got."

Forgetfully he started to enter the cabin with her. But the gently closing door reminded him, and he waited outside with Tim.

Chapter 31: THE ATTOURNEY

LEADERSHIP has always depended upon the ability to call men up to big work. Gideon Schaacht could do that. Leadership also requires the courage to crush when necessary. Gideon Schaacht had that courage, also.

It was short of midnight when Tim Flannerty and Jonathan Blair were preparing Young Chief for a trip out to the Christofferson place. Schaacht entered. With him were Major Armstrong and ex-corporals Mulvane and O'Fallon.

Schaacht was direct. "Blair, you've become a strong man. I flatter myself I made you that way. But now I need you. You're going to undo this little trap you sprung on me here. If you think I'm going before the board in Philadelphia and wring my hands and say I was beaten by a handful of farmers and a woods lawyer north of Columbus, you're crazy. You're on my side whether you like it or not."

"No, Schaacht. I'm through."

"I don't mind paying well. Together we'll put order into the West, and we'll take a fair return for the job."

"Count me out, thanks." And to Tim Flannerty, "I think that's enough blankets, Tim. He'll suffocate."

Schaacht said, "Damn you, Blair, do you think I come empty-handed? You getting so big you forgetting who you're dealing with?"

"No, sir. I wouldn't turn my back a minute." Blair grinned and said, "Tim, tuck his hands inside and make him keep them in there. It's cold out."

"Well, I'm sorry you make me do it this way. But if you won't come with me willingly, I guess I'll have to go back to the old way.

I suppose you have occasionally wondered why the bank never pressed charges for the unreturned portion of the hundred thousand dollars. Well, we were saving that . . . for now."

Blair sucked air.

"Consider yourself under arrest for the larceny of five thousand dollars which was not returned to the U. S. Bank. If you wriggle out of that, I'll sue for the interest on the entire hundred thousand while it was in your hands. And I'll keep you rotting in the Chillicothe jail until you holler for uncle Gideon."

Blair appeared not to hear. But he heard every word. He was not sure he wanted Tim Flannerty to hear any more. He told Tim to leave.

Schaacht said, "Armstrong, you want a lieutenant-colonel's leaf . . . get Blair to the Chillicothe jail. Miss this time and you'll be the highest-ranking permanent mess officer in the Army."

Armstrong turned to Mulvane. "Mulvane, you want your stripes back?"

"Yes, sir," Mulvane paused. "But I don't know if I want them *this* bad."

Armstrong didn't bat an eye. He said, "O'Fallon?"

O'Fallon moved toward Blair eagerly. Mulvane blocked him with an arm. "All right, damn it. It might as well be me."

Blair said, "Just a minute, gentlemen. You still need a warrant to arrest a man."

Schaacht grinned and reached in his pocket. "Did you think we'd overlook that?"

Blair licked his lips. He turned to Armstrong. "All right if I put out the fire? I guess we'll be gone awhile."

Armstrong nodded. Blair stooped to the fire. There was a pile of wood ashes six inches deep. Blair shovelled them up and walked to the door to shovel them out.

Suddenly he whirled and hammered the shovel against the support pole. Ashes as fine as powder filled the cabin and the eyes and nostrils of the men in it. He instantly snatched up the fur sack.

Blair was gone.

The cabin of Hope Christofferson was surrounded by Armstrong's men. If they executed this assignment well, it could be an end to the most unsoldierly tour of duty ever inflicted upon any unit in the West. Part of Gideon Schaacht's skill in life was to use the motives of other men to activate his own plans. And he believed that not many more hours could pass before Jonathan Blair would try to break through to the cabin of the shepherdess. When he did, Armstrong's men were there.

Armstrong waited.

"He's near here, you can be sure of that. He might even be within hearing distance right now."

Mulvane said, "Major, on that order of yours to fire if he won't halt, you meant fire close, didn't you?"

In an extra loud voice Armstrong said, "Fire close, hell! Fire to hit, Mulvane! Or you'll be groomin' hosses till the end of your hitch!" He leaned close to Mulvane and lowered his voice, "Didn't you hear me say he might be close enough to hear?"

Mulvane clapped his hand to his mouth. Armstrong was not angry. He was strangely thoughtful. He kept his voice low. "But I'll tell you one thing, Mulvane. How you fire is up to you. But if he slips through your damn fingers, I'm not foolin' about the horse part. I'm not even sure how I'd fire myself until it happens. I know one thing, though, I'm not gonna grow over-age-in-grade because of this damn lawyer. How I'll aim depends on how he moves. My rifle is loaded with a seven-finger charge."

The night was long in the circle of sentries around the Christofferson cabin.

It was long for the woman inside the cabin, too. She sat before her fire, upset and restless. Blair had come bursting in here earlier this evening, out of breath. He had Young Chief under his arm, and he had a kind of desperation in his eyes. He had said, "Hope! No questions! I want you to marry me tonight, and come with me . . . now!"

"Now just a minute, Jonathan. I . . ."

"No 'just-a-minutes,' Hope! Now!"

"Why? Why marry? And why right now?"

"The reasons don't sound so good. Just come," he ordered.

But Hope Christofferson had not survived in the big woods this long by jumping whenever a man yelled.

"Jonathan, you didn't ask me if I *wanted* to marry you, which I'd have liked if you had. But, even if I wanted, it wouldn't be decent to Brute, so soon after."

"Hope! What are you saving yourself for! What are you living for? Sheep?"

"Merinos. There's a difference."

"Look, Hope . . . all I know is I want you. Will you just once trust me to . . ."

But he had stopped and listened carefully at the door. He had then quickly reached for the bundle of fur that was Young Chief, and started out.

"Jonathan, if there's trouble, leave him!"

Blair had paused to look at the babe in a moment of hesitation. "No. He stays with me." And he was gone.

Shortly after his departure, Hope Christofferson had become aware of the noise outside. Opening the door she saw the silhouettes of the soldiers and she heard Mulvane's voice, "He went this way!"

They knew the open cabin-door was a question, and Mulvane yelled, "The little black ram, ma'am! He got loose!"

Hope started toward the shed, but Mulvane yelled, "Never mind. We got him, Miss Hope."

She saw the soldiers move toward the shed, and Boss came running back into the cabin. She sat by the fire. That was over an hour ago.

Yet the night seemed alive somehow. Jonathan was running from something all right. There was whisky on his breath, though. And his talk was whisky sounding.

Boss paced the floor. Hope opened the door and stood there looking out. Nothing moved, and yet it was as though the woods teemed with action and called to her.

On the following morning Hope Christofferson was surprised to see that Armstrong had such a large number of men at work around the sheep shed. And there were some spread out around the cabin finding various things to do. "Like to keep the men busy, Miss Hope," the major said. "If you don't mind."

The sun was two hours high when Hope started to hitch up the cart to go in to Hosmer's Store. Armstrong was at her side with gallantry. "We'll hitch up, Miss Hope. Or better yet, I got a man going in to the center. Can we fetch whatever you were going for?"

And on the same morning, up in the Indian town of Upper Sandusky, Gideon Schaacht painted an inviting picture of revenge for the chief of the Wyandots. He wouldn't have needed to make it so complete. The chief was getting the idea very clearly, and his tongue wet his dark lips, savoring it a little.

Schaacht said, "So we'll want you to testify, Silver Pigeon."

The Pigeon smiled, concentrated on carving a length of hickory, said nothing.

"All we ask," Schaacht explained, "is that you say that Blair came up to the Indian town and took the hundred thousand dollars. Testify, that's all."

Rontondee was standing there. He held out his hand to Schaacht. Schaacht unpocketed a handful of Spanish milled dollars that glistened. Rontondee grabbed them. Pigeon reached slowly over to snatch them. He tossed them like hickory shavings at Schaacht's feet. Rontondee started to stoop. Pigeon's glance straightened him up. Silver Pigeon knew how to make a white man boil.

"All you have to do is testify, Pigeon!"

"No good to testify. The lawyer has learn to fight back." Silver Pigeon said. "A man like that, he should be . . . he should be an Indian."

Schaacht stooped to pick up the silver and he motioned to the two soldiers who accompanied him. They mounted and rode south.

Pigeon rose, and keeping his eyes on their receding backs, he motioned with his knife hand to Rontondee. "Horses!"

And down in Mesopotamia, Gavagan was back. Matt Gavagan was accustomed to being the center of things when he came back into town after being out in the world. He brought back the few exciting things that came into Mesopotamia. And he brought back news of conditions downstate. But never had Matthew Gavagan brought back such a cargo of intelligence as today.

To the group in front of the store he was repeating his experiences in Washington. By his own telling of the story Matt Gavagan did not come out unheroically. But having so well credited himself he was generous with credit where else it was due.

". . . so this young Bolding, he stood right up there in front of those law makers like a soldier, and he told 'em. He told 'em plenty."

"The point is, Matt," Buttrick interrupted, "did the law go through?"

One rule Gavagan enforced was to tell his own story at his own pace. "So when he sat down, there was clapping even. I was watching from up in that catwalk they got, like the rifle ramp in the blockhouse. And then they thanked Bolding for what he had to say. And then the head man there, up on the big throne chair there, he said he thought they should support Mr. Schaacht in this big effort of his by voting in favor of the Schaacht land law."

"The *Schaacht* land law!"

"I'm comin' to that. This Bolding, he marches right up there. I changed my mind about him. He marched right up there in front of everybody and he whispers in this man's ear awhile. There's nodding and talking back and forth. And then the head one there, he said, 'Mr. Bolding tells me he is certain that Mr. Schaacht would want this bill known as the Blair Land Law. That's that lawyer that started that petition going through the territory, the one that blew in here by the wagon load and turned this chamber into a blizzard of paper that day.' Then there was laughing, and the man said, 'H. B. 713, the Blair Land Law.' And then right away begins the 'ayes' and 'nays,' and it was a sight to see I'll tell ya."

And when the settlers of Mesopotamia went out of Buttrick's store, known as Hosmer's Store, they left taking big steps that day . . . until Gavagan said, "Hey, where the hell *is* Blair, anyhow?"

On the second night Hope Christofferson stirred up the fire and stared at it. In the same way that she often rose in the middle of the night to look in the shed knowing that she would find a sick ram, so she felt drawn to the outside tonight. There were good reasons Blair should have been back by now. There was a sharp wind, and she threw on a log which flared up.

Out in the woods the attorney saw the orange windows in the Christofferson cabin glow brighter. It helped him silhouette the ring of sentries which stood between him and the Christofferson place. He knew, too, that if he ever got past the ring of sentries that same cabin light would help the sentries silhouette *him*.

He had made a complete circle around the cabin, and found that Armstrong had it completely ringed. Nor did the sentries stand still. They used a modification of Armstrong's combing technique. Each soldier walked casually clockwise in the circle until he met the next man. After making contact on that leg he walked back counterclockwise until he met his neighbor in that direction. It was a casual, sauntering, constantly moving circle. Blair could occasionally hear the brief interchanges as sentries met and parted.

"Anything?"

"Nothing."

"Might keep an eye on that draw there. Good cover for him if he tried to get through."

"Yeah. Been watchin'."

"Poor bastard must be freezin'."

"Yeah, and the kid, too."

Blair saw one of the soldiers break off and walk to the cabin. The door opened. The soldier entered. Apparently they would watch from the inside, too.

The bundle in the lawyer's arms began to vibrate. Blair recognized the signals. It would wind up like that for a few moments. Then it would cut loose in a screech. He hurried back into the woods, and he clamped it to his chest to drown the noise. But the strident treble seemed to the lawyer to pierce above the winds. He wondered if it did or if it only seemed that way because it reverberated through his ribs.

But as suddenly as it began, the cry ceased, and the fur bundle was limp in a kind of silent anger. Blair crept back as close as he dared to the outside of the circle of sentries.

Inside the cabin the young soldier said, "The major thought I ought to come sit with you, Miss Hope."

"Oh? Why?"

"Said I just ought to. Guess they heard noises outside. Maybe some of those red ones are down stealin' again. Anyway he said I should be with you. I'll be no trouble, Ma'am. Stay over here in the corner."

Hope looked at his equipment. "The major has you all armed tonight?"

"Yes, Ma'am. 'Case of Indians, like I said."

Hope thought about this. She opened the cabin door and looked out. She could not see into the dark. But she could hear the susurrant circle of sentries in constant motion under the wind. To the young man, she said, "What's the commotion?"

"Just men walking, Mrs. Christofferson. Major put us on the alert around the house." He added quickly, "Oh, and watching the sheep, too! Especially."

Hope closed the door and went back to the fire. More than sentries were stirring out there.

Except for the wind blasting across the top of the chimney, the room was silent. Hope had a sense of time going by, life in fact. Blair's words came back to her, "What are you saving yourself for?" And there was a yearning in Mrs. Christofferson. Nor was it a vague undefined longing. Though it was mixed with a languishing sense of wasting herself, it came mixed with a strong picture of the face of Jonathan Blair. There was frost on his breath from the heat of it this cold night, as she saw it. His lips were drawn back, breathing hard against exertion. The eyes held a kind of perpetual query about mankind. The jaw lately had a certain "be damned to you then."

These things she saw, and more. She saw now in a different light Armstrong's offer this morning to send to the store for her. She saw differently the chasing of the black ram last night. Blackie had never got loose before. If he did, he was the kind that others would have followed. And Boss would have been barking.

On this particular night it seemed important to Mrs. Christofferson to be . . . well, to *be*.

She looked over at the soldier who sat in the corner watching her. But as the flame flared up she noticed how you could hardly see the corners of the room. Looking away from the fire into the gloom, the soldier was not visible.

A sentry on the outside of the house would have the same problem. If he looked away from the light into the darkness his horizon would be pulled in to a few feet in front of his face.

It was at this moment that Hope Christofferson rose and took from a brass mug certain pedigree letters, having to do with sheep. She put these in her pocket.

The soldier alerted.

Next Hope lighted a candle at the hearth.

The soldier rose, suspicious.

"I'll just be saying good night," she said to him as she went into the other room with the candle.

It was Jim Hawkins who was on duty in the cupola of the blockhouse that night; and he was the first civilian in Mesopotamia to see the red glow in the sky out over the east road.

He hammered upon a certain large bell which had come into

Mesopotamia's possession a few months ago from Chillicothe. It was only a few minutes until cabin windows lighted up. Hawkins heard Denaro fire off his rifle. Then fainter, he heard Adams relay the shot out the west road. And shortly he heard the faint answering explosion of Fitchburg's rifle way up on the northern edge of the clearing.

It was thirty minutes before the men of Mesopotamia were moving toward the red glow over the trees to the east, carrying shovels and rifles, not knowing which they'd need.

The young soldier was alarmed for Mrs. Christofferson. "You better get any valuables out, Mrs. Christofferson!"

But Mrs. Christofferson stood in the doorway looking out beyond the ring of sentries, trying to pierce the ring of black. She held onto the door frame to brace against the wind which riffled her short hair and swirled on inside to fan the fire which was eating along the bottom of the cabin. Preoccupied with her staring she called over her shoulder, "Get the rifle and the cook pans out, and the linen." But she did not sound as though it were of first concern.

Armstrong's voice could be heard over the wind. "Get back to your posts! Nobody relieved you! I sent four men to the fire. Don't another man leave off from this circle! This is the time to keep your eyes open!"

But as they looked away from the fire the blackness was blacker yet.

Armstrong's voice came and went on the wind. "Just the kind of thing he would . . . be alert . . . remember the bell trick . . . and same thing . . . he'll be moving in somewhere along the circle right now . . . and when the confusion starts don't you move an . . . unless . . . and any man that . . . groom the hosses the rest of your life!"

Of the townsmen, Isaac Steese the tanner, was first to reach the burning cabin. He had with him a pair of wet hides for smothering flame. He arrived out of breath. But Hope said to him quietly, "Never mind the cabin. As the men come, have two or three go stand around each soldier. Blair's trying to get through, I think."

"Shouldn't we check the fire?"

"No."

The well seasoned cabins of old settlers burned fastest. And Hope was early in this country. As the flames ate the cabin down, the sentries were surprised at a strange phenomenon which began to take place. Mulvane noticed that Adams and Fitchburg and Denaro stood around him, with calm faces. "Put out the fire you damn fools! What you standin' here lookin' at me for! The Old Man won't let me move. But you could at least . . ."

Adams folded his arms on his chest. "No law against us just standin' here with ya, is there, Mulvane?"

"Can't you see the cabin is . . ."

"Yeah. We see."

And suddenly Mulvane saw a lot, too. As he looked around the circle he saw that each sentry was receiving the attention of two or three Mesopotamians, who just stood and talked with the sentries.

The cabin burned down.

Towards it walked a man who came in out of the woods through the circle of sentries who were now engaged in conversation with the men of Mesopotamia. He carried a fur bundle. The howling wind occasionally lowered enough to defer to several verses of the most poetic and tuneful profanity ever to grace the lips of a Western field-grade officer. The major's sentries stood surrounded while the lawyer walked unmolested toward the blazing cabin.

In a panic Armstrong felt the major's leaves growing permanently into his shoulders. He swung his rifle up and yelled, "Halt!"

Blair looked back, but he continued walking. "Halt! Dammit, halt!"

Armstrong leaned his cheek to the stock of his piece. But the tendons in the back of his knees were stung by the knife edge of Adam's hand. The rifle exploded into the sky. Armstrong lay flat on his back.

The town did not wish to go back to sleep. Amos Exeter opened up the tavern for their accommodation at this late hour. Young Chief slept in his fur, oblivious and exhausted, and at last . . . unhungry.

Faith Hawkins was assuring Hope Christofferson that there was plenty of room for her at the Hawkins house until her cabin could be rebuilt. Hope was listening but not closely. For in the jumble of tavern noise another voice was saying, "Hope, Young Chief and I take hardly any room. I was hoping to offer you my house."

As these things are sensed, the room quieted down and men looked over from their mugs. "Starting tonight," added Blair.

There was no answer from Hope. Blair stumbled on. "You asked for reasons before. I can give reasons enough, if you'd want to hear them. And the cabin's ready right now."

Tim Flannerty said, "I'll build a new fire in the hearth." But he waited to see if it would be needed.

Faith Hawkins rose from the tavern bench and drew herself up, "What about the girl's privacy?"

Blair said, "I guess you didn't take me right. I don't mean for her to have privacy. I've already asked Jim Dolk. He's ready and waiting; and he's studied the marriage out of his justice-of-the-peace book."

Hope colored and rose and the women of Mesopotamia saw at that time a Hope Christofferson which the men had always seen.

"I said it seemed too soon, Jonathan, for Brute."

Tim Flannerty said, "But it's late for Mr. Blair, Miss Hope. Already grey hair by his ears."

Gavagan barged in where most anyone feared to tread. "Jonathan, that young Bolding and me were talking. You trained him up pretty good. We were talking about the part of the money that didn't get turned back and how that Schaacht might nail you for it and have Hope tell how much Brute got. But he says, 'there's one way out. A woman can't testify against her kin.' "

"But that isn't the reason, Hope," Blair said.

The room was silent for painful seconds.

Hope Christofferson looked over at Young Chief's fur sack.

" 'Course, I did start the family in a way, Jonathan," she said. "And I'm one likes to finish a job that's begun."

The lawyer moved slowly so as not to worry her, but he moved steadily to show he meant to hold her to it. His hand around her waist pulled her to him, and her head bent back.

They held it right there, and right then. Mesopotamia leaned forward on the benches straining, trying to help Jim Dolk over the unfamiliar words. But even without all that help it sounded good because Tony Denaro's soft violin gave Dolk's steady voice a kind of official tone nobody had noticed before. And the presence of a squad of disarmed and truculent United States troops added dignity to the proceeding.

Denaro's fiddle stopped abruptly on a slightly discordant note as the ceremony was interrupted by the opening of the tavern door. Chief Silver Pigeon stepped over the threshold, flanked by Squindatee and Mudeater. His face was severe. But he looked over the activity, and sat down on the end of one of the benches with curiosity and dignity. Mudeater and Squindatee squatted on the floor. Denaro resumed his fiddle guardedly.

James Dolk, justice of the peace, came to the place where he said, "And if there be a person who knows good reason why these two should not be joined, let him speak now or forever . . ."

"I speak!"

Mesopotamia turned to face the standing figure of Chief Silver Pigeon.

Dolk was nonplussed. But his face asked the question. The Pigeon said, "For a man to have a woman he should be man enough to keep life in the young. That is a man's job. What right is it for . . ."

But the chief was interrupted by a muffled protest from the beaver sack. Pigeon's eye was attracted to the hearth where he saw the sack rock and shake from the angry tempest inside. The Silver Pigeon's great dark face lighted up in a grin.

"I will sit down. It is good."

On the morning of the fourth day, Saul Brooks seemed unaware of the recent concerns of the men of Mesopotamia. He looked at the town narrowly as a doctor looks, which is as it should be.

"Blair, you've got to get Hussong to dry up that hog wallow. Our fever will drop off the day that wallow dries up. It drains down southerly. And there are springs below it that are feeding an eighth of these cabins."

But Blair looked at the town narrowly, as a lawyer looks. He said, "Brooks, you've given us our twenty days. Why don't you get on back to your Chillicothe?"

"Don't worry. The sooner the better."

"When then?"

"I'll be riding out of here the minute I get the remedy for Mrs. Hosmer's shakes."

"Huh . . . she's had that ten years off and on already. Could be ten years more yet."

Like any doctor hearing a layman's diagnosis, Brooks made no reply.

A couple hundred trail miles to the south at the town of Chillicothe in the office of the U. S. Bank, Gideon Schaacht surveyed the young man named Bolding who stood opposite him. Schaacht planked his boots on the table and he said, "When you get him down here, have them double the guard on the jail house."

"But I'm not going to bring him back, sir."

"You said you were going to Mesopotamia to see him."

"Yes, sir. But I'm still going up to get his signature on my law certificate, sir."

Schaacht's feet came off the table, "What!"

The young man flinched a little, but he stood his ground silently.

"Why?" Schaacht demanded. "Why *his* signature?"

"Well . . . uh . . . just happen to think someday that'll be a good name to have signed to a man's law certificate."

"Hah! Whatever you want, then. Just be sure you get him down here, and locked up tight."

"No, sir. I'm not bringing him back, sir."

Schaacht was so tall that when he got up out of this chair as he did now, it seemed he would never stop going up. He leaned across the table and opened his mouth as if to yell, but the words came out just above a whisper in painful restraint. "Would you repeat that please, Mr. Bolding?"

"Uh . . . yes, sir. I'm not bringing Blair back. I have decided that it is impossible to prove charges of theft or anything else against him concerning the fraction of the hundred thousand dollars which was not returned."

"You w-h-a-t!"

"Not at least, sir, without risking counter charges against my own family."

Schaacht's whisper dropped to a dangerous inaudibility. "Your what?"

"That is my future family, I hope, sir. You see she actually carried the money over the threshold into the custody of the State of Ohio. She is very much a party to it."

"She?"

Bolding moved away from the table closer to the door. "Your daughter, sir."

Schaacht stood there bracing himself on the table and swaying back and forth in such a pantherlike silence that Bolding put one foot outside the doorway before closing the interview with, "You see what I mean, sir? A law student could be proud to take his preceptorship under a man like that. 'Fact I guess you took a couple lessons yourself."

Michael Stikes did not sit on Blair's bunk now that this was a married man's house. He stood. He wiped his hands on his apron and then reached into an inside pocket. He pulled out the bounty land warrant he'd got for serving under Harrison in the late English war.

"Jonathan, I hate to bother you with this any more."

"What is it, Mike?"

"Now that you got them red devils moved up on the reserve, I figure it's all right to take claim under this warrant. I got a piece in mind up there I'd like to stake out. Figured I'd sell it and get some money to buy some plate iron over at Yellow Creek furnace."

"Why?" Blair asked.

"Lot of the men are screamin' for new plow blades for spring. New scythes, new axes, wagon bolts, new grub hoes. Never saw so much activity. Gonna be a lot of new sod turned up here next spring. *Lot* of it. Gonna be more plantin' and buildin' and diggin' start here than you ever saw . . . now that a man knows who owns the ground. And it all takes iron."

"Good, Mike." Blair lighted a conestoga cigar. "That's mighty good. Yes. I'll process your warrant."

"Point is, Jonathan, I don't like to trouble you with it. But I want it processed good. Don't want any of those five-dollar lawyers."

Blair grinned.

"Now I know your fee would be a dang sight more'n I could raise, Jonathan. But I figured I got somethin' here that might even it up fairly close."

Stikes handed over a piece of wrought iron work. It was lettering, and it was also a kind of degree. One of the words was misspelled. But the letters were beautifully wrought. Blair looked at it in several different lights. "You mean I should put it up on the trail in front of the cabin, Mike?"

"That was the idea of it, Jonathan. Figure you'll be needing it now."

"But nobody much would see it. That road only goes south to Boxford's Cabin and north to Upper Sandusky, Mike."

"That's one way to look at it."

"How else?"

"Well, in a way of windin' around, it goes between Cincinnati and Detroit. So y'might say we're sittin' smack in the middle of the Republic."

Blair reached out a hand to the lanky blacksmith. "Mike, one thing about you, you see clear."

Blair took the sign outdoors, but the blacksmith snatched it out of his hands. "I'll mount it. You wouldn't likely get it straight."

Which is how it happened that travelers between Boxford's Cabin and Upper Sandusky . . . or between Cincinnati and Detroit, however you look at those things . . . became accustomed to seeing a fine wrought-iron sign in front of one of the cabins. It read:

"J. BLAIR——Attourney at Law"

ITEM:

The Territorial Historical Society has ordered and received for sale sixty dozen Jonathan Blair commemorative dinner plates from the Kettlecreek Kilns. The design and conventional border on the plates are in maroon on a white background. Etchings of the Blair High School, Blair Legion Post #25, the old Blair cabin and the Pittsburgh Iron Works are worked into the border design. On the backs appear the following interesting biography of Jonathan Blair:

Practice began in circuit court........................1803
Sub-agent Indian Affairs.............................1817-22
State legislature......................................1817-22
President, Second Mesopotamia Hog & Trust Bank......1822-26
Circuit Judge...............................1827-(uncertain)

Proceeds from the sale of the plates were planned at the last meeting of the society to be used for new books for the Blair Memorial Law Library at the university. However, Mr. John Youngchief Blair II proposed to the contrary that the funds be used to establish a law scholarship for the benefit of young men among the 730 Wyandots now living on the reserve in Oklahoma, the grant to be known as the Silver Pigeon Law Scholarship.

It was decided that this would be voted upon at the next regular meeting.

Meanwhile, Mr. Fred Buttrick announced that he has on display at the loan desk of the Second Mesopotamia Hog & Trust two pieces of the currency made from the petticoat of Angelina Steese. He said he would like to obtain a few more pieces and will pay better than collector prices for any in good condition.

SAULINA S. BROOKS
*Editor, The Society Quarterly
and Secretary of the Society*

November, 1954

NOTE: The professional or occasional historian may quickly recognize in this story the manipulations of an attorney named Charles Hammond and the circumstances surrounding the court case known as Osborne vs. U.S. and he may wonder why the writer has given the case another name. But upon reflection, he will be the first to admit that unless there is space for the whole Hammond story, the truth is too brash for fiction. For those who wish to read it in the bold, faded handwriting of the original cast, their correspondence is listed below. And if the reader has become interested in following the American silver certificate beyond Mesopotamia, he will find it in the following works which, though not intending to comprise a comprehensive bibliography, make an interesting beginning place:

The Hammond Papers at the Ohio Archaeological and Historical Society, Columbus, Ohio. Letters: Hammond-Wright, Hammond-Brown, Hammond-Henry Clay, Hammond-Worthington.

C. C. Huntington, *Banking and Currency;* R. Carlyle Buley, *The Old Northwest;* R. C. H. Catterall, *Second Bank of U.S.;* Earnest L. Bogart, *Taxation of Second Bank of U.S. by Ohio;* Gouge, *Paper Money and Banking;* Gouge, *History of Banking;* Frederic L. Paxson, *Frontier Finance;* H. M. Utley, *Wild Cat Banking, Michigan;* Liberty Hall, Jan. 20, 1817, *Defense of the Granville Bankers;* Gallatin, *Considerations on the Currency;* John Bach McMaster, Vol. IV, *History of U.S.; Ohio House and Senate Journals,* 1816-1822; Annals 16th Congress, 2nd Session, Vol. II, VII; *Memoirs of Gorham A. Worth; Wheaton,* Vol. 9, see Osborne vs. U.S.; Jacob Burnet, *Notes of Settlement of Northwest Territory; Harvard Law Review,* I (1887), XXXI, (1917-18); *Laws and Treaties,* Vol. II; *Niles,* Vol. XVII; A. J. Baughman, *History of Wyandot County;* Harmon, *Sixty Years of Indian Affairs;* Swanton, *Indian Tribes of North America;* P. J. Treat, *The National Land System;* Carl Wittke, *History of Ohio,* especially Vol. II; William T. Utter, *The Frontier State;* F. P. Weisenburger, *A Life of Charles Hammond; Laws of Ohio,* Vol. XIX; *Laws of Illinois, Michigan, Indiana, Pennsylvania* (1817-1822).

ACKNOWLEDGMENTS: For editorial and critical assistance with the entire manuscript and over the whole distance day by day: my wife, Dorothy Ann Ellis, and my partner, Frank Siedel. For a detailed written critique of the first third of the manuscript: Leo Trefzger with whom I work. For specific ideas and facts embodied in this work: Lee Templeton, Janet Hofstetter and Fred Lipp, with whom I'm proud to work. For research assistance: Mrs. Arline Colgrove, Cleveland Public Library and others in the history department headed by Miss Donna Root. Also members of the staffs of the Ohioana Library Association and the Ohio Archaeological and Historical Society. For carefully reading three-quarters of the manuscript with attention to the legal aspects: Richard Weygandt.

WM. D. E.

ABOUT THE AUTHOR

WILLIAM DONOHUE ELLIS grew up in Concord, Massachusetts, seat of the Rebellion, where history came from the lips of old-timers sitting on the sunny side of the Minute Man statue at Old North Bridge and from the records in the old homes of Emerson, Thoreau, Alcott, and Hawthorne.

With industry if not skill he polished off his first novel at age twelve; has been writing ever since. Upon graduation from college he was drafted and commanded a rifle company of the 77th Division in the invasions of the Marianas and Philippine Islands. Wounded by machine-gun fire at the battle for Ormoc Corridor on Leyte, he was evacuated for a series of surgery to hospitals, where he resumed writing.

After five years of service Ellis went to Cleveland to join Beaumont & Hohman, an advertising agency, and to free-lance. One year later he began writing documentary radio and TV programs, industrial reporting and industrial motion picture manuscripts.

In that same endeavor today, Mr. Ellis is president of Editorial Services, Inc., of Cleveland.

These illustrations are reproductions of currencies circulating in the Ohio Territory at the time of the story in this book.